THE S␣␣␣ OF THISTLES AND ROSES

THE WARRIOR QUEEN SERIES

BY KAREN GRAY

THE WARRIOR QUEEN SERIES

For King and Country
Chains of Blood and Steel
Battle of the Bannockburn
The Highland Queen
Beat the Drums of War

Copyright © Karen Gray 2013
First published in the UK 2015
Printed by CreateSpace, An Amazon.com Company

ISBN-13: 978-1514781616

ISBN-10: 1514781611

Front cover by Karen Gray (2015)
© Karen Gray, reproduced with permission.

Official Series Website — http://thistlesandroses.co.uk

ACKNOWLEDGEMENTS

I could not have done any of this without the support and encouragement I have received from my family and friends. My wonderful husband has put up with near constant ponderings, and has only encouraged me to share more of the crazy, but productive goings on in my jumbled up noggin, and for that, I am eternally grateful.

THANKS

To those of you who have taken the time out of your busy lives to read for me, and offer your guidance — Particularly Mum, Barbara, Jason, Jennifer and Steve.

SPECIAL THANKS

To David Steele for all your support, positivity, amazing advice and excellent guidance on my cover art. And to Skye Mackenzie for being my walking Gaidhlig dictionary.

LOVE TO YOU ALL

XX

PROLOGUE

The incline steepened, slowing Catrìona's progress to a crawl. She stumbled and tripped over the thick foliage as she struggled with the extra weight she carried. Skye padded along beside her, ready to act as ballast, should she lose her footing or take a dizzy spell; something, which had been happening with increasing frequency.

Over the last three days pressure had settled low in her pelvis, making it far too uncomfortable to ride any further. She sought her companion's mind with her own, *'I must rest. Can you still hear them, puithar?'*

Skye slowed to a halt and raised her majestic neck — her pearlescent mane fell long and silken, catching the sunlight; her glimmering horn gleamed and glittered in apparent competition for which was more beautiful. She flicked her long ears back, and then turned her head so she could prick them forward and focus. Catrìona's gaze fell upon the ugly scars running down the mare's sides. Her heart ached when she thought of the pain Silas, Prince Edward's Lion, had caused her companion to endure: Reflecting the pain and suffering, she herself had gone through, which in turn had landed her in her current predicament.

'I hear dogs. And I feel Silas' presence close, we must not tarry too long here,' she cast in reply and nuzzled her soft muzzle against Catrìona's cheek.

She ran her hand along Skye's neck. *'Can we rest a while? I can go no further.'*

'We do not have long, else they will gain too much of the distance between us.'

Catrìona nodded, headed for a large rock and sat to allow her legs some relief. The hard surface increased the uncomfortable pressure in her pelvis, and she squirmed in an attempt to relieve it, triggering the little life within her to kick hard in the direction of her ribs, making her gasp. 'Aye, aye, wee yin, I'll sit still, I'll sit still,' she murmured to herself, running her hand over the bump beneath her leine. Her weskit rode high on her rib cage, laced looser than normal to accommodate her bulging abdomen. Overall, she felt exceedingly uncomfortable.

Skye gave a soft snort of amusement, and swished her tail. '*Feeling rather too full, Ban-phrionnsa?*' The mare mirrored her condition to the day, but had not complained once. Catrìona on the other hand was full of whinges, about swollen ankles and feet, her sore back, and a bladder the size of a pea, among several other grievances that she felt the need to voice regularly.

'*Aye, puithar, I do. Don't you feel the same?*'

Skye snorted her response, immortal beasts had exception,ally long gestational periods, and in some instances, the pregnancies lay dormant until the mother decided it was the right time to birth. Though she was eight months into her pregnancy, she showed no external signs of the life that grew in her belly. Skye turned to look back down the path they had tramped through the undergrowth. '*Your wee laddie is with them, we must move on.*'

Catrìona closed her eyes tight, *Andrew*. She wanted to go back for him so desperately that her chest ached. Abandoning the last of her Douglas kin was one of the hardest things she had ever had to do. She had waited as long as she possibly could for him, but he had not joined her in her flight from Windsor Castle, well over a week ago. Guilt ate at her every spare moment of the day and she vowed to herself that she would return for him as soon as she could. She huffed at the irony that the boy she wished to return to save, was now hunting her down. Of course, he was not to blame; he was a child, no better than a slave to his Sasannach master.

'*Ban-phrionnsa, we must leave this place,*' Skye began to jog on the spot, nerves beginning to show.

Catrìona forced her weary limbs into motion, her muscles, stiff from overuse, protested but she pushed the discomfort to the back of her mind and slogged on. Throughout the afternoon and evening, the sound of the dogs, previously only detectable to Skye's ears, began to hum low in the atmosphere.

Fear gripped her, spurring her legs into an uncomfortable half jog, *they can't be far behind us now, and if the dogs are close, that Lion is closer.* She pushed, faster and faster through the undergrowth, until she caught her foot on a root and toppled head over heel down a dry ditch.

A high-pitched ringing sounded in her ears when she pushed herself to her knees. Her head spun, she placed a hand to her throbbing temple, and when she drew it away, it was stained with blood.

Skye danced on the embankment above her, snorting and flicking her ears back and forth. *'Ban-phrionnsa!'*

The ringing quietened and the overwhelming raucous of the hunting dogs enveloped Catrìona's senses. Alarm pumped through her veins and she moved to flee until a deep crushing pain ripped through her abdomen, tearing the air from her lungs and forcing her to crouch low, and grasp her stomach, *not now. Not now!* As the pain dwindled, she cautiously pushed to her feet. Satisfied after a few moments, that she must have pulled a muscle wrong, she clambered from the ditch, only managing to hobble a hundred yards or so before another stab of pain hit her, forcing her to bend double. 'Caoch!' she cursed as the realisation dawned that her fate was now sealed. *'I think I will die tonight, puithar.'*

'Not if I can help it,' Skye replied, turning on her heel and crashing through the undergrowth, *'I will lead them as far from you as I can, move on as soon as you are able.'*

'Skye, wait! Please don't leave me, I'm frightened.'

'You will do fine, and I will return,' Skye cast in reply, and then she was gone.

***

Cold sweat beaded on her forehead, and salt filled tears tumbled down her cheeks. The hot summer evening did nothing to soothe the tremor inducing chill deep in her bones. Searing pain gripped her like a vice, flooding her senses and snatching her breath. She desperately clung to the rock wall of the small cavern she had stumbled upon in the woods, scraping her hands across the abrasive surface in an attempt to gain some purchase, something to anchor her. The pain abated just long enough for her to gain a few short breaths before the pressure and burn again began to build with rapid succession.

'Dàirich!' She gasped breathless from the intensity of the pain. It was like nothing she had ever imagined; *now I know why all my aunts curse their husbands.*

Agony ripped through her, snapping her mind back to the present with savage accuracy. She didn't know how much longer she could last. At each peak, she could feel her consciousness dwindling, bells ringing in her ears, until finally; time stood still, breathless, pain filled. Seconds took minutes and the ripping, tearing, searing pain enveloped her as another soul pushed its passage through her; separating itself from her own soul, to form an entirely new one attached to the little body that was bursting into the world in a bloody, screaming mess between her legs.

Catrìona pulled her knife and used it to rip a section from her arisaid. Lifting the screaming child, naked and wriggling. She lay its tiny form on the cloth, knotted its umbilical and cut the physical tie between them, and drew it close to her chest. Her body shook with violent tremors in the aftermath of her struggle, and she had some trouble unfastening her top to allow the tiny bairn a feed. She grimaced as the wee one hungrily sucked at the skin of her breast instead of latching on, bringing her skin up in a path of red welts until the tiny mouth claimed its prize.

Resting her head back against the cool rock that propped her up, Catrìona sighed a breath of release. Her heart still hammered in her chest, and residual crushing cramps spread through her abdomen, keen on ejecting the afterbirth, which had not yet come.

Sharp little nails slid along the sensitive skin of her breast, drawing her gaze back to the tiny bundle in her arms, 'I don't even know what you are, wee thing,' she breathed, *I didn't even think to look.*

The soft bundle in her arms stirred in response to her voice and looked up at her through large emerald eyes.

'Now that's a wee lassie's face if ever I've seen one,' Catrìona remarked before checking that in fact, her child was female. Rewrapping her in the thick cloth, she removed the long red tartan ribbon that held her hair from her face, and secured the cloth around the child.

A deep cutting sensation in her abdomen pushed a tooth-grinding grimace from her; it rose to a peak and dropped away leaving her dizzy and breathless. Her heart had not ceased its relentless thumping in the time since she had given birth, and her body felt too heavy.

Something's wrong, the thought sent apprehension trickling through her veins. Careful not to jostle her now sleeping baby, she stretched a hand down to feel for the afterbirth. Having attended numerous births with her mother, and being well versed in birthing etiquette, Catrìona knew what she *should* find between her legs.

When her hand met nothing but slick liquid and the severed umbilical, alarm bit like cold hard steel in her gut. Grasping the slippery cord, she pulled gently but firmly. Razor heat shot through her abdomen causing her grip to fail. Sobs racked her weary body, chorused by a deep terror induced tremor. Placing baby down next to her, Catrìona forced her shaky body upright, allowing the rock face behind her to take her weight she squatted and tried to calm her nerves. Grasping the cord once more, she applied downward pressure, keeping it as constant as she could, and to her relief, the membranes gave to the traction and inched their way free of her body. A whoosh of blood followed the main body of the afterbirth, in a bittersweet release that left her feeling woozy. She fell forward onto her hands and knees panting with the strain. Her arms shook as they fought to hold her weight, the ringing in her ears intensified as a rush of heat bathed her, darkening her vision, and she slumped to the ground.

***

Consciousness returned in graduated flickers. Catrìona seemed to float in her surroundings rather than be physically within them. A dull ache in her abdomen sharpened her self-awareness, and she opened her eyes.

Shockwaves of fear bolted through her as her eyes registered the naked man's form before her, his white hair tumbling down his sculpted back, fine silver amulet gleaming around his neck, and her newborn bairn in his arms. 'I smell evil in the bairn's blood,' he said, his familiar voice deep and watery, 'much has happened to you, mo Bhanrigh.'

His salty scent eased a few of Catrìona's nerves, but not all: The Each Uisge professed their loyalty to her clan, but they were a dangerous race and warranted caution at all times. Ceò, son of their King, had taken a particular interest in Catrìona since the day of her birth, and though she exercised caution around the rest of his kind, she felt completely at ease in his presence.

Ceò rose and padded toward her, his bare feet leaving damp footprints on the dusty ground. He held her tartan wrapped bairn in one arm and offered her the other, which was cool and calming next to her fevered skin. He encouraged her into an upright position and crouched before her, the muscles of his naked body tense and hard.

Catrìona grimaced as the pain in her abdomen intensified and dropped away in response to her change in position, and her heart began to race as hot fluid began to trickle from her. Casting her gaze across the cavern to where the afterbirth should have been, she noted it gone and looked back to Ceò.

His brow twitched, 'Did you expect me *not* to devour it?' His storm grey eyes carried concern, and she knew then that she was in trouble.

'Ceò...' her voice sounded weak even to her own ears.

8

'It was not complete,' he said, expression grave.

A tiny fist grabbing at a lock of his hair that had fallen across the bundle in his arms drew his attention, and for a moment, Catrìona saw him as a mortal: His expression full of the tenderness and care of a father holding his child for the first time. *This is how Mammy said he looked when I was born.* The thought allowed her mind to register what he had called her, when he had first spoken: Not princess, but queen. Tears filled her eyes as the realisation dawned that her mother had left this world.

'The bairn looks like her, but then so did you,' he handed her the bundle of tartan and squirming bairn, and looked to the cavern's opening, 'Athair,' he said bowing his head.

Though she felt safe in Ceò's presence, his father unnerved her. He paced into the cavern in the form of a majestic black stallion, coat gleaming, enticing innocent hands to seek its sleek feel. His fine silver bridle shone in the darkness in the same manner as the amulet around his son's neck.

His presence seemed to evaporate and reform, black hair draped over his naked shoulders, a silver amulet hung around his neck. He appeared as a young man in his twenties, the same as Ceò, but in fact, he was several thousand years old, and several hundred years older than his son. His eyes, almost black pierced straight through Catrìona, and she shuddered in their intensity. 'You have broken our laws.'

'Athair –'

'Do not try to dissuade me Ceò; it is not your place. You know the penalty she is subject to for crossing the bloodlines, and with the Bastard King!' rage filled his watery voice, adding a gravelly growl to its depths.

'The Bastard King has been dead six hundred years,' Catrìona protested.

'His blood pumps through that child's veins. You have birthed the devil from your womb, child. I must stop this evil before it grows and consumes us all,' he stepped forward.

'I did not do so willingly, sir,' she said holding a hand up as if it could stop him in his tracks. 'Please, my child is innocent, she is not a devil, she is a wee bairn who knows nothing of this world. Let me raise her right and I promise you she will be everything a good, highland lassie should be. Not a devil.'

Ceò cast his gaze to her, his brows were drawn and his eyes filled with steely determination, 'It was not her fault, Athair.'

'It matters not, the child must be destroyed, as must she,' he moved toward Catrìona with fire in his black eyes.

Catrìona clutched her child close to her and closed her eyes; sure, her death was only seconds away. When nothing touched her, she opened her eyes to see Ceò between her and his father.

'Step aside Ceò.'

'No, Athair.'

'You would stand against me. You would turn your back on your own race in favour of an abomination bastard child?'

'There is good in her, Athair, I swear it. I can taste it.'

'That is as may be, but evil will out and she must die.'

'I will not let you touch her, Athair,' Ceò growled, his appearance shimmering and evaporating until he had taken his equine form. His white coat glistened even in the darkness, and he roared through his nostrils at his father, stamping a hoof in defiance.

His father's face contorted with fury and he too shifted his form. Catrìona watched in terror as the two mighty Water horses lunged at each other, kicking, biting, and roaring with rage.

Catrìona scrambled to her feet and pressed herself close to the cavern wall. Her head swam, and her limbs trembled, blood continued to trickle down her legs as she inched her way closer to the exit.

A wall of water blocked her passage, and despair gripped her heart. In a chance moment, as Ceò's father concentrated his attention on the cavern's exit to stop Catrìona, Ceò knocked his legs from beneath him, sending the black stallion toppling to the ground. Quick as a flash Ceò took his human form and ripped the silver bridle from his father's head. A shriek of fury escaped the black horse as he leapt to his feet. The wall of water covering the opening crashed to the floor and whooshed into the cavern making Catrìona jump in surprise.

'It is over, Athair, without your bridle you are powerless, do not make me kill you,' Ceò said expression grim.

The black stallion roared and leapt for Catrìona. Ceò changed form as he moved to intercept and when his father stretched out his neck to reach for the bairn, he sunk his jagged teeth deep into his father's throat and whipped his head back leaving a gaping hole, through which dark salt water and blood gushed. His father, the mighty King of the Water horses fell at his feet. Ceò snorted at the limp body then raised his stormy eyes to Catrìona's.

'*Come,*' he nickered softly to her, '*you may ride me, I will take you somewhere you can get help.*'

Catrìona felt rooted to the spot, like a tiny flower swaying in a strong breeze. Ceò padded to her and bent to his knees to allow her easy access to his back. She grasped his mane and strong crest tight and lifted one leg, sliding it over his back. She gasped at the pain in her groin and abdomen, gripping tighter to his mane, grains of sand from the roots slid beneath her fingernails, and the salty sea smell filled her nose.

'*Breathe, mo Bhanrigh.*' he soothed, '*I will not leave you.*'

'Ceò your father,' Catrìona could no longer focus her mind to send mental communications, though she could hear Ceò's messages.

'*He brought about his own downfall, I allowed him the chance to leave, and he did not.*' He rose and leapt into an immediate gallop, smooth and rolling, causing minimal jarring to Catrìona's already agonised body.

'I am sorry you had to choose.'

'*Your daughter will not walk the dark path of her father, I can feel it; she will stand against him. There was no decision to make. I knew you were special when you were born just as I know she is. I would die to protect you both.*'

Catrìona's heart felt fit to burst, and she clung to Ceò with a newfound respect and love for the beast that she should fear over all others. Ceò carried her through the forest and out onto an open stretch of ground. Catrìona flinched at the sound of dogs behind them. Ceò lunged forward, increasing his speed as his mist gathered around them. Heavy clouds gathered overhead and rained down heavy droplets with torrential force. The sound of the dogs drowned beneath the hiss and drum of Ceò's downpour.

'Ceò, I don't feel so good,' Catrìona could feel her grip weakening on his mane, and around her tiny bairn.

'*Just a little further, mo Bhanrigh,*' Ceò replied without breaking his stride, his mental voice full of concern.

Catrìona gasped as the pain in her abdomen intensified, robbing her of her wits and loosening her grip. Without warning, the tartan bundle holding her tiny newborn slipped from her arm. Ceò reacted instantly, shifting form on instinct, and twisting to catch the infant in his strong hands. The cost of his choice hit Catrìona hard as the ground rose to meet her, and she tumbled several feet, before a dyke stopped her motion.

Catrìona cried out as the pain engulfed her senses, not the pain of her fall, but the deep ripping pain within her womb, spilling blood between her legs. Ceò was with her in moments, her precious bundle cradled against his blood stained chest, his back and legs also covered in fresh blood, her blood. He crouched and passed her the now screaming bairn, anxiety plain on his handsome face. She moved her clothing to allow the child a feed, despite her fear and discomfort.

Ceò ran a smooth, cool hand down her cheek, sadness filling his stormy eyes, 'You would have made a wonderful Bhanrigh, and an even better màthair.' He breathed a deep sigh, and kissed her forehead, 'What would you have me do, mo Bhanrigh?'

'Are there people close?' her voice was no more than a trembling whisper, but he heard it.

'Aye, at the other side of this paddock, the MacDonald's: They tamed kelpies to breed with their destriers. One of your kin I believe. The bairn will be safe with them. I will watch over her always, mo Bhanrigh, I swear to you.' The strength of his conviction filled his voice, and nipped at Catrìona's heart. 'Can you walk?'

'I think so.' When baby had finished her feed, Catrìona sorted her clothing and grasped Ceò's outstretched hand, to help her to her feet. Pain shot through her when she tried to straighten, and she cried out. Her knees buckled and Ceò caught her before she dropped back to the ground. He lifted her in his strong arms and carried her toward the farmhouse.

Sobs racked her weary body once more and she buried her face in Ceò's cool chest, he kissed her hair as he walked toward the whitewashed house. His storm swirled around them, shielding them from sight until he reached the door.

'Can you stand, mo Bhanrigh?'

'I will have to,' she replied, preparing for the shock that the move would jolt through her.

Gently, Ceò placed her on her feet, 'I will not leave you. Say what you will and leave her here,' he squeezed her hand and evaporated into the storm, *'I will be waiting.'*

Catrìona's heart raced as she lifted her hand to knock the door. Muffled voices rose from within, and Catrìona hugged her sleeping bairn close as she waited for the strangers behind the door.

'Aye, aye, aye, settle down quine! All tell em tae piss aff, don't yi worry yer wee sel!' The door swung inward, and a gruff looking man glared at her, his ginger beard thick on his chin. He was stout and not much taller than Catrìona, a typical highland man, of the type she was used to. Recognition dawned in his dark grey eyes, 'Dàirich! Evie, grab some blankets!' he called. He reached toward Catrìona and she pulled back from him, grimacing at a stab of pain. Confusion joined the emotions flooding his face, 'What happened tae yi lass? How did yi get here?'

'You know me, Sir?'

'Aye lass, yer oor Ban-phrionnsa, nay oor Bhanrigh.'

Her breathing began to labour, 'Please, I do not have long, I need you to do something for me,' she said, grasping his sleeve, her hand caked in dry blood.

He paled but did not let his shock reach his voice, 'Anything, mo Bhanrigh,' he said placing his fist over his heart, a long outlawed gesture of the clans meaning 'respect' and 'loyalty': A salute to their queen.

Catrìona looked at the bundle in her arm, and longed to see her grow and develop, sadness at the knowledge that she never would pricked her eyes, and she swallowed the lump in her throat. 'Take her; do not let anyone know you have her. I am being hunted, as will she if they find out about her. So far, they have no knowledge of her existence. Please, do not ask me to stay; do not ask me to explain further, I cannot. Please raise her as your own and keep her hidden. And when she comes of age, take her to my father, but not before. If you are loyal to my mother, to me... you will do this.'

'I will, mo Bhanrigh. What is the bairn's name?'

Catrìona nodded, and kissed her child, 'Name her for my mother,' she said handing over the little bundle and straining to hold her tears back. 'Go now, close your door and forget you ever saw me,' she said.

'Mo Bhanrigh –' he began to protest.

'Go!' she cried and he obeyed, closing the door and leaving her to drop to the ground, distraught.

Ceò materialised beside her and scooped her up in his arms.

'Ceò it hurts.' She wept into his chest.

'I know, mo Bhanrigh, I know,' he hushed her, and carried her under the cover of his storm, into the forest, to find somewhere peaceful for her to spend her final moments.

FOR KING AND COUNTRY

THE WARRIOR QUEEN

BOOK 1

BY KAREN GRAY

Chapter One

PATIENCE IS A VIRTUE

As dawn broke, and the birds began to sing, Mòrag sat up in her bed. The rough woollen sheets were damp from the heat of the horses below, mixing with the chill of the air in the rafters. Swinging her legs round, she slipped her feet into her boots and pulled on her overcoat. Heading towards the rickety old ladder, which groaned and bowed under her weight, she descended towards the stalls below.

Mòrag smiled as every head in the barn raised and called out to her: thirty black faces happy to see her and eagerly awaiting their breakfast. She headed across the stone walkway towards the feed store at the rear of the building. Dust danced in the mottled light from the slatted windows that ran the length of the walls. Once she opened the shutters, light would flood the vast space. For now though, it remained in half-light. The long procession of stalls lining the walkway were whitewashed, and a stark contrast to the jet-black horses they housed. As she neared the door of the feed store, she could feel the heat from their hungry eyes on her back.

'Patience is a virtue you know,' she said feeling their impatience growing, 'I haven't eaten either.'

'*If we weren't cooped up in here we would be able to eat wherever, and whenever we pleased,*' piped up Petorius, the oldest, and most stubborn of the herd. He was always the first to complain. Most often at meal times, and whenever he was due to be ridden.

'If you weren't cooped up in here, Petorius, you would be nothing more than a common horse, covered in mud and as dim-witted as a fool,' she retorted without turning to look at him.

The barn was filled with whinnies of laughter, '*Ha!*' called Shand, '*she has a point Petorius! I'll bet you aren't getting any carrots this morning for being rude!*' The youngster was in good spirits. At three years old, he was now ready to undergo the binding.

Each of the horses was selected and bred for their enhanced mental abilities. Not originally a communicative race, the horses had been farmed for generations, to yield an animal capable of mutual communication. Through the binding, horse and rider would become one, a single entity with two intelligent minds driving it. Shand was the next step in the evolution of the breed. A horse far more suited to the field of battle than the training yard.

The goal had always been to breed an animal capable of becoming berserker. Under the control and guidance of their binder, they would be a formidable force. Shand was the first of these super-elite destriers. He would be bound to an officer, someone experienced in battle that could harness his abilities and use them effectively. If he did well at his job, he would be used to father the next generation.

Petorius snorted, '*I had better get my carrots or I'll give her a swift kick the next time she walks past my stall!*' He pawed at the ground to further emphasize his point, before freezing, ears pricked to the sound of a low, rumbling growl to his rear.

'*If you were to do that, Petorius,*' came the growl from the shadows, '*I might have to forego my venison this evening, and hunt you instead.*'

The old horse stood statuesque, unwilling to move, and too stubborn to yield.

'*Or perhaps I should eat you now?*' The growl continued, hypnotic, soft and menacing. '*Not that you would provide me much sustenance.*'

'*Bràthair, he means me no harm,*' Mòrag cast. She could feel Rannoch's consciousness intertwined with her own. She could always feel it to one degree or another, but when he was close like this, it was like having two minds in her head. Yet, she never felt more whole than when she was with him. When she gained no response, she spoke aloud, 'Rannoch, enough.'

'*Puithar*,' he replied. The disappointed tone of his mindcast was obvious, but he obeyed her with the slightest snort towards Petorius.

She watched as he emerged from the shadows behind the old horse. His emerald eyes that matched her own were trained on his (now unattainable) prey. His arched majestic neck and his thick flowing mane, added extra bulk to his already massive shoulders. Unlike the rest of the herd, Rannoch's mane did not just dress his crest: It flowed from his forelock and ears down both sides of his neck. The thick mane also covered his chest and ran between his front legs, tracing down the centre of his undercarriage.

His eyes and mane were not his only distinguishing features. Like the rest of the herd, his coat was a deep onyx, but he was considerably shorter and more compact in stature. His muscular legs were stronger than those of the others in the herd and his joints were far more flexible. Instead of hooves, he had strong paws, which concealed razor sharp claws. His face was elegant like the others but his muzzle was jowlier, with a silken tuft of hair under his chin, and concealed a set of teeth more reminiscent of a lion than a horse. His tailbone was elongated, as long as his legs were tall. It had a tuft of hair on the end rather than along its length, and from his forehead, stretched a magnificent horn. He was a beautiful yet terrifying sight to behold. No wonder the old horse was shaking.

Rannoch stalked past Petorius' quivering form before leaping up onto the hayloft platform. He padded over the heaving, creaking boards of the loft floor to his favoured spot by Mòrag's bed. As he lay himself down a shower of dust rained from above. While he was not as tall as the others were, he was certainly heavier. Whenever Mòrag walked over the loft floor, the boards breathed and flexed beneath her. As she regarded them now, they seemed to have sunk several inches in the area where Rannoch was lying, and she wondered how strong the floor of the loft really was under his immense weight.

'*Strong enough*,' was the yawning reply in her head.

Mòrag smiled as she walked over to give Petorius a reassuring rub between his large black ears, before returning to the job at hand.

The scent of garlic and mint tingled in her nose as she opened the feed room door. Whinnies of anticipation filled the air as Mòrag organised fresh oats, barley, alfalfa, a generous scoop of garlic and sugar beet pulp into each horse's bucket. She took a pestle and mortar, and a small wooden box containing baked roots of Campion from the shelf by the door. The box was a little rough underneath from many year's use, but the lid and sides were ornately decorated with mother of pearl and an exotic red wood. The enticing design swirled beneath her fingers. Setting the box down on the old oak table in the far corner of the room, and slipping on a pair of gloves from her pocket, she felt along the table's base for the trigger to release the hidden compartment. From this, she removed a finely decorated silver key. She admired the delicate workmanship for a moment, before unlocking the box with care. Lifting the fragile bundle of baked roots, she selected one and placed it in the mortar. She then replaced the bundle, sealing the box and locking it shut before replacing the key.

She ground the root to a fine powder and mixed it into Shand's feed. Her head spun and she had to grasp the doorframe to keep steady.

'*You breathe too much, puithar,*' Rannoch's mindcast was muffled in her head.

Mòrag felt too dizzy to answer. Campion root, or Dream root, was more effective on horses than people, at least in this form. Although it could still make her quite disorientated, the effects were mild and short-lived. When the drug was extracted from the petals of the flower, it was far more potent. She had to take slow, steady breaths until she felt stable enough to walk unaided.

Mòrag added carrots to every feed, then stacked the buckets and placed them on to the trolley. The noise in the barn dropped as each horse received their long awaited breakfast.

Shand was last in line.

'Big day for you, boy,' she said as she placed his bucket into his stall, 'you may feel a bit strange at first. But, by the end of today, you will have an officer bound to you. *That makes you one of the most important horses in this barn.*'

'*I will do my best, màthair,*' he cast. His ears twitched as he stretched down to eat his feed. Mòrag smiled as he raised his head and lifted his top lip, showing his teeth. '*It tastes strange, not bad. But strange,*' he remarked before stretching down once more and hungrily gobbling at the remainder of the feed.

Chapter Two

HIDDEN IN PLAIN SIGHT

Sipping from the steaming cup of tea, Randall regarded the scene unfolding before him. The summer sun was high in the sky, unperturbed by clouds it beat down relentlessly, bouncing from the whitewashed walls of the outbuildings that skirted the training arenas. The younger Tyros had completed the morning's drill training, and were now cooling off the horses in the neighbouring arena. The few older Tyros that accompanied the group were lined up along the wooden fence, eager to see the binding of a Tyro and his horse take place.

Randall relished the intense heat from the sun. The table where he sat was atop a grassy incline at the near end of the arena, and was the area best situated to observe all of the arenas at once.

Randall's grey-gold wolf Tara lolloped at his feet panting, and paying particular attention to the burly boy stomping around after the young horse in the arena below. She accompanied him for every binding, and for the most part found it a rather dull spectator sport.

'The boy has no idea what he is doing,' she cast to her partner.

Randall grunted in agreement and gave her a scratch between her large shoulders. Fletcher Raine, son of the Ninth Guard General, was about to undergo the binding of his new steed, before moving on to the graduation tournament from which he would emerge as one of the king's soldiers.

He was a handsome young man in his early twenties: Full of bravado and pride. His father was one of the most feared

Generals in the King's army. He had high expectations for his son: Perhaps too high.

Randall supervised each and every binding that took place. Each Tyro would be bound to the animal most suited to his or her particular talents before being submitted for graduation. For the Cavalry and Royal Guard, it was the horses. Officers were also allocated a horse but more often than not, had a second familiar.

Randall knew that for the binding to be accomplished and held, the binder must be stronger of mind than the animal being bound. Young Shand was the culmination of several years' intensive breeding and was the strongest and most intelligent destrier that had been produced by old Jock's stud thus far. General Raine had made it clear that his son and no other would bind this horse.

Randall had doubts over the suitability of the match, but he was no longer the decision maker. When politics became more important than warfare, he had been retired from active duty to train the Tyros.

'Well done, young Raine,' he called as the youth managed to back the disorientated Shand into a corner, 'this time do not let him pass you.'

'I *am* trying, Sir, but the damn thing won't stand still!' complained Raine.

'*He* is not supposed to stand still, Raine,' Randall sighed, exasperated, 'you are supposed to bind him. Get a hand on him. Find your connection, and make him yours.'

Eyes wide and nostrils flared, Shand's distress was obvious. His legs were splayed outward and his coat was slick with sweat. A white froth had begun to form between his legs and down the sides of his neck, matting his long mane. The effects of the baked Campion root, most favoured for animal bindings, were twofold: Enhancing perceptions while breaking down the mental defences, creating a door through which two separate minds could be bound together. The disorientation that the horse felt was intended to help the bond form with the binder, who would steady and control the horse with mind and body.

This circus however, had been going on for far too long. The young horse was becoming steadier on his feet as the drug continued to dilute. This couldn't go on much longer.

'You are a stupid beast!' Raine spat at Shand. 'To think I am to be paired with one such as you!'

'Calm yourself, boy,' instructed Randall. *The little git does not deserve this horse,* 'I think we are done here.'

Raine kicked dirt at Shand in a fit of frustration. The young horse responded by lashing out, missing the youth by inches.

'Stupid beast!' Raine shouted.

Already in motion to stop the emerging situation in its tracks, Randall couldn't believe his eyes when Raine pulled a flip knife from his pocket. As Shand lunged forwards again, lashing out with his front legs, Raine spun to the side and buried the blade deep into the destriers flank.

What followed was a sobering sight. Deep red rivers oozed from around the blade as Shand spun around to face his aggressor. The whole thing was over in mere seconds, but to Randall, the scene seemed to move in slow motion.

Raine realised he was outmatched and had turned to run as Shand, now foaming at the mouth, thundered towards him. The destriers strides were so powerful that the blade dislodged itself, landing in the thick sand of the arena and leaving a deep wound through which the red liquid of life began to torrent. Raine only managed three strides before Shand, eyes rolled back in his head and ears pinned flat clamped his teeth onto Raine's shoulder. He bit down hard, clenching his strong jaw, and tugged Raine backwards. The sickening snap of the youth's collarbone was just audible over his terrified wails. Raine had tried to protect his face and abdomen with his arms, curling into a ball, making himself as small a target as he could, but his actions were futile: The enraged horse, wild with bloodlust had torn and ripped at Raine's body. He half rose on his back legs and beating down with his front feet again, and again. The more the youth's blood seeped from his wounds, the more the horse attacked.

Kicking and biting at the object of his obsession, Shand did not rest until there was no more movement or sound coming from his victim. The only reason Raine was still alive, was that lack of consciousness rendered him still and silent.

Movement from the Tyros surrounding the arena drew the battle blind horse away from the unconscious youth's fragile body.

'Keep out of sight!' Randall commanded. The Tyros obeyed, crouching low behind the fence and keeping as still as they could.

Randall reached into his satchel for the sedation he always had with him during bindings. As Shand was circling back towards Raine at the far side of the vast arena, Randall released the dart. Hitting its mark, it served only to make Randall the new target.

'You had better go,' Tara's warning was full of intentions. She leapt out in front of him, hackles raised and teeth bared: Ready to defend him against the rampaging destrier.

'Tara, you are no match for him,' he cast, but it was too late. He could feel her muscles spring into action as she took off towards the charging horse, 'Shit!' He cursed and pulled his preloaded compressed crossbow from his blazer, taking aim.

'STOP!'

The command was so powerful that it halted Randall's finger on the trigger as well as bringing both Tara and Shand to a standstill.

For a moment, Randall was dumbfounded. A mental command of this magnitude was only ever issued by officers or the King. Not to mention that he knew all of their mental voices as well as he knew his own. This voice was alien to him, and powerful.

Scanning the immediate area his eyes locked on to a young girl, old Jock's adopted daughter, at the far end of the arena. She had dismounted her horse, jumped the fence and was now running flat out towards Shand.

'What do I do?' Tara asked. He could feel her uncertainty, *'she spoke not only to the horse. You heard her command through our link. She stayed your hand too, did she not?'*

With a jolt, the recognition of what had happened turned the pit of his stomach to lead. *How can this be? How could she have gone undetected with such strength, and for so long?* After the war against Prince Edward had been fought and won, General Raine had rounded up everyone that harboured powerful talents above the age of twelve. This had become known as the Purges. These people posed a significant threat to the Crown, and if they refused to join his army, to protect King and Country, they were executed on sight. It had been a dark and bloody time.

I need to take her in. Have her cleansed, and assess the extent of her talents. She cannot be allowed to roam free: Not with power like this. He wondered fleetingly if she was young enough to come through the Cleanse and remain whole. In any case he had to try and salvage the situation, though he would have to exercise caution, he still did not know the extent of her power.

'*He's wounded and means you no harm, she-wolf, please go back to your master,*' the girl cast to Tara. Randall heard the command echo in his own mind through their link. It was full of concern but also held command, and he felt Tara's surprise at her forced obedience. Then it dawned on him: She had said, 'she-wolf.'

Most people saw a large sable coated dog, similar to a guard dog when they looked at Tara. The more powerful familiars, like her, only showed their true form to other animals and their bound partner, if they entertained one. This girl could see Tara for what she really was.

He watched as she placed a hand on Shand's shoulder and leaned her head against his. The previously uncontrollable, battle-mad destrier was now still and calm, save for the trembling in his legs and breast from the pain that he must, only now be feeling. Adrenalin rush having passed, the full effects of the dart began to take hold of him and he collapsed in a heap at the girl's feet.

The Tyros that had been concealed behind the fence began to show themselves once more. They spoke in hushed voices, their inaudible words creating a gentle hum against the quiet that had descended over the area.

Randall's ward, Brax had begun to catch and stable the horses that had been let loose during the commotion. The young man seldom ventured from Sruighlea Castle, unless he had been ordered to do so, but on this occasion, Randall had placed a formal request for his attendance, to take the place of his usual Seeker who had fallen ill.

'Boys! To Raine. Get him to the medics immediately!' Randall bellowed. 'Quickly now boys!'

Four of the older Tyros leapt the fence in unison, and as Raine's ruined body was removed from the arena, Randall approached the girl. She was kneeling by Shand's side, tending to his wound. He regarded her with caution, but guessed from her lack of fear that she had not realised the magnitude of the situation.

If he could just get close enough, he could sedate her before anyone came to harm. There was a reason the Purges had been orchestrated, and that all 'powers' remained under direct control of the Crown: Wild power like hers was dangerous and a threat to the King.

'How did you stop him?' he asked her.

'I asked him to stop.' Without looking up from Shand's wound she spoke again, 'will *he* be ok?'

'Raine will be fine, we have powerful medics, as I am sure you know,' he replied.

'I raised Shand from a foal,' she told him, 'I have never met a sweeter natured horse. He was so excited about today.' She turned toward Randall, her bright emerald eyes were hard as the precious stone from which they stole their colour, 'I hope he's scarred for life for what he's done.'

Her admission took him by surprise. He felt for the Subjugator in his pocket. As the girl turned back towards Shand, Randall leapt forwards. He placed the gun to her neck, and felt the needle fire deep into her flesh, releasing its debilitating electric sting and subduing venom.

'Bràthair!' She gasped as her body flopped to the ground.

'Randall! RANDALL! Attention to your rear!' Tara's alarmed mental shout jolted him into action.

Spinning round Randall saw the girl's horse, bound over the fence and come barrelling towards them. He was different from the other horses here: Much shorter and stockier.

She must have bound one of her own. He stepped in front of the unconscious girl and reached for his sword.

'That's no horse!' Tara warned, hackles raised and snarling.

Sprinting to the fence and leaping it in a single fluid motion, Brax intercepted the horse before it reached Randall and the unconscious girl. Pulling a long glinting object from his sleeve mid stride, he pierced the charging animal's shoulder. Spinning round, the horse lashed out striking Brax's chest, throwing him backward to land several feet away, before faltering itself and crashing to the ground.

Randall was astounded that a wound to the shoulder had managed to bring down a destrier in full charge.

Scrambling to his feet, Brax, grasping his chest, had sped to the horse. Pulling a syringe from his jerkin he inserted the needle into the wound, administering a potent sedative. Stepping backward he grimaced as he released his hand from his chest. In place of a hoof strike, five deep gashes appeared. As the blood began to flow, Brax fell to his knees.

Chapter Three

SCRATCHING THE SURFACE

The moon was bright and round. The firs, bathed in pale blue, stood to attention flanked by luxurious grass, thick and soft under Mòrag's bare feet.

As she walked through the serene meadow, the daisies shone bright, reflecting the moon's cool glow. The sweet scent of wildflowers hung in the air, the veritable taste of summer.

A herd of wild horses came into view on the horizon. Galloping in a choreographed unit like a flock of birds, they raced each other along the channel of the glen.

The herd was a pool of diversity. Majestic animals of all colours, not like the carbon copy, onyx destriers of Jock's stud. At the rear of the herd, driving them forwards was Rannoch.

The majestic Nemeocorn tossed his mane, the helix of his horn catching the silvery rays and gleaming luminescent in the moonlight. Mòrag couldn't peel her eyes from him. As he galloped and frolicked with the wild herd, her heart danced.

Changing direction in a flurry of forelocks and feathers, Rannoch drove the herd straight up the grassy incline towards Mòrag. She was utterly transfixed, her heart pounding in her chest in time with the drumming hooves. Breaking a few yards in front of her like the negative tides of the Blue Sea, the wild horses galloped past so close; that Mòrag could feel the warmth from their bodies.

Rannoch did not alter his path and continued straight toward her. She felt as though she had not seen him in a thousand years. As he skidded to a halt, he sat up on his haunches and lifted himself up until he was standing tall on his massive back paws towering over her. He settled himself back on all fours and stood, tail swishing from side to side, nickering softly to her. He could be such a show off at times.

'Bràthair,' Mòrag reached out expecting her hand to be met by his soft muzzle. Instead of reaching out to her, his body went rigid and tense. He stood bolt upright, ears pricked, looking past her and suddenly, inexplicably, he was gone. *He didn't even look at me.* Conflicting thoughts began to rise within her, but she pushed them to the back of her mind.

She didn't know why, but she was drawn down the incline towards a whitewashed stone building. It somewhat resembled one of the outbuildings from her home, which lay in the meadow at the foot of a glen. It seemed cold; hard against the soft landscape.

Mòrag chewed her lip as she approached the colossal steel doors. The massive rusty hinges protested with a screech, as she heaved the door open. Inside, down-lighters were spaced at infrequent intervals along the walls of the corridor, giving barely enough light to see by.

She jumped as a deafening roar – a terrifying guttural sound - echoed up the corridor. *Rannoch*. The hair on the back of her neck stood on end as a cold sweat broke on her skin. She ran toward the sound on trembling legs. There, in a dark room, horn and strong legs shackled and bolted to the wall was her mighty Nemeocorn. His deafening roars reverberated through her body. He pawed at the ground and the wall, leaving deep gouges in the mortar. He reared and wrenched at his chain. He fought as if he knew his life depended on it. He did not seem to see her, nor did he respond to any of her attempts to communicate.

Six men in blood-stained overalls entered the room, their eyes trained on Rannoch. They set about him with thick lengths of chain. The dull thud of the steel on his flesh made Mòrag feel sick to her stomach. She screamed at them, begging them to stop, but like her familiar, they were unresponsive. His gleaming onyx coat was tainted with blood. Rivers of red ran down his legs and back, and still he fought.

The wall cracked from the strain, freeing his restraints, but there was no sound. He barrelled into the men knocking them down, and then took off, desperate to escape. Mòrag followed suit. She didn't dare look back, fearing that the second cost to look would be her last. Rannoch had veered off to the left from the main corridor. She found him pawing and snorting at a bright room. The sight of him standing, shadows on his back, face illuminated by the light coming from the doorway seemed to make her stop. *I've been here before.* She took a deep breath; steadying her nerves for the shock, she knew was coming.

When her eyes had adjusted to the light, she was not as ready as she thought she had been, for the horror that awaited them. Hanging along the walls were monstrous instruments of death. Strewn across the floor and along both walls were the lifeless bodies of the once majestic herd: A grey at her feet, anguished, empty eyes wide. Its coat matted with blood from a slash wound to the throat: A bay lying awkward on broken legs, a hole in its forehead. A buckskin colt, days old, too young to be stripped of its mother was trying to suckle from her lifeless corpse. Blood from ugly slashes to his body stained his coat. Everywhere Mòrag looked, she saw death and devastation.

Rannoch padded around the desolate bodies of his wild companions. He nuzzled the foal nickering sympathetically to him, encouraging him to leave his fallen dam and escape this place, but the young colt wouldn't leave his mother. *He will be killed*; she found it hard to leave him.

Mòrag followed Rannoch towards the door at the other end of the room. The blood, which should have been cold and slippery underfoot, had no sensation whatsoever. *This doesn't make any sense,* she followed Rannoch out into the cool night air.

The sound of a sickening squeal and dull thud, told her the young foal was dead. Rannoch leapt to the top of the grassy incline with ease. She scrambled behind, desperate to make it up the rise. He seemed oddly calm after what had just transpired.

Straightening, she reached out to Rannoch with her mind, '*Rannoch?*' he gave no reply, '*Bràthair please speak to me.*'

Mòrag started toward him, but a piercing pain in her chest brought her to her knees. It ripped the breath from her lungs making her gasp, and as the pain reverberated through her body, the surroundings began to dissolve.

Her eyes jumped open. She was bathed in sweat. Stained blankets stuck to her wet skin. Her heart was racing. All the equipment she was attached to was screaming. Six men in white overalls and medical masks stood around her bed. The largest of them was lifting a set of defibrillator paddles from her chest. His salt and pepper hair was cut short; beneath his mask was a stubble beard that darkened his jaw and his eyes were a deep blue that pierced right through her. 'Thought we lost you there,' he said in a flat emotionless tone. 'That would not do at all would it?'

Mòrag's chest burned from the shock she had just received. She scanned the faces of the men as they moved to restrain her. Recognition hit like a smack in the face and she felt the familiar fear rising up within her. *How many times have I woken like this since I was taken from home?*

'Time to dream again,' he said.

'Please...' she breathed, voice weak, 'please let me go'

'No, Mòrag. I am afraid you must endure until you have been cleansed.'

He disappeared out of sight for a moment, and then reappeared with a syringe. 'Dream now.'

'No! Please!' Mòrag gasped as she struggled against them. 'Don't send me back! I can't see it again!' Her weak muscles blazed from her effort to fight them but it was no use. 'Please. Help me. Somebody help me!'

The fluid felt cool as it swept through the tube into Mòrag's arm. The room began to spin and drain away. Mòrag was once again standing in her nightdress, barefoot on soft lush grass, in the sweet scented meadow, waiting for the herd of wild horses and Rannoch to appear.

Chapter Four

ESCAPING THE DREAM

It was bitterly cold for a midsummer. For Randall, the refectory offered no warmth, just a plethora of cooking smells and the hectic sounds of the cook and her assistants preparing the evenings feast. Through the rising mists of his piping hot stew, he meditated on the day's events.

Old Jock's adopted daughter, Mòrag, who should have completed the Cleanse, continued to resist. It was getting risky. Today was the third time that he had brought her back from the brink of death.

Randall inhaled a deep breath as he habitually ran his nails over his stubble beard. She was strong of mind; he had seen evidence of this with his own eyes. Although, it seemed, she was so strong of mind that her body could not keep up.

Most Initiates succumb to the Cleanse within four days. Mòrag had resisted for sixteen: Sixteen days. It was not often that an initiate failed the Cleanse. Those that did either expired or lost themselves completely and although they woke, their bodies were vacant husks. These were taken away by General Marcs to be put out of their misery. Even taking her age into account, it was astonishing that she still had fight left in her.

Randall closed his eyes and leaned into the diminishing mists of his cooling stew, letting it warm his face. The hairs on his chin stood to attention at the change of temperature. He opened his eyes, grasped his fork and dipped into the stew. Although the meaty dish looked and smelled pleasant, it was chewy and tasteless. He dropped the fork, sat back, and decided to take the matter to General Marcs.

Randall stood, smoothed the creases from his coat and set off for his office. He left the refectory by the North stair, which spiralled around a pillar of granite, upwards towards the offices or down to the initiation and medical wards. As he reached the doorway he felt something tugging at his consciousness, pulling him to the descending steps. He stopped for a moment unsure if he really had felt the summons. It had been at least four months since another mind had last brushed his own. It was a regular occurrence when another General was on the base.

At this time of year, during the cleansings, his fellow Generals preferred to take a leave of absence. The anguished nightmares and constant trials of the initiates must be quite draining to those predisposed to 'lurking' in the minds of others. Randall was glad he was only mildly mentally gifted. His mind remained open and if someone linked to it, he could communicate back and forth and he could also sever the connection with all but the King. He could not however, initiate a link with anyone else.

He decided to ignore the feeling and continued toward the ascending stairway.

'STOP!'

Randall froze, foot hovering over the first step. The girl's mindcast had force and strength behind it. It rose up from the depths and drowned his soul with authority.

Randall found himself standing in a dark room, dressed in bloody overalls, chain in hand. In front of him, Mòrag's familiar, showing his true form, was shackled to the stone wall by his horn and legs. His claws dug deep into the concrete floor as he fought against the five other men in the room. Mòrag was standing to the side of the furore screaming at them to stop.

He was stunned. In front of him was the very initiate he had been musing about only moments before. She was clad in a white summer nightdress, her feet were bare and her long auburn hair tumbled like wild fire over her shoulders. She was shouting, screaming, pleading for the other five men to stop the brutal battery of her familiar. The wall cracked releasing the chains holding the mighty beast. It turned on its haunches and knocked the other five men to the ground before it fled for the door. The girl stared at him for a split second, as if she expected him to have been knocked over with the other men, before she too fled the room.

The other five men began to fade, as did the room. Randall realised with a shock that his mind had not only been summoned but that his entire consciousness had been drawn into this girl's nightmare. Now that she was no longer in the room, it was fading fast. Randall dropped the heavy chain, which hit the dissolving floor without a sound, and headed for the door. The darkness was like a heavy blanket pressing down on him; he could hardly see, save for the slight glow from a room further up the passageway. With a hand on the soft wall of the fading corridor, Randall quickened his pace. He had never experienced anything like this before and did not want to guess at what would happen if he let himself dissolve along with the edges of the dreamscape.

He reached the doorway of the bright room. The girl and her familiar were close to the entrance so the dreamscape here, for the moment, remained solid. Randall leant his back against the wall of the dark passage and tried to connect with his physical self. He could feel the grain of the wooden stairway handrail, and the slight sway of his physical form from having one foot mid step, but he could not disengage his mind from this initiate's. The best that he could do was 'will' his body to come to his mind. The clattering of footsteps echoing up the corridor broke his concentration. The other five men had reappeared and were rushing towards the room. He could see them clearly now. They were the medics who had been working on the day this girl came to the base: The same team that had been with him when he had restarted her heart.

The five men sped past him and burst into the bright room. Randall entered behind them and the horror of what he saw shook him to the core. The floor was littered with bodies: Eyes wide, dull and lifeless. The only sign of life in the room came from the bloody footprints of the retreating girl and the frantic drumming of a young foal's hooves on the slippery floor.

Terrified of the approaching men and equally terrified to leave its dead mother, it danced on the spot on frantic little legs.

One of the five men, possibly an imagining of Major Darrow; the chief medical officer, approached the foal. He grabbed it around the neck and drew a blade from his sleeve. The frightened animal could only start to give a choked squeal before its throat was cut and it dropped with a sickening thud to the floor. The men began to search the room for the girl. Randall took the opportunity to catch up to her and strode for the door, his boots sliding on the slick and sticky blood.

As he emerged into the cool moonlight, he could see her familiar dancing at the top of the grassy incline, which led away from the building. The girl was trying to scramble up the rise but the angle of ascent was slowing her progress. Randall saw an opportunity and took it.

Lunging forward he grabbed her wrist as hard as he could. For a moment, everything went black. He opened his eyes to discover that he was once again in his physical body. He was in the initiation ward, room fifty-two. He was clenching Mòrag's wrist, and she was staring straight at him, emerald eyes defiant.

Chapter Five

BIRTH OF THE NEMEOCORN

Mòrag glowered into the blue eyes of the man that faced her. He looked as if he had seen a ghost. She moved her gaze from his weather-beaten, stubbled face, to his hand clamped tight around her wrist. More than anything, she wanted him to let go. She stared at his fist, putting the force of her desire into the stare, willing his grip to loosen. She felt heat flow from her arm under his clamped fist. To her surprise, his grip loosened. She looked back into his eyes.

'*Let. Me. Go.*' She commanded.

As his hand dropped to his side, she was once again thrust into oblivion.

Mòrag shivered, the dreamscape seemed much colder than it previously had. Random portions of the horizon looked almost rippled: As if the landscape was the top of a pond, and someone was skipping stones over its once smooth surface. The grass, which before had been luxurious and soft, now felt hard and artificial underfoot. The looping dreamscape that had been, terrifyingly constant, had become disfigured. By what, she didn't know.

Perhaps I've changed it. The dreamscape shimmered in apparent response. *Maybe I can find a way to escape this.* The sound of the thundering hooves that she had come to dread was warped and muffled to her ears. It sounded almost like the herd were galloping through thick mud, and instead of being a solid mass of moving colours, the herd appeared faded and bleached. Only Rannoch remained unaltered. Mòrag watched the scene unfold as it always had. The ghostly apparitions of the horses began to dissolve before they reached her. Rannoch skidded to a halt before her and stood up on his hind legs. This time she did not wait for him to disappear. Acting on impulsive she rushed forwards, throwing her arms around him and burying her head deep into his thick, warm mane.

'Bràthair, don't leave me!' she pleaded 'I need you, I need your strength.'

She was pushed backward as he lowered himself to the ground, ears twitching. His image continued to follow the path of the nightmare and as she stretched her hand out towards him, he was gone.

Mòrag clutched her chest, sank to her knees and cast out to him. 'Bràthair, come back,' she sobbed, 'please come back.' No. I won't watch it again, I won't. 'Bràthair, come back to me.' He will come back. 'Come back to me.'

Nothing.

She placed her head in her hands. Her face felt wet from the tears she hadn't noticed tumbling down her cheeks. Closing her eyes, she began to search her mindscape. Rannoch was always there: Always. She just had to find him.

Whatever drug they had given her had made her dizzy when her eyes were closed. Perhaps a tactic to keep her eyes open to the nightmare. Now, however, the effects were less so. She still felt a strong compulsion to open her eyes but resisted it with fierce determination.

Concentrating on her own mindscape her breathing began to slow and deepen. Her shivering body stilled as she felt the familiar warmth rising from within. *Rannoch.* She thought about every detail, everything that she loved about him. The way he would flick his tail when he was hunting, the low rumbling purr that sent her to sleep at night, the luxuriously soft mane that she would bury her face into when she needed him close: His eyes that matched her own; bewitching, burning, emerald green. Her heart ached for him.

They had been inseparable since his birth. The memory of that night was patchy from the fear and exhaustion her younger self had felt, but Mòrag focused hard: Trying to picture every little detail. She knew that if she were going to find Rannoch, it would be here.

Snapshots of the ugly scars running down the pregnant Unicorn's sides, the terror in her eyes when the tainted dart hit its mark and the roar of the enormous black Lion as it charged towards her. The thud as she hit the ground when her legs gave way, the cheers of the hunters in the dark, and the way the Lion pinned the sedated mare to the ground all flickered through her mind's eye.

The image that remained in the forefront of her consciousness was of the man that had strode triumphantly from the shadows. She would never forget the smug look of self-importance that dressed his face. The curl of his nut brown hair, and stubble that darkened his jawline, or the fire that danced in his pale silver eyes as he revelled in the distress of the beautiful creature.

A boy of around fifteen or so, his son or close relation, followed him into the clearing. The boy had the same shade of curly hair and the same pale silver eyes, yet he shared none of the man's pleasure with what was taking place.

The man regarded the subdued Unicorn for a moment before flicking his heavy woollen cloak back, and pulling a long sword from beneath his fine furs. He held it out to the boy and gestured at the mare's horn, instructing with pride in his voice, that the boy deal the killing strike. The boy, shaking his head, spoke too quiet for Mòrag to hear. Whatever he said infuriated the man. He leaned in close to the boy, growling at him to do as he was told. Again, the boy refused.

Burying his fist deep into the boy's furs, the man thrust him toward the fallen mare. He bellowed at the boy once more to do as commanded, and though he looked reluctant, the boy took aim. With effort, he swung the sword.

There was an ear-ringing clang as the steel made contact with the horn. The sound was harsh and unnatural, more similar to steel upon steel. Instead of cutting clean through, the blade lodged within the horn's glistening length. The mare started to struggle wildly beneath the Lion's grip.

'Stupid boy!' The man, now beyond outraged, had grabbed the hilt of the sword and pushed the boy to the side. 'You must strengthen your blade with your mind. Fool!' He tugged the blade free, and taking aim, he swung it with force, finally relieving her of her beautiful spiralled horn and condemning her to death.

Mòrag's physical body convulsed in response to the memory: She had wanted to run to the poor creature's aid. She had wanted to do something, anything. She had been unable to force her body into action. Fear and fatigue had set her muscles to stone.

Wide-eyed and voiceless, she remained beneath the winter foliage, watching, willing them not to see her and wishing for the monster and his Lion to leave.

'You did well to track this one, Silas,' he praised, laying a hand on his Lion's strong shoulder. 'She has been allowed to evade her fate for far too long,' he glowered at someone out of Mòrag's eyeshot. 'There is no escaping my Silas.'

The Lion had answered this with a soft growl as he had turned and padded toward the tree line.

The boy was ashen faced. It was obvious he wanted no part of what was going on.

'You do see, James,' the man said as he stooped to collect the shorn off horn, 'why we must cultivate the horns?'

'I thought the Unicorns shed their horns annually, uncle.'

'Nonsense, boy!' the man chastised. 'An old wives tale if ever I heard one!'

'Father told me.'

'Well, Father doesn't know what he is talking about,' he interjected, 'stupid boy! My brother knows nothing of the ways of this world.' The venom on his lips and hate in his eyes had been obvious even to Mòrag.

They stood, considering each other for what seemed like eternity, until the man stormed off into the dark of the forest, leaving the boy alone in the clearing. The powdery snow creaked under his polished leather boots as he approached the fallen creature. Crouching down and pulling the glove from his hand, he placed his palm on the Unicorn's neck.

'I am sorry,' he stood, unfastening the ornate silver clasp of his olive cloak. Grasping the heavy woollen material at his shoulders, he swung his arm above his head. The cloak flew elegantly through the air and settled over the Unicorn.

'Be at peace,' he said as he turned and left the clearing.

It took several long minutes and five steadying breaths, before Mòrag was able to will her body into action. The walk from her hiding place to the fallen Unicorn was filled with tears. She sobbed, for the beautiful mare and for the unborn foal. She stood for a moment, unwilling to touch the poor beast, but the shuddering of her half-frozen body compelled her. There was still warmth in the mare's body and Mòrag had pressed herself as close as she could in a desperate attempt to warm her own bones.

As she huddled tight to the mare's belly, she tugged at the luxurious fabric of the cloak that dressed the mare, pulling it around her, and could hardly believe her senses when she felt movement from within. She had been almost positive that she had imagined it until she felt a very definite kick. It's still alive!

Rummaging in her furs for her water cask, she emptied its contents and placed it to the mare's udder. Palpating it as Evelynn had once shown her, she extracted as much milk as the cask could hold. Placing it back in her furs, she then looked for a blade. At seven, all she had been allowed was a tiny blade that she could cut saplings and such with. Throwing the heavy cloak from around her, she scrambled around, in a desperate search for something sharp.

The snow chilled her fingers but she kept scanning the area until she came across a shard from the mare's horn. The man must not have cut as clean as she thought. The shard was about the length of her forearm. It was smooth, rounded at one end, and jagged at the reverse. The horn felt delicate and smooth under her fingers.

She folded the cloak and put it to one side, then taking the sharp tip she cut to the side of the mare's belly, like she had seen Jock do when a broodmare died. The hide split much easier than she had expected, and the blood, still hot, sent plumes of steam rising into the air. It mixed with her steaming breath and swirled around her cheeks and up into the atmosphere.

Gently she reached her spare hand into the wound to guide the cut. Her freezing hands burned from the mare's internal heat: As she cut deeper she could feel the foal's sack. Pinching it between her fingers, she punctured the membrane with the horn. A gush of amniotic liquid had flowed from the wound, diluting the deep red of the blood that dressed the mare's quarters, Mòrag and surrounding snow.

Placing the horn beside her, she reached both hands into the wound, extending them forwards and outwards to stretch the passage for the foal. She felt for the front legs and hooked her hands behind them, straightening them out. Next, she felt for the foal's head and eased it into position with the legs. Moving her hands back to the foal's legs, she grasped them tight and pulled hard.

Expecting delicate white hooves to appear first, Mòrag was taken aback when what emerged were soft black paws. She paused for only a moment before heaving the rest of the foal's body out into the freezing night.

It slid from its mother with very little resistance and settled with a soft thud on the blood stained snow that encircled them. Mòrag fetched the cloak and draped it over the wet, shivering newborn, and rubbed with vigour to help dry him off.

The fabric felt wonderfully soft under her tacky hands. She felt sorry to stain such fine cloth but the foal's need was paramount. It did not take long before the adrenalin in her veins dispersed, and hypothermia began to set in, sending violent shudders through her body.

She had been lucky that night: Lucky that the boy had left his cloak with the mare, and lucky that Jock had found her when he did, before the Wrathwind picked up and blew through the glen. Neither she nor Rannoch would have survived the night.

The memory faded leaving only the long track towards the grove. Her mindscape was more vivid and far safer than the dreamscape had been. It nurtured her confidence. As she emerged from the tree line into the tranquillity of the thicket, her heart leapt.

There, in the centre of the clearing, on a bed of bluebells lay Rannoch.

Chapter Six

DIFFICULT DECISIONS

Fine ribbons of smoke from embers long since dead rose in a series of swirls and loops, as if dancing toward the chimney. Randall exhaled a deep breath. He had been lost in thought for some time, and had no more noticed the waning fire than the darkening sky that he gazed past.

Leaving the window, he traversed the undulating stone floor, worn smooth from centuries of pacing inhabitants. The mahogany desk at the far wall was littered with files and folders containing the details of the current week's initiates.

Collecting the heavy iron poker from the roughly woven reed basket by the mantel, he stabbed at what was left of the cooling embers. Exerting his will towards their weakening glow, he stabbed once more. The embers sparked in response, and he placed some fresh kindling between them. *Grow.* At once, a small flame flickered into life, closely followed by another. Randall placed some dry logs around the kindling. *Grow.* The internal flame grew and flickered up through the pyre, spreading outward and upward, and roaring back to life. Satisfied, Randall left the hearth and settled into his worn leather armchair.

Lifting his left hand, he inspected the tender skin. *She burned me. She actually managed to burn me.* He rubbed at his palm with his fingertips. Her ferocious desire to free herself from his grasp had quite literally translated onto his skin, which was now red and sensitive.

The low creak of the heavy oak door heralded Tara's arrival. Randall glanced toward the door to see her padding to him. She sat in front of him and regarded him directly. She flicked her gaze towards his hand and back to his eyes, cocking her head; she gave a concerned whine.

'*Are you ok? Your mind was hidden from me for too long.*'

'*I am fine. At least I think I am,*' he cast, '*other than my hand that is.*' He held it out to her.

She inspected his palm. '*Not to worry. Nothing I cannot fix.*' She ran her tongue over it several times, before giving a small nod and resting her head on Randall's lap. '*All better.*'

The thick saliva was soothing, which almost made the stench of Wolf breath bearable. *Almost.* As the last of the heat and redness dissipated from his hand, Randall gave Tara a rub behind her ears and down her neck. The contented canine harrumphed at him and closed her eyes, enjoying the contact.

'*If you don't like it,*' she opened one eye to look at him, '*you should have tried harder at medic training when you were a pup.*'

'*I was not trained as a "pup," remember.*' Randall sighed. He had not been 'trained' at all. Not in the manner that initiates were now. He had received military training only. Things were different back then. Not that, 'then' was even all that long ago. There were no tests, no Cleanses, no military training academy at Sruighlea. Simpler times. Of course, that was before the assassinations and subsequent rebellion that led to civil war. In less than a year, the country had plummeted into darkness. It was a long road to recovery. Indeed, they were still walking it even now. '*In any case, I have no talent as a medic.*'

'*What do you plan to do about the pup downstairs?*' Tara lifted her head and regarded Randall thoughtfully. '*There is raw power within her. You risk further angering her familiar should you allow them to alter her with the Cleanse, if she even can be altered. There is only so long you will be able to prolong his slumber. And I cannot stand against him. He is the Nemeocorn, one of the higher beasts. I do not think even King James' Livia could stand up to him for long. Even with maturity and experience on her side.*'

'*I do not doubt it. If she cannot be controlled, the King will want her dead. Of that I am certain.*' He felt a pang of guilt rise within him, so strong that it made him question his resolve. He couldn't remember the last time he had felt any emotion this deep. His emotions had become significantly dulled by his link with the King, which was always kept open to some extent or another. The purchase price Randall had paid many years before, when he had become the King's right arm; his personal Berserker, was an overwhelming lack of empathy.

Since his consciousness had been ripped from his body he had slowly began to feel. The shock realisation of the guilt he felt over the fate of the girl in question had opened the floodgates. Everything had become turbulent and conflicted within his mind. Without the constant shackles around his mindscape, it flexed and expanded. His inner landscape, like a river carrying the spring thaw, was swelling and bursting its previous restraints: Guilt, loss, freedom, sickness, relief, worry, elation, anger. He felt them all rise up within him, swirling in the pit of his stomach. His skin grew hot and his throat became tight. Cold sweat beaded on his forehead as he began to pant.

'Randall?' Tara could feel it too, 'breathe deep, and slow. Calm your mind. I know it is difficult, but you must try: Everything to its rightful place.'

Randall felt as though he had just received a mindstrike.

'I will need help,' he cast. He had not ventured into his mindscape unaccompanied before. It had been the domain of the King for so long, that it had begun to feel unfamiliar to him. He had only ever withdrawn to it when commanded to do so.

'Of course,' was all Tara cast in response.

He took a deep steadying breath, and then let it out, repeating the motions until his throat loosened enough that he did not feel quite so sick. Burying both hands deep into the fur at either side of Tara's neck, he closed his eyes to the physical world. He felt her forehead press against his. As he retreated into himself, his mindscape began to form around him. A liquid landscape masked in a thick fog. Warped and misshapen plants and foliage dressed the pale surroundings. The colour seemed to have leached from everything. The distortion of his mindscape was vast and all encompassing. Not unlike the hold, the King previously had over him.

'Let me in.'

'*How? I have no talent for this, you more than anyone should know that.*'

'*Silly pup!*' She grunted, '*you only think that you cannot control your own mind, because you were always informed so. Of course, you have talent: Would I have chosen you if it were otherwise?*'

That was true. The Wolves tended to keep themselves to themselves. They were among the oldest of the communicative races and were neither impressed nor sympathetic toward people. Tara had never explained why she had chosen to bond with someone, particularly Randall. All he knew is that he seemed to be the only person who could see her in her true form. Everyone other than the King, Brax, a few members of the royal family and now this girl, saw her as a large dog. In any case, he was glad to have her in his life.

'*True,*' he pictured her form: Twitching ears, blue eyes, soft muzzle, enormous tongue... He smiled to himself as she began to materialise in front of him, wagging her tail, tongue hanging out the side of her mouth.

'*Good. Now we can fix this mindscape of yours.*' She turned and sniffed the air and wrinkled her nose in disgust, '*this way.*' Whatever she smelled, she didn't like it.

'*Where do we even start?*'

'*The source of the corruption,*' Tara replied. '*James.*'

Randall didn't know what to say. He was fiercely loyal to the King, but after seeing his defaced and shattered mindscape, he was more than a little disturbed. *How could this have happened without my knowledge?* Never before had he questioned the King's word, he had simply obeyed. *I have been blind.*

He followed Tara along the more solid areas of his mindscape, trying not to pay particular attention to his surroundings. She led him to an oak door with a gold knob for a handle. It was freestanding, unattached to any form of structure, with the door slightly ajar showing a hint of another room.

'*Enter,*' Tara instructed.

'*What will I find?*' He could feel the muscles in his legs clench.

'*It does not matter.*' She sat back on her hocks and lifted a paw to his chest, '*You must go, you must see, and then you must leave and lock the door behind you.*'

As Randall approached the door, the hair on the back of his neck stood on end. Reaching for the doorknob his hand trembled, and though he tried, he could not make it still. There was a fluttering in his chest and his feet felt like lead as he pushed the door inward. At his touch, the door swung away, revealing a small white room, devoid of anything, save for the statue at its centre.

The marble image of the King both enticed and repelled him. It was an odd sensation, not unlike the buzz when two opposing poles meet.

Randall took a step closer and studied the face of the statue. It was a perfect semblance of the King's younger self. Delicate curls dressed the face full of shock and sadness. His brow was raised. His eyes were wide and held no sparkle of life behind them. His lips were slightly parted. *This was how he looked the night his parents were murdered.*

Randall felt a compulsion to touch the face of the statue. He raised his hand. The air seemed to vibrate as he drew closer to the marble effigy. He hesitated only for a moment before stretching out his fingers to touch the soft roundness of the marble King's cheek. He pulled his hand back, rubbing his thumb along his fingertips. *Wet?* He had been crying that night.

Before Randall had time to question why a stone figure would be producing tears, the face began to change. The jaw line began to clench pulling the lips tight together. His brow began to drop until it was drawn down mirroring his lips. His eyes, no longer wide and round, were glaring, lined by tense lids.

Randall's skin began to crawl. *This is how he looked the night I finally agreed: The night he first took hold of my mind.* A quiver spread throughout his body. He knew now why he had to see this. On that night, he had not wanted to partake in the plans the King had suggested. He had not wanted another mind controlling his body. He had not wanted to become a puppet on a killing spree. He still didn't know whether he had agreed because of loyalty to King and country, or fear that even against his wishes; the matter would have been forced upon him. About one thing, he was now certain. Now that the hold over him had been released, he did not want it back.

Taking a step back, Randall bowed low. 'I am sorry my King.' He then turned and marched from the room, as fast as his quaking legs would allow.

Chapter Seven

REGAINING CONTROL

It could have been the hot breath, or the smell that woke Randall, he couldn't be sure, but the first sight that greeted him, was Tara. She was standing above him, a paw on either side of his head.

A stream of drool slid down her long tongue, and he flinched as it landed on his cheek. It rolled down the side of his face to the cold stone floor.

Randall grunted, his whole body ached, every muscle protested as he lifted his hand to wipe away the trail of saliva. His throat burned, and as he allowed his head to flop to the side, he cringed at the pool of vomit that dressed the floor.

He sat and grasped his throbbing head. 'Urgh, what happened?'

'*Your body is reacting violently to the removal of the King's binding.*' Her mindcast was like needles in his ears. She moved to his back, leaning into him supportively.

Randall appreciated the gesture. His muscles trembled and jerked at random intervals, making the chill from the cold sweat that clad his body, significantly more uncomfortable. His clothes were damp and clung to his skin, he hoped only from the sweat, though the stink of stale urine told him otherwise.

'*Can you get up?*' Tara asked.

He nodded in response. Twisting round, he grasped hold of her strong back in an attempt to steady his quaking body, as he rose to his feet. He shuddered, and fought the forces of gravity that sought to bring him back to the floor.

Slowly, and with much concentration, Randall made his way across the room, past the puddles of vomit that were soaking into the heaps of papers, scattered when his armchair toppled hitting the table. *What a mess.*

Tara stayed by his side, ready to steady him should his legs give way. After what seemed like an age, he reached the bathroom. Harsh clinical light flooded the room as he slid the glass door to the side. Randall squinted against its scalding glare.

The clean tiled interior and stainless steel fittings were a stark contrast to the rest of the castle that housed the army's training Officers and Tyros. As an Officer, one of the privileges Randall enjoyed was privacy. To that effect, the military had seen fit to deface the beautiful castle by knocking down walls to create bathrooms where the Officers could freshen and bathe in private. He thought it ugly: A useless waste of a beautiful and historic building. Now however, he was thankful for it.

Reaching the sink, he leant an arm either side of the bowl and let it take his weight. His ragged breath came in snatches and his body continued its relentless quivering. The sweat ran off him in icy streams dripping from his cheeks and nose into the sink, and running down the back of his legs and his spine making him shudder even more.

Turning on the tap, he let the water pool in his palm and sucked it back. The cold liquid dampened his scorched throat until, as he sucked back his fourth mouthful, the first hit his stomach, which instantly contracted, forcing the fluid back upwards and into the sink. Bile followed water until Randall was left retching with no result.

'*You need help that I cannot give.*' Tara's comment held a question.

He nodded, 'Brax,' he gasped.

'*I will return as fast as I am able.*' she cast as she turned to leave.

Randall slumped to the floor: Lying on his side, the cool from the tiles comforting his fevered skin. He hugged his knees close as his stomach knotted and pulsed. The last thing he could remember was the sound of the door clicking closed behind Tara.

The faint first light of the day was just visible through the heavy curtains when Randall woke. He was in bed. The black satin sheets were soft against his skin. Tara was lying by his feet snoring softly.

Lifting himself up onto his elbows, took far more strength than he had expected. Rolling to the side, he swung his legs down and shoulders up until he was perched on the edge of the mattress. Blood whooshed in his ears and lights danced in front of his eyes. *Too fast.* Sitting for a moment, he concentrated on his breathing until he felt more stable.

Opening one eye, Tara cast her gaze in his direction, '*You shouldn't try to get up yet.*' she warned. '*How do you feel?*'

Randall noted that he no longer wore his uniform. Instead, he was dressed in a simple pair of bed shorts. He ran his hand through his short hair. It felt silky and not at all matted, as he would have expected. *Someone must have bathed me* he cringed. As he ran his fingernails over his jaw line, expecting to find the short stubble that had become his habitual stress reliever, he realised that he was clean-shaven.

'*Who shaved me?*'

'*A young medic girl I think.*' She rolled on to her back and stretched her paws into the air. '*Brax asked her to care for you it seems.*'

Randall only grunted in response. He missed his beard already. He had not been clean-shaven for so long, that he felt naked without it.

There was a rap at the door. Tara woofed in response, and the door swung inward. Brax strode into the room followed by Ava Marcs, the daughter of General Marcs, one of his oldest friends. Her cheeks flushed as she saw Randall sitting at the side of the bed. He felt the heat of embarrassment flow through his body as realisation dawned that she must be the 'young medic girl' who had bathed him.

'Awkward,' Brax chuckled.

Ava's face responded to his jibe by turning a deep scarlet.

'Go on, I can take it from here,' he told her.

She gave a quick nod and darted from the room.

Brax wore a grin that immediately made Randall feel uncomfortable. 'Morning,' he said, giving Tara a pat as she padded from the room.

'How long?'

Brax crossed the room and sat himself down on the chair by the bed. 'Three days,' he crossed his long legs and stretched himself out, folding his arms behind his head, until the stretch made him wince and lower his hands back to his lap. 'You were a mess. I covered for you of course,' he winked, 'food poisoning apparently.'

'Thank you,' Randall replied. 'Have you still not healed?' he asked, nodding towards Brax's chest.

'Not fully, no,' he sighed.

'Will you still refuse the help of a medic?' Randall already knew what his answer would be: Brax was fiercely protective of his own mind and as such would not allow the medics near him other than to tend to external wounds.

'It's not up for discussion,' he said. 'They cleaned it, that's enough. I can do the rest on my own. However long it takes. So stop pestering me, Old Man.' A smile started to creep back onto his face, 'Talking about medics and old men,' he said, 'I hear Ava was quite impressed by her patient.'

'How could you Brax?' Randall's cheeks flushed.

'Don't worry so much. She's too shy to make a move on her Daddy's best friend. Unless you want her to,' he winked.

Randall couldn't think how to reply, he was weak and clearly outmatched in wit. Instead, he just sighed and reached for the tumbler of water that was sitting on his bedside table. His movements were awkward and slow. As he lifted the glass, his grip failed and it fell from his grasp, smashing on impact and splashing its contents across the floor. 'Damnit!'

'It's ok. I'll get it.' Brax rose and left the room. He returned with a dustpan and brush. 'You're going to have issues. You've not had full control of you mind for, what is it, ten years now?'

'Yes. Ten,' he replied, distracted.

'Do you think he knows?' Brax asked as he brushed up the shards of glass from the floor.

'I was just asking myself the same question,' Randall sighed. 'I do not think I would have been able to sever the connection, had he been paying attention to it.'

'That's true. Look, I'm not really wanting to drop this on you now.' Brax began. 'But both the girl and her beast are close to waking.'

'Has she completed the Cleanse?' Randall had forgotten about Jock's daughter.

Brax shook his head. 'No. She seems to still have some fight in her.'

'Perhaps I should contact General Marcs; I think I had decided on that.' He shook his head, 'I am not so sure about any of my past decisions now.'

'I don't think you should,' Brax replied. It seemed as though he had already thought this matter through. 'Look, the way I see it,' he continued, 'is that, given recent events, a powerful ally wouldn't be such a bad thing.'

'I am in no condition to deal with this just now.' He was embarrassed to admit it, 'I can hardly control my own body, let alone try to teach control to an over aged initiate.'

Brax gave a weak smile, 'I know,' he said, tone sympathetic.

'If you feel that you can take the lead on this.' Randall continued, 'if you are prepared to shadow her, test her, and train her as a Seeker, which I suspect she is... Then wake her Brax. And do it quickly.'

Brax rested a hand on Randall's shoulder, 'It's good to have you back old man,' he smiled.

Chapter Eight

INTERFERENCE

The deep rumbling breaths of the sleeping Nemeocorn vibrated through Mòrag's body. Lying amid the bluebells with her head and shoulders against Rannoch's belly, a gentle breeze tickling her skin, she finally felt safe.

Rannoch was still proving difficult to communicate with, and would not fully wake from his slumber, but would give vague answers to the occasional question. She was happy to accept the small amount of communication after such a long period of silence from him.

She had managed to work out from his vague responses, that he was not awake, he did not know where he was, and that he would quite like a fresh young buck for his supper. The last remark had made her smile. After feeling so much fear for so long, the simple comment had been like sunshine on her soul.

Mòrag was not sure how much time had passed since she had entered the dreamscape. Nor did she know how long she had spent hidden away in her own mindscape. She was well aware that time became irregular when consciousness stepped out of the physical world. She had heard stories of people becoming lost in themselves — Preferring their own internal world, to their external one.

The thought made her wonder if that was how she would end up, locked in her own mind, with an empty shell for a body. She chewed at her lip. One thing was certain. She was not going back into the nightmare.

She stretched back against Rannoch's warmth; he obviously sensed it through their connection, and emitted a contented purr. She gazed upward at the lilac sky, breathing in the faint scent of wild garlic.

A tingling in her hands caught her attention. It was an odd sensation. Lifting her hands to examine them, she found nothing of any consequence. The sensation seemed to transfer to her neck, sending a shiver down her spine. *It almost feels like I'm being watched.*

Scanning the area, Mòrag searched for any abnormalities. Anything that wasn't from her own mind should be easy to spot. Her visual exploration of the surroundings yielded no results. As she leaned back onto Rannoch once more, the clear and distinctive cry of a bird of prey pierced the tranquillity of the thicket.

Mòrag leapt to her feet, wide-eyed. Putting her weight on the balls of her feet, she prepared to run. *Where am I going to go? I'm in my own mind.*

A second, much closer cry, allowed her to locate to the rough area of the approaching threat. She stared into the dark of the treeline, waiting. Utter quiet had descended upon the clearing.

There was a rustling as something came to rest behind her. Mòrag was torn. Should she run, or stand and fight the threat? *I may not be able to find my way back to Rannoch if I run.*

'*Do not be alarmed, child. I mean you no harm.*' the tone of the mindcast felt sincere, but still filled Mòrag with dread.

Without transferring her weight from the balls of her feet, she turned slowly.

In front of her, atop Rannoch's shoulder, sat an enormous Haribon. Its head was dressed with long brown feathers that reminded Mòrag of Rannoch's mane. A deeply arched blue-grey bill and intelligent eyes of a paler shade dominated its regal face. Smooth brown feathers coloured its back, while the feathers of its undercarriage where a gleaming white. The great Haribon perched upon substantial yellow legs, which ended in large powerful talons.

'*You may call me, Sharri,*' she cast, her pale blue-grey eyes holding Mòrag's gaze '*my master would speak with you, if you would agree to let him.*'

Mòrag was stunned to silence. She could not trust this unexpected apparition, though she knew that the status quo could not continue much longer. Eventually she would have to find a way out. *What do I do?*

'May my master speak with you?' She hopped gracefully from her perch, and landed a few feet in front of Mòrag. Standing on level ground, she was past the height of Mòrag's waist. *'Your body is ailing, child, I urge you to speak to my master. He means you no harm.'*

'How can I trust what you say? I've been forced into this hell by your master and his càirdeas.'

'You need not trust me. You have felt it yourself have you not?' the Haribon cocked her head to the side, *'If you cannot trust my word, you must listen to your body, and trust what it tells you.'*

Mòrag knew it was true. She had often felt her heart flutter. Breathlessness and chest pain plagued her. Her body was slowly wilting.

'Will your master release me?'

'As I understand it,' Sharri replied, *'that is his intention.'*

Mòrag gave a slight nod. *'Aye,'* she cast, *'I'll speak with your master.'*

The Haribon aired her powerful wings. The winds she created swirled around Mòrag, who could not help but admire the magnificent bird.

'You must listen and follow my directions exactly. Do you understand, child? If it is discovered that you have escaped the Cleanse, you will most likely be killed. It is imperative that you follow my instructions. Do you understand?'

'Yes. But –'

'There is no time for me to explain, child.' She interjected, *'There will be occasion for questions later. For now you must listen.'*

Mòrag nodded in response.

'You must take yourself to the edge of your mindscape, as close as you can to the waking world. When you wake, you must lie still. If there is no one in the room, you must stay as you are. Someone will come to check on you. When they speak with you,

you must only give simple answers, as if you are insensate. They will expect you to act so. You must let them lead you to a recovery cell. I will come to you by night and take you to my master. Can you do this?'

Mòrag chewed her lip as she absorbed the instructions, *'I will do as you ask.'*

The great Haribon bowed her head, and was gone.

Chapter Nine

A FACE FROM THE PAST

It was early in the morning, roughly two o'clock. During the height of summer, the sun rose beyond the Eastern crags, no later than four o'clock. In his small quarters, situated in the West wing of the castle, Brax paced the floor. Sharri had left him almost two hours before, to fetch the girl from her recovery cell. It should have only taken twenty minutes to transfer her to his room. *What's taking so long? We're running out of time.*

Moving to the wooden stool by his desk, he sat awkwardly. It was too short for him, but was all he had. All of his furniture was too small for him. His desk was too low. His bed was not only, too low, it was also far too short for him to lie comfortably. Having asked several times for more suitable furniture and been declined, Brax had resigned himself to a life of aching muscles. It was just another show of dominance by the king and his Generals.

With his rare talents, he was an important possession of the king's army. Yet, he knew that was all he was, a possession: A tool to be used, whenever James saw fit to use him. The fact did not upset him; it had been this way since he was a young boy. He was treated far fairer as one of James's subjects, than he had been under the grasp of James's uncle Edward.

His quarters reflected his status or lack of, squirreled away out of sight, in a forgotten corner of the castle. It suited Brax just fine, *apart from the damned furniture*; he had more privacy than the top ranking officers and visiting officials.

He kept little in the way of personal items. Edward had not allowed him to keep anything for himself. If he found or was gifted an item, it had been snatched away once Edward got him out of view. It had become habit for him not look for sentiment in material objects.

There were only two items, which he treasured: The first was a leather bound notebook, given to him in secret by Catrìona, the Albannach princess, which he kept in his desk drawer, wrapped in a rough piece of cloth to disguise its importance. It was full of sketches of the greater animals and plants from the highlands and heartlands of Alba. Over the years, Brax had added the Albannach lowland, and Sasannach flora and fauna, making it the most comprehensive guide to the animal and plant life in the two countries. The second item, which he could not bring himself to part with, even for a moment, was the shorn horn of Catrìona's Unicorn, Skye.

Edward had coveted the horn as if it were the crown that he had been denied. Brax, consumed with guilt and sadness, had hidden it away, determined that the power hungry monster would not have it. He had paid in blood for his actions. James stumbling upon them was the only thing that had saved him. Then the whole world had gone to hell.

At times, when the stab of loneliness would nip at him in the dark of night, he would wonder if he had been the cause of the whole thing. The guilt ate at his soul in the quiet moments. Randall had often reminded him that whatever his actions, Edward would still have done the things that he did. What Brax had done slowed Edward down, and in a roundabout way, allowed James to escape the slaughter. Brax was not as confident of this as his guardian was.

A faint rap at the door caught him off guard, making him jump and gasp as the movement jarred his tender wound. He was surprised that his heart seemed to race as he walked the short distance to his door. *Have I done the right thing? Too late to turn back now.*

He lifted the latch and pulled the door inward. A hooded figure stood in the passageway.

'Come in,' he said, casting an eye down the passage to reassure himself that she was alone.

As she entered his quarters, a whoosh from the window and ruffling of feathers told him Sharri had returned.

'*My apologies for the delay: The child asked for some of her possessions and I thought it appropriate that she have them,*' she cast, bowing her head and stretching her wings wide.

Brax turned toward her '*A heads-up wouldn't have gone amiss, Sharri. I've been twiddling my thumbs here for hours,*' he retorted.

'*My apologies.*'

'*Never mind, I'm glad you are back. Any trouble?*'

The girl, still stood at the door, cleared her throat, 'You wanted to see me?' she asked, unknowingly interrupting his internal conversation with Sharri.

'Oh. Um yes,' without turning he strode to his desk and pulled out the stool. 'Sorry, it's been a long couple of days, please, sit.' *I suppose she's had a rougher few days than I have.*

He turned to regard her as she walked the short distance from his door, to the stool. She wore an olive cloak over her army issue clothes. Obviously one of the 'possessions' she had asked Sharri to retrieve. The sight of it stirred something inside him; it looked familiar.

Sitting herself on the stool, she raised her hands and lowered her hood. Long auburn hair that had been wound up out of the way now tumbled free down her back. The flickering light from the fire made her pale skin shimmer. Her intelligent emerald eyes studied him, as he studied her.

Brax felt as though a knife had pierced his heart. *It can't be.* The girl that sat before him was the double of Catrìona. Every detail was the same from the wave of her hair and the freckles on her cheeks, to her mesmerising emerald eyes.

He stood, open-mouthed. The last time he had seen Catrìona, she had begged him to flee the Sasannach castle with her. Edward had caught him in the wee hours of the morning, trying to sneak out of his room, which lay within Edward's chambers. Brax had been battered senseless for his insolence, at five years old; he was no match for Edward's brute strength. As he had lain on the floor next to his bed, head whirling, the last he could remember of that night was the alarm sounding that Catrìona was gone.

'I,' he faltered. 'Excuse me,' he said as he took a seat on his bed. 'You reminded me of someone I used to know. You must have questions?' he offered.

'Where's Rannoch?' she asked, concern in her voice.

'He's in the dungeon cells,' he told her, 'please be assured, it will be more comfortable for him there than you imagine. He's still asleep after all.'

'When can I see him?'

'In time, there's a lot we need to do. A lot I must ask *you* to do.' He could see her absorbing each word he spoke.

'If he wakes, he won't stop until he gets to me,' she said.

That's true. And, I doubt we would be able stop him. I only just managed to subdue him before. 'Do you think you could persuade him to stay put for a while?'

'It depends.'

'On what?'

'On what you have to offer him.'

Chapter Ten

BAD DOG

Lying flat on her back, staring at the stone celling, the firm horsehair mattress, lumpy and uncomfortable beneath her shoulder blades, Mòrag let the conversation of the previous night whirl around her.

The main point that she kept coming back to was treason. Had he really committed high treason by releasing her from the Cleanse? If that were the case, of course he wouldn't shy away from asking her to perform an act of treason in return. An internal war was now raging within her. Should she do as he asked, place herself and more importantly Rannoch in danger: Not to mention tarring Jock and Evelynn with the same brush: *Traitor to the Crown.* She knew only too well what happened to traitors.

As a young child Evelynn had often told her stories of the 'Purges,' *swear fealty to the Crown or die. The brightest minds in all of Alba systematically sought out and destroyed. Of course, the Sasannach's swore their allegiance to the Crown. It was a Sasannach King, sitting atop a Sasannach throne after all.*

Anyone who did not swear their loyalty faced the death penalty, as did the remainder of their bloodline. She would have to come to a decision soon.

Mòrag looked around her cell. Bare stone walls melted into the stone floor. All that filled the small space, other than her body, was her small bed and a chamber pot. Sharri had informed her on their journey back to the cell, that she would not be able to keep her possessions here. The bird had offered to hide them so that they would remain safe. Mòrag had agreed.

'If we're found out: If it's discovered that you've not completed the Cleanse, we'll all be killed. Do you understand Mòrag? It's vital that no one knows.' Brax had told her, 'you'll face many tests, you'll be asked to do terrible things. And you must do them without question.'

She gave a deep sigh. *What do I do? If I try to escape with Rannoch, I'll be hunted for the rest of my life, and Jock and Evelynn, who have been nothing but caring toward me, will most certainly pay for my disappearance with their lives. I don't really have a choice do I.*

She realised, that not to do as Brax asked was not an option. For the sake of all involved, she had to play her role. Perhaps she could find a way out of this mess at a later stage. For now, she would have to sit tight and wait for instruction.

Decision made, she closed her eyes in an attempt to get some rest.

Raised voices down the corridor made her jump. Rising and pressing her ear to the door of her cell, she tried to listen to what was being said.

'I'm sorry, Sir, but I cannot allow you access to the recovery cells.'

Mòrag recognised the medic's voice but couldn't place it.

'Where is she?' A deep voice boomed.

'Recovering, Sir, I am sorry but you cannot see her,' the medic insisted.

Mòrag's pulse started to race. *I hope it's not me he's looking for.*

There was a deafening smash, followed by a thud and muffled noise from the medic.

'What room?'

'I, I can't,' the medic faltered.

'WHAT ROOM?'

'F-fourth on the right,' she gasped.

Mòrag backed away from the door. The clattering from his boots as he marched to her cell was too much to bear.

With a bang, the door of her cell flew inwards. The man, who burst into the room, was clad in black. His epaulets displayed the bath star and crossed swords beneath a crown, the symbols of a General.

His lips, curled back in disdain, 'There you are,' he growled.

Short black hair framed his weather beaten face. His dark brown eyes were cold and calculating. The medals decorating his pumped up chest, jangled as he advanced towards her.

Mòrag backed away, until she reached the wall of her cell. Noting that he had not closed the door, she tried to dart past him.

Catching her easily, he slammed her back into the brick, forcing the air from her lungs. His hands clamped on to her shoulders, as he pushed her up the wall until she was eye height with him, and her feet were dangling.

He leaned in close, breathed deep, 'You smell of fear.'

Her body was still suffering the after effects of her prolonged sedation, and she could do little more than struggle weakly against the fingers that dug into her skin. The more she fought the tighter his grip became, until it made her gasp.

Drawing back, he locked her gaze; a sneer crept over his lips. 'Your parents had the stink of fear on them too. Would you like to know what I did to them? Of course, you would. But, I shan't tell you. I will show you. I am going to enjoy this.'

Hurried footfall from the corridor perked Mòrag's hope.

'General Raine,' the voice belonged to Brax.

The General's gaze was unwavering, 'Go back to your kennel, Dog. My business is none of your concern,' he growled.

'I've been sent by General Steele. This girl has completed the Cleanse and is under the care of the academy,' Brax stepped closer. 'Release her.'

'Randall has not been an acting General for years now. You know that as well as I,' although he refused to let her go, his grip loosened, much to Mòrag's relief.

Brax continued to approach until he was within striking distance. His fists were clamped tight; his pale silvery-blue eyes were like those of a wounded tiger: Equally full of fear and anger. His whole face was tense: His whole body rigid.

'He has never been officially stripped of his rank.' He spoke through gritted teeth, 'he is still a General whether you want to admit it or not. He has been placed in charge of the recovering Tyros, and *he* has the authority here.'

Mòrag hit the floor with a thud as General Raine turned to regard Brax.

'You are getting brave, Dog,' he spat. 'Your master has been absent for too long I see.'

Relief flooded over Mòrag as General Raine took a few steps away from her. With him so close, she had felt as though she couldn't breathe. He advanced instead, toward Brax. She watched as Brax backed towards the door. She couldn't understand how a young man like Brax could be out faced by a man over twenty years his senior. The General was tall, and slim compared to Brax who was built on a heavier frame, yet he still retreated, until he hit the wall by the door.

'We used to have fun, didn't we, you, Edward and I? You were obedient back then, unlike now. We all know what happens to disobedient dogs, Brax.'

Stepping in, the General buried his fist in Brax's stomach, forcing the air from his lungs. He doubled over, gasping as his knees buckled.

Leaning down, the General spoke in a quieter tone, though Mòrag could still make out what he said.

'Someday soon your master will return. You want to behave for your master like a good dog, do you not?'

The crisp white of Brax's shirt began to mottle with deep red stains.

'Poor dog,' General Raine mocked, 'you had better go lick your wounds before they become infected.' Straightening, he turned to regard Mòrag once more, 'until next time.' He said, and then strode from the room.

Mòrag sat quietly, back against the wall, absorbing everything that had just happened. Brax had leaned back against the opposite wall, and was trying hard to regulate his breathing. *He is more scared of that man than I am.* Rising slow, she approached him with caution. He looked up at her, his face much paler than it had been.

He took a few steadying breaths. 'He was lying,' his voice was hoarse from pain, 'about your parents. Randall,' he shook his head, 'General Steele arranged for them to be moved as soon as you were brought in.'

Mòrag let out a long held breath. She had been terrified for Jock and Evelynn. She offered a hand to Brax. He shook his head, gesturing with his hand that she should move back and give him more space, and with a grimace, he got to his feet.

'You're hurt.' She didn't think he had been hit hard enough to split skin.

'It's nothing,' he said, 'an old wound.'

'An old wound shouldn't be bleeding,' she insisted, 'you need help.'

'I don't need help,' he smiled, 'I need put out of my misery.'

Chapter Eleven

RUMOURS OF RETURN

'And the fact of the matter, *Steele*, is that he interfered with General Raine's business. He has no right to even be in the same room as a General, never mind order one out of the building. Disgraceful! Utterly disgraceful! The rudeness and audacity of that boy is beyond belief!'

Randall let out a long sigh. Mairead, General Raine's secretary, had been ranting and raving in his office for over an hour. The middle-aged woman was short, and plump. Her red face, hemmed by short brown hair, gave her the appearance of a baboon's backside. This image amused him. He had never noticed before. In all the years he had worked alongside her, he had never spotted this detail. Her comical appearance was not helped by the presence of her familiar, who, in actual fact, was a baboon. She was clearly offended by Brax's involvement in the matter. As she got more and more irate, her face grew redder and redder. Randall was struggling to keep a smile from his lips.

'General Raine,' she continued, 'is requesting that you transfer the girl to him for punishment. He also was adamant that the boy be suitably punished: Preferably locked up if you ask me!'

'I am sorry, Mairead,' he began, 'but I will not be acting upon any of General Raine's requests. The girl has done nothing wrong. She has completed the Cleanse, and as such, will receive the correct and proper training, as decreed by the King.'

Mairead began to huff and puff as he spoke.

'As for Brax,' he continued, 'he was acting upon my instruction. I will not punish him for doing as I requested.'

Mairead's face became a deep shade of purple.

'Please relay my apologies to General Raine: That, on this occasion, I must decline his requests. Thank you, Mairead that will be all.'

The sullen faced woman stormed from the room, followed by her familiar. As he closed the door behind her, a smile crept across Randall's lips.

'*Does she amuse you?*' Tara asked from her makeshift 'den' beneath his desk.

'*Yes, she does. I never noticed before.*'

'*You missed a lot while James was in control. I am glad you are regaining your senses.*'

'*You say that as if I was an empty husk,*' he noted, sitting himself back down behind his desk.

'*You were not yourself.*'

'*No, I suppose not.*' He thought back over the last few years. His memories were vivid but carried no feeling, as if they belonged to someone else. '*How could it have gotten so bad?*'

'*Fear; paranoia and fear: Misguidance, paranoia and fear. It will only get worse as time goes on. That is why he has affected you so. James has become withdrawn from the world. I had begun to fear you would suffer the same fate. I am glad it will not be so.*'

Randall was touched by her emotion. She could have left him at any point. She was not obligated to remain, but she had stayed by his side regardless.

'Thank you, Tara,' he said, '*I imagine, I would have been lost completely if you had not been here to keep me anchored.*'

Tara did not answer. She just wagged her tail and fell asleep.

Randall set about organising the several files and folders that littered his desk. He had a lot of paperwork to catch up on after the near week that he had spent in bed. His muscles, still full of aches and groans had protested late that morning, when he had donned his uniform and tackled the winding corridors, to his office in the North wing of the castle. It had taken him an hour to walk the distance, and by the time he unlocked the heavy oak door, it had been close to midday. The mountains of paperwork stacked on his desk had been a fearsome sight, surpassed only by Mairead barging into the room without as much as a knock.

It shouldn't be long before Brax appears to tell me his version of events. As if in response to his thoughts, there was a quiet knock at the door. 'Come in.'

After a moment's pause, the door creaked slowly inward. The young man that entered the room was pale, his forehead, beaded with sweat. He walked stiffly, clutching his abdomen. 'I'm not alone,' he said, voice tight. 'I've brought Mòrag. What I have to say concerns her too.' He held the door ajar as she walked into the room, then closed and bolted it behind her.

Brax moved to the window ledge. As he turned to lean against the sill, Randall could see that his shirt was marred red beneath his arm.

'Brax, what the hell happened?'

'Split some stitches. Not a big deal. Our friend General Raine paid Mòrag a visit.' He grimaced, 'Randall... I.' Brax seemed unsure of himself, 'I think Prince Edward means to return to Sasann.'

'What makes you say that?'

'Raine told me,' the young man's gaze was searching, as if he was trying to work out how Randall would react to this information. 'Look.' He added before Randall could reply, 'he *is* coming back. He is. And we need to be prepared. We need Mòrag to be prepared. She needs to start her training now.'

'Raine told you?' Randall couldn't keep the scepticism from his voice. He thought it odd that General Raine would not have come to him in the first instance, if he indeed had any knowledge that Edward was planning his return. 'I do not think it likely Brax. You and I both know that General Raine does not have a liking for you. It is possible, that he has told you this in an attempt to upset you. Clearly he has succeeded.'

'He's told me before.' Brax looked hurt. He obviously truly believed Edward would return.

'Yes. You have mentioned it to me more than once.'

'You don't believe me.' It wasn't a question. The young man turned away from him then, although he made no move to leave the room.

Rising from his desk, Randall approached the sullen young man. 'Oh, I believe you, Brax. I believe that General Raine told you this. I also believe that he has you convinced beyond all doubt, that Edward is plotting his return. But I am afraid, my young friend, that I do not believe this matter is anything other, than a ploy by those who seek to torment you.'

Mòrag, who had remained silent until now, stepped forward. 'It's true. I heard him say it.'

Randall turned to regard her. He had not expected to see her for a while yet. Usually initiates would spend up to a fortnight recovering from the Cleanse. Considering what she had been through, she should have still been in bed.

'I don't think he was lying.' Mòrag's eyes were red rimmed. It made them appear an even more intense green.

'Raine wanted to harm her. I can't let that happen. I *won't* let that happen.'

Randall was struck by the conviction in Brax's voice.

'There is more to this than you are telling me.'

Meeting his gaze Brax nodded, 'There's more to this than you will ever know.' He smiled meekly, 'Raine is, and has always been Edward's accomplice.'

Chapter Twelve

HAUD YER WHEESHT!

Mòrag followed Brax through the winding passageways of the old castle: The flagstone floors worn smooth over the centuries. As she followed Brax's back in the dim light, she couldn't help but marvel at how the castle had survived the Great War six hundred years earlier. As she understood it, this particular castle was already three hundred years old before the war, yet even now, its stone walls remained strong.

Looking back down the dim passageway, the memory of her nightmare lingered, and, lost in thought, she did not realise Brax had stopped in front of her. He grunted as she walked into him.

'Sorry,' she said quietly. She had an overwhelming desire to whisper.

He was panting hard, one arm clamped tight over his stomach, the other against the stone wall of the passageway for balance. *He's in so much pain.*

'I'm... ok...' he gasped, 'just... give me... a sec.' He was shaking like a leaf.

'You're not ok.' Mòrag couldn't understand how he could endure such pain and injury. The military had the best medics, and most advanced technology. There was no need for him to be in this state.

'I... just need to... catch my breath... Bloody Albannach castles.' He smiled at her then, though it did not spread past his lips, before letting out a few long sighs, 'At least most Sasannach castles... are on level ground... Let's go.'

Mòrag didn't answer she just followed behind. Warm smells began to float up the corridor towards them, making

Mòrag's stomach growl. She had not eaten since Sharri had brought her to Brax's room in the early hours. She had not noticed her hunger, until the circling aroma of the Tyro's lunches had tickled her appetite.

The hum of activity grew louder as the passage dropped away into a winding stone staircase. Brax's movements were increasingly slow and jarring. He winced as he descended each step until they reached a landing. The spiral staircase continued to descend but he moved from it to stand, back against the wall, next to a closed set of double doors.

In the brighter light, Mòrag could see how pale he had become. His breathing had not improved. He closed his eyes, leaning his head back against the wall, as he focused on regaining control of his lungs. His jet-black hair was slick with sweat, hung loose around his shoulders, his damp shirt clung tight to him, hinting at a more toned physique than she had first imagined.

He gestured, indicating she should follow him. Using his back to push the door he led her into the refectory. Hundreds of Tyros sat on wooden benches either side of wide mahogany tables that seemed endless. Brax kept close to the wall, eyes locked on the exit at the opposite side of the hall. His pace quickened as they reached the halfway point, which was when Mòrag noticed that the noise in the hall had diminished. Instead, the atmosphere filled with hushed voices, whispered questions and poorly concealed laughter.

'Hey look, the Dog's got himself a bitch!' The hall erupted with laughter.

Brax did not break his stride, but Mòrag slowed scanning the faces, to see if she could locate where the voice had come from. Halting, she locked eyes with Fletcher Raine. Obviously, *he* had not turned down the help of the medics after Shand had finished with him. To Mòrag's disappointment, he looked as though he had never been injured at all. He was among a large group in the centre of the hall. Sitting on the table, his feet on the bench. He wore a wide grin across his round face. His short brown hair was meticulously combed. His brown eyes flicked toward Brax, then back to Mòrag.

'What's the matter, Darling?' he crooned in a smooth Sasannach accent, 'Gone off your dog? Probably wise, he's damaged goods you know. Want a real man to show you a good time?'

Brax caught Mòrag's arm just as she was about to approach the group, *and do, what? I have no plan other than smacking him in the heid.* She knew it would have been a pointless manoeuvre, but it would have made her feel better at least.

'He's not worth it... None of them are,' he said under his breath.

She turned away from the group, which was roaring with laughter, and followed Brax from the room.

The laughter continued to be audible until they had descended the south stair to the dungeons.

Brax nodded at the two sentries. Returning the greeting, they unbolted the fortified steel door and pushed it inwards. The door closed and bolted behind them as Brax led the way, past several empty cells to another iron door at the end of the corridor.

'Go on.'

'Thank you.' Mòrag lifted the latch and pushed the door inward. Rannoch lay sleeping on a bed of straw in the centre of the room. There was a drip line attached under a bandage that dressed his shoulder.

Brax approached Rannoch with caution . He ran his hand through the sleeping Nemeocorn's thick mane, before starting to un-dress his shoulder.

'I don't know how long... it will take him to wake. I've never encountered one... of his kind before... I'd only heard stories.' A slight smile touched his lips, 'Only realised at the last second... he wasn't a Unicorn... He almost had me that day,' he grimaced. 'Damned hands won't stop... shaking.'

'It's no wonder, you should be in bed.' Mòrag was surprised that he was still on his feet, after so much walking with an aggravated wound. 'Wait. You can see Unicorns?'

'Yes... I'm a natural... Seeker... born with... the talent... Randall tells me... you're the same.'

Mòrag frowned, 'well, I have seen a Unicorn: Once. And I know everyone sees Rannoch as a destrier: Other than you that is. But I don't think that makes me a Seeker.'

He stopped tinkering with Rannoch's bandage and turned to look at her. 'What about Tara... Randall's familiar? And Sharri?'

'He has a She-Wolf, and you have a Greater Haribon.'

'So it's true... You are a Seeker.' He turned back to Rannoch. 'To most people... Tara looks... like a big dog... And Sharri appears... as a buzzard.' He removed clip and needle from Rannoch's shoulder. 'Call him.'

Mòrag nodded and reached out with her mind, '*Bràthair?*'

Rannoch's eyes opened, and he locked gazes with Brax. His lips curled back revealing his sharp teeth.

Brax backed away as Rannoch rose to his feet, growling.

'*He's a friend, Rannoch.*' Mòrag cast, '*At least, I think he is.*'

'*He struck me down.*' Rannoch flexed his claws, swishing his tail from side to side. '*You had better tell him to run if he knows what's good for him. I'll not be caught twice.*'

'*No, Rannoch. He released me. He risked himself to protect me this morning.*' She laid a hand on his back, '*You've already wounded him. He could have died then. Please, Bràthair?*'

Rannoch stilled then, and sniffed the air. '*He still might. That wound is festering.*' He snorted as though the smell irritated him. '*I'll do as you ask. But I can't promise I won't eat him later.*'

'*Thank you.*'

Mòrag switched her gaze back to Brax. He stood clutching his abdomen, eyes still locked onto Rannoch. He wore a near constant grimace on his pale face, and was trembling uncontrollably.

'He won't harm you: Unless you move to harm either of us.' She told him, as she approached his trembling form. 'Rannoch told me your wound is infected. You need to go to the medics.'

'*Puithar?*' Rannoch padded to her side. '*If you can hold him, I'll clean his wound. When I struck him, I wanted him dead. Something tells me he won't heal, unless I heal him.*'

'I'll... be... fine,' he gasped, 'I... just... need... some rest.'

'A skelp's what you need, you numpty!' She huffed at him, 'If you leave it festering like that you're probably going to die.'

'Would anyone care?' He lowered himself to the floor of the cell, 'I may as well give in... It would be... easier.'

Sympathy isn't what he needs right now. 'Och haud yer wheesht!' the snap in her voice surprised her, she hadn't meant to be so sharp with him. 'You've pulled me into this mess, and I'm not being left to deal with it on my own.'

'I'm sorry'

She crouched to his level, and looked him in the eye, 'I don't want you to be sorry. I want you to pull it together a little bit.' She placed a hand on each of his shoulders, 'will you let Rannoch clean your wound?'

Brax looked away. He didn't speak, and just gave a stiff nod in response.

Chapter Thirteen

UNEXPECTED BOND

It was early evening. The sun, close to disappearing beyond the western forest, cast long shadows across the empty courtyard. All the men from court were out for the last hunt of the season. Trying to catch the silver buck before the winter snows covered the valleys and the rivers turned to ice.

Andrew crept as silently as he could along the balustrade hoping to catch a glimpse of the Albannach Princess. Edward had warned him to keep out of sight, but curiosity had overridden his better judgement. He waited until he was sure that his master had left the castle grounds, before slipping from his room into the main room of Edward's quarters.

He made his way toward the grand entrance hall, and crouched behind the balustrade for what seemed like years.

'What are you looking for?'

Andrew practically jumped out of his skin, letting out a loud yelp. He spun to face the owner of the voice, and was met by the most beautiful sight, his young eyes had ever seen.

Flaming locks of auburn hair hung about her shoulders, the rest was twisted loosely up around her head, bound by bright red tartan ribbon. Her skin was paler than buttermilk, which enhanced the freckles that danced across her cheeks. Her eyes were like nothing Andrew had ever seen before: Large, smiling eyes that were a more intense green than the jewels that adorned the Queen's crown. She smiled warmly at him, and bent low in a graceful curtsy. The deep green fabric of her dress rippled on the floor around her.

'*Tha mi toilichte do choinneachadh. That means "Pleased to meet you," wee laddie.*' She winked at him, '*who might you be then?*'

Imitating her, he stood as tall as he could, and then bowed deeply. '*I'm Andrew, but everyone here calls me Brax.*' He took a step toward her, '*are you a princess?*' he whispered.

'*Aye, laddie,*' she said, '*Catrìona Margaret Elizabeth Mary Stewart, Princess of Alba, and heir to the long revoked Albannach throne, should we ever get it back.*' She lent down until they were touching cheeks, and whispered, '*you can just call me Catrìona if you like.*'

When she drew away, his cheek tingled; he couldn't help lifting his hand to touch it.

She smiled at him more warmly than before, if that was even possible. '*I think it's past your bedtime. Shall I accompany you to your quarters?*'

Andrew blinked at her. '*No?*' he said, cocking his head.

She giggled, '*lead on, young sir, wee laddies such as you, need good rest to grow big and strong.*'

Taking her hand, he led her through the winding passages toward Edward's quarters. The scene through each window they passed grew darker, until there was no light left. Andrew slowed to a stop as they reached the door.

'*Thank you for my lovely greeting this evening, wee laddie, I hope we can be good friends.*' She smiled at his intake of breath, '*you like that idea, don't you?*'

'*Uh-huh.*'

'*Good. Well goodnight for now.*' She bent down once more and gave him a gentle kiss on the cheek. She smiled as she drew back and saw the open-mouthed surprise on his face. '*Goodnight,*' she said as she turned and started back up the passageway.

Andrew stood, watching her back until she was out of sight, hand against his cheek. Slowly, and as quietly as he could, he pushed the door inwards. The main room was quiet and dark. He let out a sigh of relief, and headed to his room as quick as he could. He couldn't stop touching his cheek, which still tingled from Catrìona's kiss. As the door clicked closed behind him, the *sweet tingling was replaced by hot venomous sting. He stumbled sideways and hit the wall with a thud.*

'*I told you to stay.*'

***

Brax woke with a start. The room was completely dark save for a sliver of artificial light from beneath the doorway. Faint odour of rodent and old straw filled his nostrils. *I must still be in the holding cells.* He lay still. Only feeling a dull ache in his abdomen, he wanted to savour the momentary freedom from pain before it resumed.

He flinched as something moved through his hair. *Wait. That didn't hurt.* He forgot about whatever it was that had made him jump, and took a few deeper practice breaths. His ribs were tender, but did not flare into searing breathlessness. His stomach felt achy and tight, but not painful. He began to question the whole situation. Was he still asleep perhaps? Had someone infiltrated his mind and it was all a trick? Before he could ponder further, whatever had been moving about his head started its journey once more.

He moved his hand up, *please don't be a rat.* Instead of his fingers meeting a small furry body, they found another hand. His heart squeezed. Clutching the hand tight, he angled his head back to see who had him in their grasp.

Mòrag was sitting with her back against the wall, her head tilted to the side. Her face was soft and relaxed, her eyes closed. Her legs pillowed his head, and her hand was stroking his hair.

'*She had to hold you still.*' Rannoch's emerald eyes were all that was visible in the dim light. '*You had a lot of fight for someone half dead,*' he purred.

'*I'm sorry,*' Brax cast gingerly, '*about how we came to meet.*'

'*You mean you regret striking me.*' He could hear Rannoch's tail swishing from side to side, '*I'll tell you this once. Speak your mind as it is. Dancing around the issue will only serve to irritate me.'* He drummed his claws on the cell floor as he awaited Brax's response.

'I'll try to remember that. Can I ask, how are we linked? I don't remember making a connection.'

'I had to... re-direct your mind, to heal in the correct way.' Rannoch gave a yawn, *'Mòrag has not yet learned, what I have known since birth. I created a bond with you for that reason.'*

'You bound me.' Brax felt as though the air had been removed from the room. *Please don't let him have seen.*

'Exactly.' Rannoch stretched and flexed his powerful paws. He was now visible to Brax's adjusted vision.

His heart started to race. *What if he's seen? What if he knows? He must know. If he has bound me, he will have had free rein to explore my memories as he pleased. And with me unconscious, I was powerless to maintain the barriers.*

'You fear what I have seen.'

Brax nodded in response.

'At first your mind recoiled from my own, you became fearfully violent. Someone has done a great damage to your soul, that much is certain. Which is why you had to be bound; a link would have been too unstable. Do not worry, I would not seek to intrude on your innermost thoughts and feelings: Although, you were bombarding me with several images, some of which were impossible to ignore.' Rannoch padded towards Brax, and dropped close to the floor so they were face to face. *'Who is Catrìona?'*

Chapter Fourteen

BOGGIN'

As Mòrag opened her eyes, her temple resumed its throbbing. Brax had thrashed about while Rannoch cleaned his wound, she was lucky he had only caught her once. He was still lying with his head on her lap, and she realised with embarrassment that her hand, entwined in his hair, was clutched by his. She made no attempt to move her hand away in case she woke him. Rannoch lay in the corner, purring. She had missed that sound more than any other. It made her feel safe.

She wondered how long it had been since they had entered Rannoch's cell. Fletcher Raine and his group's harsh cackles had filled the space outside the door when the light had gone out and the lock clanked shut.

'Enjoy your night with the rabid dog. Hope you aren't afraid of the dark. Because I *know* he is.'

He won't be laughing so hard when Rannoch's chewing on his damned spine. Mòrag couldn't understand why Brax seemed to be so hated, or perhaps it wasn't hate. Perhaps he was despised. She still could not see a reason for it. From what little she did know about the military, Seekers were highly prized. A natural Seeker therefore, should be a far more precious thing.

At once, she understood why she had been kept alive: A natural Seeker. *Maybe I hold more cards than I think I do.* She wondered if her fate would be the same as his. She would have many questions to ask him when he woke.

His hand relaxed and dropped away from hers, she was about to take her hand away from his head when he spoke.

'Don't stop.'

She hadn't realised he was awake.

'I've never been good in enclosed, dark spaces,' he confessed, 'you're helping, that's, helping. Don't stop.'

'Alright,' she said. She felt oddly comfortable. Most likely because she felt safe with Rannoch so close, although, she welcomed the feeling of calm that she seemed to bring out in Brax. 'How's the pain?'

'Better,' he looked up at her, 'thank you.'

'No need to thank me. Rannoch healed you. All I did was struggle to hold you down.' She smiled at him through the dark of the cell. 'You called me Catrìona.'

He flinched at the name.

'Who is she?' Mòrag was almost reluctant to ask him. He had pleaded for Catrìona's help.

'She... I,' he began. His hand came back to hers, giving it a gentle squeeze, 'I'm not ready to talk about her yet. Not out loud anyway. Someday, but not now; if you have to know, ask your familiar.'

'No. I'll wait.'

Brax pulled his head back to look at her. He wore the oddest expression on his face. As if he didn't believe that, she wouldn't press the matter.

'It's obviously important to you.' Mòrag continued, 'you'll tell me when you're ready.'

'Thank you,' he said, 'I appreciate it.'

She smiled at him, then looked towards the door. 'So how do we get out of here? You're clearly in need of a bath.'

'Are you saying I smell?'

'Aye. You're boggin'.'

When she looked back, Brax had a silly grin plastered on his face.

'What's so funny?' she asked him, perplexed.

'Aye? Boggin'?' he chuckled.

Mòrag could feel her cheeks warming, and was glad of the dim light. 'The last time I was pulled up for speaking like a 'guttersnipe', was the morning of Shand's binding. Evelynn never did like to hear Jock's words coming from me. Not that it ever bothered me.' She felt a pang of guilt, *I've really messed things up for them.* 'Will I ever see Jock and Evelynn again?'

Brax tentatively pushed himself up to a sitting position. 'In all honesty, Mòrag, I don't know.' He kept his back to her as he spoke, 'everything is going to change, everything. And when it does, there will be nowhere to hide.'

He is talking about what that General said yesterday. Getting to her feet, she dusted herself off before moving in front of him. 'Well. We'll cross that bridge when we come to it. For now, let's focus on getting you to a bath.' She held her hand out to him.

Brax looked up at her. 'You're some girl, you know that?'

'Of course! Now come on already, your stench is burning my nostrils.' She wrinkled up her nose at him.

'Ok, ok, I get the picture.' He grasped her outstretched hand, using it to steady himself as he got to his feet. 'The first thing we need to do is move Rannoch to the stables.'

The growl from the corner indicated that Rannoch was displeased with this idea.

'He won't tolerate that. Rannoch needs his freedom.'

'Will he tolerate being separate from you for most of the day? If he will then, as long as he is careful, he could roam the land surrounding the castle. Sharri and Tara prefer that option, I just thought you would rather have him closer.'

Mòrag regarded Rannoch for a moment before speaking. *It would be the better situation for him, as long as he doesn't start stalking people that is.* 'Bràthair?'

'*I will behave,*' he snorted.

'Let him roam. He will be close enough if I need him.'

Brax nodded, moved to the door, and placed his hand over the keyhole. The sound of the lock clicking open seemed deafening in the quiet of the dungeons.

'How did you?' Mòrag knew he didn't have a key, if she had known it was that simple to open the lock she would have done it hours before.

'A little skill I learned as a boy. I'll teach you it someday.' Brax said as he pulled the door inwards.

They did not follow the same passage back towards the guards and refectory. Instead, Brax led her and Rannoch in the opposite direction. The passage began to drop away from them until it became quite steep. Down lighters were placed at infrequent intervals, and were so pale, they barely gave enough light to see by.

Mòrag stopped. 'This is...'

'The passage everyone sees at some point during the Cleanse. This is the way you were brought into the castle: Through the underground passages to the initiation wards.' Brax shuddered. 'If I can avoid it, I don't go near that area. It makes me... uncomfortable. You would have been sedated but partially aware of your surroundings when they brought you through here. That's why it remained in the forefront of your mind.'

Brax indicated she should follow him, and they continued down the passage until they came to two enormous metal doors. He pushed one side open enough for them to get through. The sound from the rusted hinges screeched through Mòrag's bones.

The morning sun danced upon the surrounding Chluaidh-Dubh loch. After the dim corridor, the bright light burned her eyes. Brax turned to her; he was standing much straighter now than the last time she had seen him on his feet. His face was relaxed and his breath came easy. He was looking much better.

He frowned as he looked at her, 'What?'

'You look as bad as you smell!' Mòrag chuckled.

'Gee thanks,' he huffed. 'If you walk up that track there,' he pointed to the dirt path that led round the side of the building, and up over the rise, 'you will reach the barracks. Randall arranged for you to be bunked with Ava. She won't train with you, at least not for the moment anyway, but she's about your age, a year older I think, so she will be a more suitable bunkmate. She'll be waiting for you.'

'Ava.' Mòrag repeated to herself, 'how will I know who she is?'

'She's the medic you met before: The one who woke you. She is General Marcs' daughter, and an acquaintance of mine. She is,' he paused, 'sympathetic.'

'Ok, I'll find her. What about Rannoch?' she asked.

'I will take him now to meet with Tara and Sharri, they will show him around and take him hunting,' he said. 'Ava will get you settled from here. Your training is to begin tomorrow.'

'Alright,' she gave Rannoch a scratch, reluctant to be parted with him now that they had been reunited, though she knew it was a necessity. She turned towards the path before looking over her shoulder and asking, 'Any helpful training tips I should know?'

'Yes,' he said. 'Don't give in.'

Chapter Fifteen

GOSSIP

Ava had been gathering medicinal herbs and mosses, which lay on the other side of the castle, and had seen Mòrag as soon as she crested the hill.

They walked together back to the barracks and chatted guardedly about meaningless things, neither of them mentioning the incident regarding General Raine, or Brax, or the fact that Ava had refused the General passage to the recovery cells, until they had reached their bunks.

Mòrag sat hugging her knees on Ava's bunk, listening to the girl talk about the benefits of natural healing as opposed to gifted healing. Mòrag wasn't too fussed by the conversation; she was just content that her situation seemed to be looking up.

Ava's thick blond hair, secured in a band behind her head, fell in long looping curls down her back. Mòrag felt her gaze drawn to its golden abundance; it pinched at that long subdued feminine side of her, who hated her own unruly, wavy red mop, with which she could do absolutely nothing.

Considering the thickness and abundance of her hair, Ava's body was the opposite. She was a slight girl. She carried little to no weight at all, though; she had full soft round cheeks and soft curves, rather than the bony edges of the half-starved.

Mòrag had to fight to stop herself from staring at her. She had the fine delicate features of an expensive porcelain doll. Everything about her seemed to scream *look at me*. She looked far younger than her eighteen years, though she spoke with more maturity and knowledge than Mòrag could muster.

Ava was kind, or seemed kind on face value, but Mòrag felt as though something was missing behind her deep caramel brown eyes, though she couldn't put her finger on exactly what.

Like the others in the barracks, Ava had no familiar. They had chosen to specialise in a particular field, and as such would not be burdened with training for the binding, and then training their new bound familiar, until they achieved the desired level of expertise.

Ava finished her lunch and went back to the infirmary, leaving Mòrag to her own devices. She had been given no instruction, other than to go to Randall's office after the day's training was over. *What am I supposed to do for the rest of the day?* She could hear shouting from the training grounds that lay to the south of the building she was in. *I might as well take a look around. At least then, I will know where I should be going tomorrow.*

Leaving the barracks, Mòrag wandered between the buildings that were dotted along the side of the main thoroughfare. She had no aim, no particular destination that interested her; she wandered without particular direction until she came to an open door. Hearing the unmistakable sound of a gossip at the height of their current storytelling venture perked her interest. *Probably shouldn't be being nosey*, she told herself as she stood, back against the outer wall next to the open door. *Although, it's not like she is trying not to be heard.*

'Outrageous! Simply outrageous!' the woman seethed, 'he should be clapped in irons and boiled in oil for laying a hand on General Raine.'

'I agree!' another voice piped up, 'the dog wants whipping!'

They're talking about Brax. But it was General Raine who beat him, not the other way around. Again, she wondered why he was so hated.

A third voice joined the others, 'So Mairead, what is he going to do about it?'

'He won't let it stand. I assure you.'

This must be Mairead.

'General Raine will take the matter to the King,' she continued, her voice becoming sleek and smug, 'The King will not be as forgiving as that has-been Steele.'

Mòrag decided she didn't want to hear any more. So far, Brax had been the only one to change her situation for the better. She had the distinct impression when she had stood with him in Randall's office, that it had been his idea to release her from the Cleanse. Even if he had underlying reasons, she was still grateful to be free of the nightmare.

Moving away from the door she followed the road back through past the buildings, towards the castle. The sun was starting to dip in the sky, and the buildings began to empty.

Mòrag watched the Tyros saunter back to their barracks before heading to the refectory for their evening meal. She fell into step behind a large group that were discussing combat tactics and cavalry manoeuvres. One boy in a green uniform glanced back at her. He slowed his pace until he drew level with her. His loose blonde curls bounced with each stride that he took. Mòrag noted that he was not as old as his height had made him seem. He must have been around twelve or so.

'Hello.'

Mòrag looked over at him. He had a soft face, expressionless. She nodded in response to his greeting.

'You're the girl that was with the Devil's Dog last night aren't you?' He now wore a grin, though his blue-green eyes remained untouched by emotion.

'His name is Brax,' she said plainly. It was starting to irritate her that people kept referring to him as 'Dog'.

'Did you show him a good time?' his grin widened further.

What is it with these people? They aren't acting like any normal person I've ever met: Saying that, I've not met that many people. But that's not the point. Morag shot the boy a look that could boil ice.

He held his hands up, 'Ok, ok sorry. Raine told us he heard all this moaning coming from that cell you and the dog were in, and... well you know.'

Mòrag had to bury her nails into her palms to keep from punching the boy. She took a deep, steadying breath before she spoke. 'Who are you?'

'Oliver,' the boy beamed.

'Ok, Oliver. Firstly, a boy your age shouldn't be concerning himself with adult issues. Secondly, his name is Brax; he is a person, not a dog, so be a good boy and use his damned name. Thirdly, Fletcher Raine doesn't know his arse from his elbow. So do yourself a favour. The next time he opens his mouth, believe the opposite of what he says. Understood?'

The boy was aghast, 'Uh, yes, Ma'am.'

'Good. Now piss off.'

Chapter Sixteen

LESSER OF TWO EVILS

Randall suppressed a yawn as he locked up the classrooms for the day. He was ready for a light supper and a long sleep, but would need to meet with Mòrag first. She would begin her training in the morning, and he wanted her prepared.

The corridors gradually emptied of inhabitants as he reached the upper levels. Turning the corner to the office block, he came face to face with Mòrag, who was standing with her back against his office door.

'You are early,' he noted as he pulled the key from his pocket.

'I had nothing better to do,' her voice was flat, and she avoided eye contact.

Randall pushed the door inwards, 'Please,' he said, indicating she should enter ahead of him.

She glanced at him as she walked past and into the room, stopping just inside and to the left of the door.

Randall followed her into the office, turning and closing the door behind him, before moving past her and settling himself behind his desk. 'Take a seat, Mòrag,' he said as he gestured to the chair opposite.

She moved across the room and sat herself down.

'Mòrag, I have asked you here, to –'

'Why do they call him Dog?' she demanded.

Randall drew a deep breath and let it out before continuing, 'Brax's story is both long and complex,' he raised his fingertips to his fresh grown stubble beard, 'I am certain that even I do not know the full extent of it. He was, for all intents and purposes, the play thing of the King's uncle. He was exploited for his gifts, and forced to hunt down both people and beasts. That is why he is known as the "Devil's Dog." He lives a rough and lonely life, hated and despised by many, particularly here in Alba, where the Prince Edward's hatred hit hardest.'

Mòrag stayed quiet for a moment, eyebrows drawn in thought. 'He had no choice?'

'None: He has been a slave to his master since he was a young child, until Edward fled to Breizh six years ago. Brax was lucky to get away with his life.'

'Then he doesn't deserve to be treated as he is,' she said looking at her hands which had red indents across the palms.

'I am glad you think so,' Randall replied, 'he could do with someone to fight in his corner.'

She glanced up at him in silent agreement, 'You wanted to speak to me about something else didn't you?'

'Yes. Your training starts tomorrow. You will find this particularly difficult, as you remain unaltered by the Cleanse. The rest of the Tyros here have been altered, and as such, will fare better than yourself. I wanted to prepare you for what is coming next.

'Your training will be split into three sections: Endurance, skills, and talents. I oversee the final 'talent' section, assessing the development of a Tyro's core and learned abilities and allocating a familiar to them based on their strengths. General Rozzen oversees the second 'skills' section. She will train your core and non-core skills and talents including combat, communication, and survival and so on. During your time with her you will also take part in bi-yearly tournaments to assess your progress.'

He let out a deep sigh, 'Unfortunately, General Raine oversees the Cleanse and the 'endurance' section. It is a brutal test of your stamina and determination to live. His tactics are no better than torture. You must pass his tests, Mòrag, you *must*. Failure is death, do you understand?'

'I don't have any choice other than to do the best I can,' she reminded him.

'That's not strictly true,' he said, 'you could run, you might even get quite far before someone noticed you were missing, even if I was to distract and stall proceedings, the news would still get to General Raine and the King. Brax would be forced to hunt you down in order to safeguard King and Country, and you would be killed. If it is discovered that he interfered with your Cleanse, he will be killed without trial. For helping you escape, I will most likely also be tried for treason and killed. So you see, Mòrag, you do have a choice. But I am afraid you must chose the lesser of two evils.'

Mòrag looked down at her hands once more, 'I'll do my best.'

'I am glad, Mòrag. There is just one more thing. The Cleanse removes the initiates of their morality. It makes them more controllable and better soldiers. Most Tyros are cold, and they are calculating. You must try hard to be the same.'

The young girl before him nodded in response. He apologised to her again, though he still didn't feel that it was adequate. When she left his office, he no longer had an appetite.

'*Are you worried that she will not cope?*' Tara seemed to materialise out of nowhere.

'*Where did you come from all of a sudden?*'

'*The hall,*' she cast in reply, '*what is on your mind?*' Padding round the desk, she sat close to his chair and placed her head on his lap.

Randall placed his hand between her soft ears, '*I am not so sure she will cope with this. Not as she is. She has handicaps that the others do not.*'

'*Have faith in her. She is made of stronger stuff than most. She would have beaten the Cleanse on her own.*'

He scratched her head and neck, '*I trust your judgement more than my own, Tara. You have never led me astray.*'

'*And I do not plan to. She will cope.*'

Chapter Seventeen

TESTS OF ENDURANCE -

STAMINA

'Can't you sleep?' Ava whispered from the bunk below.

Mòrag sighed, 'No.'

'You had best try. You will not be sleeping for some time after today.'

'Ava?'

'Mmmm?'

'What's involved in the endurance tests?' after everything that Randall had said, he hadn't told her exactly what the tests were.

'You have to run till they tell you to stop. And, when you fall they make you run more. They will deprive you of sleep, and food. Then keep you in solitary confinement. They will test your memory when you are at your lowest too,' Ava yawned.

'Is that it?' She knew she had stamina; she could go cross-country with ease for hours on end. She wasn't keen on the solitary confinement, or a lack of food and sleep, but it was all doable.

'That's it. It's much harder than it looks. I failed the physical bit, you know, the running? But, you *are* allowed one fail. At least, you were when I did it.'

Allowed one fail? Randall didn't tell me that. 'Thanks, Ava.'

'Uh huh, go to sleep,' she mumbled into her pillow.

A gong sounded across the grounds indicating stage one Tyros should gather.

Ava groaned, 'You had better get dressed and head over to Colonel Tesso's yard'

'Colonel Tesso?'

'He runs the Endurance tests when General Raine is away. I bet you are glad *he* is not running your tests.'

'That's an understatement,' she was more relieved than glad.

Jumping down from the top bunk, she pulled her uniform from her locker and slipped it on. The pale blue fabric had black piping on the sleeves and trouser legs, it was soft on her skin, but also stiff and constricting, *hopefully it would loosen through use.*

'Right then, I'm off,' she said to the heap of covers Ava lay beneath.

An arm appeared from the mound, waving to her, 'Good luck.'

Leaving the building, she followed the others who wore the same uniform as her: A group of around twenty-four, who gathered at the edge of the walled training yards. *They are all kids,* she noted with dismay.

'Hello again,' Oliver stood a few paces to the left of her. He sauntered slowly toward her.

'You again?' Mòrag couldn't hide the annoyance in her voice.

'My sister says I shouldn't have said what I did yesterday. She gave me hell about it. Says I'm an idiot. So... Sorry, I guess.' He grinned.

'Some apology that is,' Mòrag sighed, 'think before you speak next time.'

'Look, there's the Colonel,' Oliver pointed to a man dressed in a black uniform with pale blue piping down the sides of the sleeves and trouser legs, his epaulets were dressed with two bath stars beneath a crown indicating his rank as Colonel. Four men flanked him. Their uniforms were identical to his except their epaulets, which were dressed with the triple chevron.

'I am Colonel Tesso, welcome to stage one training.'

He had a young face, he was probably only in his early twenties, young compared to the other high-ranking officers she had seen. He stood around six feet tall, short for a Sasannach. His short black hair was poker straight and carried a silky sheen. His golden tanned face, dark brown, almost feline eyes and sharp but handsome features marked the foreign blood in him. His voice was soft, but firm, an odd but inspiring combination laced with his smooth Sasannach accent.

'You will be starting immediately on your stamina assessment,' he continued, 'you will run with me, following a pre-determined route. Once you have completed a full circuit, I will leave you to continue, under the observation of Sergeants Black, Johnson, Frederik and Simmons. Each lap will be timed. You will not slow your pace. You will not deviate from the route. You will not stop. Do you understand?'

'Yes, Sir!' the Tyros all shouted in response.

'Good! Now get moving!' He set off at a quick pace.

He means to have us push too hard at the start. Mòrag waited until the group had all moved into a jog before she fell in behind. None of the Sergeants moved to follow, so she kept to a slower pace, by the time they were half way round she was sure the others would slow to her speed. The route took them round the back of the castle, over rough, rocky ground, down the side of the castle, on a steep slope, through the valley below the castle, where the footing was good except for the ford, then back up the steep rise to where they had begun. The whole thing took them around thirty minutes or so to run. *I can conserve the most energy in the valley; it should help with the climb.*

As they reached the starting point, Colonel Tesso stopped running, and the four Sergeants replaced him, two at the head of the run, and two at the rear behind Mòrag. She kept her pace open and even, focusing more on her breathing than anything else. As predicted, the main group began to slow their pace. Mòrag reduced her speed proportionate to theirs, so she still lay several paces behind. She didn't need to slow so much quite yet, but it allowed her to keep a reserve as she ran.

Four laps in, and the pace had slowed considerably. Mòrag continued to decrease her speed in proportion to the main group, until the Sergeant behind her tapped her on the back with his baton.

'Faster,' he demanded, hitting her between the shoulder blades.

She increased her speed until she was in step with Oliver, who ran to the rear of the main group. He looked awful, his hair was plastered to his head, and his cheeks were crimson.

She didn't feel too fresh herself. Her muscles blazed on the inclines and over the rocks and ford. Her lungs ached and on the descending slope, her legs felt much less stable than they had only a short time ago.

Up ahead, a brown haired girl crumpled to the ground, tripping two girls and a boy behind her. The Sergeants leapt into action, screaming at them to get up and keep running. The three that she tripped, shakily got to their feet. The girl who fell did not. The sounds of the Sergeants screaming continued to drift on the breeze long after they were well out of sight. By the sixth circuit, the young tyros were dropping like flies. Mòrag was bathed in sweat. Her mouth was so dry, that she felt sick. *I'm done.*

'*No you are not.*' Rannoch's cast held power.

'*Where the hell have you been?*'

'*Hunting, naturally: There's good meat here. I did not expect you to be letting something like this beat you,*' he remarked.

'*I'm scunnered in Rannoch, my body is done.*'

'*Mind over matter,*' he cast, '*Remember the night we met. You should have frozen in the Wrathwind. Why did you not?*'

'I. I don't know. Because I didn't want to,' she cast in reply.

'*Exactly,*' he replied. '*Mind over matter.*'

Mind over matter. She focused on her breathing first, *long and steady.* The air filling her lungs seemed cooler than before, refreshing. *My legs are strong I can go further. My legs are strong I can go further.* As she repeated the phrases in her mind, she started to visualise herself running in her own mindscape. Her movements were smooth and powerful. She could feel a shift in her physical body, as though she was no longer using muscle power to move. Her body felt free, weightless. The last of the remaining Tyros fell behind her as she neared where the route began once more. Colonel Tesso grabbed her arm as she jogged past, halting her mid stride.

'Well done. Usually Tyro's don't pass this stage until day three,' his expression was approving, 'go shower and then report to the Northern barracks.'

'Yes, Sir.' Mòrag answered, and jogged off towards the showers.

The cool water refreshed her, but now that she had ceased her exertions, her body was weak. She pressed her hands against the tiles, allowing the water to beat down her back, her legs shook beneath her.

Grabbing a towel she dried herself off best she could, her stiffening muscles hindered her, but she pushed through until she was dried, dressed, and standing in front of the Northern barracks.

Colonel Tesso met her at the door, and ushered her inside, 'You will now begin your second trial,' he said as she entered. 'You will be allocated a place to stand along the wall. You must stay there until instructed otherwise. Do you understand?'

I must stand? 'Yes, Sir.'

'Sergeant Simmons. Take her in.'

'Aye, Sir!'

Sergeant Simmons was the first Albannach she had seen since she had been taken from her home. He was shorter than the Sasannach Officers, with a sandy coloured mop of hair that fell about his eyes, and a thick ginger beard that was trimmed to perfection. A set of chains and harness lay over his shoulder.

He marched her into an adjoining room. The glaring artificial light stung her eyes. There was nowhere to hide from it. The searing light bounced off the gleaming white tiles and whitewashed ceiling. There were no bunks in the room as would be expected from barracks; instead, the room was empty of all but the tyros that lined the walls.

Mòrag was marched to the far corner of the room. A large bolt on the floor and matching wall attachment caught her eye as she came to a halt.

'Feet here,' he instructed, 'hons by yer sides.'

Mòrag followed his instructions.

Sergeant Simmons placed the chains on the floor and fastened the leather harness round her waist and securing her hands tight against her sides. He then shackled her feet to the bolt on the floor, running the chain up to a pair of clips on the harness and behind her to the bolt on the wall.

'You ston here till told otherwise. Understand?'

'Yes, Sir.'

I'm not sure I will manage this. Her legs felt like jelly so she allowed the wall chain to take some of her weight.

'You there, at the end: Stand up straight!'

The shout made her and several others around the walls jump. She tilted her weight back onto her feet once more: Her tired, aching legs protested, but held their load.

Minutes seemed like hours, there was no way to tell how long she had been standing in the room. Metallic clangs rang out at random intervals as shaky legs gave way. Every sound seemed to swing between being muffled and being too sharp for her ears. The powerful lights above buzzed loudly. *Mind over matter, mind over matter, mind over matter,* she repeated to herself. It was far more difficult to tap into her mindscape than it had been on the run. Her concentration was dwindling; she had to push hard against the mental barrier that would have her give up. A boy beside her fell forward, chains clanging as they caught his weight. His body started to convulse, flailing like a fish on a line. The commotion peaked Mòrag's attention enough for her to look in his direction.

The boy's blonde hair flopped about his head in loose curls. *Oliver!* She looked up; no one was moving to stop what was happening. *Why won't they help him?* Her heart started to race as the seconds ticked by. *Failure is death,* Randall's words ticked over in her head. No one even looked at him. *If I make a scene, they will know I've not been changed by the Cleanse. I wonder. I wonder if I could connect to him like I do with*

Rannoch? She tried to focus on his face, but watching his body judder and shake was disturbing. Instead, she looked away, towards the floor, she brought the image of his bouncy curls and wide grin to the forefront of her mind. *This is difficult. If I could close my eyes, I would be able to picture him better.*

Flicking her eyes up, she realised that the Sergeants had turned their backs. *They aren't going to watch him.* She closed her eyes and drew his face to the front of her mind. *Oliver.* She pushed herself from her physical body into her mindscape. The terrain was soft and blurred, her movements, slow and clumsy; sapping her energy with each step, she took like walking in deep sand. *Oliver.* A door flickered into being in front of her. She placed her hand on the doorknob, and pushed it inwards. The room beyond was empty save for Oliver at its centre. He was thrashing about at some imaginary foe. The room shook, and she had to fight to keep her balance. She moved as quickly as she could toward him, but he lashed out at her.

'*Go away. Get away,*' he shouted, his mental voice echoed around her head.

'*Oliver, it's me.*' Mòrag reached out.

'*Get away!*' he sobbed, '*leave me alone. I want to go home.*'

'*Oliver, calm down. Your body is fitting; you need to let me help you.*' Mòrag took a step closer when he paused to think about her words. She pushed herself closer and grabbed hold of his arms. He fought her grasp, and at times, she thought he might get free, but eventually the fight drained out of him.

'*How, how are you in my head?*' he asked, looking up at her.

'*Honestly, I am too tired to think about it,*' she replied, '*you need to concentrate on your body, make it still.*'

'*I don't know how,*' he sobbed.

'*Start with this room. Make it still. Command it to be still. It belongs to you, it should do as you tell it,*' she said.

'*I'll try,*' he said, '*please don't go away.*'

Mòrag smiled at him, '*I'll wait until you wake,*' she said, '*I am struggling, myself so you need to hurry.*'

Oliver nodded at her. He closed his eyes tight and tensed all his muscles. The effort only served to make the room shake more violently.

'*Calm down, you're panicking, and that's making it worse. Deep breaths, slow and steady, slow and steady.*' She coached.

The room began to still in time with his breathing.

'*Well done.*'

'Thank you,' Oliver's voice was no more than a hoarse whisper.

Mòrag nodded her head, keeping her eyes closed. *Maybe they won't notice.*

'WAKE UP!'

Mòrag's eyes snapped open once more, it was almost impossible to focus on the man screaming at her. Oliver had managed to regain control of his body, and was upright once more, although he swayed on shaky legs. She herself had to concentrate hard to remain upright, every sound made her jump. Before long, her whole body had begun to tremble and jerk at odd intervals, and her dry eyes burned. She couldn't seem to control them any longer. They darted about at random, forcing her to clench them shut, only to snap them open when a sergeant screamed in her face.

Mòrag began to measure time in clangs and shouts, she couldn't tell how little or long the time between each was, but it allowed her something to think about, although she still jumped every time. A girl across the room began to sob, close to breaking point. Mòrag could no longer pull her head up to look in her direction. She was hanging against the chains, breathing heavy, praying someone would end the ordeal.

'Alright, Lass, yer done,' the voice was muffled and seemed to echo in her ears. 'Hear me, Lass? Yer done.'

Mòrag traced her blurred, wavering gaze, from the immaculately polished black boots in front of her, up the pressed black trouser legs and blazer to Sergeant Simmons's face, 'Sir?' her own voice sounded odd to her ears.

'Yer done,' he repeated, unfastening her restraints and slinging them over his shoulder, 'follow me.'

Before he had fully turned away from her, the room began to spin and blacken as she dropped to the floor.

Chapter Eighteen

TESTS OF ENDURANCE - SOLITARY STARVATION

When Mòrag opened her eyes, she was lying in a small stone cell: A glass of water and a small bowl of watery looking porridge sat by the door. Mòrag scrambled over and devoured them. She regretted it, as her stomach began to protest as soon as the last morsel passed her lips. She was desperately thirsty, her lips were dry and cracked, and her throat was still parched.

The large steel door of her cell was solid, save for a sliding panel at its base. The floors and walls were rough, bare stone and the only light came from a tiny barred window, high up the wall. It was cool, once the sun dipped beyond the horizon, her little cell would get cold. She wasn't looking forward to it.

The sliding panel at the bottom of the door opened and a hand retrieved the dish and glass before sliding it closed again. Mòrag's stomach growled; grasping it tight, she retreated to the thin pile of straw that had been left for her to lie on. Her eyelids began to droop, and she allowed her head to nod forwards.

She jolted awake at a metallic scraping sound. The cell barely lit by moonlight hindered her vision, and her dazed and exhausted mind could not work out where the sound was coming from. It wasn't until two legs appeared where the barred window should have been, that she realised what was happening.

Brax dropped silently to the floor, 'Good evening,' he grinned in the half-light.

'What are you? How? Why?' Mòrag stammered.

'Good to see you too,' he chuckled, 'you look like hell by the way.'

'Gee, thanks very much for your concern,' she retorted, 'you've looked worse, so don't start.'

'Huh! And here I was, thinking you might like some company and a bite to eat: Something to drink perhaps?' He grinned as she stepped toward him, 'I see I must have been wrong. Oh well...'

'Give it here you big tumshie!'

'Now, now,' he said as he reached into the sack that he had brought with him, producing a small parcel, 'No need to be rude.'

Mòrag took the package from his hand, it was warm; the steam from it making her mouth water, and her stomach growl.

'Eat it quick before it's cold,' he told her, 'I have a canteen of water and a few other things for you too.'

'Thank you.'

'No need,' Brax said, 'you've done more for me. And I'm the one who caused your problems in the first place.'

'Raine caused the problems, not you,' she interjected. 'How long was I in there for anyway?'

'Three days. I'm surprised you managed to last after that run you did.'

Mòrag drew down her brows in thought, 'Three days,' she repeated, 'at the time it seemed like years, I've never experienced such a horrible, feeling inside my own body before. Now that it's over though, it doesn't feel as though it was as long as three days.'

'That's probably because you slept for two days when they put you in here.' Brax replied. 'Now eat,' he said, sitting himself down against the wall, 'talk after.'

Mòrag nodded and sat opposite him. She opened the parcel and hummed at the warmth coming off the meat within. It had been a long time since she had last eaten hare. The strong flavour penetrated every inch of her mouth, and she savoured every bite.

Brax watched her from the opposite wall. He was looking much better: He was clean for a start, his long hair, tied neatly behind his head, hung down his back. He wore a tight pair of trousers and long sleeved top, both black. *So he can sneak about without being seen or getting caught on things most likely.* He was watching her with interest.

'Have you eaten?' Mòrag asked him.

'I went hunting didn't I?' he replied.

'You haven't answered my question,' she noted.

'I'm fine.'

'So you haven't eaten then,' *I bet he says no not really.*

'Eh, no. Not really.'

I knew it. 'Well you brought plenty, come and eat something.'

'I brought the food for *you*,' Brax replied in a flat tone.

'I understand, and I'm really very grateful. But I feel strange eating when you're not. Please. Share some with me?'

Brax sighed as he got to his feet and crossed the short distance between them, 'One day you'll learn that I'm not worth it you know,' he said as he sat down beside her.

'One day you'll learn,' she said, holding his gaze, 'that if you keep saying things like that, I might bash your head against a wall.' She smiled at the shocked look on his face.

'But, I'm, I mean. People must be talking; *you* have to live with that. And –'

'The things they say,' Mòrag cut in, 'are cruel, and uncalled for. I want no part in it: None. You have been nothing but kind to me, so I'll be returning the favour. Now eat.'

Brax took a chunk of meat from the package on her lap, 'Mòrag?'

'Mmmm.'

'Thank you,' he said, taking a bite.

Mòrag smiled, nudging his shoulder with her own, 'Any time.'

Brax smiled then, it was the first time she had seen a real smile from him, it lightened up his face, showing his youth even in the dim light. When she had seen him previously, his face had been tense, deep shadows had laced his eyes and he had a thick layer of stubble. Clean-shaven and relaxed, he looked ten years younger.

He passed her the water cask, and she half drained it before she realised that she hadn't offered him a drink.

'Sorry,' she said, 'very thirsty.'

'It's ok, you drink it, I'll get more in an hour or so.'

'You're leaving me?' Mòrag realised she didn't want to be alone; she had never truly been alone before, she always had Rannoch around.

'I was going to, yes. Let you get some sleep.'

'I suppose it's difficult for you down here, when you don't like small dark places,' Mòrag said, 'sorry, I didn't think.'

'It's not as bad as I imagined. Different when you have company,' Brax stretched his arms out above his head, 'do you want me to stay?'

'Would you?'

'Of course: Tell you what,' he said, 'I'll go get some more water now, and I'll be back shortly. Ok?'

Mòrag nodded, 'Ok.'

'Won't be long,' he said as he disappeared from the window space.

Mòrag waited for what seemed like hours, the sky outside her window space began to lighten. *He's not coming back.* Her desire to have company shocked her. She knew being in solitary confinement would be tough but she hadn't realised it would be so difficult, so quickly. She tried to call Rannoch but her communications kept bouncing back to her. *These cells have been built to completely isolate their inhabitants.* Leaning her head back against the wall, she closed her eyes, and allowed sleep to claim her.

When she woke again it was dark, the moon wasn't as bright as it had been the previous night, so the shadows played games with her vision. She had expected to be cold, it had been cold the previous night, but she felt warm. She shifted her weight against the wall, warm and soft behind her.

'You're awake then?' Brax said in her ear.

'OH HOLY HELL!' Mòrag shot to her feet.

Turning, she saw that Brax was sitting where she had been. He grinned, obviously fighting back laughter.

'Evening,' he nodded to her, 'nice sleep?'

'Brax! You,' she was lost for words, 'you frightened the life out of me.'

'Sorry,' he chuckled, 'You were freezing cold when I got back. I couldn't leave you shivering like that, and you didn't wake up when I moved you. By the way, you're giving me the stare of death right now.'

'I thought you weren't coming back.'

'I got held up,' he said, 'I'm sorry. Randall received word that General Raine knows you have begun training. He is on his way back here to "oversee" proceedings.'

Mòrag's heart skipped a beat. Brax's words circled round her, threatening suffocation.

His strong hands caught hers. 'You should have completed stage one before he gets here,' he soothed, 'in any case,' he added, 'I'll not let him touch you.'

Mòrag looked up at him; his pale eyes wore a harsh determination.

'And how do you plan to stop him?' She was dubious about his ability to stand up to someone, who had him frozen to the spot only a week before.

He waved a hand in the air, 'I'll think about that when I have to. They should be removing you from here tomorrow for the last bit of this idiotic endurance test.'

'Did you have to do all, this?' Mòrag asked him.

'Yes and no.' he replied, turning to re-take his seat against the wall.

'Yes and no? What kind of answer is that?'

'An accurate answer,' he chuckled. 'I never went through any military training if that's what you are asking.'

'...Right,' she replied. She had so many questions she wanted to ask him but swallowed them back.

Brax patted the ground next to him, indicating she should join him.

Walking over to the wall, she sat down next to him. He looked thoughtful, leaning his head back against the brickwork he closed his eyes and sighed, 'Raine loosely bases his training on "games" he and Edward used to make me play,' he smiled wryly, 'though the tests you are being put through, are far milder and less diverse. It was worse if alcohol was involved. They'd compete to see who could get me to break first. It was usually Edward. I learned pretty early on, that if Raine won their little "game," I would pay for it later. So no matter how twisted he became, I had to outlast him. I don't know how often I pleaded for them to stop, I would scream and sob and beg them to stop until it began to make things worse. Asking them to stop became their trigger to take it up a notch.'

Mòrag sat still and quiet, listening to every word. She didn't try to speak, to stop him or ask him questions. He obviously needed to vent and she didn't want to interrupt him.

'It got worse as I grew older,' he continued, 'Edward began to use more "mental" means of torture, dreams, visions, unbearable pain, and so on. He would taunt me, whispering plans he had for my coming of age. He would make me dream the things he intended to do. It would get so bad that I would try to drown out the agony within me, by provoking a physical attack from him. It was far easier for me to accept and deal with the pain when I could see a wound.

'My thirteenth birthday came and went, but he... I don't know, he was distracted by something, and spent a lot of time away, though he kept the threats coming.

'We were held up in a castle, somewhere in Southern Sasann, though I'm not sure exactly where. Randall and his men were laying siege. Neither side was gaining ground. Edward being Edward was supremely confident. Of course, he had Raine embedded within the King's troupes as a leading General. No one suspected a thing. So, they continued to sit outside the walls, and Edward lived in comfort within the walls; and my personal hell continued as it always had.

'And then I turned sixteen,' his hands were trembling, so he clenched his fists tight, 'I wanted to die. I just wanted my life over. I'd had enough. I never really believed he would take it so far until he did. Thinking back, the pain wasn't as bad as I had imagined it would be. But,' his voice broke, so he took a steadying breath before continuing, 'I decided then that if Edward wouldn't kill me, I would find someone else who would.

'That's when I found Sharri. Creatures like her are pure beings of power and aggression they don't entertain people. So, I approached her and awaited my death, but it never came. Instead, she took pity on me, binding me to her. Then she took me to Randall. The castle fell and Edward fled to Brazier. That was six years ago.

'It's taken me a long time to make peace with the ghosts and horrors of my past. I don't think I will ever fully come to terms with it. Sharri and Tara have helped a lot, Randall has helped too although up until you appeared, he was fighting his own battles. I don't know why I am telling you this; I've never even spoken to Randall about it.'

Mòrag said nothing. *What can I say? Nothing I could say would change the horrors of his life.* She leaned against him, pressing herself as close as she could to his side and wrapping her arms round his waist. She felt him flinch at first, his body trembling beneath her arms, 'I thought you could use a hug.'

She felt him lay his head on hers, his chest quivered as he sobbed silently into her hair. He put his arm around her back and pulled her closer, which she answered by tightening her grip.

After what must have been an hour or so, Mòrag felt his grip loosen a little. Pulling herself upright, she saw that he had fallen asleep. *He must have needed that. I wonder if he has ever had that much nonviolent contact.* She sat and looked at him for a while. His face was peaceful; the previous tension had all but melted away, leaving soft features. *He's quite handsome really.* She settled back down against his side, and waited for him to wake.

A few hours passed, Mòrag had not moved from her nest by Brax's side. She had never felt so comfortable in her life. The feeling shocked her. She had always been most comfortable with Rannoch but this was a different feeling altogether. *Maybe it's because of what he has told me. Or maybe it's because, now that I know more about his relationship with Raine, his determination to protect me from him means so much more,* she couldn't decide.

'Mòrag?' he said quietly.

'Aye?'

'Thank you.'

'Anytime,' she replied, giving him a squeeze.

Chapter Nineteen

TRIALS OF ENDURANCE — INTERROGATION

Brax stretched waking Mòrag from her doze, 'Is it morning already?' she asked with a yawn.

'I'm afraid so,' he replied, 'which means I must be going.'

Mòrag sat up, 'What happens today?'

'Interrogation: Another three days, but if you get through this, you're done,' he put his head in his hands, 'I hate this,' he whispered.

'What's involved?'

'A lot of yelling and screaming in your face: They will be nasty and nice only to be nasty again. Too many things to list: The worst thing they may do is make you stand in stress positions. That would be on the last day I think, the final effort to make you crumble. You should be put back here during the night, but I won't be able to visit because they will take you in at random intervals,' he let out a long drawn breath, 'I feel like I'm abandoning you.'

Mòrag regarded him; he was clearly disturbed by the idea of leaving her there. She smiled at him, 'Don't worry about me. I've made it this far haven't I?'

He returned her gaze, 'I suppose you have.'

'Well then. Will you be here when they let me out?'

'Of course,' he said.

'Good,' she smiled at him, 'because I have a feeling I may need another one of your hugs.'

He returned her smile; it was warm, 'Thank you, Mòrag.'

'What for?'

He shook his head, 'Being you.'

The unmistakable sound of jangling iron oozed through the door.

Brax jumped forwards, giving her a quick hug, 'Don't give up,' he whispered, before leaping up to the window space and disappearing from sight.

She backed away from the door as it screeched inwards. Sergeant Simmons paced into the room, 'Right, Lass. Last bitty begins th'day, shouldna be a problem far ye, worst part's over,' he grinned, 'Gid tae see a fellow Albannach doing better than all these Sasannachs!'

Mòrag blinked in surprise, but said nothing.

'Och Aye. Am here tae tell ye the words ye cannae speak,' he seemed quite pleased with himself. 'A fine strang lass like yersel will manage tae keep' em unner yer breest.' Now he was out of earshot, he was quite broad spoken, and reminded her of Jock.

'Sir?'

'Saor Alba,' he grinned.

'But Sir, that's high treason!'

'Ye'd better no repeat it then,' he said, 'they'll be by the noo far ye, just bide a bitty longer,' and with that he left the room.

Mòrag stood open mouthed. *I have no fall back. I can't say that no matter how bad it gets, never mind the demand for Albannach freedom, but speaking in her native tongue was forbidden. Either he is confident I can do this, or he is making sure that if I fail, I really fail.*

She started pacing her cell, trying to energise herself, and had reached twenty-four laps when the keys finally clanged in the lock. Colonel Tesso appeared. He couldn't hide the shock in his face when he saw her striding round her cell. *He probably expected me to be more desperate looking.* She shared a little smile with herself but did not let it show on her face. *Thanks to Brax, I am eager to get this over with.*

'Your solitary confinement is complete,' he said, 'follow me.'

He led her out of the cell and along the dark corridor, cell doors lined the walls, *twenty* she counted. *I wonder which Oliver is in.*

Colonel Tesso led her up a flight of stairs and into a room, there was a desk on the far right, around which the Sergeants stood, to the left of the room sat several chained Tyros. Some looked in better shape than others did, but all were exhausted and closed down to their surroundings.

She was marched to a space at the centre of the group of Tyros where her wrists were cuffed. The Colonel took up his position at the desk. Morag sat on the bench that ran the length of the wall. Time dragged. Raised voices trickled from the five closed doors at the end of the room. *I suppose the waiting is intended to wear you down before they take you in.*

One of the doors swung outwards and a man exploded into the room, he had a fistful of material at the neck of a Tyro, a brown haired boy, who was being forced to stumble, bent over before being thrown down at the feet of the other Tyros, 'Who's next,' he spat towards the group.

Every Tyro flinched and looked away, hoping to make themselves invisible to his searing glare.

'The red head, Major Frank,' Colonel Tesso said from behind the desk.

Mòrag kept her eyes to the ground. A meaty hand penetrated her field of vision. It grasped her cuffs and hauled her to her feet. Thrusting her ahead of him, he pushed his fist into her back.

'Move,' he growled at her.

Even knowing that this section of the 'training' should be easier than the previous trials, her heart fluttered in her chest.

The Major shoved her in the direction of a chair in front of a large table, 'Sit.'

Mòrag did as instructed, and he fastened her cuffs to the table.

Major Frank slammed the door of the room, the impact vibrated up through the table, 'You have information I need,' he snarled, 'If you tell me now, you can go back to your bed in the barracks. If not, I will pull the information from you by any, and all means necessary. Do you have anything to tell me?'

'No, Sir,' Mòrag wanted to shrink away, the presence of this man seemed to fill the room, suffocating her spirit.

'I was hoping you would say that,' he crooned wickedly, 'I have not had Albannach scum to interrogate for too long.'

Hour after hour was filled with the Major yelling and screaming in her face, taunts and threats on her life, and on the lives of Jock and Evelynn.

Mòrag kept control, she knew Randall had removed her adoptive parents from the area, and was confident Major Frank didn't know their location. His curses and threats about her and her fellow countrymen only served to anger her, making her more defiant.

Gradually the Major quietened, 'General Raine was disappointed that he could not be here to interrogate you personally. He instructed me to give you "special treatment," and I am only too happy to oblige.'

He pressed a button on the wall and Sergeants Simmons entered the room.

'Take this one for suspension. Three hours should do.'

Mòrag could feel his venomous glare on her back. Her cuffs were unfastened from the table and she was marched out of the room through a sliding door behind the desk.

The room beyond was too bright, making her blink and duck her head down to shade her eyes. Sergeant Simmons directed her towards a metal cage suspended from the roof by a rope and pulley. As he opened the front of the cage, the Major called into the room.

'On second thought,' he said, 'put her in the Strappado.'

'The Strappado, Sir?' Simmons faltered.

'You heard me Simmons, the Strappado.'

The Sergeant led her to a rope and pulley the far side of the room. He began to strap her arms together, and attach her to the rope. He was clearly uncomfortable with what he'd been instructed to do.

'Albannach scum hang with their arms to the back Simmons! You should know better.' Major Frank bellowed from the other room.

The Sergeant's jaw clenched beneath his thick beard: He unbound her hands, and rebound them behind her back. When the Major left the other room for a moment, he whispered, 'Pace yersel lass, dinna fight it, ye'll cause yersel a damage.'

Mòrag nodded in response. The rope was pulled taught, and as her arms reached their peak, her body began to tip forwards. Her muscles blazed. She wanted to pull, and kick, and bring her arms back down to a natural position, but remembered what the Sergeant had said. She allowed her body to flop forward as far as she could, taking as much of the strain off her over stretched joints as possible. She didn't notice when Simmons left the room. All she could think about was the searing pain in her shoulders.

Mòrag began to pant as her breathing began to labour. Her legs seemed to be constantly gaining weight, pulling her straighter, and stretching her muscles and sinew to their limit.

She flinched causing a sharp jolt in her exhausted muscles when the sliding door at the other side of the room flew open with a thud.

The boot steps were slow, heavy and deliberate. 'Are you ready to tell me what I want to know?'

Mòrag said nothing.

'Tell me what I want to know!' the Major roared.

She shook her head, 'No.'

The Major disappeared from sight. Mòrag felt dread rising in the pit of her stomach at the sound of heavy clanking metal. The Major's vicelike grip on her ankles prompted her to wriggle and squirm, trying to escape his grasp only to yelp at the pain she caused herself. He chuckled, attaching a thick chain round her legs, and then let it drop from his hand.

Agony engulfed her and she wailed despite herself. She could feel the terrifyingly slow shredding of her muscle fibres, and moaned in response.

The evil, satisfied chuckle behind her made her skin crawl. He hauled the chain backward, altering her position so she was hanging on a diagonal slope. Mòrag panted hard, trying to regain some of her wits.

'What are you keeping from me?' he crooned, 'Will you tell me now?'

'No.'

He swung her with force, sending her body forward and backward on a pendulum. After the fourth gut wrenching swing he held fast, jarring her to a sudden and painful stop, that left her whimpering pitifully.

He removed the chain and clenched a hand round her left ankle, tugging downwards, 'TELL ME!'

Mòrag gasped as the pain in her shoulders intensified further than she ever imagined it could, 'No,' she gasped.

'I am no longer doing this as part of your training. I want you to be clear on that. I am making you suffer for two reasons; One - You are Albannach scum, and you deserve it; and two - General Raine would like to experience a taste of what is to come,' he sneered. 'The truth is there is nothing more pleasurable than watching an Albannach squirm.'

Mòrag was panting hard, lungs and muscles blazing.

Major Frank grabbed her hair pulling her head back, 'Anything you want to tell me?' he taunted.

Mòrag glared at him, 'Taigh nam gasta ort!' she spat.

Major Frank's face contorted with rage. Clamping his other hand around her leg he wrenched it down until there was a sickening crunch.

Mòrag screamed, instinctively fighting against his grasp and her restraints. The pain washed over her like acid rain, and reverberated round her whole body from its epicentre in her left shoulder.

'Sir!' Sergeant Simmons raced into the room.

The Major released her leg from his grip and strode out of the room, 'Drop her,' he said as he past Sergeant Simmons, 'I am done with her for now.'

Simmons hurried over to the pulley attachment on the wall, lowering Mòrag to the floor.

Mòrag felt as though she couldn't get a breath. She gasped, and moaned, and sobbed as she lay in a heap on the floor.

Simmons undid her restraints, and inspected her shoulder, 'Dislocated,' he said, 'best we mend it the noo.'

Mòrag couldn't answer him; she couldn't even look at him.

'Sorry lass, this is gonnae be sair,' he said apologetically. Taking hold of her left arm, he manoeuvred it with a gentle but firm grip.

Mòrag bit back hard on her desire to scream through the pain, only letting it free when her joint, popped back into place.

She flinched as Simmons removed his belt and unbuttoned her shirt, but was unwilling to move to defend herself. The feeling of his rough hands beneath her shirt made her shudder, increasing the burning sensation in her muscles. She closed her eyes, and tried to take herself somewhere else.

She gasped as Simmons pulled tight on his belt, fastening her left arm to her side before buttoning her shirt once more.

'Best I can do he noo lass,' he said, 'that shouldnae have happened.'

He helped her up and walked her back through the room with the table, to the room where the other Tyros sat. There were not many left, most of them had either completed this section or failed it.

Simmons sat her down and moved back to the desk. She slumped against the wall and closed her eyes. The hum of a heated discussion in hushed voices perked her interest. The only voice she knew from the group was Sergeant Simmons.

'I can't believe he suspended her.'

'Simmons says he changed his mind at the last minute, didn't you Simmons?'

'Aye. He demanded the Strappado.'

'Shit, things are getting twisted aren't they?'

'Did he break her?'

'No.'

'She must have said something to him!'

'Aye.'

'What the hell did she say?'

'Something you'd be too feart tae tell him, I'll tell ye that much.'

'The girl's got guts, I'll give her that.'

Mòrag glanced across the room to see Colonel Tesso striding towards her, he placed a hand on her back, 'Come with me,' he said, his voice soft.

Mòrag got to her feet and followed the Colonel back to the room with the table. He indicated she should sit, and she did as requested.

'Mòrag?'

She raised her gaze to meet his.

'I have decided to end your interrogation now.'

'Have I failed?' she could hear her voice was no more than a whisper.

'No,' Tesso replied, 'what transpired here today should never have happened. I am astonished that you did not give in.' He regarded her for a moment, before adding, 'Come, I will take you to the infirmary myself.'

Chapter Twenty

INTERRUPTION

'Correct. When you are binding a familiar, it is not all about you. The bond is a two-way stream of information and for some, sensation. Those of you who are able to create a strong bond will be able to sense pain and emotion through the connection.' Randall scanned the room; each face was eager and excited. *After all the training, this is what most of them look forward to. A bonded familiar is the mark of a graduate.*

'Sir?'

'Yes, Dunn?'

'How do you know which familiar is best for each of us?'

'Good question,' Randall replied, 'During your final section of training, you will be assessed to determine which skills and talents are your strong points. You will be allocated a familiar type that will support and strengthen your weaker skills. The individual familiar will be chosen based upon how well it heightens your strong abilities, creating a robust partnership.'

Before he could continue, Colonel Tesso appeared in the doorway and beckoned.

'Class dismissed. Read up on connection techniques, I will be testing your knowledge tomorrow,' he said before striding from the room. 'What happened?' he asked Tesso in a hushed voice.

'Major Frank has shown his true colours. He put her in the Strappado,' Tesso hung his head, 'He waited until I had gone to check on General Marcs' Son. He had a fit during the sleep deprivation section, and then again in the cells.'

'I see. Is he stable?'

'For now, Sir, yes.'

'How is Mòrag?'

'Dislocated shoulder and broken collarbone,' he said, 'I need a superior officer to second my request for disciplinary action.'

'Of course: Consider it done.' Randall said as he accompanied Tesso to the infirmary.

Mòrag sat on top of her bed in a private room off the main corridor. Her body was wilted and dirty, and she made no move to acknowledge the medic that was buzzing around her room.

'Tesso, go write up your report, bring it to my office when you are done for countersigning. And notify General Rozzen of the situation.'

'Yes, Sir,' Tesso said, already in motion.

Randall scratched his chin. For a member of Raine's team to attack Mòrag so openly, he would have to have been acting upon orders. Frank was ruthless but not stupid. A severe breach of the rules like this would most likely see him stripped of his rank. *So why do it?*

So far, Randall had had no contact from the Sneaks he had sent out to collect information on General Raine. They were two of the best, the Quinn twins from the southern peaks of Sasann. Quick and intelligent, with a talent for camouflage, they were almost impossible to hide from and equally hard to detect.

Randall did not expect them to return any time soon, but he had expected updates, of which he still had none, other than the first, informing him of Raine's intended return to the castle.

He caught a young medic who was walking past, and as she turned to face him, her cheeks flushed.

'How can I help you, Sir?' she asked in a small voice.

Randall pushed down his embarrassment, 'How is she, Ava?' he asked, nodding toward Mòrag.

The young girl glanced in her direction, 'Exhausted. Major Darrow is deciding whether we would be better for us to heal her, or let her heal naturally. I think he is leaning towards the latter to allow her a longer break before stage two training. So, we will have to strap her shoulder up and give her a lot of pain relief. However we deal with it, it will always be a weak point.'

'It is unfortunate that this happened before she learned to heal herself,' Randall replied, 'how is your brother?'

'Fine, thanks to Mòrag: He tells me she connected with his mind while he was fitting, during the sleep deprivation trial.'

'She did?' Randall was astounded, 'unguided and fatigued and she still managed to enter someone's mind.'

'That is what he tells me. Going by the Sergeant's notes,' she said, 'she had already been in there more than thirty hours.'

'Thank you, Ava. Can you ask Major Darrow to come and see me?'

'Yes, Sir.'

Randall entered the room and sat in the seat facing the bed.

'How are you, Mòrag?'

She flashed him a look of annoyance.

'Silly question,' he admitted, 'Major Frank will face a court martial. There is no excuse for his actions and he will pay for them, I promise you that.'

Mòrag looked out of the window, 'Mmm.'

'Did he say anything to you, about why he was doing what he did?'

'He said he wanted to make me suffer: Because I'm Albannach, and because Raine told him to give me a taste of things to come. He said there was nothing more pleasurable than watching an Albannach suffer,' Mòrag's jaw was tense. 'You'd better keep an eye on him, because when Rannoch finds him, he will leave no traces.'

'We will deal with Major Frank, your familiar need not get involved,' the last thing Randall needed was a rampaging higher beast on his hands, 'does he know?'

'Not yet.'

'Can you ask him not to interfere?'

'Yes,' she said, 'but I won't.'

Chapter Twenty-One

NOT ALONE

As the light began to fail, the temperature began to dip. The sweaty midsummer night winds had moved on, giving way to the cooler air of late summer. The castle and barracks lay atop a hill on the large island of Sruighlea, surrounded by the Chluaidh-Dubh loch. The coolness of the air, which clung to the water, and the height of the grounds made parts of the castle feel draughty almost all year round.

Brax sat atop the sloping roof of the Western end of the castle. The wind buffeted his shirt and hair, refreshing him. *Won't be long now.*

The wind rustled in Sharri's feathers as she landed gracefully next to him.

'*Something on your mind child?*'

'*I'm hardly a child any more, Sharri.*'

'*You will always be a frightened child to me, boy.*'

'*Thanks. I think.*'

Brax looked down into the castle grounds. A few Tyros were milling about between the buildings, but so far, there was no sign of Mòrag's group's release from the Northern barracks.

'*You are worried about your little female.*'

'*A little, yes. Wait, my* female?'

'*You intend to make her your mate do you not?*'

Brax felt his face flush, '*It's not like that, Sharri.*'

'*No? Then why allow her to know so much about you?*'

'*I can't answer that.*'

The doors of the Northern barracks swung open. *It's over.* Brax let out a silent sigh of relief as he got to his feet. Sharri cocked her head at him.

'Off to meet with your little female?'

'Her name is Mòrag, Sharri. And she doesn't belong to me.'

Scaling the wall, he slipped in through one of the windows and descended the stairs. By the time he reached the barracks, the Tyros had begun to leave the building. Some looked better off than others did, but all were dirty and exhausted.

Brax scanned the faces: No Mòrag. He leaned against the wall of the opposite building and waited. *Where is she?*

'Looking for me?'

Brax practically jumped out of his skin, 'Mòrag! I didn't see you leave.'

Mòrag was pale, too pale. Her bedraggled hair fell in tangled clumps around her shoulders, her red-rimmed eyes carried dark shadows beneath, her cheeks were flushed and she was swaying heavily, clutching her left arm close to her side.

'That's because I left this morning,' she said, her voice little more than a whisper, 'I think I need to sit down.'

As she began to topple, Brax leapt forward and caught her shoulders, letting go instantly as she cried out in pain. She landed hard on the dusty ground, gasping.

'What the hell? What happened to you?'

Mòrag took three steadying breaths then gave a wry grin, 'One of General Raine's men enjoyed himself a little too much. I was shifted to the infirmary this morning. But they were taking too long, and you said you'd meet me. I didn't want you to worry, so I slipped out,' she winced as she shifted her position, 'I'm starting to regret it a bitty now.'

'Come on,' he said as he stooped to lift her, 'I think it's best we get you back.'

Mòrag gasped, letting out a small yelp as he shifted his grip, 'I can walk,' she said, 'you don't have to carry me.'

'You can hardly stand.'

'Aye-no, but I can walk.'

'Don't be ridiculous.'

Mòrag huffed and rested her head against him, 'Hypocrite.'

As they approached the infirmary, there was a hum of activity. Medics were dashing left and right, darting in and out of each room.

'Which room were you in?' he asked as they entered the wards.

'Twelve, I think,' Mòrag replied, 'I wasn't really paying attention when they brought me here in the first place.'

'No, I don't suppose you would've been.'

He caught sight of Ava heading up the corridor ahead of them and hurried forwards to catch her.

'Can you put me down?'

'Not a chance,' he grinned. 'Ava, what room's Mòrag in?'

'Sorry, I don't have time to stop. She's disappeared! We've been searching for her for an hour now,' she answered without stopping to face him.

'It hasn't been an hour has it?' Mòrag asked.

Ava came to a sudden stop, spinning round, 'Mòrag! Where have you been?'

'Out.'

'OUT?'

'I believe that *is* what I said, aye.'

Brax cocked an eye at Mòrag as Ava began to stutter and stammer, scolding her for leaving and not telling anyone.

'Och, I'm back now. Though apparently my legs don't work,' she said, glaring at Brax.

Ava regarded them both, 'You are as bad as each other. You know that?' She turned and beckoned, 'this way.'

Brax followed Ava to a room at the top of the corridor.

'Here. I'll go notify them that you are back. Please don't go anywhere again. You need to be treated.'

Mòrag nodded at her, 'Aye, aye, nae bother.'

Brax watched Ava leave, and then moved his gaze back to Mòrag. Her face very close to his, her green eyes seemed to ensnare him, making him catch his breath.

'Well?'

He frowned, 'Well?'

'Are you going to put me down?'

'Oh. Em, yes,' he said. 'Sorry, lost in thought.'

He placed her gently on the bed and sat on the chair opposite.

Mòrag fidgeted, and wriggled trying to get comfortable without using her arms to support her. Brax had to suppress a chuckle when she got so frustrated with herself that she actually growled aloud.

'Can I help?'

'I doubt it,' she huffed. 'Remind me, that when I ask Rannoch to hunt *him* down, I want him taken apart as slowly as possible.'

'What exactly did he do?'

'He made that Albannach Sergeant tie my hands behind my back and leave me hanging for hours. He said three but I have no idea how long I was there. He came back alone to taunt me. I may have sworn at him, I don't really remember now. So he got spiteful. Dislocated shoulder and broken collar bone apparently: Not exactly five rotting gashes to the torso. You must think me a wee saftie.'

'No, not at all. The Strappado is,' he paused, 'brutal. You should never have had to experience it.' He realised he was unconsciously rubbing his own wrists as he spoke and rested them on his lap.

Mòrag eyed him speculatively, 'Did you experience it often?'

He nodded, 'One of Edward and Raine's favoured methods of restraint.' *I can't look at her. Even now, knowing she knows. I can't look at her.*

'Sorry,' she said, 'it must be upsetting, remembering when you were in pain and all alone.'

'Mmm.'

'Brax. Look at me.'

He looked up; her face was an inch from his. *I didn't even hear her get up.*

'You're not alone anymore,' she closed her eyes and pressed her forehead to his, 'you've got me now.' she chuckled, 'I'd give you a hug if my arms worked, but they don't.'

'How do you always know the right things to say?'

'Because we're friends, and the feeling is mutual. You just need to realise its ok to let your guard down with me.'

As Mòrag straightened up, Brax wound his arms round her waist and hugged her close. He had been without any comforting human contact for most of his life, and now that she was close, he didn't want to let her go.

He felt her hand rest upon his back. A war of emotions raged within him. He desperately wanted to help her, but to do that he would have to connect to her mind. She was sure to see at least a portion of his mind through the connection. What would she think of him? Would she turn away from him, leaving him alone once more?

'Mòrag?' he began, 'I can help you, but you may see things. Things I don't want to show you. And you may not want to know me after that.'

'Not possible,' she replied, 'I told you I was your friend didn't I? That's not going to change. Sorry to let you know, but you're stuck with me.'

Chapter Twenty-Two

HEALING HANDS

Brax rose from the seat without releasing his grip around Mòrag's waist. She gasped as the sudden movement jarred her shoulders. He placed her on the bed and without breaking physical contact sat behind her.

I don't have a clue what he is doing but I think I'll just leave him to it.

'Mòrag?' His mindcast had a timid, cautious feel to it.

'Fancy meeting you here.'

'Remind me that I need to teach you to shield your mind. It's wide open for anyone to see.'

'Eh, ok then. I didn't realise I needed a shield.'

'No. Neither did I until it was too late. Can you see me, or just hear me?'

'Which would you prefer? At the moment I'm just listening to you.'

Brax blew a few breaths behind her.

'Can you show me your mindscape?'

'Of course.'

She took him to her barn. The dimness was pierced every so often by pale shafts of light from gaps in the roof. She sat atop her bed; Rannoch lay sleeping, curled up in a ball in his favourite spot, purring softly. Turning to look behind her, she found Brax sitting, as he was in the physical world, his hands still on her waist.

'Is this your home?'

'Aye.'

'Didn't you stay in your parent's house?'

'Jock and Evelynn always kept me here. Apparently my Mother was a traitor to the Crown, on the run from the –' she gasped.

'I tried to warn you,' he said, 'the likelihood is, she was on the run from me.'

I knew I'd heard that term before I just couldn't place where. 'She probably was. But knowing what I know now, I have no hate for anyone other than Edward. I never knew her. I don't know anything about her; other than she was young — Younger than I am now. She birthed me in the forest and begged Jock and Evelynn to take me in. Evelynn told me when I was a little older that I was kept in the barn in case anyone should come by asking questions.'

'How can you not hate me?'

'Because, I didn't come up the Chluaidh in a banana boat! You were forced, under unimaginable circumstance. End of discussion. No blame lies with you.'

Morag felt the bed under her physical self shift as Brax let his body relax a little. He had been sitting straight and stiff, obviously dreading the connection forming between them.

'Thank you. Really, You have no idea how much weight that lifts from my shoulders. Talking about shoulders, we'd better sort yours.'

'And how do you propose we do that then?'

'Because you are past exhaustion, I will heal them for you. But I will show you how to do this on your own when you have rested.'

He lifted his hands from her waist and placed them on her shoulders. Mòrag could still feel his hands on her waist in her physical self though he had shifted in his mental form. Underneath his hands began to warm, spreading out over her shoulders and neck.

'Warm,' she breathed.

'You're a mess. I'm going to need to sleep for a week after this. Sorry, Mòrag, I need more contact.'

Before she could ask him what he meant, his hands took up a firm grasp of her shoulders. She cried out as the agony enveloped her. Her mindscape seemed to flicker and quake in response to the pain, only abating when he released his grip.

'Are you ok?'

Mòrag shot him an indignant look.

'I suppose this leaves me little option. I'm going to shield your mind with mine. I have a far higher pain threshold so you shouldn't feel it so much.'

Her mindscape flickered and disappeared, bathing the pair in blackness for a moment before a blue sky opened out in front of her. She gasped as she realised they were in Brax's mindscape. They sat on the castle's roof, the loch below sparkled, catching the sun's rays and splitting them into thousands of dancing lights on the water's surface.

'This is where I come to think.' Brax said, 'it's where I feel safest.'

'It's beautiful!' she exclaimed, 'you can see forever.'

'Exactly.'

'Promise you'll bring me here.'

'If you like,' he smiled, 'right, I am going to try and do this as quickly as possible. Unfortunately, you will still feel some pain but it won't be half as bad. Just let me know if you need me to stop.'

'Will you be in pain by doing this?'

'I might, but it won't be for long.'

'Will I be able to see what you are doing?'

'If you want to.'

'I do.'

He stretched his hand over and covered her eyes, 'Look through mine.'

She saw herself sitting in front of him in the infirmary.

'I'm going to unbutton your shirt,' he told her, 'it helps if the contact is skin to skin.'

He seemed to sense her hesitation and added, 'I will only bare your shoulders. That's all that's needed.'

'Ok.'

The scene shifted as Brax rose and moved in front of her. She could see his shaking hands fumble with the buttons on her shirt. She could sense his heart thumping in his chest as he slipped the shirt down over her shoulders. His gaze dropped and lingered on her tightly bound breasts, making his pulse quicken all the more.

'Enjoying the view?'

'Um, I, Eh... Sorry... Sorry... I'm sorry,' his embarrassment was all-encompassing.

Brax placed a hand over the deep purple bruise that covered her collarbone. An intense burning sensation flared to life, but it was far more bearable than her previous pain had been. The burning ache began to numb and cool.

'I'm redirecting the different energies of your body to promote and quicken   natural healing: Encouraging the fibres to knit together. It's hard to describe.'

When he was satisfied that the wound was healed he moved back to sit on the bed behind her once more. Again, he placed a hand on each shoulder.

This time, the pain was much more intense, making her gasp.

'Do you need me to stop?'

'No. Keep going.'

He continued to keep the pressure on her skin. Gradually her right shoulder numbed and cooled as her collarbone had. Her left shoulder continued to emit a piercing heat.

'Mòrag, your shoulder's going to need re-aligned. It's not sitting right.'

'Do what you have to.'

'If you're sure. Ready?'

'No. Just do it.'

Keeping one hand on her shoulder, he took a firm grasp of her hand with the other and pulled keeping a firm constant pressure.

Pain exploded in her shoulder. The scene flickered and shifted as her consciousness was ripped back to her physical self. She bit down hard on her fist to stop herself from screaming.

As Brax finally popped her shoulder back into place, a wash of dizziness swept over her.

He caught her as she flopped backwards and settled her on the mattress. His forehead was beaded with sweat, his worried gaze searching.

'I'm sorry, it needed a lot of manipulation,' he said as he placed his hands over her shoulder once more, 'it should heal now.'

'Thank you,' she breathed before her eyes flickered shut and she lost consciousness.

Chapter Twenty-Three

SOUND OF MIND

It was early morning when Mòrag woke. A cool breeze from the open window, tickled her neck and shoulders. She shrugged them to gauge how painful they would be, and was pleased to find only a dull ache.

She pushed herself up to a sitting position and looked around the room. Brax was asleep. Slumped in the chair by the window, his legs stretched out in front of him, his hands clasped behind his head.

'How are you child?' Sharri was perched on the end of her bed.

'Tired, but much more comfortable thanks to Brax.'

'Yes. He has risked much on you.'

'I know he has. But what I don't know is why.'

'Only he can answer that, child.'

'Have you seen Rannoch around? We've not been apart since the night he was born. But I have only seen him once in the last month.'

'Yes, we hunt daily. He is enjoying his freedom, though he is lonely without you.'

The sound of footfall echoed up the corridor. Mòrag glanced towards the sound, then back to Sharri who leapt through the open window in one smooth motion.

The door slid to the side and Randall emerged into the room, pausing as he spotted Brax asleep in the chair.

'Oh, Mòrag, you are awake. How are you?'

'Ready to get out of here.'

'I do not think that wise. You have a lot of healing to do.'

'Brax healed me last night.'

A frown descended on his face, 'To do that he would have had to create a mindlink, and I do not think he is capable of that.'

'Why not?'

'In order to create a stable mindlink, you must be mentally sound or far more mentally gifted than the other person, but even then, the first rule stands supreme. Sadly Brax is not sound of mind.'

This comment angered Mòrag, 'And what authority are you to decide whether or not he is mentally stable?'

Randall was notably puzzled by her sharp reaction, 'You do not go through what he has been through, and come out whole at the other end. It is impossible.'

Mòrag looked over at Brax, 'Have you always doubted him?'

'Brax as a person, no. His talent as a Seeker, no. His mental stability, yes. I have always doubted that. He must be watched at all times to protect the King's interests. If he were to go rogue there would be no stopping him.'

'Even you are setting him up to fail. He's due more credit than you give him.'

'*Thank you.*' Brax did not open his eyes, but his cast held an immense feeling of gratitude. Obviously, he had not completely severed their connection, and a simple communication link remained.

'*Anytime.*' She cast back, a hint of a smile forming on her lips. She turned her attention back to Randall, 'How can I help you, Sir? You obviously came here to speak to me about something.'

Randall regarded her, 'I have had some disturbing news from one of the Sneaks that I sent out. It seems that the King is compromised. It is not clear exactly what has happened, but the King is no longer himself. Are you aware of the link you created with my mind while you were undergoing the Cleanse?'

'Yes. Although, I don't know how I did it. I just wanted out.'

'As a result of that link, you suspended the King's binding within my mind. Because of this, I am both saved and condemned.'

Mòrag was puzzled, 'Saved and condemned?'

'Yes. I had not realised how corrupt it had become until you woke me to it. For that, I am eternally grateful. Unfortunately, once he notices that he no longer has the ability to control me, I will be tried as a traitor to the Crown. Which will place you in further danger. I am amazed that so far he has remained oblivious.'

Mòrag took a moment to allow his words to penetrate. She had suspended the King's binding. The King was considered the most powerfully gifted in the two Kingdoms. *There's just no way. How could I push him out when I don't even know how I got in, in the first place?* 'Maybe he suspended it himself.'

'No. it was you.'

'What does this all mean?'

'It means,' said Randall, 'that we must prepare for the worst. We must prepare for war, though I hope it does not come to that. I am going to need you to train, and train hard. You are the only one who has a chance of countering the King. This is the reason Brax woke you from the Cleanse.'

'*You woke me to be used as a weapon?*' she cast at Brax.

'*I had many reasons. That is one of the less important ones,*' he replied.

'Are you asking me to assassinate the King? Because that's what it sounds like.'

'No,' Randall replied, 'but if he cannot be changed. If you cannot bring him back like you did with me. It may be the only option left. We cannot risk his uncle regaining control of the Kingdom. So I must ask you to rest, and heal.'

'She is already healed,' Brax said, his voice gruff from anger.

'And where have you been, Brax? You have not shown yourself in two days. I have searched high and low for you. I did not know if you were dead or alive. How am I supposed to look out for you if I do not even know where you are?' the annoyance in Randall's voice was overshadowed with concern.

'That's the trouble, Randall. You don't look out for me. All you're concerned about are James' interests, not mine.'

'Excuse me?'

'You heard.'

'Brax I never meant –'

'I was watching over Mòrag,' Brax cut in, 'which is something you should have been doing. How could you let her get caught by one of Raine's men?'

Mòrag stayed quiet, both men were anxious and irritated, and she was not willing to be drawn into the developing argument.

'You know I have no authority over Raine's men.'

'You have Tesso. He should have vetted his men more closely.'

'Tesso was caught unaware. It is a mistake he will not make again.'

'It shouldn't have happened.'

'No. But it did. I cannot change the past.'

They glowered at each other.

'Happy families,' Mòrag said in a singsong voice.

Both Randall and Brax blinked at her.

'It's no one's fault except that Major Whatshisface,' she said, 'and he will suffer for what he did to me, so stop bickering like two whining bairns, and move on.'

'She's right,' Brax said turning to Randall once more, 'we can't allow ourselves to become divided: Even if you have no faith in my loyalties.'

Randall bowed his head in agreement.

'Good,' said Mòrag, 'now that that's sorted. I need a bath, some fresh clothes and some time with Rannoch. Then I will train.'

Chapter Twenty-Four

THE SAPLING AND THE BRANCH

'I have brought you a fresh uniform and some proper underwear. Honestly Mòrag, you would think you were ashamed to be female,' Ava fussed over Morag's clothes as she soaked in the bath. 'We are soldiers in the King's army, and we are required to use every tool at our disposal to do his bidding, whether we are fighting for him, protecting him or getting information for him.

'As a woman, your body is a valuable tool. You need to learn how to use it to your advantage. Supposedly, when we are retired from active duty we will be paired with one of the Generals to birth the next generation of soldiers.'

'Aye, that'll be right! No Sasannach General's getting their clarty mitts on me.'

'Oh don't say that, Mòrag, they are not *all* bad. I hope I am paired with General Steele,' she sighed like a smitten little girl. 'He is so handsome and absurdly gentle for such a dangerous man. Wait. Why are you laughing?'

Mòrag couldn't hide the fact that she found Ava's infatuation with Randall humorous, 'Well he's nice enough; I suppose he is quite handsome too, but he's old enough to be your Father. And by the time you are retired he will be, like eighty!'

Ava gained a pink tinge to her cheeks, 'I will throw these bandages out will I?'

'No. I'll wash them.'

'Please yourself,' she said before leaving Mòrag and heading back to her duties.

Taking a breath Mòrag submerged herself fully in the bath. The water was warm and soft against her skin. She closed her eyes, listening to her heartbeat thump rhythmically in her ears.

'*Are you dressed?*'

'*No, Brax, I'm in the bath. Why? Were you hoping to see what was under the bandages?*' she emerged from the bathwater and smoothed her hair behind her ears.

There was no reply, just an awkward silence. His embarrassment was amusing to her. She imagined he would have had little contact with anyone, let alone girls while he was under Edward's control. It was probably a little cruel of her to tease him, but she couldn't help it.

'*You can come and wash my back if you like.*' She cast, grinning to herself.

'*Mòrag, I don't, I mean, eh...*'

'*Relax, Brax. I'm only teasing. I won't be long.*'

'*Oh. Ok.*'

Leaving the bath to drain she grabbed the rough army issue towel and dried herself as best she could. The uniform Ava had left her was the same style as her previous uniform only this time it was a deep red with black piping.

She dressed her bottom half and then inspected the brassiere Ava had left for her. It was lacy and black. It didn't look strong enough to hold her but she decided to try it anyway. *How can she wear this?* It was tight and cut into her back and shoulders. The fabric felt rough and itchy on her skin. *Sorry Ava. But I'll be sticking to my nice saft cotton bandages, although they need a wash before I can wear them again.*

With reluctance, she slipped the shirt on over the brassiere and buttoned it up. It was ill fitting and uncomfortable now that she was unbound.

Mòrag marched out of the bathroom and back into the medical ward, meeting Brax outside the room she had been in the night previous, 'First stop,' she said holding up the bandages as she strode past, 'is somewhere to wash these? Because this thing's got to go.'

'Wait. What?'

'Never mind, where's Rannoch?'

'Probably in the wood hunting anything that moves.'

Brax led Mòrag out of the Castle into another scorcher. Though midsummer had passed, the days were still hot and sticky, and even this early in the morning, the sun created a haze on the water. Mòrag couldn't help wondering how her horses were: Shand in particular.

She followed Brax through the castle grounds, ignoring the hushed comments and disapproving looks from the Tyros that were taking their morning break in the sun. The island that held the castle was a huge expanse of land. The enormous castle and surrounding buildings only covered a fifth of the island's footprint. Woodland swept around the castle, covering the cliff face, spreading down the slope and breaking mere feet from the waters of the Chluaidh-Dubh loch.

The only way onto the island was by long and narrow stone causeway, just wide enough for a carriage or for soldiers to ride two abreast. One lay to the north and another to the south connecting the highlands and lowlands of Alba: During the thaw, when the water level would rise a considerable distance, the only way in or out was by boat.

To the East, lay the Abhainn Dubh, and to the West the Abhainn Chluaidh. Both were vast expanses of water that fed the loch surrounding the castle.

Sruighlea Castle was the only crossing to the North and was near impenetrable making it the key stronghold for the Sasannach rulers that sought to control Alba and her people.

Mòrag had heard Jock rave about it at night, when he had had a little too much to drink. Ordinarily, he would strive to hold his tongue for fear of upsetting Evelynn. She was a sweet woman, though not born of Alba. Her father controlled several of the lowlands close to the Albannach border.

They hated each other when they met. Evelynn had been fond of telling Mòrag the story when she was a child.

'*When the Albannach princess was taken south as a hostage to control the nobility of Alba, there was widespread outrage. The highland clans conspired to steal her away home, but their plan was discovered.*

The Sasannach punishment was swift and severe. The result of which was a mass uprising that lasted two years, which only ceased with the death of the princess, and the end of the royal bloodline of Alba.

'*During the early revolt, Jock's clan had ambushed Evelynn's father and taken control of his lands. Evelynn, her sisters and their mother were prisoners in their own home.*

'*Jock was like a wild man from the woods. His brown hair was short and messy and he sported a thick ginger beard at that time. He was several inches shorter than I, which was rather odd at first. He was not finely built like other men I had met. He was stout and strong: Muscular. And he had legs like two tree trunks.*

'*I knew he was for me when all I could see in his dark grey eyes was my own reflection. At that point, neither hell not high water would see us parted. And when my father's men came to take our lands back, I left with Jock.*'

She may have fallen in love with an Albannach but she was still a Sasannach at heart and it hurt her when Jock would sing songs of rebellion and curse Sasann.

'Mòrag?'

Mòrag blinked at Brax, 'Huh?'

'You didn't hear a single thing I just said did you?'

'Um... Aye-no, I didn't.'

'Thank you for earlier. What Randall said hurt. A lot. The truth always does, far more than the lies. You felt it through our link didn't you. My... instability.'

'Honestly? A little, yes.'

His shoulders drooped at her words.

'Let me tell you something Evelynn once told me.' She walked over to an old oak tree and bent one of the branches until it began to split, 'You seem to think,' she said, 'that because something has been damaged, that it's useless or cannot be trusted. Like this branch.'

'You snapped it. I'm not really seeing your point.'

'That's because this is you,' she said gesturing to the branch, 'and I haven't snapped it. It has begun to split. It isn't broken.'

Mòrag found a nearby sapling. She stripped long ribbons of its soft bark and brought them back to the damaged branch.

'Tell me,' she said as she wrapped the sapling ribbons around the wound, and then interlocked the end of the branch with the end of a higher limb, 'what am I doing?'

'You are supporting the branch... until it heals.'

'I am the sapling,' she said pointing to the young plant.

'But you stripped it bare to fix the tree branch. It has no protection now.'

'The tree overshadows and protects the sapling from the elements. Its bark will grow back, and until that time, it's supporting the tree branch, which in turn is protecting it.' She placed a hand on his shoulder and held his gaze, 'Understand, and move forward.'

Chapter Twenty-Five

THE SOUL TRAIL

The rain lashed against the roof of the building causing Mòrag to toss and turn in her bunk. She felt cramped in the barracks and longed for the wide-open sky and Rannoch by her side. The last two days she had spent with Rannoch and Brax, wandering through the woodland, talking and hunting. In the morning, she would move into General Rozzen's training regime. She was looking forward to the challenge.

Brax had told her that the first thing they usually teach is methods of healing, then on to hand-to-hand combat techniques, weaponry and fighting as a unit. What she was interested in were the techniques of the mind, a parallel training regime that would run alongside the physical training.

She would train with Brax in her spare time. Randall had told her that there was no one better than Brax to train her Seeker abilities. She welcomed it. Having a real friend was something she had been denied her entire life, other than Rannoch that is.

The barrack door swung inward revealing the sopping wet form of Sergeant Grey. Her normally frizzy golden locks were slick to her head, and her uniform clung to her.

'Mòrag! Get dressed and report to the gatehouse immediately. You will be briefed there. Understood?'

'Yes, Ma'am,' she called, jumping from her bunk.

'Quick as you can,' she ordered before leaving the room.

'What's going on?' Ava's voice was muffled by the pillow and sheets she had buried her head beneath.

'Not a clue,' Mòrag said as she changed into her uniform and pulled on her overcoat. 'It must be urgent for Grey to have rushed over here without taking the time to dress for the weather.'

As Mòrag hurried towards the gatehouse, the rain began to torrent stinging her eyes and cheeks.

This early in the morning only the odd sentry walked the grounds. The sound of her boots on the wet pathway ricocheted off the empty buildings and was lost amid the thundering of the rain. All lights were out save for the lights of the gatehouse.

Brax was waiting for her beneath the archway he fidgeted uncomfortably.

'What's going on?' Mòrag yawned as she joined him. *He really doesn't want to be here. Saying that, its two a.m. Neither do I.*

'That boy you helped during the endurance trials.'

'Oliver?'

'Yes. He was supposed to report to Tesso this evening to discuss having another go at the trials, seen as he failed last time. He never showed. They have now discovered he's not within the castle grounds. I've been ordered to find him and bring him back. Randall seems to think you should come with me.'

'He can't have gone too far can he?'

'There have been a few merchant's caravans through today so he could easily have run further afield.'

They were interrupted by Fletcher and one of the medics; a middle-aged woman with white hair and a hard face.

'Urgh,' Mòrag complained, 'What do *you* want?'

'Watch your mouth! I'm here to make sure the Dog does his job. He can be prone to disobedience. You are to do exactly as I say, when I say it. Understood?'

'What makes you think you have authority over me like?' Mòrag seethed.

'Birth right: And of course experience.'

His smug expression irritated her no end. She was about to respond when the grim faced Colonel Tesso appeared. Water poured from his brimmed hat as he nodded to the group. *I wonder if this is the only expression, he ever wears.*

'Thank you for assembling so quickly. Brax you know your job. Thank you once again for your cooperation.'

Brax didn't acknowledge or even look at Tesso; he just stared out into the rain.

'Mòrag you most likely won't learn much tonight however, you are an important member of this team. I understand you have touched young Marcs' mind before.

'Yes, Sir.'

'He allowed you willingly?'

'He fought me at first; he didn't know what was happening. Once he discovered I was trying to help him, he let me.'

'He tried to push you out?' he seemed shocked at the revelation, 'No. There will be time for questions when you return. Out of everyone here, you are the one he will most likely trust. I need you to bring him back. Do you understand?'

'Yes, Sir.'

'Raine, Soll, you are to act as back up team. Do not interfere. You are here to observe, however, should he resist, you are to assist in his collection. You are only to use force if absolutely necessary do you understand me?'

'Of course,' Fletcher oozed.

Tesso glowered at him.

'Yes, Sir,' he rephrased indignantly.

'*Can you draw the memory of when you helped the boy?*' Brax cast as he scanned the dark horizon.

'*Yes,*' she pulled the images to the forefront of her mind. Her heart quickened as she recalled the sight of Oliver hanging beside her, his chains jangling as he fitted.

'*Show me.*'

Mòrag cast the memory towards Brax making him grimace.

'*Look closely at his internal image. When you are within his mind you can see his soul surrounding him.*'

'*It's pale yellow.*'

'*Yes. Now bring yourself back to your own mindscape, keep his soul at the forefront of your mind.*'

Mòrag did as instructed and found that her mindscape took the form of the terrain and buildings surrounding her physical body. Fletcher and the medic – Soll, stood beside her with harsh looks on their faces. Their bodies were surrounded by soul light, as Oliver's had been, though theirs was darker.

'*Good. This is the sensory plane of consciousness, looking through your mind's eye if you like. Only natural Seekers can see the soul in this way. Each soul is unique, and as you can see, the colours vary person to person: The lighter the colour, the more innocent the person.*'

Mòrag moved her gaze from Fletcher to Brax. He did not look toward her. While Oliver's soul had been a pale yellow, swirling and glistening around him, Brax's soul was jagged and sharp: It flickered in and out of existence randomly. It was a royal blue; far deeper than his silvery-blue eyes, but had even darker areas pulsing and swirling within. He tensed, obviously uncomfortable at her seeing him in this way.

'*Focus on the soul we are looking for, no other.*'

She did as instructed; the soul of the others around her faded and disappeared. She began to see a faint trail forming: It led from the barracks, through the grounds, beneath the arch of the gatehouse, down the slope and out towards the causeway.

She moved forward, reaching out on instinct to touch the faintly glowing thread. As her fingers made contact, several images flew into her mind: Waking up in hospital, Ava's concerned face, Fletcher's sneer, a girl she didn't know crying, Oliver's pale face in a mirror. Fear encompassed the images and she felt the sensation of running, through the grounds toward the gatehouse and onward to the causeway.

She didn't realise she had begun to run along with Oliver's will to escape until Fletcher grabbed her shoulder. Although healed, it had not regained the strength it once had, and remained tender under pressure.

Quick as a flash, she turned and thrust the heel of her hand upwards into his face bloodying his nose with a loud crack.

He yelped and released his grip, allowing her to set off again. Oliver's will had become her own, and she *had* to run, she *had* to keep going until she found him.

'*Mòrag, wait! Not so fast, you might lose the trail.*'

'*I'm not following it,*' she cast towards Brax.

'*Then how do you know which way to go?*'

She slowed half a stride until he was next to her, taking his hand she tugged at his mind until he allowed her to draw it to hers.

'*Can you feel his fear?*'

'*Yes. How are you doing this? This isn't normal.*'

'*Not a clue. But I'm going with it.*'

'*Ok. I'll follow your lead then,*' he cast as his mind retreated back to his own body.

Mòrag focused on nothing but Oliver. His thoughts and feelings seemed to swirl around her, spurring her on. She had no idea how or why she was experiencing these emotions, all she knew was that if she followed them she would find him.

They passed through three small villages before Mòrag slowed to a stop at a small copse of trees. She had to grasp the trunk of a nearby tree to steady her. At her feet, the pale thread had become a tangled mess of twists and loops.

'*The boy is not well.*' Rannoch's cast was gentle as he purred and rubbed up against her side.

She placed a hand on his shoulder, though she couldn't remove her eyes from the glowing mass at her feet, '*I didn't know you were here.*'

'*You were pre occupied, and I remained quiet,*' he purred at her, '*would you like me to search ahead? I will stay hidden should I find him.*'

'*Please.*'

'I don't think he is far from here.' Brax said.

'I think he's fitting again,' she said, still looking down at the twisted and jumbled thread of Oliver's soul.

'Mòrag, you said you had created a link to his mind. Can you still feel it?'

'Yes.'

'Perhaps you should see if you can reach out to him?'

She hadn't thought of trying to connect to him mentally. Any connections she had experienced, the other person had been close by, with the exception of Randall, though she had chalked that up to being a product of the situation. *The connection is already made, so maybe, just maybe, I could reach further.*

She felt for the connection; a pale yellow door within her mindscape. As she approached it, she noted the ground surrounding the door was dry and cracked. The door juddered sending a few more cracks out like fingers cutting through the earth.

Placing her palm against the unstable door she eased it inwards. Once again, the room quaked as Mòrag rushed towards Oliver. Unlike her previous meeting with him, this time he lay at the centre of the room unresponsive, his body gently twitching.

'Oliver?'

His eyes opened but did not focus.

'Oliver you need to tell me where you are. You need help.'

His gaze moved toward Mòrag, though he looked through her rather than at her.

'I need to know where you are. Give me something, anything.'

He narrowed his eyes, finally focusing on Mòrag. She felt the strain of his mind to respond. After several moments, an image flickered before her for only an instant. As the scene died away, his body leapt into another violent fit. The room shook with such ferocity that it thrust her mind back to the physical world.

'He's under a bridge: A pale grey stone bridge, next to a river. It can't be far from here.' She cast the information to Rannoch as she and Brax began to move once more.

'I've let Sharri know, we had better quicken the pace, his trail is beginning to fade.'

They ran through the undergrowth of the copse and out onto a meadow beyond. The sun was beginning to rise above the hills now, allowing them a greater field of vision.

'Puithar, Sharri and I are with him. He is in a bad way. Run straight. You will find us.'

They sped across the pasture towards the glistening ribbon of water that wound round behind it. As they crested the small incline of the meadow, the bridge came into view. Mòrag willed her legs to move faster as she and Brax sped to the base of the masonry.

Rannoch was crouched behind Oliver with Sharri perched on his shoulder, his tail swished from side to side. He was purring at the unconscious boy, a sound that always helped sooth Mòrag, perhaps it was soothing Oliver as well. His body certainly seemed still for now.

Brax leant down, assessing Oliver's condition.

'He's very weak. He may not survive the return journey.'

'I will carry him,' Rannoch offered, *'but if I am to get him back quickly I can only carry the boy, and one other.'*

'Go,' Brax said, seeming to know Rannoch's mind. He rose with Oliver in his arms, 'I am heavier, so I'll slow Rannoch too much. I will return with Sharri.'

'Ok,' she sat herself on Rannoch's soft back, clutching his silken mane as he got to his feet. 'What about the other two?'

'They will catch up during Tesso's debrief no doubt,' he said as he placed Oliver's limp body in front of Mòrag, 'Be sure to hold him tight. If he fits and falls he could break his neck.'

'I know.'

Rannoch didn't wait to be asked; he leapt smoothly into a rolling gallop. Mòrag could feel his powerful muscles beneath her, propelling them forwards. Looking back toward the bridge, she saw that Brax was already gone.

It was difficult holding on to Oliver's limp form. Gravity reached for him always, ready to drag his body down. Mòrag's left shoulder blazed from the strain of his weight, but she bit back the pain and held him firm.

The scenery flew by in a continuous stream of greens and browns until the deep dark blue of the Chluaidh-Dubh loomed into view. At the sight of the castle, Rannoch quickened his pace.

'Will I leave you at the gate?'

'*No, as close to the infirmary as possible.*'

'*As you wish.*'

Rannoch sped across the causeway towards the drawbridge that allowed access to the island. Slowing to a stop where the stone thoroughfare dropped away to the loch below. *Why is the bridge up? They were expecting us to return.*

Fletcher's smug face appeared over the wall, 'Password.'

'Och away wi ye Fletcher! Drop the bridge!'

'Stealing horses now? You are troublesome aren't you? He looks rather poorly,' he grinned, 'shame no one was here to let you through in his hour of need.'

'*You had better hold tight.*' Rannoch cast as he retreated a few strides. Turning back towards the raised bridge he leapt forwards, crouching low as his paws reached the end of the stonework, and pouncing high up over the watery void and bridge beyond.

The upward journey was far less gut wrenching than the downward one, but they landed in once piece. Rannoch did not stop to allow for a confrontation with Raine; he continued onward past several Tyros on their endurance trial, past the buildings and offices, to the main building and door to the wing, which housed the infirmary.

Colonel Tesso appeared from the building as Rannoch came to a stop by the door. When he saw Oliver's lifeless body draped in front of Mòrag, he slowed half a step.

'He's alive,' Mòrag said as she jumped from Rannoch's back, 'hurry, he's very weak.'

Tesso scooped Oliver up in his arms and rushed into the building.

'He must feel guilty,' Brax said, 'I shouldn't have been so angry with him before, he's only doing as instructed.'

'How did you get back so fast?' Mòrag was astonished he had managed to return so close behind her and had not even broken a sweat.

'Sharri is stronger than she looks,' he grinned, 'she could carry Rannoch if she really wanted to.'

Mòrag gave Rannoch a quick hug, 'Thank you, Bràthair.'

He bowed his head and padded away towards the gatehouse and the wood beyond. Mòrag watched his back as he left. No one seemed to pay him any attention, this, it appeared was one of his many talents, and she envied him for it.

Chapter Twenty-Six

ROZZEN'S INTEREST

'Welcome. Welcome to stage two training. I am General Rozzen and I will personally oversee your training. Today you will have a simple orientation. Sergeants Pearl, Mullins, Dreyer and Duncan will each take a group of you and show you around our training areas. I will meet with each of you in turn throughout the day. Pay attention to everything you are told. The hard work starts tomorrow. I expect each and every one of you to push yourselves to the limit. Carry on Sergeants!'

General Rozzen was an exceptionally tall woman. She wore a black uniform with deep red piping, her dark skin made the pale teal of her eyes seem even paler, and her black hair was cut mercilessly short.

The four sergeants moved forward and each called out ten names. Sergeant Mullins called out Mòrag's name.

'Don't you have a second name? Jus' says Mòrag on here,' he gestured with his clipboard.

Mòrag grimaced as the others in her group sniggered.

'She's a bastard, Mullins. Like the Dog, she only has a first name,' Fletcher's sneer boiled her blood; 'she's a non-person and should be treated as such.'

His eyes widened in surprise as she grabbed a fistful of his shirt and hauled him forward, 'You ought to be careful I don't lose my temper with you,' she growled, 'you might end up dead.'

The conviction of her words surprised even her.

'Save it for the tournaments you two, I'll not have fighting during orientation.'

Mòrag released him, cursing beneath her breath, causing Sergeant Mullins to throw her a warning look.

'What are you here for anyway, Raine.'

Fletcher smoothed his uniform, 'Father sent me to give you this,' he handed over an envelope, 'try not to be late this time, ok?'

Mullins frowned at the envelope in his hand before clipping it onto his board, beneath his paperwork, 'I won't be late,' he replied.

Fletcher nodded at him, sneered at Mòrag and left.

Mullins led the group around the training yard and arenas. Explaining that the main arena was used for the bi-yearly tournaments, where the Tyro's progress would be marked by how they performed in mock battle and strategy simulations. Tournaments took place in spring and winter. It also held the yearly graduation tournament in the summer, where the graduating Tyro's would fight each other until one emerged from the pack victorious. The victor was titled 'Elite' and placed into the King's personal guard.

As they entered the stables, a shiver ran up Mòrag's spine. An explosion of sound erupted as each of the horses realised who had entered the building.

'*Màthair!*'

Mòrag's heart leapt as she recognised Shand's mental voice. She recognised every face, all of the horses from her home and more who had left them over the years, but all her family. Every one of them bounced about their stalls, kicking and calling out to her.

Shand, stabled at the far side of the building, barged through his stable door and raced to meet her.

She pushed past the astounded Sergeant Mullins and ran to meet the youngster, wrapping her arms round his strong neck and burying her face in his mane.

'*I missed you,*' she cast to Shand, '*I missed you all.*'

They all neighed in response, battering on the stall doors with their hooves.

'I hear you raised each and every one of these horses.'

Mòrag spun around to see General Rozzen standing behind her, arms folded across her chest.

'Other than Petorius, Joven, Sacchi and Mex, Yes Ma'am.'

'Well... You have done a damn good job. Come, it's your turn for a chat.'

'Yes Ma'am. *Shand, go back to your stable, I will visit later.*'

The young horse turned and trotted back to his stall with his tail in the air and his head held high, as Mòrag followed Rozzen, past the open-mouthed Tyros and Sergeant Mullins, and out of the stable block.

Rozzen led her to the office block. As Rozzen unlocked her door, Mòrag could hear Brax's voice coming from the opposite side of the corridor. *He must be talking with Randall.*

'Sit please,' Rozzen said as she took her seat behind the large oak desk.

The room was almost identical to Randall's only she seemed to have less paperwork. Mòrag perched herself on the chair opposite the General who eyed her speculatively.

'You interest me greatly. It has been far too long since I have seen another woman capable of standing up to all these men. Most of the girls end up as medics and spies, they don't have a head for battle: So far, other than myself, there is only one other woman of rank.'

'Sergeant Grey.'

'Correct. I have spoken at length about you with General Steele. He believes you are a natural Seeker. Your retrieval of General Marcs' son only proves it. Unfortunately, this means you will be at the disposal of the King as of now. However, I feel there is something more within you,' she narrowed her eyes, 'Tesso mentioned you forced your way into young Marcs' mind.'

'I didn't force my way in, exactly. I,' Mòrag paused, it was hard to describe, 'I don't really know what I did.'

When Rozzen didn't answer she continued, 'He was struggling, no one seemed to care, so I, tried to help him. I tried to feel for his mind and the connection appeared. I was in before he knew I was there. He fought me at first; I think he thought I would hurt him. So I held him still until he realised I was there to help. That's about it really.'

Rozzen's gaze was piercing. Mòrag wanted to squirm free of it but forced herself to remain still in her chair.

'Let me get this correct in my mind if you will. You evaded the Cleanse for almost three weeks, finally being released from it by Randall's command.' The corner of her lips turned up in a knowing smile, 'Do not worry; your secret is safe with me. No one is more loyal to the King than he is. Whatever his reasons, I have no doubt they were the right ones.' She ran a hand through her hair before continuing, 'You passed the stamina trial in one day, granted you are older than the average Tyro attempting it, so you would have more energy to begin with. You then force your way into a malfunctioning mind after thirty six hours of sleep deprivation that directly followed the stamina trial, and not only did you get in, you controlled the soul within and calmed his body, then continued on with the remaining thirty six hours, completing the sleep deprivation trial. Is that about right?'

'Eh... Yes, Ma'am.'

'I knew it. You are far more than a Seeker. As a Seeker you should be able to see the souls of others, this ability will allow you to track them down and even determine whether they are being truthful towards you or not. And in some instances determine the course their actions may take. You should not be able to enter minds undetected or by force. That is a trait of a completely different talent: One, which at present, only the current royal family possesses. I believe you have the skills of a Reaver.'

'A Reaver?'

Rozzen regarded her with a grin, 'Yes. I will be watching your progress with great interest,' she smiled. 'You are dismissed; I expect to see you ready to begin your training tomorrow at six a.m. sharp.'

'Yes Ma'am,' she said as she left the room, closing the heavy door behind her.

She could still hear Brax's voice from behind Randall's door so she knocked quietly.

'Come,' Randall called.

Pushing the door inward, she entered the room. Brax closed the door behind her.

'Any word on Oliver?

'He has not woken,' Randall's expression was grim, 'the medics can only sustain his body for a few days, after that...' he tailed off.

'He's still in there; he just needs time to find his way out.'

'I hope you are right.'

'I see you two are talking again.'

Both men looked sheepishly at one another. The way they spoke about each other when they were apart, Mòrag imagined that they could have been father and son in another life. There was obvious admiration between them, but the flared tempers the other day had cracked the fragile surface of their relationship: Drudging up painful memories for both of them.

'I saw the horses today. Why didn't you tell me they were here?'

'To be honest Mòrag, with everything else that is going on, I forgot,' Randall replied, 'I take it you are satisfied with their condition?'

Mòrag gazed sideways at Brax through her hair; he had remained silent since she had entered the room. He sat awkwardly on the window ledge, looking at the courtyard below.

'Yes, they're all looking braw: Shand in particular. He's filled out lots. What do you plan to do with him? He won't bond with just anyone: Especially not now.'

'I was actually going to ask your opinion on the situation. Would you be able to recognise a match for him?'

'Of course,' she smiled, 'does it have to be an officer?'

'Preferably.'

'There are none that will match him.'

'You have someone in mind?'

'I do.'

'Would they make a good match?'

'They are an ideal match.'

'Alright, will you introduce me to them so I can get the ball rolling?'

Mòrag grinned and gestured to Brax.

Randall gawped at her, 'But. But. But –'

'Shand will bond with no other. It's Brax or no one.'

'Me? Wait, what? Did I miss something?' Brax said from the window.

'Mòrag, I can't do that,' Randall insisted weakly.

'Yes you can. You just don't want the hassle it'll cause you.'

'You realise it would, quite literally, be adding insult to injury?'

'I do. But you need to start stepping up and promoting one of the best people you have. And that's him,' she pointed to Brax.

Brax's expression softened, '*All I seem to be able to do is thank you for your kind words.*'

'*What I am telling him is the truth, If Edward is going to return, you are their greatest weapon, because you know him like no other. They should be acknowledging that fact.*'

Randall sighed, 'I knew you would be trouble, Mòrag, I did not realise you would be *this* much trouble.'

'You know I'm right,' she locked him in her gaze, unwavering, unblinking, and she smiled as he visibly squirmed beneath it.

'I will think it over,' Randall conceded.

Chapter Twenty-Seven

BOND NOT BIND

Mòrag crept along the dark passageways towards Brax's room. It was a little after three in the morning and the moon was bright and round, bathing the island in silver light. She knocked on his door. No answer came, so she knocked again.
'Brax,' she called in a hushed voice, 'Brax it's me,' no answer.

Mòrag huffed, he was probably sleeping. *I'll try the handle; if it's open, I'll go in. Be open, be open, be open...* there was a click as she touched the handle and the door opened.

She peeked round the door into the moonlit room, 'Brax?' no answer.

He lay curled up on top of his bed: Which was far too short for him. His hair draped softly onto the mattress behind him. He faced the wall, his bare skin reflecting the moonlight from the window. *Please don't let him be naked.* She held her breath as she crept closer, letting out a silent sigh of relief at the sight of the pair of shorts he was wearing.

Now that she was closer, she could see that he was lean, perhaps a little too lean for his build, though his muscles were well defined. Scars covered every inch of him. A silvery web that created a map of the abuse he had suffered throughout his life, some small, some far larger. There were burn marks crossing the small of his back and five wide identical scars ran diagonally downward cutting through all of the other marks.

Mòrag felt a lump grow in her throat. *How cruel a life he's had.*

He whimpered drawing his legs in closer, his body trembling.

Even now, he's in pain. She reached out to touch his shoulder. As her fingers connected, he leapt from the bed knocking her backward and pining her to the floor, one hand on her wrist, the other with a blade to her throat.

Her neck burned hot from the weapon pressed against it. She struggled against his grip, 'Brax, it's me.'

He blinked as recognition dawned on his face, 'Mòrag?'

He let go of her wrist and pushed himself off her, and onto his back beside her. He was panting hard. 'I thought I was going to die.'

Mòrag pushed herself up to a sitting position, 'You thought *you* were going to die? I think you'll find, it's me that's bleeding here,' she said touching her neck.

Brax sat up and leaned in close, 'It's just a scrape, though it could have been far worse,' he placed his hand on it, healing the wound instantly.

Mòrag gasped as she saw what lay on the floor next to her, 'Where did you get that!'

'I stole it, from Edward. I don't know how I managed to hide it from him for so long. He was so angry that it was incomplete, that he didn't pay attention to where he put it, so I seized the opportunity. No one knows I have it.'

'I won't tell a soul.'

'I believe you.' He ran his other hand along her arm; her skin tingling in response

She felt oddly self-conscious with Brax so close like this. As though she were stripped, bare and her soul laid out in front of him. There was no reason to feel embarrassment, they had sat much closer several times, though he hadn't been quite so... bare skinned.

His hand was still on her neck, he ran it up her cheek and into her hair, pushing it back behind her ear, 'I'm sorry,' he breathed, 'I could have really hurt you.'

'But you didn't,' her voice was quiet, even to her own ears.

They gazed at each other for several moments, neither wanting to break the silence that had become something other than awkward, electric almost.

Finally, Brax broke the stalemate.

'Why did you come? You must have had a reason for waiting till this time of night.'

'I wanted to show you something in private,' she felt her face flush.

Brax blinked in surprise, 'Mòrag. It would be inappropriate if –'

'No! Nothing like that,' she cut him off, mortified that he thought she had come to offer herself in such a way, 'I was going to take you somewhere to show you.' *Everything I am saying sound's wrong,* 'just come with me will you.'

Brax smiled at her, it was a warm, soft smile, and it made her heart leap. He got up and offered a hand to her.

'Do I need anything?'

'No, just you.'

He pulled her to her feet, before moving to the corner of his room and pulling on a black shirt and trousers, and grabbing his boots. She watched him as he sat to tie his bootlaces.

'Ok. So where are you taking me?'

'To the stables,' she ignored the look he gave her, 'if we're going it needs to be now. I've to be at the parade ground for six.'

He followed her from the main building, through the grounds to the stable block. There were few sentries in this area of the castle grounds, so they were able to move around with ease.

'Why have you brought me here?'

'To give you a gift.'

'Mòrag, you can't mean the destrier, Randall won't allow it.'

She stopped and smiled at him, 'He doesn't belong to Randall, or the King, or his army. They belong to me, every last one of them: Especially Shand. When his dam died, I cut him from her belly; I fed him day and night and raised him as my own. He calls me "Màthair;" mother. I trusted Randall's judgement with him once before; I won't be doing it again. He will bond with you, or I will set him free and he will bond with no one.'

'Mòrag, I can't go against his wishes, it's not in me to disobey,' he looked away from her.

She took his hand and gently pulled him toward the building, 'He never said no,' she reminded him, 'tell you what. If you're still not keen once you've met him, then I will take a step back, ok?' she smiled at him, 'I'll take your silence as a yes. Come on.'

She pushed the heavy door open just far enough for them to enter the building. The bright moonlight shone through large windows in the stonework, illuminating the stables and the black horses they held. The building filled up with whinnies and nickers of greeting.

'Can you hear them?'

He frowned at her.

'In here,' she touched his forehead.

'Oh. No, I can't.'

'You will,' she smiled, 'Shand.'

At once, the young horse leapt over his stable door and pranced toward them.

'*Who is this, Màthair?*' Shand snorted.

'*His name is Brax; he is your other half.*'

'*My other half? But I thought...*'

'*No. I will never let anyone make a decision over your future like that again. I am so sorry you got hurt,*' she rubbed his nose, '*Brax is different. He is special, fragile even.*'

'*He is important to you?*'

'*Aye, he is.*'

'*Then I will protect him with my life.*'

Mòrag smiled and rested her forehead to Shand's, 'That's my boy. *You sound like your Athair.*'

She looked back at Brax, 'Brax, meet Shand.'

She smiled as they both took a cautious step toward each other.

'He's agreed to the pairing, all you need to do is seek the connection.'

'He can open his mind on his own?'

'They all can. No one ever needed to force them, but that's what's been happening. The resulting bond is insecure, completely one sided. In reality, none of these horses swears their allegiance to anyone other than Jock and myself. Let's keep that little bit of information to ourselves though,' she winked at him. 'Go on.'

Shand made the first move, taking one more step forwards, resting his head against Brax's chest and closing his eyes. The youngster was calm, confident that Mòrag would not lead him wrong.

Brax let his hands come up to run down the sides of Shand's neck. He flinched and a shiver ran through the young horse's body. When Shand opened his eyes, they had become the same pale silvery-blue as his new master's.

'See,' Mòrag beamed, 'you're a perfect fit.'

Brax couldn't keep the smile from his face, 'That was...'

'Feels good doesn't it, when no one is being forced against their will?'

'Like nothing I've ever felt before.'

'I've seen too many of this herd suffer during the binding process. Not physical suffering, but mental. Their soul is being caged. The guilt used to tear at me, still does. I used to scream at Jock and beg him to do something, to make them see the right way to do things, but as I got older, I realised why he couldn't make a scene. The only thing keeping us safe was that they didn't know who Jock really was. Though he used to say, if they ever found out who I was that they would hunt me down like they did my mum. I know he knows who she was. I also know he will never tell me.'

'And that makes you sad.'

'A little, though I learned to accept my shortcomings a long time ago,' she smiled wryly at him. 'Time, and practice, will strengthen your abilities, but your bond is solid. He will stand firm with you for the rest of his life, protect you at all costs. Wherever you go, he will go. He will never abandon you and he will never betray you. He will die before he sees you come to harm. He's one of a kind. Take care of him.'

'I will.' He drew his brows down as he regarded the young horse, 'Mòrag, his eyes have changed.'

'Of course they have,' it confused her that he didn't seem to know why, 'when the bond is mutual you gain each other's vision, how can you not know that?'

'I've never bonded a beast before. Both Sharri and Rannoch made their own bonds while I was unconscious. I didn't know there was any other way to make a bond than the one the army uses, until now that is. It's going to be glaringly obvious what we have done.'

'Rannoch severed his binding over you ages ago. He left the link though. Maybe your bond with Sharri is more mutual than you think. You share eyes with her so the bond must be equal. You should maybe ask her about it sometime. And don't worry yourself about what we've done. Randall wants you to have him; he's just worried he will upset Fletcher, and his big bad Daddy.'

'It will. How can you be so calm about this? It's dangerous to underestimate them.'

'I'm not underestimating them. I'm just not concerned. There is no point in worrying about what they might do; I would rather just deal with the consequences when they appear in front of me.'

'You amaze me,' he said shaking his head.

'Glad to see I leave a lasting impression,' she smiled at him.

The gong sounded in the yard, 'Six already? Think you both can wait till tonight to go for your first ride together?'

'We can,' Brax said leading Shand back to his stable and giving his neck a scratch.

They left the stable block together, closing the door gently behind them.

'I have to get going, I'm already late and I don't think General Rozzen is the type to be messed with.'

'No, she can be quite harsh at times but she's always fair.'

'See you tonight,' she called as she started in the direction of the parade grounds.

Chapter Twenty-Eight

STOVIES

The parade ground was already filled with a sea of red uniforms when Mòrag arrived.

Tyros of all ages milled about here and there. Established groups gathered and were laughing and joking together, Mòrag kept to the back of the crowd, *at least no one has noticed I'm late.*

'You are late.'

Mòrag flinched as Rozzen leaned over her shoulder. She could feel the General's hot breath on her neck.

'Don't let it happen again. Understood?'

'Yes, Ma'am.'

When Mòrag turned, Rozzen was gone.

'ATTENTION!' one of the Sergeants yelled.

Every Tyro took their place in line, and stood poker straight, arms by their sides. Mòrag followed suit, inching into line behind a tall and slender blonde girl.

'Today, our newest Tyros join us. Look around you study their faces. You are to give them no second chances. Weakness will not be tolerated. Those of you who are new to us, pay attention, learn from your peers. Aim to surpass them. I have no time for Tyros with no ambition. Most of you will last no longer than six months. This training is designed to push you to the very limit of your abilities. I am looking for the best of the best.'

Mòrag eyed the Tyros around her; finally, her eyes fell upon the one person she hoped she would be pitted against; Fletcher Raine. He glowered at her with unadulterated hatred. Mòrag narrowed her eyes at him then looked away.

'Sergeants, gather your troops,' Rozzen boomed.

'Yes, Ma'am!' they all shouted in response.

Each of the sergeants carried a clipboard and began to call out the names of the Tyros in their group. Once again, Sergeant Mullins called her name, and she moved toward the group that was developing in front of him.

'Right troops: Over your time in General Rozzen's group, you will bounce between several different classes. After the Winter Tournament, you will be assigned to different levels for each group based on your ability, not age or experience. There is no reason to hold you back if you are miles ahead of the pack. For now, we will be focusing on the basics, starting with hand to hand combat and defence. Pair up and we will go over the movements.'

Mòrag's ended up partnered with a young boy of thirteen or so with scruffy brown hair and green eyes. He was clumsy and had an attention span similar to the collective intelligence of a swarm of midges.

The day seemed to drag ever slower as Mòrag's stamina dwindled. High block, low block, blocks to either side, repeated over and over and over again.

'Take five then I will test your form.'

Plonking herself down on the soft grass incline hemming the parade ground, Mòrag sighed. She longed to be with her horses and see how Brax and Shand would get on together. *I wonder how long it will take before they –*

'MÒRAG!'

Realise. She smiled to herself. Obviously, they had noticed the change in Shand. She stood up and watched as Randall stormed across the parade ground, stopping mere inches from her. He was furious, literally shaking with rage.

'My... Office... Now,' he commanded.

'Of course, Sir,' she said , bowing her head to him.

As she crossed the parade ground, she could hear the whispers and comments making the rounds.

Rozzen eyed her before approaching the still fuming Randall that walked at her back. They stopped to exchange a few hushed words. Mòrag decided not to break stride and continued to Randall's office alone.

She waited by the door until Randall arrived and ushered her inside slamming the door behind her. Sitting in the chair in front of his desk, she watched him cross the room. It was as though he was bathed in blue flames. His soul itself seemed to bubble and boil.

'DAMN IT, MÒRAG! I TOLD YOU NO!' he battered his fist on the desk. 'I had a visit from General Raine today, demanding his son have another go with the destrier. I had to take him to see the beast, only to find it completely changed, placid, no longer wild. And its eyes, no longer brown but blue, pale blue. He knew immediately that the horse was no longer bind-able. He is demanding a hearing to determine your punishment. Do you realise what you have done Mòrag?'

She pulled herself away from the state of awareness that allowed her to see his soul. *Keep calm,* 'I did right by Shand and Brax.'

'You disobeyed a direct order.'

'I didn't.'

'I told you no.'

'I think you'll find, you told me you'd think it over, which basically means yes. It *doesn't* mean no.'

'You should not have acted on your own.'

'I had to. I couldn't watch you allow that brat and his daddy to abuse *my* horse again. I won't allow it.'

'*You* are not in a position to make such decisions. These beasts belong to the King's army, not you.'

'They belong to *me* — Shand belongs to me.'

'You realise you have doomed us all.'

She didn't answer she just concentrated on keeping all emotion from her face.

'There will be a hearing in the morning you will stand before the panel of Generals including myself. I cannot save you this time. General Raine knows I had nothing to do with your actions,' he blew out a long breath, finally allowing his anger to abate, 'if you had only waited.'

'You would have made the wrong decision. I told you yesterday. You need to start protecting your most powerful weapon. That's Brax. No one knows your enemy like he does: No one. You have him hidden away in a deserted wing of the castle, surrounded by the ghosts of his past when what he needs is companionship. He needs someone he can talk to, or more to the point, someone he doesn't have to talk to. He needs to feel welcome, wanted. And he doesn't. I gave him Shand because unlike the rest of the people in this place, Shand will gladly die to protect him.'

'You're right. I should have done far more for Brax than I have done,' he shook his head, 'He deserves better than I as his guardian.'

'He has huge respect for you, but I won't lie, the way you treat him sometimes, makes him loath himself all the more. He's damaged, Randall, not broken. An unsupported wound will never heal.'

Randall drew his brows down, 'You are wiser than your years, Mòrag.'

'I only say what I see. Do you understand why I did it now?'

'Yes. And it was the right decision. Though there will be consequences.'

'I am prepared to deal with those as long as Brax is kept out of it, he didn't want to go against your wishes. I pressured him into it.'

Randall sighed once more, 'I will see what can be done. Go back to your training for now. I will call for you tomorrow morning.'

'Yes, Sir,' she said, rising and leaving the room.

She clicked the door shut and turned to leave to find Rozzen blocking her way. She gestured to her office, so Mòrag followed her in and once again took up residence in a General's hot seat.

'Care to tell me why another General saw fit to stampede through my Tyros to remove you from your training?'

Mòrag noted that Rozzen didn't seem angry, or even agitated by the situation.

'To reprimand me, Ma'am.'

'I gathered that much, Mòrag. What I want to know is *why*.'

A knock at the door interrupted Mòrag's reply. Rozzen rose and answered the door, only opening it enough for the person in the hall to see her.

She doesn't want it known that she's poking her nose in I'll bet.

The voice from outside the door was Mairead's; she was as hot headed and flustered as always.

'You have been summoned to a hearing tomorrow morning, here are the details.'

'Summoned by whom?'

'General Raine.'

'Only the King may summon me, he is overstepping his quarter. Tell Oscar that if he would like me to attend he should come and ask me personally, otherwise, good day,' Rozzen said, stepping back and closing the door with a little more force than was necessary. 'My, you have been busy. I'm willing to bet that this hearing is relating to what you were doing with Brax in the stable block, in the wee hours of this morning.'

Mòrag's eyes widened. *How does she know?*

'I have eyes everywhere, Mòrag,' she said as she took up her position behind her desk once more, 'I highly doubt you took him in there for a roll in the hay.'

Mòrag felt her face warming.

'I wouldn't care if you did. We placed an implant in your arm during the Cleanse that will prevent any "accidents" occurring, so there is no reason to hold back should you feel the urge. He is a good looking boy, just a little messed in the head, but what does that matter between the sheets.'

'Ma'am!'

Rozzen chuckled, 'You embarrass easily,' she grinned, 'by your age all of our female tyros are proficient in the art of seduction. They learn how to influence decisions and gain information using their bodies. The boys are also taught but are nowhere near as skilled. At some point, you will also need to be educated in this manner, not yet however. Alright, if you were not there for sex, what were you there for?'

Mòrag dropped her head, her cheeks were blazing, 'It's not like that. He's a friend. I took him there to bond with Shand.'

'The elite destrier?'

'Yes Ma'am.'

'The one that General Raine covets for his brat of a son?'

'Yes Ma'am.'

Mòrag jumped as Rozzen began to howl with laughter. After several moments she composed herself, 'He is not going to look kindly on that. You have just made yourself a bigger target.'

'The benefits outweigh the consequences.'

'You will not fight it?'

'No.'

'Knowing General Raine, the minimum punishment he will demand is a public lashing.'

'Fine, he can do as he pleases. It doesn't make me any less right,' Mòrag cupped her mouth, eyes wide. *I can't believe I just said that. Out loud. To* her.

Rozzen narrowed her eyes, 'You *are* an interesting one. Take the rest of the day off, and make sure you get some sleep, you obviously missed it last night.'

'Yes, Ma'am.'

Leaving the office block Mòrag decided to make her way towards the refectory. As she reached the end of the corridor, she bumped into Brax.

'I take it he found out.'

'You could say that. I didn't think he would be as angry as he is. He near enough knocked down ten Tyros just yelling my name.'

'I heard. He can over react to the smallest thing and work himself into a fit of rage in a split second. You have to be on your guard all the time around him, particularly when he gets his fitness back. I'm surprised he was so... controlled.' Seeing the confused look on Mòrag's face Brax continued, 'Randall's a Berserker. He was the first, well, not the first, but the first that they discovered. James: The King was his driver. When the royal family were,' he sighed. 'Randall was used as a battering ram. Storm in and destroy everyone in sight. I don't know many of the details. I was only a boy at the time, and had... other things on my mind.'

'Right, I did wonder when he made a scene in front of all the other Tyros. I've to attend a hearing tomorrow morning.'

Brax paled, 'A hearing? It's not only Randall that knows is it?'

'No. Can we shift and talk elsewhere?'

'Ok, lead the way.'

Mòrag led Brax toward the refectory, the smell of freshly baked bread and stew slowly cooking made her mouth water. Her stomach growled so loud she was sure Brax could hear it. Before she could push the door, open Brax caught her hand.

'What?' she blinked at him.

'If I can avoid it, I don't go in there.'

She turned to face him, 'So *that's* why you're so skinny,' she regretted the comment as soon as it left her lips.

Brax's cheeks flushed and he looked away, 'I'd rather escape the confrontation. I don't really have much of an appetite anyway. And Randall drops me in some food every so often.'

'If you'd rather not go in, I can get some stuff and bring it to your room,' she offered.

'I'd prefer that.'

'Anything you want me to get you?'

'No. Not hungry.'

Mòrag narrowed her eyes at him, *my arse he's not hungry,* 'Ok, won't be long,' she said, leaving him to his delusions.

The refectory was deserted, though it wouldn't be for long. The Tyros would soon flood the hall for the lunch break. She asked the cook (a plump little woman with brown curly hair, rosy cheeks and a strong highland accent) for a small sack and some containers, once she had collected the items she wanted and two canteens of tea, she thanked the cook for her help and set off for the West wing of the castle.

Brax was waiting by his door when she arrived. He raised an eyebrow at the sack in her hand, as she moved past him and sat on his bed. He moved to the window, perching on the little chair.

Mòrag smiled as Brax's stomach growled in response to the smell from the open container in her hand.

'Still not hungry?'

'Maybe a little.'

'Good. I got you stovies.'

'Stovies? Really? Actual stovies?'

'Aye,' she grinned, 'amazing what you can get if you ask the right people.'

'I didn't think they offered any Albannach food.'

'They don't, but the cook is accommodating for her own people,' she beamed.

Brax was beside her in moments, she handed him the container and a fork, and smiled as he got stuck right in. When he had finished he flopped back against the wall giving a more than satisfied sigh. 'That was good, really good.'

Mòrag was still picking at her meal, she was finding it difficult to keep the hearing out of her mind. *The least he will demand is a public lashing. I wonder how I'll cope with that.*

'So how much trouble are we in?'

Mòrag took a deep breath, before she spoke, 'I am hoping it will just be me that's punished. Unless Randall or General Rozzen let on that they know who Shand is bonded with.'

'You can't take the blame yourself. Wait Rozzen knows?'

'She apparently finds the whole thing hilarious. She doesn't seem to like General Raine at all. She said the least he would demand is a public lashing. I told her I didn't care. Why did I say that? To a General of all people, Brax am I going mad?'

'No, you're stubborn as an ox though,' he chuckled, 'but if Oscar tries to whip you in public I'll take his head off his shoulders.'

Mòrag pushed herself to the back of the mattress so she was level with Brax, 'No you won't. You won't endanger what I'm trying to save in the first place. Let him have his moment, however hard it is on me, and then I'll let Rannoch have him.'

'Mòrag I can't just sit here and –'

'You can, and you will. The whole point in matching you and Shand was to keep you both safe.'

'I'm not making any promises,' he said before lifting one of the canteens to his lips.

'Rozzen thought I took you to the stable block, to, um, you know...'

Brax almost choked on his tea.

Chapter Twenty-Nine

ʻTHE HEARING

Randall flicked his eyes from the empty seat beside him, to the door and back again. Raine and Marcs were here, but not Rozzen. In all the years he had known her, she had never once been late. In fact, she was always the first to arrive, yet today, at a hearing for one of her own Tyros, she was nowhere to be seen.

'Shall we begin?' General Raine's smug voice cut through the silence.

'We should wait for Rozzen,' General Marcs noted. He looked exhausted, his face a few shades paler than usual, his blonde hair unkempt and jawline uncharacteristically darkened by stubble.

'You know as well as I, Marcs, that if she is not here early, she is not coming at all.'

'I suppose you are right, but for one of her own.'

'Women are fickle. Am I right Steele?'

Randall frowned, unwilling to speak against her and unable to speak for her.

'It's settled then,' he said, turning to the guards at the door. 'Bring her in.'

The small room was empty save for the curved table that accommodated the four generals and the elaborate throne that sat on a raised platform behind. Mòrag was ushered into the room; she paced gracefully across the floor, to the centre of the room, coming to a stop directly in front of them.

Marcs sat forward in his chair; he had been keen to meet Mòrag since his son returned to him, though until now he had not had the chance.

'You have been called here today,' began Raine, 'to be held accountable for your actions on the seventeenth night of September.'

Mòrag stood tall and straight before them, and carried an indignant look on her face. It was clear to Randall that she absolutely would not admit fault. After their meeting in his office the previous day, she had been adamant over the correctness of her actions. Her contempt for Raine was obvious. *That will only rile him up more.*

'I charge you with misconduct of the highest order! Interfering with objects outwith your control is unacceptable!'

'He is not an object,' Mòrag's voice was clear, calm, unwavering.

'You will only speak when asked!' Raine boomed.

Marcs exchanged a glance with Randall, his blue green eyes saying far more than the expression on his tired face. *Yes Daniel, she is brave, but she is also reckless. Mòrag, behave yourself.*

'As you wish, *Sir*,' she retorted, bowing her head a fraction in feign respect.

She is not going to behave. She does not care what the outcome is here. What can she possibly hope to gain? Or does she hope to make him so angry at her he is blind to Brax's involvement?

'Did you or did you not enter the stable block on the seventeenth night of this month?' Raine growled.

'I did.'

Sir.

'Did you interfere with my son's destrier?'

'No.'

Sir!

'You did not bind a destrier on that night.'

A faint smile laced her lips, 'Correct.'

Rudeness is not going to help you, Mòrag.

'Watch it girl! Address me correctly!'

Another feigned bow. Randall paled, *she's goading him!*

'If you did not bind the beast then why is it changed?'

'Starting without me are you?' Rozzen's smooth voice dominated the room with ease.

She stood in the doorway, arms folded across her chest and a calculating look in her eyes. Randall and the two other Generals were speechless. *She must have something up her sleeve; otherwise, she would have been here on time.*

She stepped into the room, Brax at her heel; she exchanged a hushed word with him before moving to her chair between Randall and General Marcs. Brax moved to stand with Mòrag.

Impossible: How does she know he is involved? What are you thinking, Patricia?

'What is *he* doing here?' Raine's repulsion was clear; he gripped the table in front of him until his knuckles were white.

Rozzen didn't even give Raine a respectful glance. As she spoke, her sharp eyes were on Mòrag and Brax in the centre of the room, 'He is directly involved. I thought General Steele would have told you that. How strange he did not,' her tone was mocking.

'Involved, how?' Raine's rage was barely contained within him.

What are you doing? You have been itching to get your hands on Brax for years, though I have never allowed it. If he is tried and punished here, you will never have the chance to train him. What's your play?

'He is bound to the destrier. It belongs to him now.'

Panic began to rise within Randall until he looked at Brax. In this situation, under the impending wrath of General Raine, he should have been worried, frightened even, but his face was calm, and he stood with an unspoken confidence.

'Steele, did you know about this?' Raine screeched.

Rozzen answered before Randall, 'Of course he did. I spoke to him about it on several occasions. How can you have forgotten to tell him,' she shoved his arm, 'Were you listening to me at all?' she huffed.

Randall blinked at her, 'I. I must have forgotten.'

'You see, Oscar,' she smiled as he glared at her use of his first name. 'I told Mòrag to help bond the horse to Brax. They are a perfect fit, far superior to the original match. So, as you can probably tell, this hearing is unnecessary. I suggest, that the next time you have an issue with one of *my* Tyros, you approach me personally.'

Randall watched Rozzen with admiration. *How could I ever have doubted her?*

Raine was so furious he was shaking, 'You should have cleared this with me first. That beast was reserved for *my* son. And why do it at that time of night, it's as though you meant to make a fool of me, Rozzen.'

'There was no need to concern you with such matters, as General Steele is in charge of beasts and I am in charge of the Tyros in question. The decision lies with us alone. I did not want Mòrag to miss any of her training so I instructed her to complete this task in her own time.'

'He is NOT military, he has no right!'

'Which brings me to the second point on my agenda: Seeing as we are all gathered. I would like the approval to induct Brax into the military as an official Tyro under my training. I am sure you all agree, the fact he has been able to bond with this horse, that even the son of our great General Raine could not tame, has earned him his place.'

'No,' Raine seethed, 'absolutely not!'

'That's one no and one yes. Marcs?'

Randall looked over at his fellow General. He looked tired. He had spent several nights by his son's bed hoping he would wake.

'My answer is yes, though I have one condition. I am sure you can guess what it is.'

'Consider it done. General Steele, you have the deciding vote,' she locked him in her powerful gaze.

She hasn't looked at me like this in a long time; she still makes me catch my breath.

'My answer,' he glanced at Brax and Mòrag, who were watching him, 'is yes.'

Rozzen clapped her hands together, 'It's settled then. Brax, beginning tomorrow you will be joining my troop.'

'He should be starting with my exams,' Raine threw in.

'I do not think there is any need for that,' General Marcs replied, 'he has been through far worse than your sadistic "endurance trials." He should go straight into Rozzen's troop.'

'I agree,' Randall called, supporting Marcs.

'Three to one: A clear majority. Are you willing to accept?' Rozzen did little to hide the glee in her voice as she spoke.

'If I must.'

Marcs addressed Mòrag and Brax, 'You are both dismissed. Brax, collect your uniform and accompany Mòrag to my office.'

Randall had guessed Marcs would ask them to see his son. His days were running out and he was getting desperate.

Mòrag and Brax called, 'Yes, Sir!' in unison, then left the room.

Raine rose from his seat and stormed from the room. Marcs followed him, leaving Randall and Rozzen alone.

'I should have known you would have something up your sleeve.'

She smiled at him, 'The girl is more than just talented. And we both know I relish any opportunity to get an advantage over Oscar.'

'You cornered me into giving you Brax.'

'You would never have agreed otherwise. You are possessive over him, though you are not protective. I do not know what happened to you over these last few years. You became distant, too distant. It is nice to see some life back in your eyes.'

'A lot has happened. I was lost for a time. I feel much more myself now.' *Would it be safe to tell her? She used to be the only one I could trust, but we have grown apart in recent years. I suppose the blame must lie with me. If I had noticed the change in myself because of my link with the King, could I have done something? Probably not: His hold over me was far too tight.*

'Patricia.'

Rozzen's expression softened, 'Yes?'

'I have reason to believe that Oscar is controlling the King.'

Chapter Thirty

LEAPING INTO THE UNKNOWN

'Thank you both for coming,' General Marcs said as Mòrag and Brax reached his office.

He had been waiting for them outside his door and as soon as they arrived, he led them back up the corridor. Mòrag exchanged a glance with Brax as they followed behind.

Marcs said nothing more until they reached the door that led to the infirmary, 'My son has until this evening to wake,' he clenched his fists, 'once his time is past they will no longer support his body and he will leave this world behind.' He turned to address them directly, 'You both are my last hope. A father should be buried by his sons, not the other way around. Please.'

Mòrag watched as Brax nodded to Marcs, 'We will do everything we can, Sir,' she said.

'Thank you. He is in the last room on the right,' he said, holding the door open for them.

Brax moved through first and Mòrag followed close behind. Reaching the door at the end of the corridor, she grasped the handle and slid it open.

Oliver lay under thin cotton sheets, tubes from his arm were connected to two hanging bags of fluid, a mouthpiece sat between his lips, the connecting tube was attached to a piece of equipment that beeped and whooshed at regular intervals.

'Is there anything we can do for him?'

'I'm not sure, his body is weak and his soul is almost fully withdrawn. Look at him in your mind's eye.'

Mòrag did as instructed. Oliver's pale yellow glow was gone, his body no longer covered in its soft light. Mòrag looked deeper, past the superficial layers of skin and muscle until she found the only light that remained, behind his eyes.

'Can you see it?'

'Yes,' she replied, 'how can we return it to how it should be?'

Brax retrieved a chair from the hallway and placed it next to the bed, 'Sit here,' he said, then moved the chair by the window to the opposite side and sat in it himself.

He took Oliver's hand in his own and indicated to Mòrag that she should do the same. It felt heavy, cold against her skin.

'I don't remember much from my early childhood,' he frowned, 'I have little memory of my parents or my home, other than damaged images that don't seem to fit together. I remember seeing my mother and father, sitting like we are now. There had been a lot of fighting; a man lay across the table where we ate our meals, and he was still, as if he had died. But I could see the glow behind his eyes. I cried,' he let a sad smile touch his lips. 'My mother told me to hush; I was to be a good boy, and I shouldn't be frightened. That together, she and my father could save the man. So I was quiet, but I didn't stop crying, I was too afraid. I stayed quiet and I watched what they did.'

Mòrag listened quietly. Brax had never spoken much about his own life and never mentioned anything before he came to be with Edward. It was clearly painful for him, but he continued to speak, so she sat silent and still.

'First they held his hands: My mother to his left and my father to his right. Then they reached out to him, not physically, not mentally, but somewhere in between.'

Brax's soul began to glow, then fine tendrils stretched out from his hand into Oliver's, moving up his arm. Mòrag breathed deep and reached for the place between thought and the physical world, where she could sense the souls of others. She looked down at her own hand, bathed in an emerald green glow, she willed the light to spread as Brax's had, nothing happened.

'Don't push your soul,' Brax said, 'seek Oliver's.'

At once, she understood. She closed her eyes and reached for him, she could feel the heat from her hand travel up his arm. She found herself in a barren wasteland, Brax by her side; they each held one of Oliver's hands in their own.

'*Why are you here?*' the boy's words carried no sound, his image did not even move its lips.

'*To bring you home,*' Mòrag squeezed on Oliver's hand. She could feel that he was frightened. He was more frightened of waking up, than he was of Brax's presence.

'*I'm not going home. It's not safe. It's safe here.*'

'*Oliver, your dad's waiting, Ava too,*' she could feel his soul trying to pull away.

'*It's like hot needles in my head. I can't keep control. Everything aches. It's so painful. I'm safe here. It's numb here.*'

'*You're body is dying,*' Brax's communication was as gentle as possible, '*you're being supported by the medics, I'm sure you know how hard on your sister that'll be.*'

'*Ava? I don't want to hurt Ava, or father. But I can't control myself.*'

'*We'll help you,*' Mòrag assured him, '*have I ever lied to you?*'

'*No.*'

'*Will you come with us?*' Brax asked .

'*I will try.*'

'*Take it slow Mòrag; retrace your steps at Oliver's pace.*'

'*Are you ready Oliver?*' he asked.

'*No, but I'll try.*'

Mòrag eased her way back, at first, she noted resistance but gradually, Oliver's soul began to ease outward. *We're doing it. It's working.* She opened one eye and glanced over at Brax, sweat beaded on his forehead and he was panting hard. *How am I finding this easier than he is?*

She reached her free hand over and grasped Brax's. His fear almost enveloped her, then settled behind her in the form of a small boy. Though Oliver continued to advance as planned, she was now aware of Brax at her back, images from his mind whirled around her.

The closer Oliver's soul came to the surface, the more vivid the images from Brax became, until she could see the man lying on his table, Brax's mother and father on either side of him. The boy was sobbing behind her.

As Oliver's soul reached the boundary to the physical world, Brax gripped her hand tight. The image almost blocked her view of Oliver. Brax's parents were writhing against an unseen force; the little boy began to scream as the man sat upright on the table, a wicked smile on his lips. Brax's parents dropped to the floor, all life gone from their now empty eyes.

As the man lunged at Brax, the scene disappeared from her mind. He had let go of her hand and fled the room.

Immediately, Oliver's soul slipped backward. Mòrag didn't think she grabbed blindly for his other hand, finding it she felt for his rapidly retreating soul, no matter how hard she tried, she couldn't keep it in her grasp.

'Oliver?'

'Where did he go? What happened?'

'Never mind that: You are on the edge, I need you to wake.'

'But my body will –'

'I'm here, I won't let you go. I promise.'

She felt him make a decisive push towards her, but still she couldn't reach him.

'Oliver?'

No answer came. She searched for him, reaching out as far as she could.

A hand on her shoulder jolted her and she opened her eyes.

'Time's up,' Major Darrow said, 'thank you for trying.'

Ava stood by the window, her face buried in her hands. General Marcs stood behind her, his face was grim, his eyes red rimmed as he watched a medic remove the tubes from Oliver's arm.

'Wait. No. Oliver's in there, he wants to wake up he just needs a little more time. You can give him a little more time can't you?'

'I am sorry, we cannot. He has already had more than double what is allowed for.'

The medic reached to remove the mouthpiece and breathing tube. Mòrag lunged forward, gripping his arm tight, 'He needs more time.'

A small-scale struggle ensued, ending with General Marcs pulling Mòrag to the back of the room.

'I'm afraid; even I cannot ask for any more time.'

'You have to, Sir! He is still in there. Damn it, Oliver wake up!'

Marcs was fighting hard to hold back tears, 'Mòrag, don't.'

'Oliver wake up!' she struggled in his father's grip as his mouthpiece and air tube were removed. 'Wake up, *please!*' she closed her eyes, reaching for her link with Oliver, the door to his mind was wide open but the walls and floor within were crumbling and dissolving. In the centre of the room, there was no more than a tiny, pale yellow flame. Mòrag hurled her mind towards it catching it and pulling herself close to it.

She opened her eyes and sat bolt upright, desperately sucking in a deep breath of air. Her throat and lungs blazed. Her vision was blurred, and her head ached.

As her vision cleared, she realised that she was staring at her own body, hanging limp in General Marcs' arms. *How did I?*

She could already feel Oliver's body wanting to rebel. Searing pain spread through his skull, his vision began to flicker. Oliver stood with her, holding her hand. Since she had taken control forcing his body to live and breathe his soul had re-formed.

Mòrag grasped Oliver's head with his shaking hands; she could feel the earthquake beginning within. Major Darrow darted from the room, returning moments later with a syringe. Mòrag felt the deep sting of the needle pierce Oliver's skin as the sedation was administered. Slowly, the pain began to melt, the terrifying shudders that had begun within him stilled. His head felt heavy, weariness dragged at his eyes, so she let his body flop back onto the bed.

Is it over?

I think so. Do you think you can take control? I'm struggling here.

How did you?

I don't know, but I can feel myself being pulled back. Can you manage on your own?

I'll try.

The draw of her own body was impossible to resist, the mindscape seemed to whirl around her until she was looking at her own feet.

As she straightened her legs, taking her own weight once more a wave of nausea swept over her. She pushed General Marcs' arm away and threw herself at the sink in the corner of the room, allowing her stomach to turn itself inside out. When the retching had stopped, Mòrag wiped her face on her sleeve and turned to see Oliver still awake. His father stood where she had left him, open mouthed, glancing between her and Oliver.

'Fa... ther?' Oliver's hoarse little voice was slow and slurred.

General Marcs dashed to his side, grasped his hand and kissed his forehead, 'I thought we had lost you.'

Ava threw her arms around her brother and wept. The medics were talking by the door, formulating a plan for his continuing care.

'Sir?' Mòrag said in a quiet voice.

General Marcs squeezed Oliver's hand and smoothed his son's hair back, then turned towards her.

'May I check on Brax?'

'What happened? He bolted past me, he was white as a ghost, I thought the worst, but then you were still here.'

'For him it was,' she said, 'old demons.'

'Go. And Mòrag,' he placed a hand on each of her shoulders, 'thank you. I owe you both a great debt.'

Mòrag bowed her head and left the room. She had to make sure Brax was alright. Shockwaves reverberated through her body as she recalled the face of the man who had murdered his parents.

It was the same man she had seen kill Rannoch's mother, she was sure of it. Understanding dawned like a knife in the gut. Edward. Even thinking his name made her shudder. One other thing leapt out at her from his memory that she hadn't noticed at first: The green-blue tartan that clad the lifeless, soulless bodies of his parents.

Mòrag sped through the passageways toward Brax's room. She found him sitting on the floor between his bed and the wall, his head to his knees and his arms hugging his legs close to his body. He hadn't noticed her come into the room.

That memory was terrifying for me. But it actually happened to him. I can't imagine what he's going through right now. She moved toward him, and kneeling beside him, she placed a hand on his shoulder. He flinched at the contact.

Mòrag sat and pulled him down until he lay beside her, his head resting on her lap. She ran her hand through his hair. *This helped him before.* Several long minutes passed before he spoke.

'You saw,' it wasn't a question. 'I have spent nineteen years trying to forget that night. It's the only memory I have left of my parents; I have no other memories of them, only the sight of them lying there on the floor, lifeless, lightless: Dead. I'm sorry I ran. I let it get hold of me.'

'It's ok, you don't need to apologise for that,' Mòrag soothed.

'Is he, did I...'

'Oliver's awake, they have him sedated, but he's conscious.'

'It worked,' he breathed, 'then it was worth it.'

Chapter Thirty-One

ᴛHE SOUL BLADE

Frost lay thick on the castle grounds. The seasonal shift had been extreme this year, the blistering heat of the summer seemed to have switched to sub-zero chill in less than two days, though in reality it was a gradual change over several weeks.

It was still early, only four a.m. or so, and the barracks were full and silent. Mòrag replaced the heavy slat of the shutter, lifted a towel, her bandages and her uniform, and padded softly on bare feet towards the shower room. She placed her uniform on the wooden bench that ran the length of the room opposite the five shower cubicles. Setting the water flowing, she retrieved her bandages and shook them out before carefully rerolling them. Setting them on top of her other clothes on the bench, she undressed as fast as she could and hopped into the steam filled cubicle. The shower room held a colder atmosphere than the rest of the building, which in summer was cool and comforting, however, now that the weather had turned, Mòrag appreciated the uplifting heat of the water on her back.

She pressed her forehead and palms against the cool tiles, and closed her eyes, enjoying the drum of the hot rain on her back. She allowed her mind to drift, though it settled where it always seemed to settle these days, on Brax.

In the month since the hearing, she had spent every spare moment with him. He was an escape of sorts, someone who she felt completely comfortable with. With him, there were no rules, no expectations. They enjoyed each other's company pure and simple.

Brax was doing well with Shand. He and the young destrier were a perfect match, each levelling out the other's personality. They were so in tune that there had been no need to back and train either Shand or Brax in the usual manner. From the very first, once mounted they moved as one. It thrilled Mòrag to watch them, reminding her of her own bond with Rannoch.

I wonder if Oliver will ever recover enough to bond a familiar. In the month since his waking, she and Brax and visited the young boy every day. He seemed to have no memory of what happened within his body before he took back full control. Ava, Major Darrow and the other medics had not seemed to notice the switch from Mòrag to Oliver either. Mòrag was secretly grateful of this. She didn't want any of them asking questions she didn't have answers to.

Their father on the other hand had figured out exactly what had happened. Like Mòrag, he didn't know the how or the why, but he knew she had somehow transferred herself to Oliver's body and back again.

The General had shown up at Brax's room to 'escort' her back to barracks. In fact, he wanted to determine how much she knew about what had happened. He had taken her to a sealed area of the castle. The large, locked door was decorated by an ornate carving of two unicorns with a shield between them.

'Mòrag I am sure I do not have to spell it out that what you have done tonight is not normal. As head of intelligence and defensive strategy, I have an in depth knowledge of all the talents and their subsequent skill sets. It is of course my job to monitor and analyse the development of such powers. I have however, never come across anything like what I saw you do tonight. I must ask you to keep this to yourself, tell no one, not even Brax, I'm sorry, I know you are friendly with him. But if this information got into the wrong hands you would be placed at significant risk. I will see what answers I can acquire from the old records. Until then, please mention this to no one. If you need to talk, come to my office at any time,' he left her by the door of the restricted wing to walk back to the barracks alone.

Mòrag sighed, *all this stress and secrecy, and the winter tournament starts in a few days*, she turned off the shower and dried herself quickly with the rough towel, wrapping her hair up in it, she dressed her bottom half. Mòrag lifted her bandages; the soft material was twice the width of her palm and had a slight stretch to it.

Moving to stand in front of the tall mirror, she held the end of the bandage flat across her chest. She unfurled the material until it covered the beginning edge, taking care not to crease or twist the bandage. She then used her spare hand to smooth the material as she rolled it across her skin, diagonally downward until she reached the point above her hips. She then began to wind the material back upwards until she reached her bust once more. She wound five more rounds across her breasts only moving half an inch upwards each time so it provided a firm support, and tucked in the tail. She smiled to herself as she always did, it amused her that this was the same method she used to bandage the legs of the horses when they were training or to support an injury.

Mòrag let out an exasperated sigh, 'You waiting to give me a lecture, Ava?'

With an unimpressed look, Ava appeared from the shadows, 'Still binding yourself I see. What happened to the bra I gave you?'

'I gave it to Randall so he could sleep better at night.'

Mòrag grinned at the horror on Ava's face.

'Mòrag you didn't!'

'Aye, I did. He said he wants a red one next time.'

Ava's face turned a deep shade of scarlet.

Mòrag smiled wickedly at her, 'Keep yer heid, I'm only messing. It's in yer locker.'

'Mòrag you are wicked!'

Mòrag chuckled, well you're the one whose lurking, you deserved it,' she winked at her, 'I can't wear that thing. It's painful on my shoulders and too tight round my middle. We aren't all as skinny as you, you know.'

'But binding, Mòrag: You should be presenting yourself not covering up. That aside, I'm sure it's damaging to wrap your body like that.'

'Probably,' she stretched, flexing, checking the support and tension of the material that gently hugged her body. 'If you had seen how it used to be done you would have had a hairy canary fit.'

'How it used to be done?'

'Up until I was fourteen I was bound so tight I looked like a boy. My hair was chopped short too.' Mòrag pulled the towel from her head and combed through her wavy hair, gathering it up behind her head and securing it with a band. 'It got too painful, so I would take the bandages off in the forest where no one would see, and replace them myself at a comfortable tension.'

Ava was aghast, 'Why?'

'Just,' *to hide me from you lot because of my 'traitor' mum, but I can't tell you that.*

'That's awful! You must have hated your parents.'

'No. Jock and Evelynn did the best they could for me, and all I've brought them is trouble. Anyway the point is, these support me where as that doesn't support you,' she said pointing at Ava's chest.

'It's very supportive,' she protested.

'Oh? Jump up and down then.' She sniggered when Ava declined, 'I didn't think so.'

Flinging the shirt over her back, she padded back to her bunk with Ava.

'Where are you going?'

'To meet Brax of course.'

'At this time?'

'Well I'm not going to sit and wait till later am I.'

'You are going to get in trouble.'

'Only if you tell... which I know you won't.'

Ava huffed, 'Here,' she said tossing a thick scarf from her locker at Mòrag, 'don't catch a cold, you'll get me in trouble.'

Mòrag grinned at her, 'Ta. I'll try not to.'

She fastened her heavy olive cloak round her shoulders, wrapped Ava's fluffy pink scarf round her neck and raised the hood.

'So fashionable,' Ava remarked.

Mòrag turned with a wave of her hand and a smile on her lips and headed for the door.

The sky was pitch black; the moon was still high and cast a silvery glow over everything in sight. The crunch of the frosty ground beneath Mòrag's boots reverberated off the buildings. Except for the mist of her own breath, the air was crisp and clean. It nipped at her cheeks and Mòrag pulled Ava's scarf a little higher up her face.

Brax was stoking the fire when Mòrag arrived at his room, the small space held the heat well and she felt choked in her cloak and scarf.

Brax glanced at her sideways, 'I didn't think pink was your colour.'

'It's Ava's,' she replied, stretching and rubbing her eyes.

'Still having trouble sleeping?' he asked sitting himself on the old threadbare rug by the fireplace.

Mòrag nodded.

'When you first start developing the various skills of any particular talent, your brain goes into overdrive, although I would have thought that you would have recovered by now.'

'Do all skills and talents have the same effect?'

'No, the more difficult the skill, the longer it will take you to master and recover, although with practice it should become second nature. Perhaps we should choose another day for you to learn about the soul blade.'

'I'd rather do it now.'

'It takes a lot of concentration; though once you know how to do it it's really easy to master. Rozzen told me once that it's a skill specific to natural Seekers. That's probably true, though I know of one exception to the rule.'

Mòrag sat cross-legged in front of him, 'So Reavers can do this too then?'

'They don't seem to be able to no, other than Edward. Wait. Who told you about Reavers?'

'Rozzen: She didn't tell me any details, she just mentioned that the current royal family are Reavers.'

Brax gave her a funny look, it was obvious he had something on his mind, but whatever it was, he didn't say. 'Making a soul blade isn't as hard as it sounds. You're already partially doing it when you're strengthening a hand held weapon. The difference is that you and I can take things to the next level. Move yourself into the sensory plane like we've been practicing.'

Mòrag did as instructed; emerald green light bathed her, she looked up at Brax who for once didn't look away.

'I'm getting used to you seeing me like this. It still makes me feel uncomfortable, but not ashamed anymore.' He let out a long breath, 'ok, watch closely,' he said holding up his hand.

Mòrag watched as Brax's soul began to shift like ripples on a pond, flowing toward his hand, until it formed a red-flecked blue sphere around it.

'This is the first stage. I'm sure you can already see the first danger of using the soul blade.'

'Your soul hasn't swollen at your hand,' she noted, 'it moved there. Does that mean it's not covering your body somewhere else?' She scanned his body but couldn't see any area that was uncovered.

'It's not covering an area on my back. Obviously, the section of our soul that's always outside our body, encasing our skin, is a natural protection, a barrier that protects us automatically. By moving it to gather at my hand, it has left an unprotected area. I am sure I don't have to tell you my surface protection has taken a lot of damage, so this method would only produce a weak blade, and if I were attacked it would most likely fail immediately, so it's not the one I use.'

Mòrag sat for a moment absorbing what he had told her, 'What method do you use?'

He allowed his external soul to retreat to its original position. 'I don't use the soul blade unless I *absolutely* have to,' he said as a sphere surrounded his hand once more, only this time it was a crisp royal blue. 'Any time you do this you are using some of your body's protection to construct a weapon.

Instead of using my weak outer soul, I use the protection that surrounds my vital organs. I retain my outer protection but the risk is greater. This can be moulded and shaped as you wish from an orb like this which is near on useless, to a blade of whatever type you prefer,' the orb around his hand seemed to melt and stretch out before him, thin and sharp. 'The more you train the more varied your style can become. And with experience you can use more of your soul to strengthen or grow the blade. The strength of your resolve hardens and sharpens the blade. So for example,' he swung the blade at her allowing it to pass through her body and emerge from the other side.

Mòrag flinched, expecting more than the warm tingling sensation she felt. 'You cut me last time,' she said.

Brax let the blade melt away and ran his hand through his hair, 'Last time,' he said, 'the blade was focused, and you woke me from a nightmare. That's not a very clever thing to do. My body reacted instinctively. I still think about that. I could have easily killed you.'

'But you didn't,' she pointed out. 'So the horn focuses the blade then?'

'Exactly: Though there is some resistance when I use it from the residual power left within. That's what happens when the animal is murdered. Its horn becomes tainted. I'm actually still surprised I can use it.'

'May I see it again?' She noted his discomfort at her question, 'I have a theory, and I want to see if I'm right.'

He considered for a moment, then rose and retrieved the horn from beneath his pillow, handing it to her with only the slightest hesitation.

'It's quite precious to you isn't it?'

'Very. It's the horn of the familiar of the last Albannach monarch. Her name was Skye, and she was the gentlest creature I have ever known. I couldn't let him have her horn, not hers. So here I am, still petrified he will find me and discover I have it,' he smiled wryly.

Mòrag inspected the horn; it glittered and glinted in her hands, 'How did it get damaged?' she asked.

'James didn't want to kill her. His blade got stuck.'

'It's funny,' she said, 'I don't remember seeing you when Rannoch's mother was killed,' she watched him as she spoke, 'I do remember being petrified *I* would be seen. I remember Edward. I didn't realise it was him until I saw your memory of him. I remember how his face turned from annoyance to fury when the blade stuck. I remember the pain in her eyes, how she struggled beneath the black Lion's claws. And I remember the desperation that I felt when I realised her unborn foal was still alive.'

Brax had turned several shades whiter than his normal pale colour, 'She was...'

'You can imagine my surprise when what I cut from her wasn't a unicorn foal, but Rannoch.' Mòrag reached into a makeshift pocket she had sown onto the inside of her cloak and pulled from it an item wrapped in a soft leather cloth. She unfolded the material and lifted the shard of horn that had split from the main part. 'This is what I used to cut him free. If James hadn't split her horn, Rannoch wouldn't have survived. I doubt she would have out run that Lion as heavily pregnant as she was.'

'You must only have been six or so, how did you know how to...'

'Seven. I'd seen Jock do it before; though I won't lie I was bricking it.' Mòrag placed both sections of horn together, the seams melted as the horn became whole once more. She smiled at Brax and handed him the now flawless horn.

Chapter Thirty-Two

GENERAL DISCUSSION

Randall held open the door to his chambers, allowing Marcs, Rozzen and their familiars to enter into the sitting room. Randall closed the door behind them and ushered them to the table. He had only cleared the area of folders and files moments before they had arrived. The papers now piled neatly along the wall and behind the settee.

Tara 'oofed' softly in greeting to her two companions, who bowed their heads to her in reply.

Rozzen's silver Cadmean Vixen, Seline padded to the floor beside her chair, she was never far from her bonded mistress, though it was rare to see her openly. In all the time Randall had known Rozzen, he had only seen Seline on a handful of occasions.

Marcs' Black Panther, Nyx preferred to lie stretched out in front of the fireplace. The large cat was not fond of the cold, wet winter weather and slept through as much of it as duty would allow.

Randall had prepared some shortbread, two fresh brewed pots of tea, two cups and a large mug for Rozzen. She was quite the tea jenny and could happily drink gallons of the stuff.

Rozzen scanned the room, 'It is more cluttered than I remember,' she said giving Tara a scratch between the ears.

'I'm not surprised. It has been a number of years since you were last here. And you were not so concerned with the contents of the room,' he replied, pouring out the tea and taking his seat.

'I think we all know why we are here.' Marcs said, 'Mòrag has caused quite a stir since she first came to the academy. I would like to know your thoughts on the matter.'

Randall considered his words before he spoke; he had known Marcs since they were children. Even as a boy he always did like to get straight to the point and didn't care much for stories full of pointless twists and turns. Mòrag's story was nothing but twists and turns. 'She has an incredibly strong mental authority. During the binding, when the destrier went berserk and charged me, Tara took up the challenge. I was about to shoot the beast down and with one mental command: One word. She stopped all three of us in our tracks. I have only ever felt that kind of power from King James.'

'Do you think she knows she has that level of authority?' Marcs asked.

'Honestly, no. She seems to have an exceptionally strong will to endure. She fought the Cleanse with such ferocity that she actually pulled my consciousness into her mind. Her power to command me was absolute. Her hold was so strong that I am now no longer actively bound to the King. She seems to have dislodged his hold of my mind.' Randall noted the shocked faces of the other two Generals.

'Why did you neglect to tell us this?' Rozzen demanded.

'At the time I was in no fit state to talk to anyone. Unfortunately, Daniel your daughter could tell you more about the aftermath of the event than I can.'

'Ava told me you had food poisoning when she was caring for you.'

'Yes, that is what Brax told her. Only he knows what happened to me. Mòrag does not seem to remember. Not that I am surprised, considering the nineteen day ordeal she went through with the Cleanse.'

'From what Tesso tells me,' Rozzen said, 'she performed exceptionally during Oscar's ridiculous trials. She has saved your son, Daniel, not once, but three times now.'

'You do not have to remind me, Patricia,' Marcs replied, 'I will never be able to repay the debt I owe that girl. On that subject I must apologise, I have kept certain aspects of that night from you. I withheld the information until I could do some research on the subject.'

Randall refilled Rozzen's mug and narrowed his eyes at Marcs, 'Are you saying that Mòrag and Brax did not bring him back together?'

'That is indeed what I am saying. Brax fled the room a good forty minutes before my son came back to us.'

'Forty minutes?' Rozzen repeated, 'On her first try, to be left in the final stages of a retrieval and maintain it to the end is astonishing.'

'That's just it, Patricia,' Marcs replied, 'the retrieval failed.'

Randall couldn't believe what he was hearing. *It failed. How then is Oliver alive?* 'Daniel, how did she...'

'I am not sure exactly. His time was over; Mòrag made a scene of course; she had tried her hardest and failed; I had to hold her still so they could let him be at peace. Essentially he should have died. One minute she was struggling in my arms and the next her body went limp, and my son sat up. Only it was not my son. I could see it was Mòrag and not Oliver. It was clear she didn't know what had happened, she told me as much when I spoke to her about it later that night. She somehow removed herself from her own body and took over Oliver's, allowing him enough time to gather his strength.

'Darrow administered a sedation while she was still in control, and when she came back to herself, my son was able to remain conscious. It took a lot out of her, she was sick and disorientated afterward, and I have been told she is still having difficulty sleeping. I am sure you will understand that I wanted to find out more about this power before speaking to you both.'

Randall exchanged a glance with Rozzen, 'I assume from your request for this meeting that you have come across the information you sought.'

'Indeed,' Marcs said, 'I searched our records spanning the past century and found nothing. I looked back over the last four hundred years, and found nothing. I found no record of a skill similar to the one Mòrag used, until I came across the ancient tomes that record the histories before the Great War.

'The damaged and faded text had sections ripped out or tainted and unreadable. However, I gained three key facts about the origin of the skill Mòrag has shown. Firstly, the skill involves transferring the person's entire soul into another body. Secondly, the talent has no name, as there has only been one documented occurrence in our known history, up until Mòrag that is.

'The talent is formed when the Royal bloodlines of Alba and Sasann merge, creating a Seeker/Reaver hybrid. Lastly, but most importantly, the owner of this talent, Reginald I: The Bastard King, was the cause of the Great War that almost wiped out humanity. He perfected the talent to such an extent, that he was able to leave his original body behind, and exist in a host body indefinitely. By the time he was defeated he had reached one-hundred and fifty-eight years old.

'In truth, there is no proof that his soul was destroyed, though there are no further mentions of him throughout our history. I have found a few texts warning of his return, and just as many discounting it. Though I have found several tomes and texts predicting a recurrence, which will be marked by the birth of a higher beast, they called the Nemeocorn,' he scratched his floppy golden locks, 'It describes the beast as half Unicorn, half Nemean Lion. I do not know how reliable these ancient writings are, but even I must admit that there are too many coincidences to ignore the possibility that this girl is the second coming, so to speak.'

'She is most definitely of the Stewart dynasty; of this I have no doubt in my mind.' Rozzen said, 'There are only two bloodlines that possess the inherited Seeker ability; the Douglas Clan and the Stewart Clan. Each has particularly distinct features. Mòrag is no Douglas.'

'How can you assume that, Patricia,' Marcs asked, 'The Douglas Clan was wiped out almost two decades ago? No one remembers what they look like.'

'Not true. The Albannach people remember; every one of them. And so do I, Daniel. I do not easily forget when someone pays me a kindness. I am surprised neither of you have noticed what you had in your midst all this time.'

Randall and Marcs now took a turn to exchange a glance, 'I never thought you were a sympathiser, Patricia.'

'I never thought you could be so blind, Randall. There is only one living member of the Douglas Clan left, and his resilience is a testament to their honour. Yet after escaping Edward's claws he has been squirreled away in a hidden corner, to be forgotten other than when you decide you need him.' Rozzen's words held venom behind them.

Randall blinked at her, unsure of how he should respond, or even if he should respond at all. Rozzen was prone to the occasional hot temper, though it took a long time for her to boil over, when she did however, it was a formidable sight, 'I am not making excuses, Patricia,' he said, 'but, I am sure you already know that I have not been myself for quite some time. I have done the boy a disservice which I will try to make up for but I can't change the past.'

'I must admit, Patricia, that Brax fell short of my radar until very recently and I am sure you can appreciate I have had far more important things on my mind,' Marcs said.

Rozzen huffed and drained her mug, sliding it over the table for Randall to fill, 'Men. You are full of excuses for your inadequacies. You should count yourselves lucky I am fond of you both.' She sighed, 'ah well, I am sure we can leave the worrying about the supposed second coming until the Nemeocorn appears.'

'He already has,' Randall said scratching his chin, 'He is the beast that injured Brax the day she came into our hands.'

'I thought it was a destrier that had been wearing war cuffs,' Marcs said.

'No. It was the Nemeocorn. To this day I do not know how he managed to bring the beast down, but he did.'

'And you still never noticed him for what he was?'

'Patricia, I was not myself,' he said, meeting her steely gaze with his own.

General Marcs looked from Randall to Rozzen and back again, 'I think we ought to be discussing how we should proceed from here rather than dwelling on the past, don't you both agree?'

Rozzen let out an exasperated breath, 'You have a point. In my opinion the girl is essentially kind-hearted, though she does not seem to recognise authority in any form,' she smiled 'she certainly knows how to rile Oscar up.'

'I was surprised by her actions at the hearing myself. I have found her genuine and fiercely determined,' Marcs added, 'but I have not had a great deal of contact with her.'

Randall refilled his cup, 'She is as you both say. Mòrag fights for what she feels is right. She is wilful and optimistic. But... I believe there is a darker side to her, I have not seen evidence to support my feeling yet, but I think we will need to watch her closely. One thing is abundantly clear. If we are to regain our King, I do not think anyone other than Mòrag is capable of the task.'

'Surely Brax is more than adequately skilled.' Marcs said.

'He is Daniel, but I am afraid neither of them wants anything to do with the other. Mòrag is the only one who can take up the task. Also, amid rumours of Prince Edward's return she has openly sided with Brax. She has formed a strong friendship with him, and should Edward return, I believe she will be one of our strongest weapons against him. I only hope we can release Oscar's hold on the King before then.'

Chapter Thirty-Three

TEAM TOURNAMENT BEGINS

Mòrag stood in line with Brax outside the large building that lined the parade ground. It held sparring practice and other activities of the sort during the winter months. It was still dark and the stars shone brightly in the sky. Mòrag felt a deep trembling in her bones; she would have preferred a lap of the castle to all this standing around in the cold.

Inside there was a huge noticeboard set up to the left of the hall. Pinned on it in groups of four, were several white cards, though she could not make out their inscriptions from this distance. The Tyros stood at ease in groups according to their level. Mòrag looked round at Brax. He was paying attention to the Generals at the opposite side of the hall.

'What do you think they're talking about?'

'Not sure,' Brax answered, 'but they keep looking at you.'

'Well that's just braw now isn't it? I'm really getting fed up with all this attention.'

'I don't blame you,' he replied, 'Rozzen's going to speak.'

Rozzen left the other three Generals and strode up a small set of steps onto the raised platform at the far side of the hall. Sergeant Grey called everyone to attention before Rozzen spoke.

'Today marks the commencement of the winter tournament. I expect each and every one of you to push yourselves to the limit.' She scanned the sea of red uniforms in front of her focussing on Brax for a moment, before looking away towards another group. 'As per usual there will be a team section and an individual section to the tournament. Each of you have been assigned to a squad of four, details of your allocated unit can be found on the wall to your left.

'Your team will be provided with a basic map, directions, and objective. On the table to your right is a selection of basic provisions. Each unit is permitted only six items. You will all be allocated a weapon based on your level. You have three days to complete your objectives. The Sergeants will take you to your designated starting points in one hour. Be ready.' She turned and marched from the platform, as her foot left the last step Sergeant Grey called for the Tyros to fall in.

Mòrag watched the generals resume their heated discussion for a moment, and then followed Brax to the left of the hall. She scanned the cards for her name, finally finding it in the lower centre of the board. *Lennox, Oswald, Cowrie, Mòrag.* She sighed, Cowrie's name was written in messy script next to a name that had been blacked out, *I don't have a clue who any of these folk are.* Mòrag looked to see who Brax had ended up with but he had disappeared from sight.

A young boy of twelve shouted out next to her, 'Cowrie, Lennox to me!' he turned and stared at Mòrag, 'you too.'

Mòrag blinked at him, this must be Oswald. Taking charge from the outset: That was either very good, or very bad, she couldn't tell but followed along behind him anyway.

They collected their map and sealed envelope, containing details of their task and vague directions, then followed Oswald to the enormous table covered in provisions. There was a wide variety of items available for the taking, Food packs including a loaf, some cheese, tough meat and a canteen of water; lengths of rope; grappling hooks; compass; first aid kit; waterproof sheets; canvas sacks; lengths of wire wound round a bottle of oil, flint and cooking pot; matches; kindling; blankets and so on.

Oswald's pale green eyes scanned the tables in front of him. Mòrag waited for him to speak but he stayed silent. *He doesn't know what to take.* She caught him glancing sideways at her. 'What do *you* think?' he asked.

Mòrag was pleasantly surprised. It was the first time someone had asked her genuinely for her opinion, even if he was a child. 'First aid kit, rope, wire and oil, knife, waterproof sheet and blanket.'

'I think we should take a food pack each,' Cowrie said, 'I don't want to starve myself for three days.'

You have a point,' Oswald agreed, 'we won't last if we don't eat.'

'Who said anything about not eating? What do you think the wire, oil and knife are for?'

'That's if you can catch something... which I doubt.'

'Units six and nine, to me,' Sergeant Grey shouted.

'Nine. That's us,' Oswald said leading the way.

Mòrag followed behind her team through the crowded red uniforms toward Sergeant Grey, who was standing with clipboard in hand and a face like fizz.

'Cowrie, you are to transfer to unit six. Brax, take his place in unit nine.'

'Why, Ma'am?' Cowrie asked the red-faced boy regretted his question as he came under Grey's broiling glare.

'None of your damned business, Cowrie! Transfer to six. Understood?'

'Yes, Ma'am,' he said.

'*What's going on?*' Mòrag cast to Brax as he moved to her side.

'*I'm not sure. It seems I was supposed to be in this unit and someone changed the lists. Rozzen is practically spitting acid.*' He gave her a quick smile, '*I'm glad I've been moved back. I wasn't looking forward to this. It will be more bearable with you around. Just.*'

'Oi!' she gave him a soft shove.

'Ok team, let's get our supplies,' Oswald said, 'we need to leave soon.'

'I take it you are taking point then?' Brax asked.

'Got a problem with that, Dog?' He growled.

'No. He doesn't.' Mòrag retorted, 'but I do. You and your wee buddy there don't know the first thing about surviving outdoors in winter. If you want to play Simon says that's fine with me, but don't expect *us* to save *your* arse when you won't listen to *our* advice!'

The boy stared at her, shocked that she had spoken to him in such a manner.

'And another thing, Dunderheid. You need to learn how to address people by their names.'

'My name's not Dunderheid. It's David.'

'Well until you learn that *his* name's Brax,' she snapped, 'you're Dunderheid. Got that?'

'Mòrag, it doesn't bother me anymore,' Brax said placing a hand on her arm.

'*Don't lie. I know it bothers you,*' she cast. 'Well you may not care anymore but I do.'

Oswald looked from Mòrag to his feet to Brax, 'Yes, Brax, I will take command of the unit.'

'Good, good. Let's get the stuff and get going then,' Mòrag said striding back to the tables of provisions.

In the end, Oswald decided to take her advice on the provisions, and they left the hall with Sergeant Mullins. He led them down to the causeway where they descended the steps at the base of the structure to the water's surface, where a boat was waiting.

Mòrag's legs felt unsteady as she boarded the simple craft. Brax offered her his hand as a stabling aid and she gladly took it. Mullins seated and blindfolded them before the vessel set off. The cold air of early winter was frigid at the water's surface. Mòrag could feel her muscles beginning to stiffen and throb. Her left shoulder carried a near constant ache. She couldn't class it as painful yet, but by the time the unit had spent the night outdoors she was sure it would be ten times worse.

Time dragged as their journey progressed. Someone, Mòrag wasn't sure who had succumb to seasickness and was retching to the right of her. Her throat tightened in response, making her feel nauseated herself, so she blew a few deep breaths.

'*Where do you think they will take us?*' she cast to Brax.

'*Downriver somewhere,*' he replied distracted.

'*Oh aye! I never thought of that,*' she retorted sarcastically.

Brax chuckled and shunted her shoulder with his.

The remainder of the journey passed much quicker, as she and Brax cast mildly witty banter back and forth.

Without warning, a harsh voice ordered them up. Unseen hands ushered the group off the small boat and onto a jetty. Mòrag raised her hands to remove the blindfold only to have them smacked away.

'You have to walk first,' the voice was flat and held no emotion. Its owner prodded Mòrag in the back indicating she should move forwards.

She stumbled and tripped her way over rough stony ground for about a quarter of a mile before the harsh footing gave way first to soft grass, then thick undergrowth. They travelled another quarter mile before Mullins instructed them to stop. 'Wait here until you hear the call, then you can remove your blindfolds. Understood?'

Mòrag didn't answer along with the rest she was too busy listening to his footfall. He circled the group twice and then left the area directly behind her. Minutes dragged out in awkward silence until someone touched her right shoulder.

'You may remove your blindfolds now, and proceed towards your objective.'

Mòrag let the material fall from her eyes. They sat in a small dell surrounded by well-established trees and other greenery. Twisting to look at the person who had spoken to them, Mòrag found no one. She frowned and looked over at Brax who pointed up at the canopy.

'He's up there. If I remember rightly, during exercises and tournaments like this, units are followed by watchers, who continually assess your moves and decisions. I could be wrong. This is the first time I have had to pay attention. Ra...' he corrected himself, glancing at the two boys across from them, 'General Steele talked about it once.'

Oswald set about the envelope with stiff fingers. The young boy looked far less confident in himself out in the wilderness. He was a tall boy, a hair shorter than Mòrag's five feet and four inches if she was lucky. He was thin, though not unhealthy looking, not yet at least. Nothing a few pies and pudding couldn't fix at any rate. He scratched his hand through his short sandy hair while he sifted through the contents of the envelope.

Lennox stood to Oswald's left. He had not spoken a word since the team had formed. His feathery blonde hair fell round his face curtaining his hazel eyes. His stance was notably submissive; his head remained in a semi bowed position and he crossed his arms in front of his body. Though he carried more weight than Oswald did, Lennox was at least a head taller, making him appear a more slight build than he really was.

'Well, O' glorious leader.' Mòrag made a wide swooping gesture with her arm, 'what's the plan then?'

Oswald narrowed his eyes at her, 'We are to work out where we are and make it to here,' he pointed out coordinates that corresponded with a red mark on the map. 'Then we have to find a flag of some sort and get it without being seen. We've to take it here, he pointed at a blue mark on the map. That's it. It says we should try not to be noticed but not to worry about being seen by the watchers who are wearing white tabards.'

Mòrag looked round at Brax. She knew he would know where they were and how to get to where they were going. Both of them were proficient at hunting, and he was more than proficient at sneaking about undetected. *If it had been, a unit of two we could have been done and dusted by tomorrow.*

'Ok, well we should go as far as we can as quickly as possible, so we have more time at the end. Brax knows where we are so you should probably get him to lead the way.'

'I was going to,' Oswald huffed at her. 'You know where we are. Don't you D... eh, Brax?'

Brax took the map and black marker attached to it, and put an 'X' to show where they were. He then drew a dotted line across the terrain until it met the area marked in red. 'That's the way we need to go,' he said.

'How can you be sure?'

'Let's just say I've had a bird's eye view,' Brax replied. He grinned at Mòrag as Sharri let out a hunting cry far above them.

Mòrag fiddled with the training bow and blunt arrows she had been given. Huffing to herself over the stupidity of whoever had allocated it to her. It had become obvious during training that she couldn't wield a bow. Her shoulder just could not tolerate the tension required for accuracy.

The unit set off following Brax's - rather, Sharri's designated route through the undergrowth along the edge of the woodland. Although the terrain was more of a challenge, they preferred to keep under the cover of the mature trees lining the river road. Mòrag decided for the time being to keep to the back of the group. From this position, she could gather anything she thought they would need without catching the attention of the others and slowing their progress.

During the course of their journey Mòrag had been collecting long bramble stems; she used the hunting knife to make a slit in the centre of four of the stems and passed another four through them, making a cross. She weaved other lengths of stem in and out between the spokes that the eight crossed lengths created. It was far fiddlier to weave while keeping pace with the others, but after a while, she did find an even rhythm.

As Lennox began to drop back from the others, Mòrag called a halt. The boy was shattered. Oswald was red faced and mad at Mòrag for taking authority from him once again. Mòrag shrugged it off, 'If you had been paying attention to your team member instead of trying to outpace your navigator, I wouldn't have had to now would I?'

Mòrag sat on a boulder next to Lennox, 'We will only rest here a bit. The further we get today the better,' she said. 'Don't feel like you can't say if you need a break though. We're a team after all.' She stretched, and got back to her feet, 'I'll go get you something to eat.' She turned to the others, 'I'm going to find some food while you lot rest, won't be long.'

'Do you want company?' Brax asked.

'No thanks,' she said, '*I think you should keep an eye on Mr Boss man: Just in case he does something uncharacteristically stupid.*'

'*Be careful. I get the feeling the mix-up this morning was intended.*'

'*You are full of rainbows and sparkles today aren't you.*'
'*So I'm told.*'

Mòrag chuckled to herself as she left the other three behind. She went in search of birch trees. It didn't take her long to find some; they were dotted throughout the forest. What she was really after was the tinder fungus that liked to grow on these trees. She harvested several large pieces and placed them in her basket. She also gathered some oyster mushrooms, nettles, chickweed, medlar fruit, cow parsley, pine needles and moss, which she cut in wide sections before returning to the group.

Chapter Thirty-Four

SETTING UP CAMP

The cloudless sky was beginning to darken from grey to black indicating that time was progressing quicker than Mòrag had realised. Thousands of stars pricked and speckled the darkness. Tonight would be especially cold. Weariness dragged at her limbs, and not for the first time since they set off again, she regretted having gathered so much, so early and not taking more time to rest herself.

The landscape had changed somewhat from thick forest to grassy hummock. The treeline beyond came into view when they reached the top of the rise. Brax and the two boys widened their stride, keen to get back beneath the cover of the trees, but Mòrag could no longer keep pace. Her legs felt weak as she followed them down the gentle decline. Once they reached the cover of the forest, she willed her tired limbs to move faster. It was like walking in a shadow world; everything appeared a different shade of charcoal. It took a while for her eyes to adjust, as she travelled beneath the canopy.

They approached a natural hollow in the trees where a large oak had been struck by lightning, cleaving it in two at its base, and had fallen to the ground knocking two neighbouring trees down with it.

'Let's make camp here for the night,' Mòrag called. She had fallen quite far behind the other three and though she had forced her movements to quicken, had not been able to catch up.

'We should go further,' argued Oswald.

'Let's stop here,' Mòrag repeated. 'A team is only as strong as its weakest link. Well, right now that's me. If you want to lead, you need to learn to look. Lennox is not going to manage much more either,' the boy was panting almost as hard as she was.

'We will go a little further,' Oswald insisted.

'Aye, very good.' Mòrag said as she caught up to them. She plopped herself down with her back to the fallen tree, 'You'll be going without me then. Tattie bye, I'll no be missing ye,' she said, waving her hand in the air for dramatic effect.

Oswald huffed at her and turned to leave, 'Leave her there. Come on, let's go.' When no one moved to follow him, he stormed off in a fury.

Brax placed a hand on Mòrag's head, 'You should have rested longer earlier on,' he said. 'I'll go get us something to eat, and bring *him* back.'

As Brax disappeared from sight, Lennox sat beside her; he had recovered his breath with remarkable quickness for being so exhausted only moments before. He placed a satiny soft hand atop hers. Before she could question him, she felt a warm soothing heat spread up her arm and throughout her body. Her muscles relaxed, no longer heavy from fatigue. Her lungs, aching from the constant gasping of frigid air calmed in moments. Even her shoulder, which had been blisteringly painful, eased to a dull ache. Mòrag stared at him in surprise. He was replenishing her by using the healing technique. She didn't know a Tyro this young had mastered the technique. She herself still wasn't proficient enough to perform it as well as this boy was doing now.

'Thank you,' she said, 'That feels a lot better.'

He nodded, unwilling to look her in the eye.

'Let's get a fire started before they come back.' She shuddered, now that she was no longer moving she noticed just how cold the night had become. 'Can you gather some stones? About the size of your fist would be good. I'll get a shelter sorted.'

Lennox nodded meekly and did as he was asked. Mòrag grabbed as many long branches as she could and propped them against the huge trunk of the fallen tree, interlocking them with some of its own branches. She then weaved in several pine boughs making it much more wind and watertight. She covered the shelter floor in the tiles of moss she had cut earlier and placed the waterproof ground sheet on top. Taking the stones from Lennox, she placed them at the front of the shelter and stood back to admire her work. She handed him the cooking pot, 'Could you get some water for me?'

The boy nodded and headed down toward the river. Mòrag busied herself setting the tinder fungus on the stones. She had soaked the pieces in oil when she collected them earlier in the day. They caught a spark from the flint almost instantly and produced a satisfying hot, clean-burning flame.

When Lennox returned from the river, he hung the pot above the flame on the cross branch Mòrag had placed for that very purpose.

She sprinkled pine needles into the water and taking the hunting knife, moved to the branches of a neighbouring birch tree, felled by the death of the enormous oak. Selecting the straightest branch, she marked a section, testing the blade. It made a notch but as she expected, it wouldn't cut through the woody material. Focusing on the blade edge, she willed it to become sharp and serrated. She half smiled in satisfaction as her emerald glow lined the knife-edge, effectively turning the tool into a miniature saw. *This is so much easier now I know how to make a soul blade; I hardly have to think about the knife in my hand at all.* She moved the blade back and forth across the birch limb, cutting clean through it. Bringing the branch back to the shelter she cut a small notch into the wood, scoring round its circumference until she reached the start point. Banging the section several times with the handle of her knife, she then began to twist the outer bark free. She twisted it back and forth, sanding the inner surface smooth against the natural grain of the branch. With a smooth motion, she removed the ring of outer bark from the branch. Cutting an inch wide section, from above where she had removed the outer bark, she used the knife to shave away at its surface, until it fit snug into the end of the bark ring. Satisfied with the makeshift cup, she made three more.

After what seemed like hours, Brax and a sick looking Oswald appeared back in the clearing. 'You've been busy I see,' Brax exclaimed.

'I had plenty of time to twiddle my fingers. What took you so long? And what's wrong with him?'

Brax grinned and revealed a section of the waterproof sheet he had cut before he left. He placed the makeshift sack at her feet and knelt beside her.

Within the bundle, she found several cuts of venison, 'My hero!' she said, 'You even butchered it before bringing it back. What about the rest?'

'I left it for Sharri,' he said. 'This one's not a tough as he looks. Passed out when he saw the blood,' he sniggered.

Oswald ignored the comment and moved to the back of the shelter to sulk.

'Tea?' Mòrag said, offering Brax a cup as she began to skewer the meat.

'You're full of surprises aren't you?' Brax said in an appreciative tone.

'Naturally.' Mòrag replied, 'I'm female after all.'

***

Randall sat behind the desk in his office and scanned through the reports from the supervisor for each unit. He frowned as he realised the report for unit nine was missing. He had sent Tesso to watch over the Unit containing Mòrag and Brax. His reasons for this choice were twofold: One – The young man felt responsible for what had happened to Mòrag during her interrogation and now felt obliged to watch out for her; and two – General Raine still believed that Tesso was under his control, so he was far less likely to interfere.

Tesso was never late with a report, *perhaps the group has run into difficulty*. At that, there was a smart knock at the door.

'Come in,' Randall called.

Colonel Tesso appeared from behind the door.

'Has Unit nine completed their objective already?' Randall asked in genuine surprise.

'No, Sir. I have been relieved of my post.'

'By whom?'

'General Marcs, Sir. He said he needed to stretch his legs, so he decided to relieve me of my position,' Tesso explained.

The young man was clearly put out about being replaced. He had leapt at the chance to go out into the field once more. Tesso had always relished the physical workload and teamwork involved in training the troops. He was never happier than when he had gained the rank of Sergeant. He took great pride in his job until General Raine began to view him as a threat and took him away from his loyal soldiers and active duty.

'I should have known,' Randall sighed. 'I'm sorry; I know you have been itching to get your hands dirty for a while now.'

'Am I to go back to the offices now, Sir?' he asked disappointment clear on his face.

Randall thought for a moment. *Alright, Daniel, two can play your game.* 'No. I want you to go back to unit nine. But I want you to remain hidden from sight. And I want you to evade General Marcs. Are you up for the challenge?'

The young man's face lit up, 'Yes, Sir!' he exclaimed.

Chapter Thirty-Five

PILFERED FEAST

Bright shafts of golden light pierced the foliage as the sun brimmed the mountainous horizon beyond the treeline. Brax slowed to a stop up ahead of the group. Mòrag noted how he again looked to the left and behind them. *'What are you looking for?'* she asked.

'The watcher is over to the left,' he told her. *'There's someone behind us too.'*

Mòrag resisted the urge to turn and look. Now that Brax had mentioned it, she was all too aware of the glowing lime green soul far behind her. *'I can't believe I never noticed,'* she cast.

'You aren't used to looking for trouble. I wish I knew what that was like.'

'Think we should leg it?'

'No, I think it's the watcher we had before the new one came. I just can't work out why they came back.'

'Now I know someone is there I will keep watch.'

They journeyed through a valley and stopped for a rest at a small pond next to a copse. Mòrag sat on a boulder by the pond. She lifted her cup of pine needle tea and took a few sips then replaced the cap. She had made a cap for each of the cups with a tab in the top for easy removal, so they could have drinkable liquid with them at all times.

The landscape looked much warmer than it actually was, the crisp air nipped at her cheeks and the chill wind that picked up a gust every so often set her eyes running.

The previous night in her makeshift shelter had been an awkward one. Lennox had yet to speak. Oswald spent the night grumbling about how Mòrag was undermining his leadership, and glared at her and Brax any time they sat even remotely close. She and Brax had spent the night talking without a word passing their lips. And once the boys had fallen asleep, they had moved closer to one another, sharing each other's body heat. Curled into his side, with his arm round her, Mòrag found the long awaited sleep that had eluded her since Oliver had woken. Perhaps it was exhaustion from the day's exertions, or, more realistically, it was because he made her feel so utterly safe.

Her shoulder carried a deep and intense ache that shot buzzing pains down the length of her arm right to her fingertips. She rubbed her hand: It throbbed in response to her shoulder, though the flesh was completely numb. It was an odd sensation.

Brax sat on the boulder behind her and leant his back against hers, 'Not long now,' he said. 'Four hours, maybe five and we'll be there.'

Mòrag lent her head back against Brax and sighed, 'We'd best get going then,' she said, pushing herself up. She turned to look at him. He looked worn out. She narrowed her eyes at him, 'Did you sleep at all last night?'

Brax shook his head, 'No. You needed the rest more than I did, and someone had to keep watch. I'll rest a bit tonight.'

'You'd better.'

He made a face at her then went to check the others were ready.

'*Bràthair?*'

'*Puithar,*' Rannoch replied.

'*We aren't too far from you now, Brax says five hours at most.*'

'*Good. There is plenty of shelter around the camp for you to remain hidden. You may have trouble obtaining the flag you seek during daylight hours. However, it is poorly guarded during the night.*'

'*Then that's when we'll take it. Thank you, Bràthair.*'

'*I will wait for you here. I have not been close to you in too long.*'

'*I know. I feel the same way.*' She felt their connection become silent. Both she and Brax had taken full advantage of their bonds with their familiars. Mòrag was unsure if they had broken the rules, but at no time had anyone mentioned the use of familiars, they probably haven't even considered it.

The first couple of hours passed without incident. Oswald continued to grumble and grouch at every given opportunity, as only a twelve year old could. Mòrag was utterly sick of the sight of him.

Valley grew into munro and munro fell into glen. The day became dull and overcast. Heavy grey clouds seemed to press down on them as they traversed the undulating landscape. When they reached the edge of the forest surrounding their destination, the rain began to plummet. Fat droplets of bitterly cold water fell in an unrelenting torrent that drummed the ground so ferociously, they bounced back up at least a foot in the air. Mòrag relished the smell of the damp undergrowth that hung thick in the air as they trudged through the forest.

Brax slowed to a stop as a break in the trees became visible on the horizon, 'We're here,' he said. 'We should rest up a bit and then scout round the area.'

Oswald's face puckered as though he was eating a sour sweet, but he said nothing. It was mid-afternoon and already the light was fading. Mòrag sat herself next to the sullen would-be leader, under the shelter of a large ash. 'You know,' she said, 'you would probably feel less left out if you worked with us rather than working yourself into a mood because you aren't fit to lead the group.'

Oswald's face was set in a scowl and he avoided her gaze. 'You won't let me make any decisions,' he huffed.

'You can decide as you like. But no one will listen when you're only thinking about yourself.'

When he didn't answer, Mòrag decided to leave him to his thoughts. She joined Brax and Lennox who were checking over the instructions once more. The young boy looked awkward and uncomfortable. At any other time, it would be

Brax who felt and acted this way around others, Mòrag smirked at the irony of the situation.

'Ready to take a look?' Brax asked.

'Aye, what's the plan? Split up or stick as one unit?'

'Stick together,' Oswald suggested. 'Lennox and I aren't good at moving about in here and trying not to be noticed.'

'Do we really need to bother scouting?' Brax cast, 'Sharri and Rannoch have already sussed the place out for us.'

'I know,' Mòrag replied, 'but we should at least go through the motions for their sake.'

'You're getting quite into this military thing aren't you,' Brax noted.

'Shut it, you!' she retorted sardonically.

'Good plan! We'll go with that.' Mòrag chimed a little more enthusiastically than was necessary, prompting a smirk from Brax.

Oswald was obviously clueless as to how to respond to her so he just said, 'Thanks.'

'We had best go now while this rain is still on. It'll help hide us,' Brax suggested.

They all nodded and set off together towards the encampment. Mòrag and Brax conveyed their mental notes to one another as they made the journey around the treeline that skirted the tents. Once they had retreated to a position they felt was safe enough, they set up a rough shelter in a hollow between five large trees. The bottom shoots of these trees spread wide and created a natural den. All they needed to do to make it more inhabitable was brace the branches above them so they had enough height to sit, and spread out their ground sheet.

They chatted about the formation of the tents and placement of the guards and patrols. Oswald's manner relaxed as they chatted and talked out different approaches.

'It may be an idea to do this at night you know,' Mòrag suggested.

The two boys frowned at her, 'But it will be dark!' Oswald exclaimed.

'It will. But there will be fewer guards and we could sneak in and out much easier. Brax and I can move around easier in the dark.'

'What are we supposed to do then?' Oswald asked.

'Stand guard,' Brax said, 'Let us know when it is safe to move and when it isn't.'

'And when we have the flag,' Mòrag added, 'you can take it to the extraction point. We'll hang back and create a diversion if needed. How does that sound?'

The option of being the one to hand over the flag became the swaying factor for Oswald who agreed without hesitation. They then agreed to rest over the next eight hours, each taking turns to watch while the others slept, so they were refreshed for the challenge ahead.

Mòrag took the first watch with Lennox. They left Brax and Oswald to sleep, and walked slow laps around the small area around their den. Two to three hours into their watch, a delicious aroma began to waft through the trees. Mòrag and Lennox's stomachs growled in united response to the meaty scent. 'Urgh,' Mòrag complained, 'that smell's killing me, how about you?'

The boy gave a timid smile in response to the question.

'Do you ever speak?' she asked.

Lennox shook his head.

'Can you speak?' she asked.

Again, the boy shook his head.

'Oh! Sorry. If I'd asked earlier you maybe wouldn't have felt so out of place.'

Lennox half smiled and gestured to her.

'Um... You need the loo?'

He nodded and she laughed.

'I'll be here,' she said to his back as he left.

Lennox had not returned after almost an hour. Mòrag began to worry. She waited another ten minutes or so and then turned back towards the den to wake the others.

'Brax, Oswald, wake up.'

Brax opened his eyes, as though he had only been dozing, 'What's wrong?' he asked, 'is it your turn for a rest?'

'Lennox is gone,' she said, 'he went to relieve himself and never came back.'

'When?' Oswald demanded jumping up and hitting his head on the roof of the den.

'Over an hour ago: I gave him the benefit of the doubt for too long.'

Before they could move to go in search of Lennox, there was a rustling behind Mòrag. She jumped forwards in surprise. When she turned round Lennox was crouched in the entrance of the den.

'Where the hell did you go?' Mòrag demanded.

Lennox tilted his head to the side a fraction then tapped his nose and dropped a large sack in front of them. It fell open and spilled its contents onto the ground sheet. He grinned at the gasps of his three comrades, as their eyes took in the barbequed fowl; roasted potatoes; carrots and swede; a glazed ham shank and four large canteens.

'But... How?'

He held a finger to his lips, then grabbed a leg of fowl and took a bite. No one else needed a telling and they all dived into the pilfered feast with gusto.

As she ate, Mòrag stretched her consciousness out around her. Brax eyed her as he felt her mental shift.

'Apparently Lennox can't speak,' she explained to him. 'I was thinking I could cast to him but I can't really find him. It's odd. Normally I can feel where I should be looking for a door: But, with him... All I can find is a window.'

Brax took a moment to feel for himself, 'You're right. How strange!' he exclaimed. 'It may be worth asking Randall when we get back.'

Mòrag agreed. After their meal, Brax and Oswald took up the watch, allowing Mòrag and Lennox some long awaited rest.

Chapter Thirty-Six

DESPAIR

Crouching low in the undergrowth Mòrag watched the far side of the encampment. Oswald and Lennox had concealed themselves on the North and East sides of the tents, perfectly positioned to keep watch. Brax was crouched low next to her. They were waiting for Oswald to signal that the sentries were on his side before they made their move.

'You know,' Mòrag whispered, 'I'm really looking forward to getting back to my lumpy mattress on its squeaky bunk in the barracks, and a nice hot shower.'

'You aren't the only one,' he replied, 'look, there's the signal.'

He crept up to the first tent. Mòrag followed at his heel. She felt more than a little conspicuous in her red uniform. Thankfully, it had stopped raining, and had remained overcast keeping the camp in shadow. Mòrag and Brax had left their jackets and over trousers in the den. The red material had become mucky during their journey, making it less bright and noticeable. Nevertheless, the extra bulk restricted their movement and the toughened outer shell rustled loud enough to wake the dead, so they decided to go without.

'I can't stop my teeth chattering. And I can't feel my feet!' Mòrag complained

Brax's chuckle echoed in her mind, *'It was your idea to come without boots.'*

'I must have temporarily gone mad I think.'

'It was the right choice; the boots would've been too noisy. We'll get in and out as quick as we can. I promise. Keep an eye on

the tents to the left. I'll watch the right. Sharri says the flag is on a barrel by that red tent there.'

The tent to the left of her housed four glowing souls within. Mòrag guessed they were sleeping from the lack of any movement. She and Brax snuck toward the red tent at the middle of the encampment. As they reached the next row of tents, an owl hoot sounded to their right; Lennox's signal, blown through cupped hands, indicating that they should wait. They crouched low behind four water barrels. Mòrag held her breath as she listened for any sign of movement. Boot steps approaching from behind were the last sound she wanted to hear. She began to turn but Brax pushed her down further, leaning in close and in one smooth motion threw a blanket over their heads.

'Where did you get that?'

'It was on the ground,' he replied . *'Keep still, hopefully we will blend into the shadows.'*

It was warmer beneath the thick blanket, but not warm enough to stem the shudder of her muscles. Her feet throbbed, so cold now that they felt as though they were burning. She stiffened as the boot steps slowed to a stop right next to them. She again held her breath, willing them to move on once more. When they did, she fought the urge to gasp for breath, sipping it slow and steady instead.

Another owl call from Lennox. The coast was clear. Tentatively Brax pulled back the blanket and checked the coast was clear. Satisfied, he folded and replaced the blanket where he found it.

'Let's go,' Mòrag cast, *'Before my feet fall off.'*

They kept low and moved as quickly as they were able across the thoroughfare to the barrels by the red tent. Sitting atop the centre barrel was a black flag with a red number nine stitched onto it. Mòrag lifted it and stuffed it into her shirt. She glanced up to where Oswald was hiding. He was practically jumping up and down, gesturing furiously for them to leave.

Mòrag wasted no time, *'Leg it!'* she cast to Brax who was already in motion.

By the time they made it back to the den, they were a jittery, sweaty, elated mess. Mòrag grabbed her outer clothes and practically dived into them. Dusting off her feet and pulling on her socks and boots. She was tightening the laces when Oswald and Lennox appeared.

'You did it! I can't believe you did it!' he squealed.

'*We* did it,' Mòrag corrected him. 'Without you both, we would've been caught.' She pulled the flag out and handed it to Oswald, whose face lit up. 'I told you, you could take it didn't I?'

Oswald grinned, 'Thank you.'

'Did they notice?' Brax asked.

'Nope, no one has a clue anything has changed.'

'Good,' Brax replied, 'we will still hang back just in case. We will be about twenty minutes behind you. Do you know which way to go?'

Lennox nodded.

'We'll get there. See you soon,' Oswald said. 'Don't get caught,' he added grinning.

He and Lennox turned together and set off towards the extraction point.

'*Well done,*' Rannoch's cast was sleepy and detached. Obviously, this whole thing bored him.

'*Thank you, Bràthair. I really appreciate the help.*'

'*I'll be going now, if you do not require my assistance?*' he yawned.

'*No. We'll be fine. Thank you.*' Mòrag replied. She was desperate to see him, but knew she had to finish their task first. It wouldn't be long until they were back at Sruighlea, and she could bury her face in his thick warm mane once more.

'Rannoch is heading back.'

'Sharri's already there. She left when we arrived.'

'So we're alone then,' she mused.

'Hardly, we have each other and the boys.'

'Not what I meant and you know it,' Mòrag retorted. 'I mean free from familiars. It feels strange knowing they aren't lurking in the trees, watching. Talking about lurkers, we really are alone.'

Brax looked around. 'You're right,' he said. 'Maybe they've left us alone and followed the boys, because of their age?'

'And they have the flag,' Mòrag added. 'That's probably it. We'll catch up soon enough.'

'Let's go. It's almost dawn and if they haven't noticed the flag's missing, I don't want to spoil that by letting them see us.'

'Good point,' Mòrag agreed, getting to her feet and following him from the den.

Brax led Mòrag back toward the encampment. The sky had lightened to a dull charcoal, lightening the shadows and hiding places. A quick scout about confirmed that the troops in and around the camp were still oblivious anyone had been even remotely close to the flag, never mind swiping it as they slept. 'That was almost too easy,' Mòrag whispered.

'Don't complain,' he said nudging her. 'For all we know it's a fake flag and we've failed.'

Mòrag threw him an indignant look, 'You're such a pessimist!'

'Can't be helped, it's a lifelong habit.'

'Well change it, Grumpy guts!' Mòrag teased.

Brax shook his head and smiled at her. 'Come on, we'd best catch up to the others.'

They skirted the camp leaving on a track to the West. Brax snapped a pine branch and dragged it behind them, disguising their footprints. A trained tracker could find evidence of their passage but to the untrained eye, the path looked clean and unused. The boys had not thought about disguising their tracks. *At least we know they've gone the right way.* They travelled up the path on a steady incline. The sun had risen in the distance as they reached the top. A wide valley spread out below them. Mist gathered in pockets across its expanse and although the sky above and behind them was now clear, the horizon was covered in thick heavy cloud.

They began the descent in high spirits, glad to be on the home stretch. When they reached the halfway mark, Mòrag felt a presence to her right. Stopping she stared into the dark of the treeline and found two dark brown souls. 'Brax,' she breathed.

'I know,' he replied, 'they're on this side too.'

From the dark, dirty colour of their souls, it was obvious they were not friendly.

'*Do we run or fight?*' Mòrag cast.

'*The last thing I want is to get into a fight,*' Brax replied. '*But, if we run we will endanger the others and expose our backs. Fighting seems unavoidable.*'

'No think it's a bit cowardly to hide in the shadows?' Mòrag called.

Brax flinched as a large buzzard swooped from the trees and landed in front of him, screeching. A puma stalked its way from the undergrowth before Mòrag, followed by a man dressed in black. His brown eyes were trained on her, his skin was a deep golden colour, his dark hair no more than long stubble on his head; he reminded her of an older Colonel Tesso. He was at least a head taller than Brax and came to a stop just outside striking distance of Mòrag. He towered over her, forcing her to crane her neck to look him in the eye. Behind her, Brax was facing up to his own opponent, another black clad, young man, also tanned, sporting a matching hairstyle of a lighter brown.

'*These are the King's men, elite graduates. Something's very wrong here.*'

Mòrag retreated half a step so her back was touching Brax's. She felt too exposed without Rannoch and without a proper weapon. She still had the hunting knife strapped to her leg but the training bow was useless to her.

'Our superior begs an audience with you,' the man in front of Mòrag said in a deep Sasannach accent. 'If you would be so kind as to accompany us please.'

'*Rannoch I need you.*'

'*On my way.*'

Mòrag took a step toward her aggressor, 'And who's your superior then?' she asked. 'How do I know it's worth our while?'

'*Mòrag what are you doing?*' Brax cast anxiously.

'*Not a clue. I'd quite happily be legging it right now. But if it's going to come to a fight, I'd rather know what's going on, IF I can get them to tell me.*'

The man in front of her raised an eyebrow and cocked his head at her, 'You're a frisky one aren't you.'

'So they tell me,' Mòrag retorted.

'You have poor choice in companions. Can you imagine, Rex, they have initiated our master's dog into their ranks. They must be desperate!'

Mòrag could feel Brax's panic begin to rise through their mental connection; every muscle in his back went rigid in response.

'Enough, Tesso,' said the other man, 'you are letting your mouth run again.'

'My apologies,' he replied in a dry tone.

'Tesso?'

'It's his brother Raymond.'

'Well that explains his looks, but not his ego.'

'We're way out matched, Mòrag. We're going to have to do as they say and hope Sharri and Rannoch get to us quickly.'

'You will come with us whether you like it or not,' the other man, Rex sneered. 'Move,' he strode forward and shoved Brax ahead of him.

Stumbling forwards Brax already looked defeated. All the confidence he seemed to have gain since she knew him, diminished in an instant.

Rex moved to shove Mòrag in the same direction. As he thrust his hand towards her back, she spun to the side and buried her knee deep in his crotch. Raymond was howling with laughter before Rex's knees met the soil.

'LITTLE BITCH!' Rex yowled stretching his hand and grasping her ankle.

Pain tore through her mind. It felt as though she was being ripped apart from the inside out. She couldn't breathe, she couldn't think. All she could do was grasp her head in both hands and fall to her knees gasping for breath.

The pain dissipated leaving Mòrag disorientated and breathless.

Raymond had grabbed Rex's arm breaking his concentration. 'She is to suffer,' he said. 'But not by your hand, nor mine.'

Rex glowered at him but conceded.

Brax helped Mòrag to her feet. She clung to him at first, legs trembling. She couldn't seem to coordinate them, which was only exacerbated by being forced to walk before she was ready.

'*You shouldn't have done that,*' Brax's cast was full of concern.

Mòrag grimaced as his words ricocheted around her mind, '*Couldn't help myself — didn't think.*'

'*I'll find a way out of this. I promise.*'

'*My hero,*' she replied in jest.

'*Feeling better I see.*'

'*What was that?*'

'*A weak version of a mindstrike.*'

'*Weak? Are you kidding me? I could hardly breathe!*'

'*You don't want to know what a real one's like.*'

'Oi, You two, pick up the pace!' Rex jeered, shoving Brax hard in the back.

Mòrag couldn't understand how he accepted the treatment so willingly. They drew close to a brook at the bottom of the hummock, where another man was waiting. There was something hanging in his hands, it wasn't until they were a few feet closer that she could make out the links of chain. It was then, that Brax dug his heels in. He backed right into Rex who shoved him forwards once more.

'No, no, no, no, no, no, no, no, no! I'm not putting that on! You can't make me put that on!' Brax's face had become ashen, his eyes wide.

The three men laughed at him. Rex and Raymond grabbed an arm each and dragged him forward. He fought wildly but his movements were panic driven and uncoordinated.

Mòrag moved to help him, but was caught by an unknown force. She yelped when pain flared in her shoulder as her arm was twisted behind her back. She was lifted into the air and thrown backwards, slamming into a tree and landing hard on the ground.

Major Frank pressed his boot onto her chest and sneered down at her. 'It is about time we finish what we started. Wouldn't you say?'

Mòrag looked in Brax's direction; he was still struggling with Rex and Tesso, and the closer he got to the restraints the more ferociously he fought them.

'I am the one you should be paying attention to,' Frank leered. He grabbed her left arm and hauled her to her feet, twisting it behind her and slammed her front into the trunk of the tree.

Mòrag grimaced as he twisted her arm even tighter.

Frank pressed himself against her, leaning close to her ear he whispered, 'You are going to pay for humiliating General Raine and his son. And when I am done you will be begging for death, but it will not come. I want you to suffer for the inconveniences you have also caused me. This will not be quick, and it will be anything but painless.'

Terror was pooling in her belly like liquid lead. She squirmed beneath his grip, which only jolted her shoulder more. As he leaned in close to speak, again she threw her head back with enough force to bloody his nose, though it left her dazed from the blow. He grunted, then hauled her weak arm with all his strength, tearing it once more from its socket. Mòrag wailed. She couldn't help herself; the sound was out of her mouth before she could stop it. He dropped her then, leaving her whimpering at the base of the tree, her wits temporarily scattered to the wind.

***

Mòrag's cry brought Brax back to his senses. He had been so wrapped up in his own fear that all else had been emptied from his mind. Rex and Raymond were wrestling him to the ground, but they had no weapons drawn, neither did the man who stood holding the pronged collar he dreaded.

Calm down, calm down. You know what they can do and what they can't. Use that. Brax allowed himself to go limp as though he had accepted his fate.

Immediately, Raymond's grip reduced to minimal pressure as he began to make smug comments. Rex's grip loosened but remained tight enough to hold him, though Rex could be taken by surprise. He gathered some energy to his right palm, fingers and elbow, calling on it to grow like thin needles. As the other man stepped forward, chains jangling, Brax attacked.

In one fluid motion, he snatched his arm from Tesso, hit Rex's arm just above the wrist, swung his palm back to connect with the other man's temple, and brought his elbow back to Raymond's chest. Leaping to his feet, he sped across the space between him and Mòrag.

Frank caught him mid stride. Brax could feel his mental grip around his neck, forcing him to halt. I can't fight him one on one. 'Mòrag? Mòrag are you ok?' She didn't answer.

Major Frank's nose was bloody but he sneered through red tainted teeth. 'Have a soft spot for her, do you, Dog? I've never seen you so focused when your collar is around,' he chortled. 'This is going to be more enjoyable than I thought.'

Brax glared at Major Frank as he lifted the hand he didn't have stretched out toward Brax and gestured at the collar and chain. At once, it sped through the air toward Brax. At the last moment, he brought his arm up to defend his neck, knocking the collar to the floor. By this time Raymond, Rex and the other man had regained their wits and strode to restrain him once more.

'What the hell did you do to us?' Rex demanded. The hand that had gripped Brax so tightly hung limp from his forearm.

Raymond was wheezing hard: Sucking in as much air as he could. The other man's eye was puffy and bloodshot. Brax allowed himself a small smirk. He had used his soul to inject a command into their bodies; turning the switches of the nerves, muscles, and more importantly soul energy off, rendering that body part useless, at least for a short period of time. He had the ability to make injuries like this permanent, but not under these circumstances.

'Fools!' Frank bellowed. 'You let him catch you off guard! Get that damned collar on him so I can get back to work!'

A high-pitched shriek from overhead signalled that Sharri had arrived. She folded her wings and plummeted towards Frank, throwing her talons forward as she neared him. Frank leapt to the side, narrowly escaping her grasp. His loss of concentration released Brax who was off his mark immediately and ran the rest of the distance to Mòrag's side.

Sharri whooped at the four men, hissing at them as she leapt back into the air: Hovering just above them.

'Hawke! Don't just stand there, fool! Call them!' Frank screamed at the man who Brax didn't recognise. He lifted his hands and called something in Frangach. Large creatures of every type appeared from the treeline. Several shrieks filled the air as hawks, buzzards and large owls circled around Sharri. A flurry of feathers and high-pitched shrieks ensued as the flock launched its attack on the outnumbered Haribon. Sharri was far stronger but with their numbers the flock out manoeuvred her at every turn.

Brax leant down to Mòrag, 'Are you ok?'

She groaned as he helped her up, she was pale and breathless, 'We aren't doing so well are we?'

'No, not really.'

Raymond's Puma leapt into Brax, knocking him sideways to the ground and sinking its teeth into his arm. He could do little to release himself from the large cat, the pain in his arm made it near impossible to concentrate on any form of mental attack or defence.

Out of nowhere, a yellow mass of black-spotted fur barrelled into the Puma knocking it from him.

***

Mòrag staggered to her feet, *'Bràthair where are you?'*

'Close.'

'Please hurry.'

Rannoch didn't reply but she could feel him pushing himself harder, forcing his strong limbs to quicken.

She backed away clutching her arm close to her side as Frank, Rex and Hawke stalked towards her. Frank drew a vicious looking mace from behind his back. He swung it towards her. She jumped backwards dodging swing after swing until her foot caught on a rock and she tumbled to the ground. Rex and Hawke were laughing behind Frank who stretched a hand toward her.

Mòrag felt her body being lifted into the air for a second time though no one had a hand on her. She switched into her sensory perception. Frank had soul energy flowing from him in long tendrils that wrapped around her body, clamping her arms to her sides. It was not so much part of his soul, more like a shadow embodiment of his will.

Frank lifted his mace ready to strike her, 'Let's see if you can still run with a broken leg,' he jeered.

She closed her eyes tight and waited for the pain. Instead, Frank grunted in surprise. At once she was released, and landed with an awkward thud on the ground behind Oswald.

***

'I see you are climbing the ranks little brother,' Raymond smirked. 'You're not looking quite as fit as you once did. Spending all your time behind a desk are you?' The effect on his lungs had worn off and he was breathing easy once more.

'Can you fight?' Tesso asked Brax.

'Yes,' he replied.

'Buddying up to my kid brother are you, Dog? Interesting: So what do you plan to do? Ruka already has the upper hand over Meraii, so she won't be joining you. Will you have my master's dog act as a familiar now?'

'I don't want to fight you, Ray. Your orders are corrupt and don't come from our King.'

'Oh, little brother, little brother: You are so naive. It will be your downfall.' He drew his broadsword and lunged with frightening speed towards his brother.

'Stop this, Major Frank!' Marcs demanded. 'That's an order!' His massive black panther growled deeply.

Lennox stood behind Mòrag, healing her shoulder to the best of his ability. It had popped back into the joint much easier than she remembered from the last time, although adrenalin probably had something to do with that.

'I'm afraid, *General*, you no longer have any authority over me.'

'You are refusing to end this quietly?'

'I am,' he said. 'Rex, Hawke.'

Both men leapt into motion, whatever Brax had done to them earlier had worn off and they were fighting-fit once more. Working together, they edged General Marcs back, away from Frank, Oswald and Mòrag. Their familiars set about Marcs' with savage ferocity forcing him to retreat.

Lennox and Oswald stood defiant beside Mòrag, 'You should run,' she told them, 'he's too strong.'

'Are you going to run?' Oswald asked

'No.'

'Then neither are we,' he said.

Frank looked at each of them in turn, a wicked expression of amusement on his face. 'What do you think, Zeal? You and I, against two unarmed children and an injured girl? It doesn't seem fair does it?' The large reptile by his side was reminiscent of a crocodile though it had a lengthier neck and longer, more agile limbs. It hissed and clawed the ground, eager to be let lose upon its prey.

***

The last bird dropped from the sky, and Sharri swooped low, hovering above the field of battle. Brax could see her assessing the situation from her vantage point high above them. He and Tesso were struggling against Raymond. Even two against one, they were fighting a losing battle. Tesso's cheetah had been wounded by his brother's puma and was now being backed into a corner.

'Help her, Sharri, if you can wound him, it may affect his master.'

Sharri answered with her actions. Diving low, she let out a piercing shriek and shot a jet of flame towards the oblivious puma. Grabbing the burning beast in her talons, she tore it from the wounded cheetah and tossed it several yards distance. The sound of its agonised screams as it ran to douse itself in the brook sent shivers down Brax's spine.

As expected. Wounding the puma had forced Raymond's concentration to break, slowing him enough for Tesso to get a jab in knocking him over. He leapt back to his feet, enraged that his younger brother had managed to get a hand on him. He focused all his energy on Tesso, forgetting Brax, and more importantly, forgetting Sharri. She plunged from the sky, talons forward and dug them deep into his chest, lithely hopping backwards to perch on Brax's shoulder.

'Ha! If you think a wound like this is going to stop me you've got another thing coming!'

'Stop Ray: Have you not noticed what she is?' Tesso said his expression grave.

Ignoring his brother, he sprang forward. Sharri flexed her talons, and he fell writhing on the floor.

'Feels like you're burning doesn't it?' Brax said. He glanced at Tesso; his brows were drawn, expression set hard. 'If you come quietly, I'll let you live.'

Tesso gazed at him in astonishment, then back to his brother, 'Ray, please.'

His brother managed a pained, 'Yes.'

'Sharri,' Brax said. The Haribon relaxed her stance and Raymond fell silent.

***

Lennox was wrestling with Frank's familiar, which snapped and slashed at him, though it had not yet made a connecting blow, he had lured it quite a distance away, allowing Mòrag and Oswald more room to manoeuvre.

Mòrag lunged at Frank with her hunting knife. He parried it easily and beat her away with his shield. As she readied her next attack, she saw General Marcs, who was fighting at the far side of the field, pierced by Rex's rapier. He grasped his side and jumped back from his two attackers.

Oswald Spun in a three hit combination of jabs towards Frank who laughed and knocked him several feet backwards with one hit. A twelve-year-old boy was no match for his strength, *for that matter, neither am I.*

'You best give up now, Marcs,' Frank shouted. 'How can you possibly hope to overpower us when you are so hopelessly outmatched?'

The smile drained from his face at the ground-shaking roar that followed. *Rannoch!*

The Nemeocorn emerged from the trees behind General Marcs, bearing his sharp teeth. Marcs' face paled as Rannoch did not attempt to hide his true form. Rex and Hawke began to retreat, but Rannoch caught them with a short, sharp, pulsing roar, rooting them to the spot. Their familiars turned on their heel, leaving Marcs' Black Panther in their wake and sped to protect their masters. A torrent of beasts emerged from the trees, heading straight for Rannoch. He cut through them like a knife through warm butter. But it slowed him enough for Rex and Hawke to regain their senses and retreat toward Frank. Sharri swooped out of nowhere, emitting a piercing shriek and raining down a stream of flame upon the two men.

Seeing what was about to happen Frank grabbed Oswald. The boy yelped, struggling desperately beneath the vice like grip. 'Call off the beasts, girl.'

'Let Oswald go and I'll call them off.' The boy had turned sheet white.

'No. No I don't think I will,' he said as Oswald's body began to rise into the air. The boy began to whimper, then cry as his arms and legs were pulled in opposite directions.

'Come now, boy,' Frank crooned, 'die with some dignity.'

Oswald's cries became screams. The high-pitched sound wound its way deep into Mòrag's soul; she stretched her arms out toward him.

Sweat beaded on Frank's forehead as he exerted his will. The wet gurgling, ripping sound was horrific. The contents of the young boy's body fell drenching Mòrag in hot, wet despair.

***

Mòrag's scream shook Brax to the very core. He had never heard a sound like that from her before. He reached Marcs first. The General's face was ashen, his eyes wide. He had never expected any of this, but then, neither had they. Rannoch turned from Rex's torn body, and looked with sadness in his eyes, toward where Mòrag stood in front of a manically laughing Major Frank. Brax started toward her but Rannoch stopped him.

'I suggest you look before you move. I had hoped she would never learn how to do this.'

Brax looked across the field. Mòrag's emerald green soul licked and curled like green fire around her. Her eyes fixed not on Frank, but on his soul. Her outstretched hands stopped shaking and dropped to her sides. She slid one leg back, half turning to the side, and gesturing with her hands in a fighting stance, that Brax had only seen one other person use. Edward.

Frank stopped laughing and lunged toward her. Her body evaded his with ease. She circled him as he lashed out repeatedly, failing each time to land a blow. He swung hard at her head; instead of avoiding the blow, she caught his arm, halting his motion mid swing. Frank became rooted to the spot. She had grasped not only his arm, but his outer soul. She placed her other hand over his eyes, clutching the seat of his soul. In one clean movement, she ripped it from his body, leaving the empty shell of Major Frank to crumple on the ground at her feet.

Chapter Thirty-Seven

RAMPAGE

The encampment was an uncontrolled deluge of voices and movement: The large red tent at its epicentre seemed cramped with so many people stuffed inside it. Brax sat on the bench at the back wall. Lennox sat to his left. The young boy was staring blankly at the medic who had come to check him over. Other than a few small cuts and scrapes, he had come out of the whole mess in the best condition.

Mòrag was to his right. She lay beside him with her head on his lap. When she had regained her senses, she had been distraught, utterly inconsolable. Even Brax had struggled to control her. Over time, her fear and anger had ebbed leaving only hopelessness and sorrow. Brax knew he could do little to help her. He could only sit and stroke her sticky, blood-matted hair.

General Marcs sat himself down on the next bench along. His haggard expression spoke volumes. Medics buzzed about him like flies, ignoring his complaints that he wanted left alone. He still seemed shocked that he had taken a hit, *a serious one at that,* Brax noted. Rex had always been a dirty fighter, never without a trick up his sleeve. He was fond of lacing his blades with either poison or a campion derivative to subdue and paralyze. Brax couldn't tell which Rex had used, but the General was using copious amounts of energy to fend off its effects.

'Why did you let Tesso live?' Marcs' voice was tight.

'I'm no killer.'

'Strange you think that after all the lives that were ended by your hand.'

'I had no choice.'

'Not true. You always have a choice.'

'Not with him,' Brax regarded Marcs for a moment; the General's expression had become grave. 'You suspect me because I let him live. Is that it?'

'Something like that,' Marcs said.

'You need to stop blaming me for your own ignorance,' Brax was surprised at the annoyance that laced his voice, 'You had Mòrag and I placed in the same unit and then not only sent a Colonel, but you yourself, a General, came in pursuit. You wouldn't have done that without good reason. Which means one of two things. Either, you suspected an attack, placed us in the same group, and followed to protect Mòrag. Or, you were using us as bait.'

'We were not using you as bait,' Randall's voice broke the tension that had been building between Brax and General Marcs. 'That, I would never allow. I thought you understood that, Brax.' He seemed almost hurt. He moved further into the tent, Rozzen at his heel.

She strode forward and when she reached the benches, crouched in front of Brax. 'How is she?'

'Withdrawn,' said Marcs, 'I have never seen anything like what she did. Yet again she had dumbfounded me.'

'Apparently that's not hard,' Brax said beneath his breath.

Marcs shot him a steely glare: Which he ignored.

'Perhaps it would be kinder to wipe this from her mind,' Marcs mused. 'I am sure she would be happier for it.'

'I doubt you would manage to omit it from her memories, you were never able to do it to Brax when he first came to us. And Mòrag is,' Randall glanced apologetically at Brax, 'more mentally sound.'

And there it is. It hurts every time, old man. Brax felt Mòrag squeeze his leg. *'Are you ready to talk?'*

'No.'

'I'll be ready when you are,' he replied, allowing his hand to brush her cheek as he stroked her hair.

Rozzen eyed him speculatively but said nothing. The General's conversation over Mòrag had continued without Brax's involvement.

'Do you think she actually knows what she is?' questioned Marcs.

'I doubt it,' Rozzen replied.

'Perhaps its best –' Marcs began.

'Gonnae no talk about me like I'm not here,' Mòrag said in a flat tone, sitting up so she was face to face with Marcs. 'No, I'm not alright. No, I don't want my memories wiped. No, I don't know how I did what I did. No, I don't want to know how to do it again. No, I don't know what I am, or who I am. I made my peace with that a long time ago. Any other useless questions you want me to answer can wait. I'm going to wash that innocent boy's blood off my skin before I tear myself apart.' She pushed herself up from the bench and strode from the tent.

Brax squeezed Lennox's shoulder, 'I'll be back,' he said, then turning he glared at the three shocked Generals and set off after Mòrag.

He found her by the water barrels at the edge of the camp, frantically scrubbing at her hands, tears were streaming down her face, carving thin channels through the dried blood that covered her.

'Mòrag?'

'It won't come off. It won't come off. It won't come off. It won't come off. It won't come off!' she scrubber harder and harder as her self-control crumbled.

His heart bled for her; he had been in similar situations many times throughout his life. Stepping forward he grabbed her hands and looked into her eyes. He wanted to tell her it would be ok, that he would protect her from the blackness eating at her from the inside, that she would forget, but he couldn't. He couldn't do any of those things. All he could do was be there for her, as she was for him. 'Come on, let's get you to a bath,' he said giving her hands a supportive squeeze and leading her back into the camp.

***

'Did he reveal anything, Daniel? Did he give some clue as to why he made a move?' Rozzen asked.

'I'm afraid not, not to me in any case. The attack unit consisted of Major Frank, a Frangach soldier and two of our elite graduates: Rex and Tesso. All dead save for Tesso, who Brax allowed to live. His brother has him in custody. We may be able to extract some information from him but I doubt it.'

Randall let out a deep breath, 'Where do we go from here?' *We have our suspicions but yet no proof. Unfortunately, our main suspect has the King in his pocket, rendering us practically powerless.*

'We are going to have to press Oscar for answers,' Rozzen said. 'He cannot deny that Frank is *his* man, and that the two elite were under his command.'

'I don't see him accepting the blame do you?' Randall replied.

'No. I don't.'

Raised voices caught Randall's attention. He hushed the others and listened. One of the voices was Mòrag's and the other... 'He's here.'

'Who's here?' Marcs asked confused.

'Oscar,' Randall said as he left the tent. He strode between the tents, toward where the argument was taking place.

General Raine was standing with his aide at his side. He scoffed at the accusations and curses Mòrag was hurling at him. Brax had her caught round the waist, holding her back as best he could.

'Let her go, Dog. Just see how long she lasts when she relives what she has done over, and over, and over again,' Raine taunted.

Mòrag began to scream, no longer aiming her aggression at General Raine; she flailed wildly in Brax's grip.

'Raine, stop this!' Randall demanded.

'If you would control your subordinates, I would not need to take measures like this.'

'Release her!' *How can he be so smug about all this? He is to blame for everything that has happened to that girl, to Brax, to me.*

'You really are a poor excuse for a General, Steele.' Raine jeered.

'Release her!'

'You are not really a General at all. You were only named thus because of your bond with the King. Tell me. How long has it been since you severed your connection with him? My guess is quite some time.'

Randall was knocked of kilter by Raine's revelation. *So he's known for a while.* 'Release her NOW!' he bellowed.

The corners of Raines mouth twisted upwards in a haughty grin, 'No.'

***

Oswald's petrified screams curdled her blood: The ripping and shredding of his fragile form bearing bloody rain, hot bloody rain over her body. The feel of Frank's soul beneath her fingers, stirred something within her soul, how easy it had been to bend it to her will, how little effort it had taken for her to tear it from his body. The blackness of the aftermath enveloped her like a damp blanket, heavy and suffocating. The loop beginning anew with Oswald's screams...

Mòrag regained her senses as a stunned General Raine landed in a heap, several feet back from where he had been standing. Brax leapt forward to restrain Randall, *Randall? When did he get here?* General Rozzen and several large soldiers had also arrived to subdue the wild General. Even four against one, they were struggling to control him.

Raine's jaw set hard. He rose and glared at Randall, though he didn't open his mouth to protest, clearly afraid of what the repercussions might be.

She regarded the enraged Randall once more, the muscles in his neck were chorded, and he seemed to have grown in size, though it was more like an aura of rage that grew around him.

'Guards! Guards!' Mairead screeched from behind Raine.

'Do not do this Steele! Randall! Control yourself! You are playing right into his hands!' Rozzen's words fell upon deaf ears.

Randall had only moved toward the other General a few inches or so, due to the wall of bodies blocking his path. Raine seemed to draw some confidence of his own safety from this, and he laughed openly at Randall, fuelling his fury even further.

As much as I want to see Raine beaten to a pulp, now is probably not the best time. She felt for the connection to Randall's mind; the door flew open before she requested it to do so. She had never intentionally connected with him but the link that had been established while she was enduring the Cleanse had remained active and strong.

One by one bodies hit the floor. Brax, who had an arm around Randall's neck, and a hand on his arm, was thrown several feet in the air, before he met the ground at Raine's feet with a heavy thud. Randall caught General Rozzen with a savage back hander, striking her temple. She hit the ground hard, stunned, leaving him, face contorted with rage and blood lust, free to move as he pleased.

He was mid stride toward General Raine who could do nothing but await his fate, when Mòrag cast to him, '*Enough, he's not worth it. Stop now before you regret your actions.*'

Raine's eyes widened as Randall skidded to a halt nose to nose with him: Narrowly missing Brax who had scrambled out the way at the last moment. Randall's roaring breaths were the first sign that he was not quite as subdued as she had hoped. He buried a fist in Raine's blazer, lifting him from the ground with no visible signs of effort.

Mòrag got to her feet and walked the distance to Randall slow and deliberate. She gave Raine a disdainful look, and then placed a hand on Randall's shoulder, 'Enough,' she said keeping her voice soft, 'enough.'

Comprehension returned to Randall's eyes, he looked down at her, his expression was so sad she could hardly bare it.

'Let it go,' she soothed.

Randall lowered Raine to the ground, giving him a firm shove as he released his grip, causing him to stumble backwards.

He turned away from Raine then, as did Mòrag. She didn't want to see his smug face, for fear she had made the wrong decision in halting Randall.

'You've' done it now Steele!' Raine spat, now that it was clear Randall's rage had dissipated. 'You've sealed your fate. Expect a summons to the council of Generals within the month!' he turned and stormed toward the red tent, calling on General Marcs, who had not appeared during the commotion.

Randall was helping Rozzen to her feet. He stroked her face gently, his expression paining as she grimaced from the touch.

'It's been several years since you last landed a blow like that on me, Randall,' she said, 'I don't remember it being quite this painful. I must be getting old.'

'I'm sorry,' he said hanging his head.

Rozzen gave him a nudge with her elbow, 'Think nothing of it. It was my fault for getting in your way when you we on a rampage.'

'That doesn't make me feel any better about it.'

'It's not meant to,' she said.

'I've really messed up this time. He will twist this so the focus is on me instead of him.'

Mòrag turned her attention to Brax who was sitting on the ground at the side of one of the tents. He was only now regaining his breath after having been winded on impact. She crouched beside him, 'You ok?'

He nodded, 'how did you get him to stop?'

'I asked him nicely,' Mòrag replied.

'That's it?' Brax blinked at her astonished.

'That's it,' she confirmed. 'I asked and he listened.'

Chapter Thirty-Eight

ROYAL BLOOD

It was dark when Randall woke. The empty bottle of whisky on his bedside table gave him cause for concern. He hadn't had a drink in years; it lessened his self-control too much: He could find himself in a fit of rage with little or no reason, so he usually avoided alcohol like the plague.

He sat up slow; his aching head was spinning and throbbing, each sensation battling the other to see which could make him feel worse. His throat was dry, reaching for the glass of water he sucked back a large mouthful, which he immediately spat in a flurry of droplets across the room. *Vodka?* Swinging his feet down, they met more empty bottles by the side of the bed.

Clothing was strewn all over the place; one of the curtains had been ripped from its rail; the armchair lay on its side by the far wall. 'What the hell did I do?' he mused aloud.

'You made a scene, that's what you did.'

Randall leapt from the bed in surprise. Rozzen's hearty laughter radiated round the room, 'Your face is a picture!' she noted, cocking her head, 'as for the rest of you... it's just as I remembered.'

'I, eh, um...' *Shit... I'm naked! We must have... But we can't have... But then why would she be here, naked in my bed if we hadn't?*

'What do you remember?' she asked him as she rose and went in search of her clothing.

Randall righted the armchair and plonked himself into it. *What do I remember? Not a lot. Raine, Mòrag, the journey back to the castle, Mairead screeching, finding the crate of booze*

237

by my door, knowing I shouldn't take it and taking it anyway: After that, nothing. 'I'm drawing a blank, I'm afraid.'

'Oscar set you up to fail. You shouldn't have started drinking, Randall. You know it just makes you more volatile.'

'Did I hurt anyone?'

'No, luckily there were not many people around, I was in an entertaining mood, and you were more than willing to switch your focus from work to play.' she said as she pulled her trousers over her long legs.

'I didn't force you did I?' Randall asked, worry rising within him.

'Of course not,' she laughed. 'You were in a bad place: A very bad place. I instigated the whole encounter.' She buttoned her shirt and walked towards him.

She really is the most beautiful creature I have ever seen. What she sees in me I'll never know. He found everything about her attractive, from the way she walked to the glares she would throw him when she was annoyed. The darkness of her skin; the paleness of her eyes; how she could be so soft and caring while being cold and calculating in the same breath. She was a walking contradiction and he loved every inch of her.

It had been a long, *long* time since desire had stirred within him. He hadn't realised that part of him had almost ceased to exist while he had been under the King's command. Now that he was free of James' mental restraints, it flared to life within him. He wanted her; he wanted her more than he wanted anything else.

Rozzen raised an eyebrow as she looked down at him, 'Oh no! No, no, I'm busy. You can get *that* thought out of your head *right* now! And don't expect me to come running to lick your wounds every time Raine kicks you in the balls. This was a onetime thing.'

Randall pushed himself up out of the chair, 'It can't be,' he said, a smile creeping onto his lips. 'I don't remember it, so it never happened,'

'Good. It never happened. I'll be going now,' she said turning away from him.

Randall caught her around the waist, 'Won't you remind me what I missed? How will I know if I enjoyed it?'

'Oh you enjoyed it,' Rozzen said, half-heartedly pushing him away.

'I want to remember,' Randall breathed, kissing her neck, moving slowly down and along her collarbone, breathing her scent.

'I'm busy,' she protested weakly.

'Then why are you still here?' he teased.

'You're incorrigible,' she breathed, turning in his arms and pressing her lips to his.

***

'Mòrag,' Sergeant Grey called as she entered the barracks. 'Collect your effects and report to General Rozzen's office.'

'Now, Ma'am?' Mòrag asked confused, it was well past ten o'clock at night. An odd time to move her to new quarters.

'Yes, now.'

'Yes, Ma'am,' Mòrag called.

The empty barracks seemed much larger than usual. Most Tyros were still out on their last day of the team section of the tournament. Even with everything that had happened, Mòrag, Brax and Lennox had arrived back at Sruighlea a day earlier than expected. Mòrag sighed as she packed her things into her military issued backpack.

I wonder how Lennox is coping. I'm struggling to keep a lid on my emotions most of the time, but he's only twelve. He's just a bairn.

Mòrag ripped a corner from one of the notices on the wall, she scribbled a short note to Ava saying thanks for her friendship and she was sad to be moving, and slipped it under the girl's blanket. She slung her heavy pack over her right shoulder and made her way to Rozzen's office.

Mòrag knocked the door and waited, but no answer came. She knocked again: No answer. *Maybe I'm just supposed to go in.* She tried the handle: Locked. *Strange, Grey wouldn't have sent me here if Rozzen weren't waiting for me.*

As if summoned by the thought, Rozzen sauntered into the corridor, 'Oh, Mòrag, here already.'

'Yes, Ma'am,' Mòrag said looking Rozzen up and down. Her top three buttons were undone showing a hint of cleavage. *That's not like her, she's normally so formal.*

'Something came up,' she said, 'I needed to give it my undivided attention. Have you been waiting long?'

'No, Ma'am.'

Rozzen unlocked the door and ushered her inside. 'Take a seat, Mòrag.'

Mòrag placed her pack by the wall and sat as requested. Rozzen sat herself behind her desk. There was something different about her, other than her apparent inability to button up her shirt.

'You seem to be doing infinitely better than when I first saw you this morning. However, I know things are not always as they seem. How do you feel you are coping?' She touched her neck as she spoke, running her fingers down and along her collarbone. The movement was an unconscious one, but it caught Morag's attention.

'I feel numb. When you first saw me this morning, I suppose I was trying to make sense of everything. I don't even really remember most of the morning after Oswald was...' she paused to swallow the lump that was building in her throat. 'Then General Raine did, whatever it was he did. He made me see it again and again, and again. And I think I accepted it for what it was: A tragedy that should never have happened.'

'I see, given the circumstances I will allow for yourself, Brax and Lennox to skip the individual section of the tournament. You have already proven yourselves worthy of a high grade.'

'No. I'll take part.'

'Mòrag, given your strength I would have to place you against one of my top Tyros, you could very well end up against Fletcher Raine for example. He is highly skilled and as ruthless as his father.'

'And I will beat him none the less.'

'You seem overly confident.'

'In a fair fight I won't be beaten. Not by *him*.'

Rozzen fell silent as she considered this. Her hand gravitated to her neck once more, touching the same area. 'I will consult my fellow Generals before making a final decision, but if you want to take part, I see no reason to hold you back. I just have to find you a suitable opponent.

'Now,' she said straightening, 'After a deep and meaningful discussion between General Marcs and myself, we feel that today's incident was a direct attempt on your life. We do not feel you are safe in an open and exposed environment such as the barracks. I have decided to move you here, into the main building: In the same wing where Brax resides. Your familiar is most welcome to join you there, as well as in the castle grounds. It is abundantly clear that keeping you separated would be ill advised.'

'Has Brax said anything? About what happened when it was just us against Major Frank and his men?'

'He mentioned they were under Raine's orders and you were their main priority, because of who you are.'

That must mean Brax knows something I don't. 'Because of who I am?'

Rozzen sighed. 'I suppose now is as good a time as any. Mòrag, do you know the origins of the Seeker gene: The bloodlines that carry it?'

'No, up until I came here I had never even heard the term Seeker before.'

'The skill can be learned by strong sensory types, but only two bloodlines carry the gene that produces a natural born Seeker. Both are Albannach. Both are extinct, at least as far as the general population is concerned they are extinct. Though I am sure you realise by now that you and Brax are both natural Seekers and you are not related. So we can come to the conclusion that the two bloodlines live on in each of you.'

'Ok,' Mòrag said, thinking over what Rozzen had just told her. 'I still don't see why that would be reason to target me.'

'I am not sure exactly how much Brax knows about his family. They were good to me when I was a girl. Instead of killing me, which they were well within their rights to do, they took me in. I've never known such kindness.

'I was there when his mother brought him into this world; when they named him; when he took his first steps, and I was there when his family was slaughtered and he was taken. His name is Andrew Douglas; he is the last living descendant of their clan. Edward gave him a pet's name to de-humanise him. He is so used to it now I doubt he would be able to accept being called by his birth name.'

'Andrew Douglas,' Mòrag echoed, 'there are songs about the Douglas clan. Jock called them the Stewart's bedfellows: Branch family of our Royal line. Do you think he knows he essentially has Royal blood? The Stewart family ended with the death of Princess Catrìona. Surely, that means the Douglas clan would gain the right to the Albannach throne by default. No wonder Edward wants him.'

'For someone so sharp you are equally naive aren't you? The other family which bears natural Seekers, the family from which you are descended, of this I have absolutely no doubt: Is the Stewart clan: The Royal line.'

'No, surely not.' Mòrag scoffed. 'My mother was a traitor on the run, not a member of the Royal family!'

'When were you born?'

'August.'

'The twelfth?'

'Yes, but –'

'The day she died.'

'Impossible, I can't be.'

'Brax was the last one to see her alive. If anyone knows what led to her death and if she had a child, it's him. Has he ever mentioned anything?' Rozzen asked, 'has he ever said anything that links you both?'

Mòrag's eyes widened as she remembered all the times he had called her Catrìona, the sadness in his face when he thought about her. *I can't believe I never connected him calling me Catrìona to Princess Catrìona.*

'I see he probably *has* referred to you in some way, calling you by her name perhaps, on more than one occasion?'

'Yes.'

'I have told you all this so you know the danger you are in. With Edward threatening his return, you would be target number one. For now, I want you to continue as you have been. Do nothing differently. Train and become strong, gain allies and crush your enemies. And, when the time is right for you to make your claim on the Albannach throne, you can count me among your supporters. After all,' she said. 'I swore fealty to your family many years ago, my loyalties lie with you.'

I don't really know what I think about all this. I don't want to think about it. But I know one thing. They weren't there for me. 'May I leave, Ma'am? It's getting late.'

'Of course,' Rozzen said, 'go and get settled in.'

'Yes, Ma'am,' Mòrag rose and lifted her pack, as she reached the door she turned back toward Rozzen. 'I think you need to reassess your sources of information. Frank's unit was there for Brax, I was just a bonus.'

All the way to Brax's chamber, Mòrag ruminated over her conversation with Rozzen. *Me? Princess Catrìona's daughter? Don't be mental! It can't be true. But what if it is? Well there's a twist in the tail I never saw coming. I wonder if it's true.*

Rozzen's words spun round in her head, 'Brax was the last one to see her alive. If anyone knows what led to her death and if she had a child, it's him.'

Only one way to find out: But it would change everything. Do I really want that? Sure, I want things to change, but not like that. Do I really want to know?

Mòrag rapped on his door and waited. He opened the door and regarded her closely, 'What's the bag for, you decided to move in? I suppose it makes sense seeing as you spend most of your time here anyway,' he chuckled.

'Rozzen told me to pick a room. She is moving me over here so I'm "safe".'

Brax nodded, 'Probably wise. You coming in or are you just going to stand there?'

Mòrag followed him into the room. She moved straight for her favoured spot by the fire. He took her pack and sat it by the window then joined her on the rug.

'How are you holding up?'

'I'm actually coping ok. Still numb I think.' *Now would be a good time to ask him, if I'm going to.*

'I take it Rozzen was asking the same question.'

'Yes,' *now's an even better time to ask him.*

'Did she ask about what you did to Frank?'

'No. I think she wanted to though. I would have told her that I couldn't remember what I did, if she had asked.' *What's wrong with me? Ask the damn question!*

Brax narrowed his eyes at her, 'That's not strictly true is it?'

'No. I know what I did. And I think I know how I did it too. I don't want *them* to know that though. They'll think I'm a monster. I'm only telling you because you...' *Come on Mòrag don't get side tracked.*

'Have experienced it before?'

'I got that impression, yes.' *Well that's it. The moment's gone now.*

'You're anything but a monster, Mòrag.'

'Not true. People shouldn't have this kind of power. I don't want it. I wish I never had it. Don't you?' *I don't want to know.*

'I can't do what you can do.'

'How'd you mean, we're both Seekers aren't we?'

'Yes. No. It's complicated. It's not the skill of a Seeker.'

Mòrag flopped back onto the floor and let out an exasperated breath. She was fed up not knowing what everyone else obviously knew. 'I don't care,' she said, more to herself than to Brax. *I do care.*

He chuckled at her, 'About what?'

'Everything,' *do I really, not want to know?*

'Have I ever told you, that you make no sense?'

'Brax?' *Come on Mòrag! Just ask him.*

'Mmm?'

'Never mind,' *I'm such a feartie.*

Chapter Thirty-Nine

RISING TO THE OCCASION

Rannoch stretched, yawned and got up to shuffle himself round, then flopped down on to his other side, scattering dust across the floor in a mini airborne tidal wave. Mòrag let her hand flop down the side of the bed so she could give him a scratch between his soft ears, *bliss*. She had missed the mornings most of all. Half-waking too early to get up, and giving him a scratch before turning over and going back to sleep.

Mòrag swung her legs from the bed and sat up. *The individual section starts today. I can't just lie in my bed.*

'Ready for today?' Rannoch asked sleepily, rolling onto his back and bearing his stomach to her.

'As ready as I can be,' she replied, sinking her toes into the deep warmth of his coat. His deep, rumbling purr wrapped round her as she moved her feet back and forth. 'Want to go for a run?'

'Always,' he purred, 'do you have time?'

'I'll make time.'

Mòrag enjoyed taking an early morning run with Rannoch. Sometimes she ran and sometimes she rode, but she always made sure she had time to spend with him.

Today's run had been particularly brisk, as she needed to report to the arena a full forty minutes early, to register her attendance, collect her opponent's name card and find out her assessment time.

Mòrag joined the ranks of Tyros by the notice boards just inside the large hall next to the parade grounds. *This is where I met Oswald. He should have been here.* She felt rooted to the spot, unable to will herself to move on. She spotted Lennox next to the large pin boards. His face was calm; no emotion pricked its surface. If he was enduring the same emotional struggle that she was, he was hiding it well.

All three remaining members of the unit had decided to continue with the tournament: A subconscious drive to, in some way, allow Oswald to finish with them. At least, that was how Mòrag looked at it, yet she still couldn't move her feet.

She felt a hand squeeze her shoulder.

'Having second thoughts?' Brax asked.

'No, just taking my time.'

'Oh, so that's why you have been standing here for ten minutes then is it?'

Mòrag threw him a look of indignation as Sergeant Grey strode through the crowd of Tyros to pin six notices to the board. She then traversed the hall and laid out the name cards on the tables that had previously held the weapons, and other items for the team section.

'C'mon,' Brax encouraged, 'you want to see when you're up and who you're fighting don't you?'

Mòrag nodded and followed him toward the sheets on the notice board. She scanned the timesheets, finding their names on the last sheet at the end of the day, the last three. I suppose that makes sense, they had removed us from the list and then had to add us back in.

A furore erupted at the other side of the hall. Fletcher Raine appeared to be having a poorly concealed tantrum. He spotted Mòrag, Brax and Lennox watching him, and stampeded his way across the hall.

'What gives you the right to special treatment?' he demanded. 'There's nothing special about a bastard, a defect and their dog! You aren't worthy of fighting in the same arena as elite fighters like us,' he gestured to his friends who had come to join him.

'What's got your knickers in a twist like, fighting one of us? I hope so, you deserve to be taken down a peg or ten,' Mòrag retorted.

'I wouldn't be seen alive fighting the likes of you.'

'You've got that right at least.'

'Mòrag, he's not worth the hassle, let him have his tantrum. You don't need to involve yourself,' Brax said beneath his breath.

'Speak only when spoken to, Dog!' Fletcher spat, stepping forward and facing up to him, 'You should know your place by now. Or do I have to remind you?'

Mòrag could see Brax mentally stepping backward before his body moved. She stepped into the space that had opened up between them, 'Just give me a reason Fletcher, just one.' She felt for his mind, and found him, as expected, completely focused on her. The door to his mind sported heavy bolts and reinforced locks. She had a sudden urge to scout the surface of his mind. She followed the instinct and found a window. Similar to the window in Lennox's mind, only this window was open. This entrance into his mind felt much more natural than she had expected.

'I've had just about enough of you,' he sneered, lifting his hand to strike her.

He has no clue whatsoever that I've reached his mind. Mòrag projected her will towards him, halting his action just before his fist could make contact. Stepping in close she gave him a wicked smile, 'I think it's about time you left.'

Fletcher's face was a mixture of fear and rage, 'How?' he demanded.

'None of your business,' she cast, her smile turned gleeful, as it dawned on him how she had stopped him. 'Tattie bye,' she added. Waving sweetly to him, and commanded his body to turn and walk from the building.

His friends, more than a little confused by his actions, followed him from the building, leaving Mòrag, Brax and Lennox alone once more. 'You're nothing without your mental power,' Fletcher's cast hissed, 'I'll get you eventually.'

'So you say,' Mòrag cast back before she released her hold on him. She groaned and raised her fingers to her temples, 'I have such a headache.'

'Did you just?' Brax asked, astonished.

'Well I wasn't going to stand around and let him hit me was I?'

'I suppose not. But he has really strong mental defences. It's one of the things he's best at.'

'Really? Well obviously no one's looked for the side door before then, because it was wide open.'

'Another door?'

'It was a window actually, but it was wide open.'

Brax gave her a disapproving look, 'You shouldn't get too cocky about your ability to worm your way into people's heads.'

'I wouldn't do it to just anyone. Besides, would you rather I let him hit me?'

'No.'

'Well then,' she said.

'Come on,' Brax said changing the subject, 'we had best go see who we're up against.'

The name cards were laid in six sets of double lines across the tables, corresponding to the six time sheets. Each Tyro was matched with another of his or her own level. Walking to the end of the table Mòrag searched for her name. Her headache strengthened, but she ignored it and scanned the names. She came to Lennox's card first: The card underneath read Sgt Dixon. A Sergeant, maybe they didn't have enough Tyros left to pair him with one. Brax and I will probably be against each other then. Moving along she came to Brax's card: The card underneath did not display her name as she had expected instead reading, Gen Marcs. Marcs? Shifting her gaze across to the card beneath her own, she paled as she read the name it displayed, Gen Rozzen.

All of a sudden, her headache worsened a thousand fold. 'I think I need to sit down,' she breathed as her legs began to buckle. Brax caught her and helped her to a seat by the wall.

'Are you alright?'

'I feel like my head's in a vice, I can't focus at all.'

Lennox disappeared during the first fight leaving Brax and Mòrag alone in the hall. She kept her eyes closed until the whirling, weightless feeling lifted leaving only the heavy throbbing in her head. After a short while, the headache had lessened even more, leaving a mild ache. Mòrag breathed a sigh of relief. 'I don't have a clue what caused that.'

'Over stretching yourself,' Brax said. 'Mòrag, you really need to be more careful.'

'I know,' she sighed. 'I know.'

The fights took place in the other half of the large building. Only the assessor and combatants were allowed in at one time, to cut down outside influence on the fights.

Mòrag spent most of the day at the infirmary with Oliver. The young boy was responding well to treatment and was now well enough to try walking again. She enjoyed his company, and it seemed to help his confidence when she was around so she tried to make time to visit as often as she could.

She returned to the hall in time to wish Lennox good luck before his assessment. While she was waiting, she walked laps of the hall, stretching and flexing, paying particular attention to her left shoulder. Brax appeared just as the doors opened and Lennox came into view. He looked tired but was clearly pleased with himself.

'Did it go well?' Mòrag asked.

Lennox nodded.

'Well done.' Brax said clapping him on the shoulder as he strode past on his way to his own assessment.

'Good luck!' Mòrag called after him.

The minutes seemed to drag now that it was only her left. After fifteen minutes or so, the doors reopened and Brax emerged.

'How did it go?'

'As I expected,' he said giving a small smile. 'Good luck.'

'Thanks,' she said, walking through the double doors and into the unknown.

Rozzen was standing in the middle of the floor. Marching to her, Mòrag stopped a few feet away and awaited instruction.

'You may go, Grey, I will assess her myself.'

'Yes, Ma'am,' Sergeant Grey called, turning and marching from the room.

'At ease,' Rozzen said. 'We call a halt at first blood. You may choose a weapon if you like. When you are ready to begin, take up your position across from me.'

Mòrag looked at Rozzen. She was wearing a skin tight suit: She obviously didn't want material hampering her movement. She was not holding a weapon, though Mòrag supposed she may have one concealed somewhere.

Mòrag surveyed the rack holding various weapons. Swords, axes, bows and quivers full of fine tipped arrows, a mace. Mòrag took two steps back at the sight of the morning star; it threw her off and she turned away from the rack unarmed. I always have the soul blade if I need it. She strode to her mark and stood ready.

'Are you happy with your choice?'

'Yes, Ma'am.'

'Alright,' Rozzen said moving into a fighting stance, 'begin!'

The General was quick off the mark, as was Mòrag. They exchanged a few blows, each testing the water. Mòrag blocked a low jab and ended up staggering backwards when Rozzen kicked high and caught her shoulder, jarring it painfully.

As time drew on Rozzen increased the strike rate and speed until she had Mòrag retreating at a steady pace.

Spinning low, Mòrag dodged one of Rozzen's savage blows and leapt across the hall to give herself more room.

Pulling her attention into the sensory state she favoured during combat, she watched the shimmering teal of Rozzen's soul energy swirl around her. The General attacked again, but this time Mòrag blocked her efforts. As long as I can see which way her soul is going to go, I can block her. How will I land a hit though? Rozzen pulled a large dagger from behind her back. I knew she'd hidden something! Mòrag was only just able to form a soul blade to parry Rozzen's dagger, at the last moment. She shuddered as the sensation of the blade contacting her soul resonated through her, making her ears ring.

She began to tire far quicker using the soul blade; she had never used it in combat before and it was becoming obvious to her that she wouldn't be able to use it for long. I need to go on the offensive, if I can't I'm done.

Finding herself more space she changed her stance, decreasing the blade in her right hand and growing one in her left, she then attacked in short bursts, changing position as often as she could, trying not to fall into a pattern that Rozzen could read. Simultaneously she felt for Rozzen's mind and came up against a stone wall, no door, no window, just a vast stone wall.

Rozzen increased her speed once more, all Mòrag could do was defend herself.

Out of nowhere, Mòrag saw an opening and took it. Pushing forward she swung her blade with all her strength. Instead of contacting, as it should have, Rozzen simply vanished. Mòrag stopped confused. Feeling a presence behind her, she turned to find Rozzen mid attack. The assault hit its mark, throwing Mòrag across the room and into the wall.

***

'Wasn't that a tad excessive Rozzen?' The high-pitched ringing in her ears muffled General Marcs' voice.

'Welcome back,' Rozzen said, smiling down at her. 'Ready to get up?'

Mòrag's head was spinning. 'I think I'll just sit here a minute if that's alright, Ma'am.'

'I thought long and hard about whether I should allow you to continue onto the individual assessment or not. You have power, Mòrag: There is no denying that. But, you have become overconfident in your mental abilities. Power is not everything. You are poor at physical combat. No. That is not quite true. You are adequate, which in a serious fight counts for nothing.

'You said in a fair fight you wouldn't be beaten. When you are fighting for your life, Mòrag, it is *never* a fair fight. I am, however, impressed by your ability to think on your feet. General Marcs also tells me you are a natural leader,' she looked down at Mòrag and smiled. 'Ok. Get yourself a rest and come to my office in the morning. We have a few issues to discuss.'

'Yes, Ma'am,' Mòrag said, her voice almost inaudible even to her own ears. She rose slow, trying hard to quell the deep quivering in her body, but failing miserably. One shaky step after another, she made her way back to her room. She felt miserable, caked in dust that had settled on her sweaty skin.

Though she wanted nothing more than to fall into her bed, she couldn't bring herself to lie down without first taking a shower. *It might end up making me feel better anyway.* She collected her things and headed off to the shower room.

The hot water beating hard on her back did little to sooth her. *I feel so sick. I really shouldn't have pushed it today. No. I'm fine. I'm fine. I'm ok. Breathe just breathe.* The ringing in her ears intensified as a sensation of dizziness swept over her. Then everything went black.

***

'Mòrag? Mòrag?' Brax's worried voice seemed so distant.

What? He's sitting on the wall... What's he doing sitting on the wall? She let her gaze shift. Oh! I'm on the floor. My head hurts. 'How long have I been lying here?'

'I don't know. I came to see you and you weren't in your room. So I popped down for a shower and found you like this. When did you come in here?' he asked, retrieving her towel and placing it over her.

Mòrag hugged the towel close, 'I don't know, around seven maybe. I was only in the shower a few minutes before I found myself lying here.'

Brax scooped her up in his arms, 'We'd best get you checked over,' he said. 'From the sounds of it you've been unconscious for over an hour.'

'I'm fine, really. I just pushed it too far today: Stupid mistake.'

'Still,' he said, 'I'm getting you checked.'

'Whoa! Wait, wait, wait, haud yer horses. I am not going to the infirmary in the buff, no way, not happening!' She began to smirk.

'What's so funny?'

'Your hand's on my bare arse.' She giggled despite herself. Nervous laughter had taken hold and wouldn't let go. The rapid reddening of Brax's cheeks made her laugh even more.

'I think I am fine to walk you know.'

'I can't put you down right now.'

Mòrag regarded him closely, 'Why?' she asked, raising an eyebrow at him.

If it was possible, he turned an even redder shade, 'I just can't.'

Mòrag had to look away from him, as pink heat radiated to her own cheeks. I wonder if it's possible to die of embarrassment. 'Could you just take me to my room please?'

He nodded in response; opening her door, he gently placed her on her bed before leaving the room as fast as he could.

Mòrag rolled over and buried her face in her pillow. Kill me now. Just kill me now! She pushed herself up in a bid to get dressed in case he came back to check on her, but felt too woozy to stand and walk across the room. Instead, she pulled her cover over her, closed her eyes and hoped the world would stop spinning. She floated in and out of consciousness until a quiet knock at the door stirred her.

Oh hell, he's come back, and I'm still lying here in the bare nuddy. 'I'm fine Brax, really! I'm just going to try and sleep it off, ok? No need to check on me.' Please let him leave. The door creaked as it swung open causing a fluttering of nerves in her stomach.

'Feeling awfully exposed are we?' Ava chuckled as she shut the door behind her.

Mòrag popped her head out from beneath the covers, 'You have no idea how relieved I am that you aren't Brax.'

'Yes,' she said. 'He came to tell me you needed some help. He maybe should have waited ten minutes though.'

Mòrag groaned.

'Naturally, I got my own back on him for making fun of me in front of General Steele,' she giggled. 'He is mortified.'

'He's not the only one!'

'What happened anyway?' she asked.

'I pushed it too far today that's all. My head's louping, and the room's birling but I'm ok.'

'You need to be more careful about using abilities that you have only just learned. They take a huge toll on your body,' Ava said placing her fingers on Mòrag's temples and sending some healing energy toward her.

The spinning room began to slow and her throbbing head dulled to a mild ache. 'That feels a lot better,' she said. 'Thank you.'

'My pleasure, now,' Ava said, gaining a cheeky glint in her eye, 'let's talk about Brax.'

'Eh, no, let's not.' Brax was the last person she wanted to think about, how am I going to face him again?

'I think he likes you. And I am fairly sure you like him too.' Ava said as she fetched a nightdress from Mòrag's dresser.

'Well obviously, we're friends.' Mòrag said, taking the garment from Ava and slipping the soft fabric over her head.

'But you want to be more than friends, don't you?'

'I have no idea what you mean, Ava,' Mòrag said, her tone full of sarcasm.

'How did you feel when his hands were on your bare skin?'

Mòrag could feel her cheeks warming, 'Oh, gonnae no, Ava, it's embarrassing.'

Ava grinned; showing a wicked streak Mòrag never knew existed within her. She lumped herself onto the end of Mòrag's bed, golden curls bouncing, and crossed her legs. 'Oh come on, Mòrag! Admit it; you would have been quite happy if he had been a little more adventurous with his hands wouldn't you?'

'No Ava. I think I would have died. I almost died when I realised that he... you know.'

'Had risen to the occasion?' Ava smirked.

'Something like that.'

Chapter Forty

IN THE HOT SEAT

'Stop sulking,' Rozzen instructed from her perch on the large oak desk. 'And stand up straight. You need to *look* confident at the very least.'

'That's easy for you to say,' Randall retorted, 'you are not the one in the hot seat here.'

Rozzen hopped down and helped him into his blazer, smoothing the fabric and buttoning him in. 'You have lost weight since the last time you wore this,' she noted.

'I did not have the best of diets during the last few years. I've been wasting away in more ways than one,' Randall said, lifting his sabre and fastening its scabbard to his belt. He ran his hand along its cool leather casing, and felt a pang of regret. *This sword has saved the King and I more times than I care to remember. One stupid mistake and now I face losing it.*

Rozzen hopped back onto the desk. 'If I had known back then, I would have put a stop to it long ago,' she sighed.

'As would I.'

Marcs popped his head round the door, 'Time to go, Patricia. I'll see you in there, Randall,' he said, a hint of tension in his voice.

'One minute Daniel,' Rozzen said, taking Randall's face in her hands as the door clicked shut. 'Do you trust me?'

'You are the only one I trust.'

'Then stop worrying,' she said, kissing him on the forehead and leaving the room.

Randall had received the summons only a week after the winter tournament had concluded. He, Rozzen, Marcs and Mòrag had ridden to Dùn Èideann, to board the enormous steam powered locomotive, which would carry them to the great border city of Cathair Luail, where he would have to stand and defend his honour before the Council of Generals.

He had spent the journey fretting over the possible outcomes while Marcs and Rozzen coached Mòrag on the do's and don'ts of a hearing of this magnitude. Many of the Generals were unsympathetic and biased against the Albannach people, and because of this, Rozzen had asked her to speak with the utmost formality, and in as neutral an accent as she could possibly muster.

Randall paced the room. He was overtired which, along with his nerves, added to his irritability, no longer quelled by Rozzen's calming influence. He kept one hand on the haft of his sword; the textured horn always seemed to calm him, allowing him to focus when his mind was clouded.

There were not many Unicorn horn-hafted swords left in the two Kingdoms. Only the most skilled natural Seekers could forge and imbue both the Damascus steel and horn to create the powerful weapon. Due to the near total annihilation of the Douglas and Stewart clans, seemingly leaving only Brax and Mòrag, neither of whom were sword smiths, the few swords in circulation had become irreplaceable.

A young Lieutenant arrived to bid him to stand before the Generals, 'They are ready for you, Sir,' he said, holding the door to allow Randall passage.

Randall followed the young man down the corridor towards the hall allocated to the Council. 'What is your name?' he asked as they approached the large set of double doors.

'George, Sir,' the young man replied as he opened one of the large doors.

'Thank you, Lieutenant George,' Randall said stepping past him and into the hall.

Four Generals sat at a semi-circular table set for five. Generals; Wells, Desmond, Finch and Porter had been chosen from across the Sasannach Kingdom to act as judges, headed by the council's superior; General Brooke, who was waiting for him at the door.

The silver haired man was the eldest and most respected General on the Council; he was also Randall's mentor and lifelong friend.

'Hand me your sword, General Steele,' Brooke said.

Randall obeyed, unfastening the scabbard from his belt and handing it to General Brooke.

'You have been summoned here to defend your honour, which has been called into question. Let this sword act as your honour and may you be judged upon it.' Brooke said authoritative. He then took up his place at the centre of the table, placing the sword horizontally in front of him and leaving Lieutenant George to usher Randall to his seat at the opposite side of the room.

Randall could barely stifle the fluttering of nerves within him. He took a deep breath and let it out as the Generals called the first witness.

General Raine walked to the centre of the room, swore an oath to speak only the truth, and laid his accusation down as thick as he could.

'Not only did General Steele assault myself, he also injured several soldiers, a Tyro and assaulted General Rozzen.'

The more he spoke, the more irritated Randall became. *He's doing this on purpose. He is now bringing up instances where I have lost my temper when he was not even there.* He tried digging his nails into his palm to give himself something else to think about, but the sensation only strengthened his irritation.

'I am sure my fellow Generals; you can understand my concern over the wellbeing of our children under General Steele's care. Not to mention the helpless women he could attack. I hear tell of an alcohol-fuelled altercation with General Rozzen later that same day. I dread to think about how that ended.'

Randall had heard enough, he would happily walk into prison once he was done with Raine, he could feel his inner rage building, his self-control beginning to melt away.

'*Calm down,*' Mòrag's presence in his mind shocked him enough to break his downward spiral.

Randall glanced at the soldier that stood to the side of the door to the hall. He didn't seem to have noticed Mòrag's communication. 'Mòrag?'

'You need to calm down before I punch someone. Why is your anger affecting me?'

'Affecting you? I don't know; it's never transmitted through a link before.'

'Well I was two seconds away from smacking the next person that looked at me funny, which would have been awkward.'

'Yes, I can imagine. Our link must be deeper than I first thought; there is a soldier in here who has the job of detecting any play; abilities, communications and so on. He has not noticed our conversation. I'm glad. I was about to do something particularly ill-advised before you spoke.'

'Aye, I can tell. Has he finished stirring things up yet?'

'Yes. Just. General Marcs has been called in.'

Marcs testified to Randall's professionalism, and the care and attention he gave each individual Tyro, not only under his own command, but any that Marcs or Rozzen had difficulty with. He then went on to mention Major Frank.

'Unit nine had completed their objective a full twenty-two hours early, and had split up to disguise their tracks, as the younger Tyros made their way to the extraction point. When no one came to meet the young boys, Colonel Tesso and I retraced our steps. We assumed the older Tyros were caught somewhere, close to the encampment by our assigned troops. Instead, we found Major Frank, an unknown soldier, and two of our elite graduates, openly attacking with intent to kill or seriously injure, the two Tyros we had backtracked to find.'

'This attack unit; who was their commanding officer?' General Finch asked.

'General Raine. None would accept my authority when I arrived on scene, and they continued their assault, which led to the death of a young Tyro, David Oswald. The remaining three Tyros sustained injuries, as well as, Colonel Tesso and myself.'

'I see,' said Finch. 'Do you have anything further to tell us?'

'I believe that is everything I have to divulge on the matter.'

'Thank you, General Marcs, you are dismissed.'

Randall noted the tension rising in the room, this hearing was obviously far more complicated than they had realised. *I see Daniel and Patricia are ready to play the same game as Oscar. There is no telling how this will end.*

Rozzen's intense gaze locked onto his as she entered the room, cool and confident as ever. She swore in the same manner as the other Generals and laid down the law according to Patricia Rozzen. For as long as Randall had known her she had the ability to talk her way into, and out of any situation. She was supremely confident, and prided herself in knowing more than anyone else, so she could retain the upper hand at all times.

Not only did Rozzen quash all reliability of any insinuation of rape; she also provided detailed reports from herself, Colonel Tesso and others, of the underhanded behaviour of General Raine and his subordinates.

'Honestly gentlemen, it is nigh-on unthinkable, that you would pay credence to a wildly outlandish claim such as this. General Steele can be volatile at times but he is not a sexual predator. All of you have known him for years: None more so than yourself, General Brooke. Do you really believe he is capable of such an evil?'

'I do not,' he replied without a moment's hesitation, triggering astonished looks from his fellow Generals.

Trust Patricia to turn the tables and interrogate the judges. I doubt anyone else would get away with that.

'I thought as much. General Raine has been systematically targeting one of my Tyros since she completed his ridiculous Cleanse. This is the same Tyro he targeted in order to provoke General Steele into an attack. I am sure you will agree gentlemen, that only an utter imbecile would provoke a Berserker, never mind one as powerful as General Steele.'

Randall noted that Rozzen paused just long enough to allow her audience to ruminate the information she had just delivered them, before providing yet another morsel set to tip the scales in her favour.

'If you refer to the reports I have provided, you will find General Raine's procedure for the stage one training of Tyros, laid out in excruciating detail; from the supposed Cleanse of their minds to the atrocity he calls interrogation training. The casualties of his methods are numerous and include children from your own circles, along with the Tyro I have been referring to, and General Marcs' own son; who almost died as a result of these brutal techniques; which are, gentlemen, no better than torture.'

Randall had to hand it to Rozzen, she was a formidable opponent, whether on the battlefield or in a meeting. It was no wonder she held so much authority and respect from her fellow Generals.

'The Tyros being submitted to his cruel regime are children, children: Twelve years old, with no experience of the world to speak of. Your own children, and in some cases grandchildren,' she said glancing at Brooke, 'are being forced into irreversibly damaging mental turmoil. I can relate to those children. Let me ask you gentlemen: What were you doing as a twelve year old? General Brooke?'

'Playing in the street no doubt, or at school,' the old man replied. 'All of us would answer the same.'

'Would you like to know what I was doing at twelve? No. I'm not sure you would stomach what I had to do as a child under the control of the then young General Raine.'

'Would you say you held a grudge against your former commander, General Rozzen?' Finch asked.

'My dislike of the man runs deep. But, that is not why I bring these things to your attention now. As you well know I have been attempting to address you on the matter for some years now: Though not one of you saw fit to return even one of my letters.' Rozzen looked at each General in turn. 'This hearing is an example of how backward our society has become. That General Steele is hauled here to be judged in front of you for defending one of my Tyros from General Raine.'

'Is that all you have to say, General Rozzen?'

'Yes. I have informed you of the facts to the very best of my knowledge.'

'Then you are dismissed,' Brooke said, 'Thank you, General Rozzen.'

She inclined her head toward them and left the room. Randall watched her leave, and longed to follow her. *She really has thrown a spanner in the works.* He noted that instead of calling in the next witness; Raine's aide Mairead, they spoke amongst themselves. When eventually the tubby, curly haired, hot-faced woman, waddled into the room she found the five judges less than accommodating to her whines.

'*How's it going?*'

'*General Raine's aide is giving testament,*' he stifled an internal chuckle as Mairead was reprimanded for going off topic. '*She is getting a frosty reception. I think General Rozzen has just carpeted your path, you should not have issue when you are called.*'

'*Are you feeling more confident about the outcome of this hearing?*'

'*I don't really want to get my hopes up. If I escape with a sanction I will be extremely lucky.*'

The Generals dismissed Mairead from the room within minutes of her arrival. Her hot-headed attitude was not tolerated by even one of them.

'Show the next witness in, Lieutenant George,' General Porter instructed.

Randall watched as Mòrag entered the room. The confidence in her stride surprised him. She held her head high and did not glance round the room as a young Tyro would. *She looks like she has been taking notes on Patricia.*

'What is your name child?' Brooke asked.

'Mòrag, Sir.'

'Just Mòrag?' Porter asked.

'Yes, Sir.'

'That is unfortunate. We have called you here to give testimony on the allegations of assault brought to our attention by General Raine. Will you assist us with the truth to the best of your knowledge?' there was the tiniest hint of tenderness in Brooke's voice.

'Yes, Sir.'

'We have been told that General Raine attacked you in a bid to provoke General Steele into an attack. What do you make of this claim?'

He is referring to Daniel and Patricia's claims, not Oscar's.

'It is true that he attacked me, though I am unaware if it was a bid to provoke General Steele, or whether he has just decided to target me.'

Her whole demeanour has changed. Her language and accent are practically unrecognisable as Albannach!

'Has General Raine targeted you before child?' Brooke asked.

'Why's he calling me child?'

'Because you are female: He means well, he is just set in his ways.'

'He has targeted me twice directly, and twice indirectly, Sir.'

'Twice indirectly?'

'Through Major Frank, Sir.'

'I see. And in these instances, how did he treat you?'

'With violence, Sir.'

'All four times?'

'The first three times were physical violence, Sir. In the last instance he bombarded me with looped images, of the trauma I had just experienced.'

'Can you detail this violence?'

'Yes, Sir.'

Randall felt a surge of sympathy for her as she described how Raine had exploded into her recovery room intent on harming her, and being saved by the arrival of another Tyro, though she didn't mention Brax's name. She then went on to tell them in great detail, what she had gone through at Major Frank's hand during her interrogation and finally to the event that led to his death, taking care to share her horror with them though she omitted the cause of Frank's demise.

'And this last instance, in which General Steele defended you; you were shown the previous conflict on a loop?'

'No, Sir, only Oswald's body being torn apart.'

The expressions of the judges were universally grim. 'Thank you, child,' Brook said, making no attempt to hide the kind tone in his voice. 'You are dismissed.'

'Thank you, Sir.' Mòrag said before turning and striding in a Rozzen like fashion from the room.

Randall was called up to stand before them. He felt like an insecure schoolboy in front of the panel of Generals.

General Brook spoke first. 'I think my fellow Generals will agree there is no need to hear your testament, General Steele. We all know it is the nature of the Berserker not to have clear recollection of events during a rampage. We have received more than enough information to deliberate on: If you would step outside please.'

Randall's heart sank, *so they will not even allow me to speak to defend myself.* 'Yes, Sir,' he said and left the room.

The deliberations went on for half an hour or more before General Raine was called back to the hall. He sneered at Randall on his way past. When he again emerged through the double doors, he stormed down the corridor in a fit of rage.

'They will see you now, Sir,' Lieutenant George said.

'Thank you, Lieutenant George.'

The first thing Randall saw as he entered the room was the haft of his sword pointed in his direction. Relief flooded over him.

'We have deliberated and found these claims against you to be unfounded. This matter will go no further. Please regain your honour, General Steele.' General Brooke instructed.

Randall stepped forward and clasped the haft of his sword, lifting its familiar weight and fastening the scabbard to his belt once more.

'Further to our discussions' continued Brooke, 'we have stripped General Raine of his authority with regard to the Academy at Sruighlea. He will no longer be permitted to take any part in the training of our children.

'We have, in fact, decided to leave you in charge of the whole process, and as such, General Steele, we have decided to name you Sruighlea's Commandant. You will have authority over all other officers, with regard to training our young Tyros, until they graduate and leave your care.

'Additionally, after much discussion on the issue, we have decided to recommend you for the position on the Council of Generals, which will become available when General Hannmon retires in the spring of next year. Will you accept this honour?'

'I will, Sir. Thank you, Sir.' Randall said astonished.

'I am sorry for the disruption and stress this hearing must have caused you and your associates, General Steele. I only hope this comes as some consolation. You are dismissed.'

'Thank you, Sir,' Randall said, turning and striding from the room.

Chapter Forty-One

THE WRATHWIND

The mighty locomotive made a tremendous clattering racket as it thundered along the track on the return journey to Dùn Èideann. Mòrag sat on the floor of Rannoch's stall, with him lying curled around her, claws dug into the wooden floor. He growled whenever the coach lurched one way or the other, throwing them off kilter. Mòrag felt unsettled by the enormous contraption too, and stroked his thick mane to ease both his tension and her nerves. She had never seen a locomotive before, never mind been carried within one. There were only four in Sasann, which ran up and down the midline of the country, stretching into Alba but reaching no further than Dùn Èideann.

'I thought I would find you here.'

Mòrag looked up to find Randall watching her from the next stall.

'I came to check the horses, but it appears I needn't have bothered. You have beaten me to it.'

'Do you travel on this thing often?' she asked as the carriage rocked side to side, unsettling her.

'Not as much as I used to,' he said. 'I take it you are not a fan?'

'Not really, no. Neither Rannoch or myself are fond of enclosed spaces,' she said. 'How are you feeling about your new position?'

'I am honoured. Truly, I am. I never imagined this whole mess would end in General Raine's expulsion from Sruighlea and my promotion to Commandant of the Academy.'

'And the recommendation to the Council of Generals,' Mòrag reminded him.

'You are not supposed to know about that,' he said.

'You were practically singing it in your head. I couldn't ignore it. How come you are affecting me so much? I've never experienced a link like this before.'

'I am not sure. When the King was my driver, I would feel his emotions and his will particularly strongly, but I do not think he ever felt anything like that from me. At least if he did, he never told me.'

'It's an odd sensation. Like when you were getting angry before... so was I.'

'I have been wondering for some time now if you were capable of becoming a driver: Though, I never considered myself as your Berserker.'

'Another classification?'

'Driving is a skill many sensory types can master; one which would be worthwhile learning. When we get back I will talk you through some of the basics and we will see if the link you instilled within me is the link of a driver.'

'You make it sound like I force bound you.'

'You did, after a fashion. Though your body and mind were under tremendous strain, I think you were crying out for help. At least, that is the best explanation I can come up with.'

'So how do I release you?' she asked.

'I think it is best, for now at least, for you to maintain the link. I can be unpredictable at the best of times, yet you seem to manage to keep me calm with little or no effort. Let's just see how it goes. I must ask you to keep this to yourself though. Can you do that?'

'Aye, I can do that.'

A strong shudder reverberated through the coach as the breaks began to slow the monstrous machine. Mòrag flinched at the suddenness of the change in motion: As did Rannoch who let out a low growl in response.

'You had best collect your things,' Randall said. 'We will be arriving shortly.'

Once the ramps were in place, Mòrag and Rannoch were first in line, eager to leave the unfamiliarity of the rickety enclosed space, for the comfortable openness of the outside world.

Once everything had been removed from the locomotive, Rozzen and Marcs saddled up their horses, and Randall saddled up Petorius while Mòrag sat atop Rannoch. Randall's own destrier was killed in action during the battle against Prince Edward so he had enlisted the services of Petorius for this voyage.

Mòrag watched as they fitted their saddlebags and mounted their steeds. She had never even considered using tack on the Nemeocorn and had always ridden him bareback. *I don't think he would accept a saddle and bridle anyway. It would restrict his movement too much.*

Although Rannoch appeared very similar to the destriers, his spine and other joints were infinitely more flexible allowing him to move smoothly over distance in the same manner as his equestrian acquaintances, but also allowed him to pounce and leap great heights from a standing start. He could also turn on a pinhead. Tack would never be an option for him.

It was early morning, the sky still pitch black save for its dotting of stars and the crescent moon. Their breath hung thick in the air, which nipped at any exposed skin it could find, reddening their cheeks.

Once the others were ready, they set off at a comfortable pace, allowing the horses to gradually warm and stretch their muscles. The squeak of the cold leather reminded Mòrag of learning to ride as a child. Jock would saddle up Petorius and have her sit like 'still water' in the saddle, while the horse performed all of the parade movements. It took years before Mòrag understood what sitting like 'still water' meant: For long enough, she had not even understood how water *could* be still, though she now found herself using the term whenever she was instructing Brax.

'You must sit quietly, calmly but you must be fluid and move with the horse at all times like "Still water." Water is strong, its movements flow effortlessly, but you must be strong enough to control the motion you possess, keeping your body quiet and where Shand in particular is concerned, you must keep your calm.' Unlike her, it had not taken him long to grasp the meaning within the words.

As they picked up the pace, thoughts of Brax flooded her mind. Since their night of great embarrassment, he had avoided her like the plague, and although at first, her desire to avoid him was just as strong; she now desperately missed his company.

'*If you want to see him, then go see him,*' Rannoch cast, '*The only thing stopping you is you.*'

'*That's easier said than done.*'

Rannoch didn't answer; he didn't need to. Mòrag knew he was right. The only thing stopping her going to see Brax was her embarrassment, and fear that he might want something more than she did.

'*He probably feels the same fear I do. It's silly really. I'll go see him when we get back.*'

'*Good.*'

By the time, they had ridden half the distance and stopped to give the horses a break, it was mid-afternoon. The sky had gained a thick cloud covering which hung low and heavy on the horizon. The West wind had shifted and was now blowing from the North, and becoming stronger. *We're going to get caught in a blizzard.*

Mòrag slid down from Rannoch's back and crouched next to Randall who was watching Rozzen fill a small cup with tea from a flask and grumble about the size of the portion.

'The weather's going to turn, we need to move on.' She said.

'Surely there is enough time to let the horses rest?'

'Not from the looks of it. Pasha and Frik can make the distance easily without a break, Petorius is old and decrepit so we may have to leave him behind,' she said glancing over her shoulder at the old horse.

He pawed the ground and snorted in response. '*Nonsense: Utter Nonsense!*'

'Ok, ok, you are both fitter and faster than Pasha and Frik,' she conceded in as posh a tone as she could muster, 'I do apologise most profusely!'

'Do they understand you?' Randall asked.

'Of course: You didn't think they *only* understood mental communication did you?'

Randall's blank expression told her enough.

'You need to learn a few things about *my* herd. Firstly, they understand *exactly* what you say to them whichever way you say it, and secondly they are ready to move *now* before we are caught in too heavy a snow. I don't fancy camping out do you?'

Randall shook his head at her. 'Ok, I take your point. I'll get everyone ready to move.'

They had been riding less than an hour when the thick flakes of snow began to flutter to the ground, creating a soft white carpet that covered everything in sight. The snow, falling soft and sparse creating a light dusting on the ground, rapidly developed into a full-blown blizzard. Gale force winds buffeted the freshly laid snow, into deep drifts lining the all but disappeared road.

The group slowed to a stop as visibility dwindled.

'We need to make camp!' Marcs called over the howling wind.

'*Mòrag, a Wrathwind like this will only get worse, we must press on.*' Petorius' concerned cast swirled within her mind.

The old horse had seen many of the wilds of the Albannach countryside, more than any other in the group and Mòrag trusted that if he said they shouldn't stop, then they shouldn't stop.

'No,' Mòrag called. 'We keep going!'

'Mòrag, we put our lives at too great a risk traveling in this,' Marcs asserted.

'*He is a fool, Mòrag we must continue.*' Petorius insisted.

'*Pasha, Frik?*' Mòrag cast to the other two horses.

Rozzen and Marcs straightened as they heard her voice through their link with their mounts. Showing equal surprise when both of their supposedly unquestioning steeds answered '*Aye,*' in hearty and enthusiastic Albannach accents. Up until that moment, both Generals had only experienced silent communication with their destriers, more similar to a wordless mutual understanding than actual messages.

'We keep going. I'm sorry, Sir, but...' she shrugged. *I am probably going to be seriously reprimanded for disobeying them but I'd rather be punished than dead. If Petorius says we mustn't stop, then we mustn't stop.*

The winter Wrathwind was a little known Albannach phenomenon: It had ability to not only strip your body of all warmth, but could also strip your mind of its senses, which was as deadly as the cold itself. It blew randomly over the years and had not shown its ugly face since the night Rannoch was born ten years previous.

The three Generals clung to their horses as they continued on their journey at a quicker pace than they were comfortable. They allowed their mounts to carry them along at whatever speed they decided was best, after it became clear that trying to slow them down was not an option.

Mòrag's eyes streamed and her hands burned from the cold, but she clung on to Rannoch's mane determined not to let go.

'*I know we can keep going, but can you?*' he cast; it was obvious that he was concerned, that Mòrag's perfect balance, was becoming increasingly unstable.

'*I hope so,*' she replied.

The blizzard intensified further the closer they came to Sruighlea. Morag could no longer see or hear any of the others. '*Let the horses take you home, stay alert, stay awake, and trust them,*' Mòrag cast wide. She knew her message would reach Randall though she was unsure if either Rozzen or Marcs would have picked it up. Her concentration dwindled as the frigid Wrathwind clawed at her consciousness. *Concentrate stay awake.*

'*Hold on,*' Rannoch cast, '*we're almost there.*'

Mòrag clung to him, every fibre of her wanted to let go and allow the blizzard to take her, but she hung on. The first she knew they were home was when the great doors of the main hall swung closed behind them.

Now out of the wind, the warm air seemed to blister her skin. She was utterly worn out: So worn out, that she could not even bring herself to release her grip of Rannoch's mane.

Glancing to the side she realised her fellow travellers were in the same boat. The horses were heaving their breath in and out of their lungs; thick, matted snow plastered their manes and the clothing of their riders.

Randall was the first to dismount. He placed a hand on Petorius' neck, 'Thank you,' he said, then led him around the hall on shaky legs. Rozzen and Marcs followed suit and walked their horses off to stop their legs from seizing up. No one spoke: No one had the energy to speak.

Rannoch lowered himself to the floor; the Nemeocorn was done in. Mòrag did not intend to remove herself from his back just yet. Summoning the last dregs of energy she had left, she cast to Randall. *'Tell the grooms they need to watch the horses all night, and make sure their drinking water is body temperature so they don't get a chill.'*

'Boy!' he called to the groom that had rushed in to help them. 'Wake the others. Three grooms on four hour shifts through the night to care for these horses.'

'Yes, Sir!' the boy called and scurried away to wake the other grooms.

Mòrag allowed her eyes to close and gave in to exhaustion.

When she opened her eyes again, she was in her own room. She still clung to Rannoch's back like a limpet; he lay, purring softly in front of the fireplace. A heavy woollen blanket had been thrown over them and the pre-lit fire was roaring; radiating it's warmth around the room.

Mòrag loosened her fingers from Rannoch's mane. They were stiff and sore from the clamp like grip she had maintained for too long. Pushing herself into a sitting position, she scanned the room. It was dark and empty save for Rannoch and herself.

A chill ran through her, she was still dressed in her snow-covered clothes, which were now soaked right through. Getting up, still wrapped in the heavy blanket, she stripped and changed as quick as her stiff aching muscles could manage.

Rannoch rolled onto his side. The exhausted Nemeocorn was practically snoring. Mòrag threw the woollen blanket over his back once more, he didn't really need it for warmth, but

Mòrag hoped it would wick some of the wet from him, allowing him to dry a little quicker.

Her door creaked as it was pushed open and Brax stepped into the room. From the look on his face, it was obvious that he had expected her to be asleep. He paused only a moment, before walking to her small table and placing a large, steaming bowl of soup, a small loaf and pot of tea on its surface.

'I thought you'd be hungry,' he said.

He can't even look at me.

Brax turned to leave; he was clearly still uncomfortable in her presence. She didn't want him to go: She didn't want to continue in this dance of embarrassment. She wanted her friend back.

She caught his arm as he walked past her, 'Share the soup with me.'

Every muscle in him was tense, 'I've eaten,' he said, still not meeting her gaze, 'you enjoy it.'

'Well. Sit with me then. Don't go running away because you are too embarrassed to look at me. It was my arse you got all excited over; you weren't the only one who was mortified!'

'I'm sorry.'

'What for? You didn't hurt me. Your reaction just knocked me off balance, and then I didn't know what to think,' she said. 'I couldn't ask you about it because I didn't even know how I felt. I still don't. I was woozy and honestly the thing I remember most was the look on your face.'

'It shouldn't have happened. I'm not, I can't.' He took a breath, 'I don't want something like this hanging between us. I don't want you thinking that I see you as an object.'

'Why would I think that?' Mòrag moved in front of him, 'Look at me at least.' Finally, his gaze met hers. 'I miss you. I don't care what happened on "the night of great embarrassment," I want my friend back.'

'I feel the same,' he said. 'I miss your company.'

Mòrag smiled and let out a sigh, 'I feel *so* much better now. Soup?'

'Sure.'

Chapter Forty-Two

DEATH WARMED UP

The snow that had started with the Wrathwind had continued to carpet the landscape for weeks. Everything in sight of the castle was sparkling white, save for the thoroughfares around the grounds and the causeways to the North and South. The Chluaidh-Dubh loch had partially frozen over, and vast expanses of water were now covered in snow-topped ice.

Mòrag sauntered the hill path behind Ava and her mother, who had come to visit her children for the mid-winter solstice celebrations, which would take place in a few days. It seemed all the Tyros had family visiting at this time of year, and she felt a pang of regret, that she could not spend the festivities with Jock and Evelynn. *This will be my first solstice on my own. I wonder how Brax feels about the celebrations.*

Mòrag smiled at Oliver. He was coping well today, spurred on by the presence of his mother. He was very quiet, keeping his concentration focused on movement rather than speech, or any other less useful function. He was now able to walk short distances using two sticks; today he was pushing his limits.

'Have a rest while they're chatting, you can walk more later,' Mòrag encouraged.

He looked up at her and nodded, golden curls dancing. Mòrag helped him settle into his chair and wheeled him along behind his family.

'What are you wearing, Mòrag?' Ava's mother asked.

'Me, Ma'am? Eh, my uniform.' Mòrag replied, confused.

The blonde woman shared a hearty laugh with her daughter, 'No silly!' she said. 'What are you wearing to the dance?'

'Dance, Ma'am?'

'There is always a dance for the solstice festivals; I thought you would have known that at your age.'

'Mòrag only joined us during the summer, Mama,' Ava explained.

'Oh! I'm terribly sorry. I assumed that because of your age that you had started around the same time as Ava, I did wonder why I had never noticed you before. That hair of yours stands out a mile.'

I'm not quite sure how to take that, 'Eh. Thank you, Ma'am.'

'She is very proper for an Albannach girl isn't she,' she said to her daughter. 'You speak very well. Although,' she said leaning closer, 'I am willing to bet that when you are in familiar company you speak as broad as my husband's ego.'

Oliver began to giggle.

'Yes, I thought as much. I do not know who comes out better there: You, or my husband. Now, what were you planning to wear?'

'I don't think I will be going, Ma'am.'

'Nonsense,' she said. 'The dances are a requirement. You must have a few frocks to choose from?'

'Eh, no, Ma'am.'

'Have you ever worn a dress, Mòrag?' Ava asked.

'No.'

'No?' Ava and her mother repeated, aghast.

Even Oliver was looking at her as if she had just slapped him in the face.

'What did I say?' Mòrag asked confused.

Ava's mother looked Mòrag up and down. 'Notepad, Ava!'

Ava pulled out a small leather bound notepad from the breast pocket of her coat and handed it to her mother along with a pencil. Her mother looked Mòrag up and down, scribbling as she went, 'Unfasten your coat dear,' she said. 'Don't worry, I won't bite! Come along, I don't have all day.'

Mòrag did as instructed. Ava's mother pulled a long tape from her own coat and reached round Mòrag's back, measuring her hips, waist and bust, causing Mòrag to blush.

'Ah, yes. It's as I thought.'

'These measurement's aren't right, Mama,' Ava said pointing to the last set she had taken, before leaning close to her mother and whispering in her ear.

'Does she really?' she said looking over at Mòrag, 'Have you tried to change her mind on the matter?'

'Frequently.'

'A different approach then.'

Ava followed her mother, who was practically skipping off in the direction of the barracks, leaving Oliver and Mòrag alone on the hill.

'Your-r in for it n-now,' Oliver smirked.

'I'm getting that feeling myself,' she said, turning his chair and pushing him back toward the main building.

This was the first days break from training since their week's rest after the Winter Tournament. They were permitted a week off, though Mòrag hadn't realised she would be required to take part in any festivities, *least of all a dance!*

After settling Oliver back in his room in the infirmary, she went in search of Brax. She planned to teach him the beginnings of the parade movements that were the foundation of the actions used in battle.

The stable block was dark when she arrived. All its residents called out to her as she flipped the lights on. *Where's Brax? He's never late.*

She took her time greeting each of the horses: Reaching Shand last, she gave him a scratch on his neck. *'Have I missed him?'*

'No, Màthair, I have not seen him today at all.'

That's not like him, 'I will go see if I can find him. I won't be long,' she said giving him another scratch and heading back to the West wing of the castle.

She found Brax's door locked but could hear movement from within the room, so she knocked and waited. When he opened the door, he looked terrible: Heavy black shadows hung beneath his half-shut eyes and his forehead was tense.

'Are you alright?' she asked. 'You look like death warmed up.'

'I feel like death warmed up,' he said in a small voice. 'My head's killing me, I can't even see straight. I was trying to sleep it off but it's worse when I lie down.' he pulled the door wider, 'come in.'

Mòrag walked into his room. In order to keep it as dark as possible he had hung the blanket from his bed over the top of the closed curtains. His fire remained unlit, creating a chill atmosphere that hung heavy in the air.

'You're a bit of a dafty sometimes, Bigyin, you know that?' she said, moving to light the fire. 'If you've got a head cold the last thing you should be doing is sitting in a freezing room.'

'It's too bright.'

'So don't look at it, Numpty heid!'

He gave her a disdainful look, but didn't say anything further, moving instead to sit at his table, flopping forward so his upper chest and forehead pressed against its surface.

Once the fire was lit, and she was happy that it was licking hungrily at the logs she had placed within the hearth, she rose and sat next to him on the table. He didn't look up at her. His shoulders were tense Sliding into the sensory plane; Mòrag noted that the scars and damaged areas that usually floated on the surface of his soul had convened around his head. *How odd. I wonder if I can re distribute his soul the same way I grasped Frank's.* The thought of his name made her shudder.

Her first instinct was to take hold of the damaged section, but when she moved to touch it, something within screamed at her to stop. Instead, she placed her hand at his shoulder. Exerting her will she pictured his soul like liquid, swirling and mixing, diluting the scars and dispersing the damaged material throughout.

She felt hot and sweaty from the effort but was glad to see his shoulders begin to relax. He breathed a long sigh of relief as the last of the congealed red-black marks dissipated.

'Better?'

'Much,' he said.

Now that he didn't have to deal with pain, exhaustion dragged at his eyes, and weighted his movements.

'When was the last time you had a full night's sleep?'

'Don't know,' he said.

'Ok,' she said jumping up, 'I think you should get some rest.'

'It's ok, because when you wash them they turn green, so you don't need to feed them to the horses.'

'Um... Aye... Bedtime for you, Bigyin.'

'I'm fine.'

'You're making no sense, bed.'

She helped him over to his bed, his weight heavy on her shoulders, stumbling as he walked across the room. She helped him onto the bed and before his head hit the pillow, he was already snoring. She lifted his legs onto the mattress and retrieved his blanket with some difficulties, from across the window. Draping it over him, she noted how relaxed his face had become. She smoothed back a few stray strands of hair that had fallen over his cheek, double-checked that the fire would burn for a good few hours, and made the return journey to the stable block.

Shand whinnied as soon as her hand touched the door. *'Sorry Shand. He's under the weather today. I'm afraid you will have to put up with me for mucking out and feeding. However will you cope?'*

The young horse snorted at her, *'I always enjoy your company, Màthair.'*

'It's just as well, isn't it?' Mòrag replied as she collected a wheelbarrow and some tools from the locker by the door.

Mucking out was hot work. By the time she was only a third of the way through, she was bathed in an itchy mixture of sweat and straw dust. Brax obviously liked Shand to have a bed twice as deep as the other horses had. *'You are well loved, boy, that's for sure.'*

Shand whinnied in response: It was obvious that the feeling was mutual.

Mòrag continued with her work; shaking out and moving the clean straw to one side, leaving the saturated straw and droppings to gather in a pile ready to be removed. By the time she had wheeled the last barrow full out to the midden, it was past suppertime. She fed the horses, tidied away the tools and made her way to the refectory.

The large dining hall was chock full of Tyros and their parents, all chatting amongst themselves. Collecting a tray Mòrag lifted two canteens of tea, and moved to the service window where the dirty dishes gathered.

'Aggie?' she called, hoping the cook would hear her.

'Och, Mòrag ma wee lamb! How're yi keeping?' Aggie replied

'No bad, no bad. You?'

'Weel, yon hip's been giving me gip but I'm braw none the less. Craving something mare tasty?'

'You read my mind.' Mòrag smiled.

'Just gi me two ticks,' Aggie said, scurrying away. She returned with a tray of wrapped parcels. 'Far yersel an thon lang haired laddie aye?'

'Aye.'

She pointed to each pair of parcels in turn, 'Kailkenny, clootie dumplings an some treacle toffee I made the morning.'

'You're an angel Aggie.' Mòrag exclaimed, taking the parcels and placing them on her tray.

'Mind and bide along the night afore eh dance. Ah cannae do extra on that day, but I'll have haggis neeps and tatties far you the night afore.'

'Aggie, I could kiss you.'

'Och away wi yi the noo!'

Mòrag had made her way back to Brax's room with her tray of parcels. Pushing the door open, she was pleased to see him still asleep. She placed the tray down on the table and stoked the dying fire.

'Brax. Brax, wake up.' Mòrag approached him, he looked so peaceful she was loathed to wake him, but he hadn't eaten all day so she placed a hand on his arm and rocked him gently, 'Brax?'

He woke with more of a start than she had expected, 'What happened?'

'You were sleeping.'

'Oh, right,' he obviously caught a whiff of the meal she had brought him and groaned. 'I think my stomach thinks my throat's been cut.'

'I thought as much,' she said. 'Dig in.'

Chapter Forty-Three

FOR KING AND COUNTRY

The pop and crack of wood in the hearth mingled with the muffled laughter coming from the bedroom. It was rare for Marcs to stay at the Sruighlea, but like the other Generals; he had allocated chambers none the less. The rooms were meticulously clean and tidy.

'I can't get over how big your rooms look.'

'They have far less in them than yours, Randall. Of course they look bigger.'

'Helena seems to be enjoying herself this year,' Randall said.

'She still has the odd day where she is inconsolable, but yes, she is doing much better. I think she is putting on a brave face for the other children, particularly Oliver. I honestly don't know how we would have coped if we had lost him too. I owe that young girl more than I can ever possibly give.' Marcs let out a breath, 'Will you join me for a drink?'

'No, Daniel, I had better not. You know how I get when I drink. Nothing good ever comes of it.'

Marcs grinned, 'That's not strictly true is it?'

'Does she know you know?' Randall groaned.

'Probably: Patricia seems to know everything about everyone. I wish I did. How is it going between you both?'

'I have absolutely no idea.'

'Ha!' Marcs chortled, 'trust Patricia to keep you guessing.'

'Indeed. Though, I can hardly blame her for being cautious.'

SO-CALLED-SHOES

Helena stormed into the room looking flustered, followed by Ava who looked like she would rather be anywhere else than here with her parents, interrupted their conversation.

'Daniel dear I have a conundrum of the highest order. I cannot find a single frock out of Ava's vast collection that can be altered to fit her little Albannach friend. Not one. Not one, Daniel. I am terribly vexed by the whole situation. Can you tell sweetheart? I am terribly vexed.'

Marcs gave Randall a harassed look, *'Not a word,'* he cast making it even harder for Randall to stifle the laughter that was welling up inside him.

'Is it really that important, Dear?' he asked, a hint of exasperation in his voice.

'Important, of course it is important, Daniel.'

'I get the impression Mòrag is not a dress and heels type,' Marcs sighed.

'Nonsense, Daniel,' Helena snapped, 'every girl wants to be a princess, at least for one night.'

Marcs and Randall exchanged a glance.

'Leave it with us, Helena,' Randall said. 'We know of some dresses that would suit. A wonderful seamstress such as yourself will have no problem altering one to fit.'

'Helpful and flattering as always, Randall,' she replied. 'Alright, I will leave it with you boys then. Do not let me down.'

'Of course not, Dear,' Marcs said to her back as she returned to the bedroom with Ava. 'So much for my night off,' he sighed, 'come on, before she boils us alive for not moving quick enough.'

Randall chuckled as he rose and left Marcs' chambers with his irritated friend. After the loss of his eldest son almost a year before, Marcs had been slowly scraping the fractured pieces of his life back together. The tragedy had hit the family hard, Helena worst of all; throwing her into the deepest pits of despair. Thomas' death was still largely unexplained, a supposed training accident, though Marcs was never convinced. They had been coping much better until the situation with Oliver arose, bringing the memories of Thomas'

281

loss flooding back. Once again, they were just about reaching an even keel.

Randall and Marcs made their way to the East wing. A heavy oak door, carved with two unicorns holding a shield, blocked their passage. Randall pulled an old key from his pocket and placed it in the lock, which gave a loud clank as it released its hold on the door.

'I have not stepped past this door in eight years,' he said.

'What made you seal it in the first place?' Marcs asked as he pushed the door inward. A rush of air flew past them as the corridor within seemed to suck in a breath, scattering the particles of dust that had lain dormant for almost a decade.

'These rooms belonged to Princess Catrìona before she was taken as a hostage. Though we reassigned uses for all the other rooms when we took this castle, I couldn't bring myself to take these from her. She had already been stripped of so much.'

'She was dead, Randall these rooms serve her no purpose.'

'Is that what you will tell Helena about Thomas' room in years to come?'

Marcs gave him a scalding look that softened as Randall spoke.

'I still dream of the night we found her body. I could not save that child. I was charged with her protection and I failed her. Some Royal guard I was. I could not save Catrìona; I could not save the King and Queen, or Prince John. All I could do was smuggle James away to be crowned in secret. Then I slaughtered half a nation for King and Country. I can never atone for that bloodshed. Had I done my job in the beginning, none of this would have happened.'

'You cannot be sure of that, Randall.'

'But I am. I collected her belongings from Windsor and brought them home for her. In any case, I have kept these rooms locked to preserve something of what should have been, and never will be.'

Marcs considered Randall's words, keeping silent as they walked along the passage to a room at the end. Randall placed his hand on the brass door knob, 'I think, when the time is right,

Mòrag should have access to these rooms. If for no other reason than to show her she has a heritage.'

'I agree,' Marcs replied. 'When the time is right.'

Turning the handle and pushing the door inwards Randall stepped to the side and ushered Marcs inside. 'In the wardrobe to the right, there should be several suitable dresses. I'll wait for you here.'

'Are you going to make *me* choose?'

Randall didn't reply; his heart was beating too fast; he stayed in the passage taking deep breaths. Memories of the night Catrìona died came flooding back to him, memories long since suppressed.

Randall followed Edward's search party led by Brax; the young boy was tired and reluctant to follow his master's command. He led the main body of the search party past through the thick mist, past and away from his mark's location.

Randall hung back. He still couldn't understand how he noticed that the boy had found her and continued past on, when Edward had not. When the others were out of sight, he trekked through the ferns and other thick Albannach foliage to find Catrìona lying in the hollow of a fallen tree, curtained by thick ivy. Her eyes widened when she realised he had found her.

His first reaction had been to call out to the others that he'd found her, but she leapt for him, knocking him from his feet to the forest floor.

She looked so sad; her pale skin had a deathly shade about it though her cheeks flushed pink. The tartan fabric surrounding her dress had a section ripped out of it. The inside of her legs were bathed in blood, as were her hands and she had a deep purple bruise on her temple.

'I must get you to a medic,' he told her, but she shook her head.

'I am well past the point of no return, Steele. I have been bleeding for hours now.'

'We have strong medics with us, they will save you.'

'Don't you understand, Steele? I won't go back. I do not want to be saved. I was hoping I would be long gone before he found me.'

'Before who found you, Princess? We are here to bring you home.'

She gave a short laugh, 'Windsor's nae my home and you know that fine well.'

'What happened to you?'

'He must never know. He must never find me, and he must never know she is his. Promise me, Steele. Promise me you will not let him find me,' her desperation strained her voice.

'Who, Princess?'

'Edward! He must not know she is his. He must never know she exists. Please, Steele, promise me.'

'A child?'

'You will find her with the MacDonald's,' she unfastened her necklace and handed it to him. 'When she comes to you give her this. The clans will know her by it. She will no doubt need their protection at some point.' She grimaced, gripping her abdomen tight.

It was then that Randall heard the commotion of the search party returning to the area.

Catrìona grabbed his blazer, 'I need you to help me leave this world, Steele.'

'I cannot do that, Princess. I am sworn to protect you.'

'You failed in your duty, Steele. You failed to protect me from him. Don't you understand? If I am found, they will know that I had a child, and he will know she is his. How could she not be, I have been touched by no other man. Crossing the bloodlines is forbidden. To hide his secret he will hunt her down. I will not let that happen. Please, Steele. Please help me.'

'Princess, I can't.'

'Do this and all is forgiven. My life, to protect my daughter's life: It is a fair trade. Will you help me? Will you swear to protect my daughter as you should have protected me?'

The memory tore at his heart as he recalled how easily his knife had bitten into her. She had given no resistance and she did not cry out. Her last act was to raise her hands to his face and say something in her native language, the language her Sasannach rulers had forbidden. Her sweet voice locked the memory of the event away in his mind safe from prying eyes until her daughter had need of him.

Randall had to fight hard to stop the tears from welling in his eyes. Not only had he not protected Catrìona, she had died by his hand. *I will not allow her daughter the same fate. I will protect her with my life.*

'Alright, Randall I think I've found one,' Marcs called from within the room. He gasped, 'Look at this, Randall. I have never seen anything like it.'

Randall stepped into the room, Marcs was pointing to a necklace that lay on a red velvet cloth on the dresser. It was fine silver, elaborately looped and knotted in the Albannach fashion. Delicate thistles and unicorn horn patterns could be seen weaved within the metal loops that formed ornate points around the necklaces circumference. It was the necklace Catrìona had handed him the day she died.

Randall crossed the room and lifted it gently, 'Yes,' he said. 'I think it is about time she had this.'

Chapter Forty-Four

SO-CALLED-SHOES

'A bit more direction; sit tall; that's it. Weight to the back, hands light: Now ask him for impulsion. Yes! That's it. Good... Ok, let Shand stretch a bit and then we'll do it once more,' Mòrag called.

'They appear to be improving quickly,' Rozzen noted behind her.

'Are you spying on our training session, Ma'am?'

'Please, Mòrag give me some credit, I was passing when I heard your dulcet tones. So I thought I would see what you were up to.'

'I see, just messing about really. I know he isn't really supposed to learn the passage till spring, but they did it by accident so I'm pushing them a touch.'

Shand began to leap about, tossing his head and pounding the ground with his hooves. The young horse leapt into a gallop straight across the arena towards Mòrag. He skidded to a halt in front of her, ducking his head and throwing Brax several feet in the air. He landed with a thud beside Rozzen. Shand snorted and pawed the ground.

'Brax are you ok?'

He didn't answer; he was too busy clutching his head. Shand continued to snort and roar until Mòrag forcibly released his mental link with Brax. She gave him a rub and handed Rozzen the reins.

'Your head again?'

Brax nodded. 'It's worse this time,' he said in a hoarse voice. 'Maybe I was concentrating too hard.'

'Maybe,' Mòrag said, placing her hand at his shoulder and redistributing the throbbing darkness around his head once more.

'Has this happened before?' Rozzen asked.

'A few times aye, he seems to be suffering headaches a lot recently.'

Brax let out a sigh of release as the last of the dark patches dissipated. 'I don't know how you do that, but it's better than any healing technique I know. You can get the pain to die back to a dull ache. I'm done in,' he puffed. 'Did I hurt Shand?'

'No. You didn't hurt him, though I do think he felt your pain and panicked.'

Rozzen looked him up and down. 'Brax, I want you seen by the medics. These headaches have come on too suddenly for my liking.'

Brax said nothing.

'Need a hand up?' Mòrag said, offering him her arm.

Brax nodded and took her hand. He gripped her shoulders tight in a bid to keep his balance, making her grimace.

'You, medics, now,' Rozzen said. 'Go with him, Mòrag. Make sure he doesn't get lost on his way. I will organise a groom for the destrier.'

'Yes, Ma'am,' Mòrag said leading Brax away.

His movements were uncoordinated and heavy; he stumbled repeatedly as they walked the short distance to the infirmary. By the time they reached the double doors, Brax wasn't the only one who was out of puff. He let the wall take his weight and lifted his arm from Mòrag.

'I just need a minute,' she puffed. 'How's your head?'

'Getting worse again, I just need my bed.'

'Aye, but you'll no sleep. Rozzen's right, you need to know nothing else is causing this.'

'I don't want them poking about in my head,' he said in weak protest. 'If I wasn't so dizzy I would leave on my own.'

Mòrag considered the situation. Brax had no love for medics, which had been plain to see since the first day she met him. He would rather deal with the pain on his own than see a medic, though he had let Ava help him before. As she was thinking, Brax grimaced and gripped his head. A thin stream of red ran from his nose and dripped to the floor. *Decision made. I'm not letting you out of it this time.* Mòrag pushed one of the doors open and seeing a medic in the corridor called for her help. When she turned back to Brax, he had slid to the floor. The medic came running with a chair and they both helped Brax onto it.

He was wheeled to one of the communal rooms full of curtains on runners to give any residents privacy during examinations or when sleeping. Mòrag was relieved that this room was empty; the tyros here were cruel whether they were sick, injured or well and she didn't want Brax to have to deal with snide remarks when he was feeling so low.

The medic handed Brax some tissues for his nose and left to call her superior to assess him. Mòrag sat on the bed next to him, 'How's the pain?'

'Painful.'

'Oh, haha! It can't be that bad if you're making jokes.'

'It's bad enough,' he made a face.

'Taste the blood?'

He nodded.

'No wonder. You're leaning back.' Mòrag hopped from the bed and helped him straighten up in the seat, 'Tip forward, chin more toward your chest. It should run away from your throat now.' She ran her hand over his forehead and smoothed back his hair, his skin was feverish to touch.

'What has been going on here then,' Major Darrow asked as he appeared from the corridor. He was a tall man with short, silvered hair and friendly brown eyes. He strode confidently toward Brax and crouched down to his level. 'How long have you had these symptoms?'

'Today or in general?'

'Today.'

'About an hour, maybe more.'

'His nose only started bleeding when we got here, Sir,' Mòrag added.

The Major nodded to himself and pulled the stethoscope from around his neck. He listened to Brax's heart and lungs; he then wrapped a cuff round his arm to check his blood pressure. 'How often do you have these headaches?'

'Every day, for the last couple of months,' Brax admitted.

Mòrag practically growled at him prompting him to add that the pain had only gotten this bad in the last two weeks.

'And how much sleep are you getting?'

'Next to none.'

Darrow removed the cuff from Brax's arm and checked his nose. 'It seems the flow has stopped. My honest opinion is that lack of sleep is the most likely culprit.'

'That's it?' Brax asked astonished.

'That's it. Before I do any other in depth tests, you should try to get more rest. If that alleviates the problem then you have your answer. I'm going to give you a kick start,' he said rising and unlocking a cabinet at the far side of the room. He reached in and pulled out two small bottles. Into them, he placed a selection of tablets from larger bottles within the cabinet, before locking it once more. 'Take two of these,' he said holding up one of the bottles, 'on an empty stomach before bed. There is enough here for three days, then I want you to come back and see me. I want you to take this one when you get back to your room,' he said holding up the other bottle, which had only one tablet inside. 'It will help you to relax for the rest of today.'

'Thank you, Sir.'

'Help him back to his room would you, Mòrag?'

'Of course, Sir,' she said, taking the bottles and placing them in her pocket. She helped Brax steady himself and they made their way back to his room. He was a little more coordinated on this journey, making it far easier on Mòrag's now very tired shoulders.

'I can manage fine myself from here.'

'Sure you can,' Mòrag retorted, pushing his door open and ushering him inside. 'I think you should lie down for a while. I'll get the fire going, its chilly baltic in here.'

She settled him onto his bed and set about lighting his fire. Brax remained quiet while Mòrag worked. When she was done, and the fire was hungrily devouring the logs, hissing and popping like hot corn and emitting a powerful woody aroma, she moved to sit beside Brax. A knock at the door stopped her half way across the room. 'Expecting anyone?'

'No.'

Mòrag opened the door to find Randall stood in the hallway. 'By the look on your face you weren't expecting to see me were you?'

He composed himself quickly, 'I came looking for Brax; Rozzen mentioned he was under the weather.'

'Nothing I can't handle old man,' Brax called across the room.

'Hmmm. I came to tell you, that if you were feeling poorly you could give the dance a miss.'

'Both of us or just him?' Mòrag asked, hope building.

'Just Brax. Your attendance is required.'

Mòrag pulled a disdainful face, 'Do I *have* to? Ava and her mum are plotting my demise I'm sure of it.'

'Yes I heard they were intent on frills and heels,' Randall chuckled.

'No way! Not doing it. If *he* isn't going, then *I'm* not going.'

'Well that's not a very polite way to ask me to take you to the dance now is it?' Brax said.

Mòrag looked at him in surprise before noting his silly grin and glaikit expression. *He's practically half cut. He must have taken that medication as soon as we got back.*

Randall looked back and forth between them, 'So you *are* going?' he asked Brax.

'Yup,' he said with a chuckle and a wicked glint in his semi-glazed eyes, 'I want to see her squirm because she's being forced to wear a dress.'

'Oi, Traitor! That's not fair!' Mòrag protested which only made Brax chuckle even more.

'Is he alright?' Randall asked her.

'He was given something by Major Darrow, to... relax him.'

'Ah, I see. Well I will leave you to it; I have a few things to attend to.' He turned and left the room.

'You!' Mòrag seethed, but Brax had already dozed off. She let out an exasperated sigh, covered him with his blanket and left the room.

With nothing to do and most of the day to fill, she wandered aimlessly throughout the passageways of the castle. Every now and then, she would pass other Tyros walking with their parents, talking about how they had progressed and which training paths they were interested in.

Passing through main door, Mòrag made her way to the barracks to see if she could find Lennox. Since the tournament, she had been spending time with him. Mostly they walked while she talked and he nodded along with the conversation. The last time she'd seen him, almost a week before; she had attempted once again to make contact with his mind, and discovered his image behind the window. It had remained locked but he had acknowledged her presence, which was a huge leap forward.

As she reached the barrack door, she felt a familiar presence approaching from behind her.

'I've been looking for you *everywhere!*' Ava exclaimed.

'You obviously didn't look very hard then,' Mòrag replied smiling.

'Can you come to my father's rooms? Mama wants to check something.'

'This isn't to do with a dress is it, Ava, I'd rather not,' Mòrag protested, though she knew her efforts were futile.

'Oh please,' she pleaded.

'Lead the way,' Mòrag said exasperated.

Ava led her to her father's chambers in the lower North wing of the castle. Mòrag felt uncomfortable and out of place in the lavish surroundings. There were carvings all around the roof, where the ceiling met the walls. Albannach knots and long since faded golden prancing unicorns, interspersed with foliage and thistles. Even the furniture was ornately carved in Albannach patterns. She stepped toward the fireplace and ran her fingers across its smooth surface. Two rearing unicorns adorned the sides of the mantle, the real horns of their once living brethren set into the stone glinted in the light from the large window across the room.

'Welcome, Mòrag, welcome,' Ava's mother said shepherding her towards the sofa.

'It's nice to meet you again, Ma'am,' Mòrag said.

'Call me Helena, please dear, I am not fond of being referred to as Ma'am.' Her deep brown eyes were smiling, and slightly glazed, matching her daughter's.

'Sorry, Ma'am — Helena,' Mòrag corrected herself.

'Would you like some tea? Or perhaps some wine?'

'No thank you.'

'Try the wine,' Ava said dropping onto the sofa beside her, 'it's divine.'

Mòrag looked from Ava to her Mother and back again, *I wonder how long they have been drinking already,* 'Do I have to?'

Ava giggled. 'If you don't want me to pester you all night, then yes.'

'Alright,' she sighed, 'just a little.'

Ava chatted excitedly about the dance while her mother collected three enormous brandy glasses, and filled them to the brim with crimson wine. She handed a glass to Ava and one to Mòrag.

The fine crystal of the glass in Mòrag's hand sparkled brightly, its rich crimson contents smelled deeply fruity. Taking a small mouthful Mòrag grimaced as she swallowed the liquor down. Though it smelled fruity, it had a more metallic taste.

'Have you tried wine before?' Helena asked.

Ava grinned at her, 'I'm betting no.'

'Sip it slowly, the taste will change.'

Helena leapt back into her in-depth tale about the jewellery she had chosen to match her dress. Mòrag sat quiet, sipping away at the fishbowl of red liquor in her hand. By the time she had sipped half of the glassful, Ava and her mother were filling their second. Mòrag allowed herself to sink into the sofa, the soft leather hot at her back. The metallic tang of the wine had indeed lessened the more she drank, until the rich fruity flavour enveloped her senses, sending a lightness throughout her body and warmth across her cheeks.

In contrast to how light and floaty the rest of her body felt, her head felt heavier. It was an odd sensation. Mòrag rested it back on the sofa to compensate and continued to sip from her glass, no longer cautious; she now desired the sweet intoxicating flavour to pass her lips.

'What do you think, Mòrag?' Helena asked.

'Eh?' Mòrag blinked at her, she had been completely unaware that the woman had been talking to her.

'Did you hear anything I just said?'

'Nope,' she shook her head in an over exaggerated movement and felt an irresistible urge to giggle.

Ava grinned, 'Mòrag, I wanted to show you some shoes. They are really pretty.'

'I have shoes,' Mòrag said lifting her foot. 'See, pretty black ones!' she exclaimed causing an eruption of laughter from Ava and her mother.

'I think that is quite enough wine for you, my dear,' Helena said reaching out for Mòrag's glass.

Mòrag tossed the remaining half glass of the wine back and grinned stupidly at the woman, as she handed her the now empty glass.

'Mòrag, you are terrible.' Ava announced.

'*You* gave it to me. Don't complain. What like are these shoes then?'

Ava and Helena placed their glasses down and led Mòrag to the bedroom. An enormous mahogany four-poster bed dominated the room. Like the reception room, this room was also laden with carvings and other Albannach decoration, though Mòrag no longer cared enough to examine them. Along the wall was an ornate wardrobe, on which hung three gowns each covered in a satin sheet, to protect the material inside from dust: Below sat three sets of overly fancy looking shoes. *I don't know how they can call those shoes; they are no more than a leather sole with a needle to balance on, held on by some sparkly laces. Not what I'd call a shoe.*

Helena lifted the pair of 'shoes' from beneath the furthest away gown, and presented them to Mòrag.

'Aren't they perfect?' Ava asked excited.

Mòrag looked at the crystal-encrusted loops of leather in Helena's hands, 'They're something alright. What do you want me to do with them like?'

'Wear them silly!' Ava exclaimed.

'Nae chance!'

Helena began to chuckle, 'Oh Mòrag, you are so funny. Come now,' she said directing her to the chair by the window, 'sit here and we will see how these fit you.'

Mòrag allowed herself to be manhandled into the 'so-called-shoes.' Looking down at them it struck her how odd they looked with her uniform trousers. She began to giggle, and then she began to laugh, 'I don't think they go with my uniform!' she howled.

Still laughing, Ava urged her to try walking in them. Pushing herself to her feet she felt unnaturally high up, her legs contained an internal tremor that threatened to become worse with movement. *I challenge you to a duel legs! If I can walk the length of this room, I get a prize, and if I fall, you get a prize... deal?* Naturally, her legs gave no answer.

'Try walking dear,' Helena said. 'Shoulders back carry yourself tall and graceful: Watch Ava.'

Ava had attached her own set of skewers to her feet and was mincing across the room in a fashion that reminded Mòrag of a hen trying to impress her flock. The thought of the prominent breast of the bird and its tail feathers waggling back and forth was too much for Mòrag to bear, and again she giggled uncontrollably.

'Right,' she said, barely composing herself and taking a wobbly step, 'walk like a chook.' She had hardly taken three steps when her ankle buckled and she toppled to the floor in a wriggling, giggling heap.

'Perhaps we have been a touch ambitious with the heels,' Helena said helping Mòrag to her feet. 'Try again love.'

Mòrag yelped when she put weight on her right foot and her ankle protested with a searing, gripping pain, 'I'm done.' She pulled the straps over her heel, ankle still throbbing, and slipped the 'shoes' from her feet, then hobbled over to the chair.

'Sorry Mòrag,' Ava said. 'I thought you might take to them a little easier. Does it hurt much?'

'Aye... much.'

'More wine!' Helena announced, as she retrieved the bottle and glasses.

Eventually, Mòrag didn't care much about her twisted ankle, she laughed and joked and sang with Ava and Helena atop the lavishly soft bed, until sleep claimed her.

Chapter Forty-Five

PRINCESS OF ALBA

The light that shone through the undrawn curtains was far too bright and forced Mòrag to shadow her eyes with her hand. She groaned as she sat up, her throat blazed and her skull throbbed savagely. Ava and Helena lay sprawled across the bed next to her drooling and snoring. *Now, that's not a sight I thought I'd be waking up to.*

Tentatively she rested her feet on the floor, pain flared in here ankle almost instantly which was echoed by the aching in her head. Holding onto one of the bedposts, she pulled herself up to standing and allowed her centre of gravity to regain its rightful place, before hobbling stiffly out of the room in search of water.

The reception room was quiet and dark. Only glowing embers remained of the once roaring fire. Mòrag limped across the room and threw a few logs into the hearth.

'Enjoy yourself last night?' came a voice from the darkness behind her.

Mòrag spun round, placed too much weight on her tender ankle and crumpled to the floor with a thump. When General Marcs flipped on the light, it almost blinded her.

'You look a state,' he said.

'My throat's as dry as a badger's arse,' she replied without thinking. 'Eh, I mean. What I meant was –'

'What you *meant* was exactly what you said,' he said with amusement on his face.

'I'm sorry, Sir, it was rude of me.'

'Calm down, Mòrag. You do not need to be so formal here. You are not formal with General Steele. In fact you are so comfortable around him you call him by his first name.'

Mòrag could feel her cheeks begin to warm. She had never thought about how she referred to Randall, and he had never corrected her, so referring to him as Randall, had become habit.

'It is perhaps something to do with your lineage. Royal blood is Royal blood, and we instinctively respond to it as such.'

'I'm not who General Rozzen seems to think I am.'

'No? I beg to differ. If you require proof, you need only look to our journey back from Dùn Èideann. You naturally took charge without a second thought, and we; three Generals of the *King's* army followed *your* command over our own. That would not have happened had you been anything other than Royalty.'

'Blood is blood, it doesn't make a person. Whether I have Royal blood or not makes no difference. I'm still just Mòrag, and always will be. And I'm more than happy with that.'

'As you wish,' he said. 'I will let the matter rest.'

He is saying that as if I 'commanded' him to stop talking about it. Mòrag pushed herself to her feet and limped to a chair to put on her boots. She fastened the laces of her boot much tighter over her tender ankle; the strong leather stopped just below her knees and once laced up tight, supported her ankle well.

'Escaping before they wake?' Marcs asked.

'I have intruded too long. I'm sorry we kept you from your bed. Please tell them I enjoyed myself.'

'I will,' he said. 'Can you manage on your own?'

Mòrag moved to the door, 'I think so. Thank you for your hospitality, Sir,' she said, and then left the room.

With her boot laced and secured, she felt only mild discomfort as she moved through the passageways. Her head still carried an intense ache and her stomach growled at her so she headed toward the refectory. After a quick chat with Aggie, and an apology for not turning up for her haggis, Mòrag left for her room with a flask of tea and some wrapped up haggis rolls for her and Brax. Stopping by his room, she noted the door was ajar. She pushed the door open and gasped at the devastation she found.

Clothing and bed sheets were strewn about, his mattress was dipped in the middle where the timber had given way and snapped, and his pillow was covered in dried blood. Mòrag dropped the flask and parcel of rolls, and spun round into Brax's chest.

'Good morning,' he said cheerily.

'Good morning, good morning? How can you say good morning when your room's like this? What the hell happened?' she groaned as her alcohol abused brain recoiled from her outburst.

'I don't have a clue what happened. I woke up to it like this. Maybe I went walkabout in my sleep, who knows. I must have had a nosebleed at some point, but quite honestly, I don't care. I had the best night's sleep I've had in years,' he grinned. 'Oh. I didn't realise I'd cracked the bed. I must have been bouncing off the walls. By the way,' he added, 'why do you smell like a brewery?'

Mòrag groaned once more. 'I got collared by Ava and her mum. There may have been sparkly shoes? I *know* there was wine. I have brain ache and no amount of healing energy seems to be helping.'

Brax chuckled at her, 'Self-inflicted, you're getting no sympathy from me.'

'Fine,' she snapped, 'then I'll just keep your haggis roll for myself.'

'You wouldn't dare.'

'Try me,' she challenged, lifting the parcel of rolls and hiding it behind her back.' Though her head ached, she still felt a little giddy and was fully prepared to run off with his breakfast should he be game to chase her. *I'm such a bairn.*

Before she could run he grabbed her and pulled her close so her chest was against his and her hands, hidden behind her back, were in easy reach. He used one hand to hold her and the other to snatch the parcel from her grasp.

'No fair,' she protested, 'you're bigger than me.' She moaned, 'I have such a headache.'

'Excuses, excuses.' He grinned and held the prize far out of her reach.

'Urgh, gonnae no, I feel rotten,' she said leaning her head against his chest. His skin was cool against her aching forehead, *soft skin*. Then it occurred to her that his chest was bare. She felt mercilessly close to him, so close she was afraid he might hear her heart hammering in her chest. *Why do I feel so nervous around him sometimes and not others? Maybe it's the wine.* 'You've put on a lot of weight,' she said. When she looked up at him and saw his expression she took a step backward, hurriedly adding, 'What I *mean* is you're looking really healthy.'

'What did you expect when you've been forcing me to eat and train with you?'

'You weren't eating enough.'

'I had no appetite before.'

'Before what?'

'Before you,' he said, and then stiffened.

Ok, now it's getting awkward.

They gazed at each other for only a moment before Brax unwrapped the rolls and handed her one. He stooped to retrieve the flask and handed it to her, 'I think we had best eat in your room, there's not really anywhere to sit in here. You go ahead; I'm just going to throw a shirt on.'

Mòrag nodded and made her way out of the room, she let out a sigh of mild disappointment as she unlocked her door and stepped into her room. *I wouldn't mind if he stayed bare chested... What the hell is wrong with me?*

As the day progressed Mòrag's brain ache diminished, much to her relief. She and Brax had spent the morning attempting to reorganise his obliterated room and were now attempting to mend his ruined bedframe.

'Couldn't we just pinch a bed from somewhere else? It's not like anyone would notice, all these rooms and only you and I share the space.'

'I wouldn't feel right just taking one.'

'Well you can't sleep on this. I say we "borrow" one and then tell Randall tomorrow that yours broke. It can always go back you know. Or, we can go ask him for one now.'

Reluctantly Brax agreed and they left the room in search of Randall. They traipsed across the castle to his office, which was locked and silent. They did not find him in the refectory either, so traipsed to his chambers. They knocked on his door, but no answer came.

'Where is he?' Mòrag mused, 'I suppose I could just ask him couldn't I?'

'Why didn't you think of that before?' Brax asked.

'Because people keep telling me not to rely on my mind, so I'm trying not to.'

'That's true. Ok, I'll let you away with it.'

Mòrag held Brax in a mock glare and then felt for her connection with Randall. Usually when she tried to contact him, his attention was peaked instantly, today however she found his mind distracted and unwilling to tear itself from its current focus. *What are you doing?*

Mòrag's thought drew her to his mind, showing her the object of his current obsession: Dark skin, soft as silk, his fingers running lightly across its surface: The intertwined warmth of two bodies that wanted to be one: The touch of her lips. *I don't want to see this. I don't want to see this!*

Her vision snapped back to Brax who was looking at her more than a little confused. 'Eh. He's busy, let's go.'

'Busy? What's he doing?'

'Rozzen,' was all she could reply as she pulled him away from Randall's chambers and fled down the corridor.

When they reached the main door, they stopped running to catch their breath. Brax laughed openly at the shocked and embarrassed expression that dressed Mòrag's face. 'I thought they were done for good,' he gasped. 'He's really changed since you appeared.'

'What's it got to do with me? It had better not be anything to do with me.'

'I don't know,' he said. 'People just seem to show their true colours around you.'

'There you are, Mòrag. We have been looking all over for you.' Ava called from behind her. The cheerful girl bounced toward her, soft golden curls dancing around her shoulders.

'If you are here to initiate round two count me out. No more wine for me.'

Ava laughed in a musical tone, 'You are such a lightweight, Mòrag. I came to help you get ready; Mama says she wants to help you into your dress.'

Mòrag gave Brax a pleading look, *'Say something to save me please,'* she cast.

'Not a chance,' He replied, *'I already told you. If you're being forced to wear a dress, I want to see you squirm.'*

'I'm going to make you pay!'

'I look forward to it.'

'Do I have to, Ava? I'm not really a "dressing up" kind of girl.'

'Yes,' General Marcs said appearing behind her, 'you have to.'

'I need to go have a shower; I'll see you after that.'

'I thought you'd say that,' Ava said grinning, 'Mama says you've to use her bath; so you don't run away.'

Mòrag gave Brax a disdainful look as Ava grabbed her hand and led her away. Marcs had stayed behind to talk to him, obviously intending to leave Mòrag once again at Ava and Helena's mercy.

Mòrag was ushered into the bathroom as soon as she reached General Marcs' chambers. The immaculate tiled room was spacious and bright, the polar opposite of the Tyros washing facilities. It didn't fit the theme of the rest of the apartment, but Mòrag didn't care too much. The soft calming aroma from the bathtub at the centre of the room drew her attention. Helena had already drawn the steaming hot water and saturated it with lavender scented foam. The freestanding tub had a rolled top decorated in Sasannach roses painted along its circumference. It rested upon four gilded feet shaped like lions paws.

'Alright dear, let's get you out of these clothes,' Helena said turning her to begin unbuttoning her shirt.

Mòrag recoiled, 'I'd rather be alone, if that's alright.'

'We are all the same, Dear, no need to be shy,' Helena said.

'Helena, let the poor girl be,' Marcs called from the main room, much to Mòrag's relief. 'I am sure you pestered her enough last night.'

Helena let out an exasperated sigh in response to her husband. 'There are plenty of products on that shelf there, use whatever you need. Once you are ready, Mòrag, join us in the bedroom,' she smiled, and left the room.

Mòrag stripped and bathed, spending more time than she perhaps should have, deep in the hot, scented water. When eventually she peeled herself from the bath, and dried herself, she found to her embarrassment that her clothing was missing, in its place lay a neatly folded, silken, silver dressing gown. Wrapping her hair up in a towel, she slipped the delicate silver material over her shoulders and tied the sash around her waist.

Heading for the door, she examined her reflection in the long, partially misted mirror: The dressing gown left very little to the imagination. Mòrag opened the door a crack and was relieved to see that the room was empty. As quick as she could, she made a beeline for the bedroom.

The room was dim, lit by small lamps at either side of the bed where Ava was sat. She was wearing only a lace brassiere and matching lace pants, rolling a sheer stocking up her leg. Mòrag felt deeply uncomfortable, she backed away to the seat in the corner and hoped no one would notice her there.

'Finally, Mòrag,' Helena called from across the room, 'I thought you were going to be in there all night.'

'My clothes were moved.'

'Well of course dear, I couldn't have you putting that dirty uniform back on now could I?'

'I suppose not.'

'They are over there on the dresser. Now come here and we will get you into this dress.'

Mòrag hobbled across the room, her ankle throbbing again. Now that the heat from the bath had dissipated, it had begun to stiffen once more. Helena handed her a fancy pair of black pants and nude stockings. The material was soft and trimmed in lace. Mòrag was relieved to see they were not as close cut as the ones Ava was sporting, though they covered far less than anything she had worn before.

'I'm glad you didn't hand me a pair of those,' she said gesturing to Ava.

'I didn't think you would be keen on Frangach knickers so I settled for these. They should be comfortable yet enticing.'

'Enticing? Who do you think's going to be seeing them like?'

'Well, you never know do you?'

'Are all Sasannachs sex mad, or is it just the people in Sruighlea?'

'We just don't let sex get in the way of what's important dear. We all crave a bit of skin at some point or other. There is nothing wrong with that. Now be a good girl and put your pants and stockings on.'

'You have been living a sheltered life, Mòrag,' Ava said. She was now sliding into her dress. She unclipped and discarded her brassiere, once the gown was high enough to cover her bust. The dusky pink, silky satin fabric hugged her body close draping elegantly to the floor. It was simple yet effective, accenting each curve of her body, and to Mòrag's surprise, left her back uncovered. Ava slipped the strap over her head and arranged herself within it. 'Well?' she asked twirling.

'You look absolutely ravishing dear.'

'You look bonnie,' Mòrag said, 'really bonnie.'

Ava beamed and pranced over to her, 'Your turn,' she sang, pulling at Mòrag's dressing gown.

Mòrag's stomach clenched. She was confident in most situations, to the point that at times, she could be over confident; but not when it came to her body. She had spent so many years hiding herself that 'dressing to impress' was a totally alien concept.

Helena removed the gown from its hanger and held it for Mòrag to step into. It looked a lot of material all gathered at her feet and Mòrag wondered fleetingly if it would be heavy to wear.

Stepping into the ring of fabric, Mòrag stood as Ava and Helena lifted the bodice up around her.

Ava held a towel to Mòrag's front, 'To protect your dignity,' she smirked as her mother removed Mòrag's dressing gown. 'Clip the fastenings at the front together and make sure your breasts are comfortably positioned. Then hold it tight to your chest.'

Mòrag did as instructed and Ava removed the towel. The bodice felt soft beneath her fingers. It began to constrict as Helena tightened the laces running down the back. After ten minutes or so, Mòrag no longer had to hold the dress to her, it hugged her on its own.

'Breathe in dear and hold it would you?'

Mòrag did as instructed and Helena tugged the bodice down half an inch, then instructed her to breathe as normal again.

'That's better. You had it a little high at the front.'

'I feel like I'm going to fall out of it,' Mòrag protested.

'Oh you won't fall out,' Helena said. 'Not when I have finished tightening it you won't.' A further twenty minutes of cord pulling ensued before Helena announced that she was finished.

Mòrag felt surprisingly comfortable. The bottle green velvet draped softly around her feet, the bodice hugged her gently. Running her fingers over the soft fabric, she found detailed embroidery that enticed her fingers to discover each pattern and shape the thread depicted.

Ava took her hand and led her to the mirror. Before her stood a beautiful young woman, clad in a velvet gown of bottle green. The embroidery that had enticed her fingers looped and danced across the bodice in the form of intricate thistles: The ornate stitching glinting in the lamp light.

'Now you *really* look like a princess,' Randall said from the doorway. He, Marcs and Rozzen stood smirking at her.

'No men allowed while the girls are dressing,' Helena commanded.

'Now, now dear,' Marcs said taking his wife's hand and leading her from the room, 'they look about ready to me.'

'Ava, do you mind if I have a word with Mòrag alone please?' Randall asked.

'Of course, Sir,' Ava replied leaving the room and closing the door behind her.

Mòrag's cheeks flushed as she remembered the vision she had gleaned from him earlier, but she decided to talk to him about it at some other time. She limped across to her pile of clothes, and retrieved a long red tartan ribbon from her pocket. Moving back to the mirror she began twisting the majority of her hair loosely up around her head, intertwining the ribbon and tying it to hold the tresses in place, though she allowed some to hang loosely around her shoulders. Satisfied she turned to regard Randall.

'You look just like your mother. You even dress your hair in the same way.'

Mòrag didn't know what to say. Half of her wanted to believe what the Generals had told her, and the other half didn't want to acknowledge it.

'There are a lot of questions you will want to ask, I promise you I will answer them as fully as I can, in time. For now though I have something for you.' He stepped forward and presented a velvet pouch.

Mòrag looked up at him questioningly.

'Your mother asked me to give you this,' he said pulling the silver necklace from the fabric. He moved behind her, placing it around her neck and fastening the catch. 'I want you to keep this with you at all times. If you cannot wear it, conceal it on your person. It is your gateway to safety should you ever need it.'

'It's beautiful, but how can you know it was meant for me?'

'I will explain in time,' he said, 'there are many things that are only now coming back to me. I promised her as she breathed her last breath that I would give my life to protect you. Had I only realised what was in front of me sooner you would not have had to suffer such ills. For this I can only apologise.' He drew his sword and knelt before her, holding the naked steel up to her on the palms of his hands. 'My life is yours. On my sword and my honour I give them willingly to keep you from harm, Princess of Alba.'

Chapter Forty-Six

SOON...

Garland and ribbon dressed the castle's entrance hall. Tiny lanterns hung from the balustrade and around the walls. In the centre of the hall an enormous conifer stood, decorated with ribbon and twinkling lights. The space was buzzing with families, friends and couples, meeting and leaving for the hall next to the parade ground where the dance was being held.

Brax had made his way towards the entrance hall early, and had stood behind the balustrade for a good twenty minutes or more, scanning the crowd of people below for any sign of Mòrag.

'What are you looking for?'

Brax practically jumped out of his skin, letting out a loud yelp. He spun to face the owner of the voice, and met the most beautiful sight his eyes had ever seen.

Flaming locks of auburn hair hung about her shoulders, the rest, twisted loosely up around her head, bound by bright red tartan ribbon. Her skin was paler than buttermilk, which enhanced the freckles that danced across her cheeks. Her eyes were intoxicating: Large, smiling eyes that were watching him intently. She smiled at him with a warmth that only she could possess, and bent low in a graceful curtsy. The deep green fabric of her dress rippled on the floor around her.

'Tha mi toilichte do choinneachadh,' she said. 'That means—'

'Pleased to meet you,' he replied astonished.

Mòrag rose and held her hands out to her sides, 'Well?' she said, 'what do you think?'

His heart was racing, standing before him was his closest friend, yet she was the image of Catrìona. The dress was the same; every detail of it matched his memory perfectly. Her hair was secured in the same way, with the same ribbon. She even wore Catrìona's necklace. *But she's not Catrìona.* There were subtle differences he hadn't noticed until now. *Mòrag's hair is a deeper shade of red, and her eyes larger, more almond than round, and a more intense green than Catrìona's.* She was taller too, her body more developed than her mother's had been, though that could account to the difference in their ages. When he had met Catrìona, dressed as Mòrag was now, she had only been thirteen or fourteen, Mòrag was a good three years older than that and fully developed. He tore his gaze away, as he realised he had let it drop to her breasts, which sat softly cradled by the bodice of the dress. Her hips more pronounced than Catrìona's were accented by the contour of the bodice. *She's prettier than her mother.*

'Are you alright?' she asked, concern lacing her words, 'you look a bitty pale.'

He smiled at her, stepped forward and took her hand in his. *I never thought I would ever see anything as lovely as Catrìona. I was wrong.* Raising her hand to his lips, he kissed it gently and said, 'You are the most beautiful thing I have *ever* seen.'

Her cheeks flushed at his words. 'I never expected you to say that.'

'What did you think I would say?' he smiled.

'I don't know. The same as everyone else I suppose: That I'm the image of my mother. No one seems to see me, just her.' She smiled at him though he was sure he saw a hint of disappointment behind her eyes.

He felt a little guilty for thinking what everyone else had obviously been telling her. Taking one more step toward her, eliminating the gap between them, he ran the back of his hand down her cheek. 'Yes, you and Catrìona are very alike, especially when you are dressed like this. But you are not the same. All I see is you.'

Mòrag wound her hands around him, embracing him in a hug, 'Thank you.' She said. She lingered with her hands around him, 'You look really handsome,' she added looking up at him.

As long as I live, I will never love anything so much as her.

'Getting cosy are we?' Ava called from behind them.

Though Mòrag never made a sound, he felt her mentally groan at the interruption, which brought a smile to his lips.

'Mama thought you might feel a touch *exposed*, so she sent me to give you this,' she said holding out a long sheer silk ivory scarf. 'You can drape it about your shoulders or wherever. Personally, I do not think you need it, but Mama insisted I give you the choice.'

'Thanks, Ava,' Mòrag said, taking the scarf. 'If you see your mum before me, will you thank her for me?'

'I surely will. I will leave you to it, I have a man of my own to meet,' she said striding gracefully away.

'She's like a swan on stilts, I have no idea how she manages to keep her balance on those things and still look graceful,' Mòrag cast to Brax as she slid the scarf behind her neck, and under her arms before knotting it at the small of her back.

He chuckled. 'Are you going to show me yours?'

Mòrag grinned and pulled up the fabric of her dress, to reveal her laced, knee high uniform boots.

'You're something else,' Brax exclaimed.

'If I wasn't, you'd be bored of me by now,' she retorted with a smug expression.

'Not a chance,' he said, offering his arm, which to his pleasure, she took eagerly.

***

Randall stalked around the training hall, Tara at his heel. The festivities were in full swing. Tyros and their families were dancing and making merry. It pleased him to see the friendships blossoming and alliances forged among his troops.

There was also however, a darker side to these gatherings that took the form of political games played throughout the ranks. Competition and ambition walked hand in hand here. Stripped of most or all of their moral fibre through the Cleanse, the Tyros were ruthless in their pursuit of power. This meant that the Generals had to be ahead of the political games of their subordinates at all times, particularly on nights like this when clashes were most likely.

Tonight, Randall had his work cut out for him. The recent goings on over General Raine's dismissal from Sruighlea and the deaths of Oswald and Major Frank had sent ripples through the ranks, resulting in a divide forming throughout the troops. On one side, Fletcher Raine was gathering as much support as he could muster. On the other was Mòrag, who was earning respect and support throughout the troops, particularly from the officers who had more knowledge of her background.

Randall was sure she had no idea of the severity of her situation, which made his job even harder. Not to mention Rozzen's near constant presence, threatening to tear his attention away from the job at hand.

Tara nudged his wrist, indicating he should pat her. He, of course complied with her request. *'Try not to worry too much. Sharri, Rannoch and Nyx are stalking the grounds and of course, Seline and I are on watch here. You should try to enjoy yourself. I see your mate is showing more skin than normal.'*

Randall glanced across the hall to where Rozzen was standing, observing a selection of young Tyros, who were attempting to cajole their parents into dancing. She wore a sleek silver satin gown that accented her breasts and buttocks. When she realised Randall was watching her she eyed him suggestively.

'Is she trying to drive me crazy?'

'I think that is highly likely,' Tara replied. *'Go on, we will keep an eye out for anything amiss.'*

He gave her another scratch to thank her and started across the hall. As he passed Sergeant Simmons and the cook, he overheard their astonished gasps, and turned to look at what had grabbed their attention: Mòrag. *Of course! They are both from the highland clans. Dressed as she is and wearing Catrìona's necklace they are sure to realise who she is.*

'It cannae be,' they said in unison.

Randall leaned in close to the pair and kept his voice low, 'Keep this to yourselves, and inform any other Albannach who recognises her to remain silent. Now is not the time to make her claim public knowledge. Understood?'

'Aye, Sir,' they said together.

'Good. Enjoy your night,' he said and continued on his way across the hall.

**

Mòrag watched the dancers in the middle of the hall. Ball gowns of all colours floated on the air as the girls they clung to twirled and pranced with their partners. *They're all so confident. I wish I was.* She saw Brax watching her from the corner of her eye and turned to regard him.

'Do you *want* to dance?' he asked as if he knew what she was thinking.

'Not really,' she said. 'Well, no. That's not true. I would *like* to, but I don't know the steps, and I'm,' she sighed and cast, *'afraid I'll make a fool of myself.'*

'The steps aren't hard,' he said taking her hand and pulling her to the centre of the hall.

'No, Brax wait, I'm not ready to –'

Too late: Brax ignored her protests and led her around the floor. He grinned at her as she realised that she didn't look like any different from the other girls dancing with their partners. She was dancing of her own accord before she knew what had happened. When the band stopped for a break, she followed Brax across the festively decorated hall, towards the drinks table, where they met Helena and Oliver.

'Here to sample the mulled wine dear?' Helena asked.

'I think I'll give wine a miss for now. I'll stick to something a little less intoxicating.'

'That is probably wise,' Helena agreed.

Mòrag gave Oliver a quick hug and told him he was looking well, before pulling Brax back to dance, when the band began to play once more.

'Getting the hang of this are you?' he asked when they eventually took a break.

'I'm enjoying myself.'

'Good,' he said. 'So am I.'

Fletcher Raine did not show his face the entire night, which pleased Mòrag no end. She had worried he would try and make a scene in front of all the Tyros and their families, but it seemed, for one night at least, that he was letting matters lie.

By the time the bell chimed in the hall signalling the end of the evening it was three a.m. The hall was empty save for a few small groups that had become so engaged in their conversation, that they had not noticed the time passing.

Brax stood and offered his hand to her. Rising, she took it, and followed him from the hall into the snow-covered grounds.

The sky sparkled with twinkling stars, flickering around the wide crescent of the almost half-moon. Their breath misted in the air around them as they made their way back to the West wing of the castle. The air chilled her exposed skin making her shudder. The small movement enough to stop Brax in his tracks and drape his blazer round her shoulders.

'I should have given it to you before,' he apologised.

'Thank you.'

His blazer smelled of him, a scent she had noted before but tried to ignore. Now it surrounded her, and she breathed it in. It still carried within, the warmth of his body, comforting her chilled skin, and she couldn't help wishing it were his arms around her instead.

'*It seems you have reached the point of no return, Puithar.*' Rannoch purred within her mind, '*Shall I stay away tonight?*'

Mòrag ignored his comment. She could feel his amusement within her mind as he informed her he would not return until the following night, and she was glad of the chill night air that cooled her warming cheeks.

As they turned into the passageway that led to their rooms, Mòrag's heart began to flutter in her chest. She was suddenly more aware of the heat of his hand around hers, the scent of him on his blazer, the memory of his bare chest the morning before. Reaching her door, she felt him pull her forwards.

He twirled her as if they were dancing then he bent low and kissed the back of her hand once more. 'Thank you for a wonderful night. I'm glad you persuaded me to accompany you.'

Her skin tingled where he had kissed her and she found herself wondering if that was the only place, he was willing to kiss her. 'How did I persuade you?'

'I wanted to see you squirm from being forced to wear a dress. You didn't, but I enjoyed myself none the less.' He moved closer, so close she could feel his breath.

Her breathing quickened and she suddenly became very aware of her breasts, which, held secure by her bodice, rose softly upward as she breathed.

Brax half smiled, he seemed to have noticed the same thing. Lifting is hand he ran his fingers down her cheek and neck and then along the front of her bodice, barely touching her skin.

Desire flared within her. She wanted him to touch her; she wanted him to press his lips against hers. She was done with the notion that they could ignore the attraction they both obviously felt.

As his fingers reached the other side of her neck and slid up to her cheek, she rose up on the balls of her feet and brought her mouth to his. He returned her kiss with equal desire until they fell into each other's arms panting hard.

Mòrag ran her hand between the buttons of Brax's shirt, craving the feeling of his bare skin against hers.

He caught her hand, stopping her from venturing further, 'I think we should stop,' he said, voice hoarse.

Embarrassment descended upon her, 'Oh, ok,' she said, her voice no more than a whisper.

He pressed his lips to hers once more, then said, 'I *mean*, we are still in the corridor.'

Oh! Mòrag you numpty!

Brax kissed her cheeks, her hair, and her neck as she twisted in his arms. Retrieving her key and unlocking the door.

'Where did you hide that?' he mumbled into her neck.

'Never you mind,' she breathed as his wandering lips set a fire within her.

Turning so she was facing him once more, she took his hands, intertwining her fingers with his; she backed away slowly, paying no particular attention to anything other than his eyes, and his lips.

She reached for him with her mind, up until now they had only shared a partial connection for communication purposes, but she desperately wanted to bring herself closer to him, body and mind.

She reached out and to her surprise, he reached for her too, their mental images grasping hands, and pulling their mindscapes together to form one. Their shared mindscape, for the moment, took the form of their current physical surroundings.

'*You realise you may see parts of me that even I don't wish to remember.*'

'*And it will change nothing,*' she cast, her image unbuttoning the shirt of his, and kissing his bare chest, her physical body copying the motion.

He cupped her face in his hands and returned her affections, and it thrilled her. She felt as though the warm tingling rush of emotions could dance around them forever as they sank deeper towards each other.

'*I see you have begun to fantasise about Catriona, I suppose you reached that age a while ago now.*' The unfamiliar, deep, commanding voice seemed to whirl around their mindscape until it settled a few feet away, taking the form of a man.

She had never forgotten the smug look of self-importance that dressed Edward's face. The curl of his nut-brown hair, and stubble that darkened his jawline or the fire that danced in his pale silver eyes. His image was not as young as she remembered. She looked at Brax; he was sheet white and could not remove his gaze from the wicked man from his past.

'*You were always infatuated with her of course, always trying to get close to her, trying to keep her from me. Absurd really, I never wanted her in the first place,*' he chuckled wickedly, sending shivers up Mòrag's spine in the physical world as well as the mindscape.

'He thinks you're your mother,' Brax whispered. 'Do *not* do anything to make him think otherwise.' His image in their mindscape remained still and silent, staring at Edward.

I don't understand. If this is a vision from his mind, why is he so afraid?

'Does it hurt? Knowing that she will never be yours?' Edward's image began pacing towards them as he spoke. 'Does it tear at your soul knowing that I took her from you?'

Brax placed himself in front of Mòrag, keeping the distance between her image and Edward's.

'You will never have her. You will never enjoy her,' he said circling them. 'Not like I enjoyed her... And Brax,' he locked gazes with him, 'I enjoyed every inch of her. But, you know that don't you, because you were there. Cowering in the corner like a whipped puppy, trying to ignore her screams.'

The pit of Mòrag's stomach turned to lead, as she understood what he meant. She pressed herself to Brax's back, hoping to offer him some moral support, as the image of Edward continued its onslaught.

'Do they wake you at night, those desperate, agonised screams? Does she still call to you from the abyss?'

A single tear rolled down Brax's cheek.

'I thought so. You caused her suffering boy. If you had remained quiet, she would never have gotten in my way. You are the reason she thrust a knife into her gut. You will never be rid of her: Just like you will never be rid of me. Very soon now Brax, you will be back cowering at my feet, like the dog you are.'

GLOSSARY

ALBANNACH TERMINOLOGY

Away wi ye - Don't talk rubbish
Aye-no - No
Bairn - Child / kid
Bide - Come
Bigyin - Big one
Birling - Spinning
Boggin' - Dirty
Bonnie - Beautiful
Braw - Great / Awesome
Bricking it - Frightened
Cannae - Can't
Chilly Baltic - Freezing
Chook - Chicken
Clarty - Dirty
Clootie Dumpling - Pudding boiled in a cloth
Caoch - Shit
Dàirich - Fuck
Dafty - Idiot
Dunderheid - Idiot
Feart / Feartie - Afraid / Coward
Gip - Discomfort
Glaikit - Foolish / Vacant
Gonnae no - Stop it / Don't
Guttersnipe - Tramp
Half cut - Tipsy
Hod yer horses - Wait
Hawd yer wheesht - Shut up
In the bare nuddy - Naked
In the buff - Naked
Kailkenny - Potato and cabbage dish
Keep yer heid - Calm down

Leg it - Run
Louping - Painful / Sore
Mental - Mad
Midden - Muck heap
Mitts - Hands
Nae chance - No chance
Neeps - Turnip
Numpty - Idiot
Numpty-heid - Idiot
Och - Oh
Och away wi yi the noo - Don't be silly
Saft / Saftie - Soft / Softie
Scunnered - Weary
Skelp - Smack
Stovies - Potato dish with other veg and beef
Ta - Thank you
Tatties - Potatoes
Tattie bye - Goodbye
Thon - He / she / him / her
Tumshie - Turnip
Weel - Well
Whatshisface - Used when name is forgotten
Yersel - Yourself
Yon - That

OLD ALBANNACH WORDS

Abhainn - River
Athair - Father
Ban-phrionnsa – Princess
Bhanrigh – Queen
Bràthair - Brother
Càirdeas - Friends
Màthair - Mother
Puithar – Sister
Leine - Long shirt/tunic worn under arisaid and weskit
Weskit - Laced waistcoat
Arisaid - Woman's of great kilt

OLD ALBANNACH PHRASES

Soar Alba - Free Alba
Taigh nam gasta ort - Fuck off/Go to hell
Tha mi toilichte do choinneachadh - Pleased to meet you

FAMILIARS

Frik - General Marcs' Destrier
Rannoch - Mòrag's Nemeocorn
Livia - King James' Nemean Lion
Seline - General Rozzen's Cadmean Vixen
Ruka - Elite Soldier's Puma
Shand - Brax's Elite Destrier
Meraii - Colonel Tesso's Cheetah
Silas - Prince Edward's Nemean Lion
Nyx - General Marcs' Black Panther
Skye - Princess Catrìona's Unicorn
Pasha - General Rozzen's Destrier
Tara - Randall's (General Steele) Wolf
Petorius - Jock MacDonald's Destrier
Zeal - Major Frank's Comodo Dragon

PLACES

Breizh - Northern region of Frangach.
Cathair Luail - Great Border City which lies between the Albannach and Sasannach Kingdoms.
Dùn Èideann - Capital city of Alba. Sasannach military stronghold. Historical home of the Douglas Clan.
An Fhraing - Neighbouring country to Sasann across a body of water. Part of a larger collection of countries somewhat controlled by the Sasannach throne.

Sruighlea - Heart of Alba, Sasannach military strong hold and training academy, and gateway to the Albannach Kingdom. Historical home of the Royal Stewart Clan.

MYTHICAL BEASTS

Cadmean Vixen - Enormous fox, exceptionally cunning and rarely seen.

Destrier - War horse originally bred from the Kelpies by the Clans. After Sasannach occupation, Jock MacDonald was ordered to breed them for the Sasannach army.

Elite Destrier - War horse; capable of becoming berserker under control of their rider. Only one is in existence at present who's dam was bred to a Water horse

Greater Haribon - Higher Mythical Beast; bird of legend who inspired stories of Dragons and Phoenixes.

Nemean Lion - Higher Mythical Beast; gigantic Lion whose skin is impenetrable other than to its own claws and the Unicorn's horn. Companion animal of the Sasannach Royal family.

Nemeocorn - Higher Mythical Beast; hybrid between Nemean Lion and Unicorn, displaying strong traits of both beasts. Companion animal of the Hybrid Royal line (mixed blood but both parents from opposing Royal families.)

Unicorn - Higher Mythical Beast; Usually a white mare, though males and other colours appear on occasion. Can compel most beasts to slumber, and has exceptional healing powers. Companion animal of the Albannach Royal family.

Each Uisge - Higher Mythical Beast; Can appear in equine or human form. If robbed of its bridle/amulet, it is stripped of its power

CHAINS OF BLOOD AND STEEL

THE SAGA OF THISTLES AND ROSES BOOK 2

BY KAREN GRAY

Chapter One

A Spade's A Spade

Cold steel slapped against Mòrag's arm causing her to curse. The resulting sting from the flat of the blade added to her irritation and distraction.

'Pay attention.'

She glowered at Tesso. The young Colonel danced around her with ease, throwing blow after blow with increasing speed, so much so, that she could no longer parry the attacks.

'Focus and counter my attacks, you will never learn anything standing around letting me strike you.'

I think you'll find it's you that isn't giving me a chance here, I'd counter if I could. His smirk and the sting of the steel irritated her beyond imagining.

'Quit standing around and attack me,' Tesso ordered as he swung his blade toward her with lightning speed and precision.

Mòrag by this point had given up on physical attacks and slid into the sensory plane: The field of vision where she could see the soul. Lifting her free hand, she caught his effortlessly before he landed the blow.

Tesso's eyes widened as his body ceased to move with his will, frozen mid strike.

Mòrag stepped in close to him, invading Tesso's personal space on purpose to further emphasise how vulnerable he had become. When she was nose-to-nose with him, she locked him in a glare, 'You're not giving me a chance,' she said, releasing her grip on his soul with just a little push so he would lose his footing.

Stumbling backward he toppled to the ground as expected, landing with a thump. 'I thought we agreed not to use mental abilities, Mòrag.'

'If you want me to learn, *Sir*, then you need to give me a chance. You're clearly too quick for me. If I could match your speed I wouldn't have *had* to resort to mental abilities.' She retorted.

Tesso got to his feet, 'Perhaps I have underestimated how much I could slow my own body,' he sighed. 'I have spent so many years forcing my body to move faster, that I find it difficult to take a step back sometimes.'

His admission shocked her. Tesso, for the time she had known him, had always been a private person. He did not offer much in the way of personal information to anyone, yet here he was admitting self-doubt.

He indicated she should follow him to the bench that ran the length of the training hall. Sitting, he regarded her for a moment before he spoke. 'I never used to be quite so quick. It was always my weakest point. Technical ability in both physical and mental attack and defence were never an issue, but speed,' he shook his head. 'If I had been a fraction quicker, I would have beaten Ray, my brother, during the graduation tournament, and been named the youngest Elite in the King's guard.'

'How old were you?' Mòrag asked.

'Fourteen, Ray was twenty-four; he had taken the extra time to specialise as a Sneak. He was furious I had been allowed to compete, never mind beat the competition to face him in the final. At that point, we were still fighting a war against the King's uncle, so they needed as many of us on the front lines as possible, even if it meant child soldiers. Though, as it turned out I ended up being the youngest.'

Mòrag sat quietly; she knew Tesso felt responsible for what happened to her during her interrogation six months earlier. He had no reason to feel responsible, Major Frank was the one who dislocated her shoulder and snapped her collarbone, not Colonel Tesso.

'General Steele noticed my potential as soon as I arrived on the front lines,' he gave a short laugh. 'He actually thought

General Brooke, who was running the training academy at Cathair Luail at the time, was trying to mess with his head. "He can't possibly have graduated. He's just a child." I sat outside the command tent listening to him demanding someone contact his mentor for confirmation. Anyway, he passed me over to General Rozzen's troop and she gave me these.' He unbuckled one of his bracers and handed it to Mòrag.

'Bracers? I don't see what bracers have to do with –' instead of a toughened leather support sitting lightly in her hand. Tesso's bracer was abnormally heavy, so heavy that Mòrag dropped it in surprise and it hit the ground with a loud thud. 'Michty-me! Do you wear those all day long?' She asked stooping to retrieve it.

A small smile crept across his face, 'Of course not,' he chuckled. 'I trained with them during strictly timed sessions. When I first started, the plates inside were much lighter, only half a pound or so. As I got used to them I gradually increased the weight. What you are holding is around seven and a half pounds; I have greaves of the same weight too.'

'Thirty pounds, you must be joking surely?'

'No. I train with the greaves and bracers on alternate days,' he said taking back the bracer and strapping it to his arm. 'I have gone off topic. I think the reason I have been asked to train with you in a one to one situation, is to increase your physical skills. Accuracy is important, but so is speed.' Tesso reached into the satchel he had beside him pulling out a pair of bracers and a pair of greaves, and placing them on the bench between him and Mòrag. 'This was the first set General Rozzen gave me. They should fit you well enough until I can have a set made for you. I want you to wear them when we train. When you no longer notice the extra weight, I will swap the plates for heavier ones.'

'So, basically, by training in these and allowing the weight to become part of me, I should get quicker by removing them at a later stage?'

'Exactly. You will never match the speed of someone like General Rozzen though. Speed is one of her blood talents, like your Seeker ability: Others can learn the bare bones of the skills involved in your talent but they can never actually see the soul like you can.'

'So, what you're really saying is you can't slow down so I need to speed up?'

'Something like that,' he said.

Sergeant Simmons appeared at the outer door. The ginger bearded burly Albannach officer nodded at Tesso, and some unspoken communication took place.

'Excuse me, Mòrag; I have some business that needs attended to.' Tesso said, leaving her in the training hall and striding after Sergeant Simmons.

With little else to do for the rest of the day, Mòrag lifted the items he had given her and went in search of Brax. He had been avoiding her since the Winter Solstice Dance; when they had both realised their feelings for each other and taken the next step toward becoming something more than friends. He seemed to think that by avoiding her, he was somehow protecting her. *It's not* me *that needs protecting.*

His previous master, the now exiled, Prince Edward of Sasann, had warned them on that night through a projected mindcast, that Brax would soon be back under his control. He mistook Mòrag's presence in Brax's mind, as an imagining of the late Albannach Princess, Mòrag's mother, Catrìona. Evil taunts and visions had swirled around them. Mòrag had tried to ignore the awful images and terrifying memories of Brax's tortured past, but try as she might, she could not force herself to close her mind to them. *And why should I have? He was having to relive one horrific moment after another, the least I could do was be there to hold his hand and bear witness to the awful things that happened to him behind closed doors.*

When the visions ceased and Edward's communication fizzled out, Brax broke down. Mòrag had seen his deepest darkest moments, his master had vowed to haul him back into his own personal hell once more, and he had no idea how to deal with any of it.

She had held him close the entire night, hoping to offer him some comfort, but could do little to stop the ghosts of his past re awakening to haunt him once more. In the morning, he threw himself into training and had focused on that ever since. He had now been avoiding Mòrag wherever possible for almost eight weeks.

Mòrag too had felt the need to push on with her training. *Edward will not have him.* The only way she knew to protect him was to develop her own powers no matter how frightened of them she was.

Stepping out of the training hall into the smirry rain, she pulled her hood close to her head and jogged up through the grounds toward the castle's main entrance hall. Weaving her way through the passages toward the West wing where she and Brax were roomed, she stopped at his door and listened for movement beyond. Slipping into the sensory state, she could see Brax's soul within. Satisfied she tried the door: Locked. Placing her hand over the lock, she sent thin tendrils of her soul in search of the tumblers, moving them gently until the lock clicked open.

She edged the door inwards and peered into Brax's room. As expected, his drawn curtains left only the dying fire to light the room. The soft wheeze and pop of the wood was no more than a whisper, over shadowed by the whistling of the wind high up in the chimney. Brax was sitting on his bed staring into space with so sad an expression on his face that it made Mòrag's heart ache.

She picked up a few logs and tossed them into the fire, removed her wet coat and sat softly next to Brax. Leaning against him, she rested her head against his shoulder; he remained quiet, resting his head against hers in automatic response.

'Don't you know what a locked door means?' he said quietly.

'It means you're brooding and don't want told off,' Mòrag replied.

Brax let out a small, amused huff, 'Trust you to see it like that.'

'A spade's a spade Brax. What's on your mind Bigyin?' she asked, running her hand down his arm and weaving her fingers through his.

'You. Always you,' he said giving her hand a gentle squeeze. 'The problem is *he* is there too. Always. And I can't...' he sighed, 'I will never be rid of him.'

'Are you still dreaming of him?'

'Every night: Even with the medication, Major Darrow gave me to help me sleep. It just means I can't force myself to wake from the nightmares. I've also started seeing him during the day. It happened this morning with my sparring partner. His face changed and all I saw was Edward. I lost it, in front of everyone, I lost it,' his grip intensified on her hand. 'I'm slowly unravelling. I don't think it's safe for you to be close to me.'

Mòrag pushed herself away from his side so she could look at him. He did not meet her gaze; keeping his eyes instead, toward the fire. His dark hair fell soft down his back; the few shorter strands dressed the sides of his face. 'I think you need to speak to Randall.'

Brax jumped up from the bed, his flight-response kicking in. 'No. I can't. Mòrag you know I can't. He'll think I'm a spy, he'll assume I have always been on the enemy's side. He'll have me locked up; he's already weary of me. Please, Mòrag, tell me you haven't told him. Please don't tell him,' he dropped to his knees in front of her, grasping her hands, 'please. I would rather die than be thrown in that dungeon, where I can't escape. It's as good as handing me back to Edward bound and gagged'

His pale eyes were fighting back tears; he was clearly terrified at the prospect of incarceration. Mòrag pulled him towards her, moving his hands so they were round her waist. She ran her hands over his cheeks and through his hair, smoothing the shorter strands back behind his ears, before taking his face in her hands and kissing him on the forehead. 'I won't let him.'

'But, Mòrag –'

'I *won't* let him,' she said holding his gaze until the tears he had been holding back flowed free. She enveloped him in a hug, 'Promise me you won't push me away any more.'

'It's not safe for you to be around me, what if he sees you.'

'You really are glaikit sometimes, Bigyin. We share a mindscape remember. If he pokes around your mind, he will find me anyway. What's the use of pushing me away when it will make absolutely no difference to whether he sees me or not?'

His body tensed as he realised she was right. 'Mòrag you have to –'

'No way, not doing it. I am yours and you are mine, and if Edward wants you that badly, he will have to go through me before he can have you. I don't see that ending well for him. Rannoch feels the same. I doubt that Lion of his could stand up to a Nemeocorn, let alone a Nemeocorn, a Greater Haribon *and* Shand.'

'You shouldn't underestimate them.'

'I don't. You shouldn't underestimate us,' she smiled.

'You're some girl, you know that?'

'So you keep telling me.'

COMING DECEMBER 2015

44398894R00186

Made in the USA
Charleston, SC
22 July 2015